The American Utopian Adventure

SERIES TWO

THE FAMILISTERE

The Familistere

A NOVEL

BY MARIE HOWLAND

Author of "A Shield of Glass", "Tymie Bonnet", "A Bicycle Romance", etc.
Translator of "Solutions Sociales" and other works by M. Godin

THIRD EDITION

WITH A NEW INTRODUCTION BY

ROBERT S. FOGARTY

———"Wisdom is humanity;
And they who want it, wise as they may seem,
And confident in their own sight and strength,
Reach not the scope they aim at."
—W. S. Landor.

PORCUPINE PRESS

Philadelphia 1975

First edition published 1874 under the title *Papa's Own Girl*
Second edition, 1885
Third edition, *The Familistere,* 1918
(Boston: Christopher Publishing House, 1918)

Reprinted 1975 by
PORCUPINE PRESS, INC.
Philadelphia, Pennsylvania 19107

Library of Congress Cataloging in Publication Data

Howland, Marie.
   The Familistere.

   (The American utopian adventure ; ser. 2)
   Reprint of the 3d ed. (1918) published by Christopher
Pub. House, Boston, which was originally published in
1874 under title: Papa's own girl.
   I. Title.
PZ3.H844Fam15   [PS2039.H2]   823'.4   74-32134
ISBN 0-87991-024-0

Manufactured in the United States of America

THE FAMILISTERE: RADICAL REFORM THROUGH COOPERATIVE ENTERPRISE

"Papa is a radical, they say, so are we. We believe in love, not hate; in happinees, not in misery." With that declaration of philosophy Clara Forest affirms her lineage and sets the tone for her self-fulfilling career as "papa's own girl." In this utopian romance, first published in 1874,* it reflected the varied career of its author, Marie Howland, and when reprinted in 1885 as part of Lovell's Library, it served to direct attention at two utopian experiments, one successfully established, the other soon to be launched for failure. The two communities were the "Familistere" at Guise, France and "Pacific City" at Topolobampo, Mexico.

Marie Howland's reform career spans a forty year period and the central figures in the novel reflect that history. It began in 1845 in New Hampshire where Marie Stevens early struggled at "developing the self reliance which during her life has been one of her characteristics." According to her second husband, Edward Howland, the early death of her father placed burdens on Marie particularly in the care of her twin sisters who figure in *The Familistere* as Linnie and Leila. She worked at a cotton factory at Lowell and while there learned phonography which helped her gain employment at subsequent periods. In the early eighteen fifties she moved to New York City where she taught school, finished Normal School and married the radical lawyer Lyman Case. During the late fifties she lived at Stephen Pearl Andrews' cooperative boarding house, "Unity House," where she moved in a radical circle and had among her friends Jane McElheney, the famous "Ada Clare," and Edward Howland, the publicist, who was to be her second husband. According to one source, Howland and Mrs. Case lived in Europe during the Civil War and at J. B. Godin's "Familistere" during one of those years — probably in 1864.

In 1866 the Howlands returned with Edward working as a free-lance writer (he was to write a biography of Grant) and she as a secretary. During 1868 they moved to Hammonton, New Jersey, where they maintained a lively radical household with Albert Brisbane a visitor, and "Ada Clare" buried at Hammonton after her tragic death in 1874. And, in fact, the Hammonton house may have been the "Progressive Colony" referred to in some sources. It was in 1874 that Albert Kimsey Owen, the railroad entrepeneur, visited the Howlands at Hammonton and it became the center of publicity for his railroad and colony venture which was to be located at Topolobampo Bay, Mexico with the glorious name "Pacific City". The Howlands edited a variety of publications for Owen and in 1888 joined the colony. They lived there until 1894 with Edward an invalid in a wheelchair by that time and Marie having an affair with C. B. Hoffman, a millionaire socialist, and backer of the colony. When the Topolobampo Colony failed she moved to another colony, this one the Georgeist single-tax settlement at Fairhope, Alabama, where she acted as the colony librarian and wrote a regular column for the *Fairhope Courier*. During her later years she was supported by Fiske Warren, a wealthy George supporter. She died in 1921 at the age of 85. There is more to her career as an edited collection of her letters should reveal; yet it is primarily her experience at Guise that forms the basis for this novel.

The "Familistere" was the project of Jean Baptiste Godin born in January 1817 at Esqueheries, Aisne to a laboring family. As a young man he worked as a smith before turning to the manufacture of heating apparatus in 1837. In 1840 he patented a stove and developed a successful business by creating new models and anticipating new trends. During this period he studied the writings of St. Simon, Owen and Cabet and found them wanting, but in 1842 he was attracted to Fourier's ideas. And in 1848 he underwrote a third of the cost of the ill-fated Icarian experiment in Texas. The idea of "Familistere" took hold around 1856 with Godin striving to improve his workers' conditions by improved housing and a better organization of the services of production, education and recreation.

From 1856 to 1859 it remained an idea; however, in April 1859 he built the first wing of the "Familistere," or Social Palace. In 1861 the first building was roofed and occupied; in 1862 a central court was begun. It grew slowly and Marie Howland based her impressions on her 1864 visit and Godin's *Social Solutions* which she translated in 1873. Although Godin was elected to the National Assembly in 1871 he found politics unsatisfactory and devoted his life toward cooperative activities at the iron works in Guise. From 1880 until his death in 1888 he edited *Devoir* (Duty) which printed his writings and other social commentary. Paradoxically his wife divorced him during this period and the project was slowed down by the necessity to make large settlement payments to her; yet when he died in January 1888 the Social Palace was completed.

There were five branches of the "Familistere," each intended to complement one another so as to form an integral community promoting collective well-being but respecting individuality and privacy. The five branches were: 1) a collection of united buildings, the Social Palace; 2) a group of cooperative shops (bread, fuel, food); 3) an educational service (a nursery, plus elementary education up to age 14); 4) a system of profit sharing based on seniority and a guild concept; 5) a system of mutual insurance for sickness and old age.

At the height of the community's activities there were some 1500 — 1700 employees with about 350 living in apartments in the Social Palace. In addition, a branch establishment, near Brussels, was begun in 1887 on the same principle. A good view of the community was given by Edward Owen Greening, the English cooperator, who visited Guise in the 1880's and wrote this account for the *Cooperator News:* "The French Society we have come to visit not only includes a cooperative store, with departments for grocery, baker, confectionary, drapery, boots and shoes, butchery and every other article of prime necessity, but it furnishes its members with employment in a gigantic ironworks, houses them in palatial buildings, nurses their babies so far as the mothers desire its help in that important department, educates their children, provides library, news-room, billiard room, refreshment saloon, theatre, music master, doctor and dispensary; assists them by machinery to wash and dry their clothes, insures them against the needs of old age, the accidents and ailments of life, and the loss by death of the wage earner; furnishes them with a newspaper devoted to their principles, with baths, and many other luxuries in life, including a glorious co-operative garden filled with fruits and flowers."

Greening was impressed with every aspect of the "Familistere" — particularly the nursery and educational system run on the Froebel method. In the nursery they used an igenious system to catch waste in the children's bassinettes. An absorbent bran mixture was placed under the sheets and the set lump of bran was removed at the end of each day, a child's kitty litter in fact. But beyond that there were the real accomplishments of a successful cooperative factory run on reliable business principles and utilizing a large labor force. The Howlands' visit must have affected them profoundly since her reform work from that point on and up to her involvement with Topolobampo all speak to her dedication to the "Familistere" principles. She was not, like the Claflins, a summer patriot but one who worked at reformation throughout her career. The aspirations of that career are best expressed in this novel which came during the early stages of her life, ran through three editions and was widely hailed as a major reformist tract for the times.

The Familistere is a classic romantic novel where good triumphs over evil, where the characters represent moral abstractions and where the plot serves the needs of didactic rather than stylistic necessity. Though it follows the conventional forms its content clearly marks it as a novel radical in its social philosophy and dramatic in its presentation. Arthur Morgan, in his biography of Edward Bellamy, states that *Papa's Own Girl* may have served as the prototype for *Looking Backward* and there are numerous points of comparison, most clearly in the person of Clara Forest, the self-willed and independent woman who closely resembles Bellamy's Edith Leete.

Yet the novel does not stand solely on historical comparison, but on its forceful presentation of women's rights, cooperative living and social radicalism. "Papa", or Doctor Forest, is at the novel's center and serves as its most didactic voice. He is the beloved local physician who, though "liberal", is held in great respect because of his integrity, intelligence and concern for his patients. Dr. Forest defies local conventions and his conventional wife by encouraging his daughter, Clara, to seek her own way: "Independence, honest self-support by honest productive industry is the thing for women as well as men." He puts other notions abroad which shock Mrs. Forest and set the radical tone for the novel. For example, he asserts that the first condition for broad development in a woman is "the loss of respectability as defined by hypocrites and prudes." Supposedly such assertions had the 1874 edition banned from the Boston Public Library and others.

Though Clara has been encouraged to follow a radical career she does marry and to a respectable physician, Dr. Delano, whom Clara loves with a purified passion. After their marriage he disappoints her by pursuing another woman and that sets the stage for her true love affair with Count Frauenstein ("Ladies Rock"). As a counterpoint to Clara's efforts at self-fulfillment there is her profligate brother, Dan, and the poor girl he brings to ruin, Susie Dykes. Susie's development from a "fallen woman" to a self-confident and successful businesswoman makes her a spiritual daughter to Dr. Forest who initially harbors the pregnant girl and encourages her to study and make her way in the world. She does so by establishing a nursery business, "Delano and Dykes" which she and Clara run with an eye toward profit and social advancement: ". . . The firm of 'Delano and Dykes' were sworn never to employ a man where a woman could be found to do the work required."

While Dan wanders the countryside in disgrace drinking himself into insanity, the two women resolutely move ahead though Clara has separated from her husband and Susie has a child to raise. In short, they are self-willed and independent women just as "Papa" had raised them to be. Minor characters play stereotyped roles, but always within a broader context of benevolence and reform. Dinah, the Negro servant, is wise about sex and Susie's friend in the Forest household; yet, she is treated as a social equal by Dr. Forest in front of scandalized neighbors. Miss Marston, the schoolteacher, is respectable, earnest and won over to the reformers' cause because it is both intelligent and honorable. Too Soon, a Chinese cook, is shown to have virtues and talents in a town that scorned his "foreign" ways. When Too Soon is given an opportunity to work with respect, his abilities shine forth in a productive and aesthetic fashion.

Mrs. Forest and her circle of friends represent conventional wisdom at a niggardly and self-protective level. They are the town moralists who are scandalized by the doctor and Clara, who are eventually won over by the pragmatic accomplishments and superior achievements of the reforming group. There is more to these characters than the stereotype suggests since they mirror social conventions and practices which Marie Howland confronts directly. For example, Mrs. Forest is scandalized by Susie Dykes' pregnancy and forces her out of the house, then punishes her husband by withdrawing her sex to show disapproval. Double standards exist everywhere as Howland plays one standard against another to highlight society's hypocrisy and fraud.

There are only two characters who stand completely above societal pressures and embody a higher morality, Dr. Forest and Count Frauenstein. Frauenstein is modeled after Jean Baptiste Godin; yet there are clear embellishments on the historical figure. Frauenstein has degrees from Cambridge and Heidelberg, a regal lineage and a two million dollar fortune. His entrance into a provincial New England town stirs passions and he is immediately attracted to Clara. They are a natural pair and soon a scheme is hatched to build a grand social palace after the "Familistere" at Guise, France: "I must help to build up a society of men and women who can be honest and free . . . I found more intelligence, more faith in humanity among the workingmen at Guise, than I ever met among any set of people in my life."

Workers are paid in labor script, plans for an industrial center are organized and the magnificent palace is opened as the novel closes. It is, of course, dazzling to the New Englanders since it contains, under one roof, all that is needed for any community. A grand banquet inaugurates the Social Palace with Count Frauenstein proclaiming, as had Godin on numerous occasions, about the dignity of labor and the importance of cooperative idealism. Clara and the Count's crowning moment comes with the announcement of their child's birth as the palace opens. They had been married in an impromptu ceremony presided over by the benevolent and law-giving doctor. The novel ends on a triumphant note with the Forest family living in the Social Palace (even Mrs. Forest reforms and becomes a temperance leader) with the principles of women's rights, cooperative living and social radicalism vindicated in the process.

It is a grand, sweeping novel which — contrary to the utopian novel tradition — is eminently readable and, like *Looking Backward,* offers a practical, common-sense solution with a magical device (in this case it's Frauenstein's millions) against a backdrop of personal greed, social inefficiency and hypocrisy. But there was more than just romance as the facts of Godin's experiment at the ironworks indicate. In fact the novel, like Godin's own tomb at Guise, serves as a memorial to his hope in the future. On one face of the tomb there is a portrait bust of Godin; on another face a young woman points toward the portrait while holding a child in her arms; on another, a moulder in his working dress; and above the bust the figure of immortality stands. And inscribed on the tomb are the following words:

COME TO THIS TOMB
WHEN YOU HAVE NEED TO BE REMINDED
THAT I FOUNDED THE FAMILISTERE
FOR BROTHERLY ASSOCIATION AND PARTNERSHIP
REMAIN UNITED BY THE LOVE OF HUMANITY
PARDON THE WRONGS WHICH OTHERS DO TO YOU
HATRED IS THE FRUIT OF EVIL HEARTS
LET IT NOT ENTER AMONG YOU
LET THE REMEMBRANCE OF ME BE FOR YOU A BOND
   OF BROTHERLY UNITY
NOTHING IS GOOD OR MERITORIOUS WITHOUT
   THE LOVE OF HUMANITY
PROSPERITY WILL ACCOMPANY YOU IN PROPORTION
   AS CONCORD SHALL REIGN AMONG YOU
BE JUST TOWARD ALL AND YOU WILL SERVE AS AN EXAMPLE.

Robert S. Fogarty
Antioch College
Yellow Springs, Ohio

*The first edition was published under the title *Papa's Own Girl.* The third and last edition, here reprinted, was published under the title, *The Familistere.*

FOREWORD

The Familistere, at Guise, France, has been undoubtedly one of the most successful social experiments ever attempted. Marie Howland's visit to Guise, her experiences at the Familistere, where she lived for a time, her personal acquaintance with its founder, M. Godin, (author of "Solutions Sociales," translated into English by Marie Howland) have all had their influence in shaping the plot and developing the characters of "The Familistere."

When this first appeared it was hailed as "unquestionably the best labor novel of the day," and Harper's Magazine said of it: "No novel has yet appeared so comprehensive in its range, bearing upon the great social questions of the day, the position of woman, and the conditions of labor." It soon went into a second edition, and the further demand is met by this, the third edition.

In reply to Mrs. Howland's inquiry as to the fate of the Familistere since the war, a recent visitor writes her as follows:

"The news is much less bad than it might be. Although the Familistere was, very early in the war, occupied by the Germans and many of the workmen were caught there and remained in the hands of the enemy; yet no great harm, as far as we know, has been done to them; nor until very recently was much harm done to the buildings or works, when the Germans destroyed a part of the machine moulding department, breaking the apparatus they could not carry away. We know that the director and his family were well, waiting with courage the hour of their deliverance.''

Marie Howland has not only made a close study of the Familistere in France, but has been actively identified with many efforts to establish better social conditions in the United States, to which work she has given many of the years of a long life, and the attainments of a broad culture

CONTENTS

I.—AN OLD LETTER_____ 5

II.—THE SKELETON IN THE GARRET_____ 11

III.—DR. FOREST AT HOME_____ 17

IV.—ONE OF DR. FOREST'S PATIENTS_____ 25

V.—THE TATTOOING_____ 37

VI.—CLARA AT STONYBROOK COLLEGE_____ 45

VII.—DAN'S BUSINESS OPERATIONS_____ 54

VIII.—PHILOSOPHY VANQUISHED_____ 64

IX.—THE LION'S DEN_____ 73

X.—CLARA'S RETURN.—THE DRAMA IN THE DOCTOR'S STUDY_____ 83

XI.—FAITH AND WORKS_____ 98

XII.—CLARA DECIDES BETWEEN RELIGION AND PRINCIPLE_____ 112

XIII.—PAPA'S OWN GIRL_____ 122

XIV.—DAN'S MONEY RETURNED—THE DOCTOR CONQUERED_____ 132

XV.—THE DOCTOR'S LETTER.—DAN REJECTED 144

XVI.—THE VISIT OF THE DELANOS_____ 152

XVII.—COSTLY GRAPES_____ 165

XVIII.—HOW DAN GOT MARRIED_____ 175

XIX.—THE BABY.—LOVERS' ADIEUX_____ 187

XX.—CLARA'S WEDDING_____ 199

XXI.—THE NUCLEUS OF THE FLOWER BUSINESS_____ 208

XXII.—THE FIRST CLOUD................................... 220

XXIII.—THE INVITATION TO THE WHITE MOUN-
TAINS 236

XXIV.—A SPASMODIC MOVEMENT OF LOVE............ 244

XXV.—LETTERS.—A CONVERSATION................... 253

XXVI.—THE CRISIS.. 266

XXVII.—THE SANCTITY OF MARRIAGE................ 278

XXVIII.—THE EFFECT OF DR. DELANO'S FOR-
GIVENESS 291

XXIX.—THE COUNT VON FRAUENSTEIN............. 301

XXX.—OUT OF THE JAWS OF DEATH.............. 314

XXXI.—INTO A BETTER WORLD....................... 330

XXXII.—THE DISTINGUISHED VISITOR.............. 343

XXXIII.—LEGITIMATE, OR ILLEGITIMATE.......... 360

XXXIV.—THE SLAVE OF THE LAMP.................. 375

XXXV.—THE SLAVE OF THE LAMP OBEYS......... 387

XXXVI.—THE COUNT'S SPEECH TO HIS WORK-
MEN 405

XXXVII.—POETIC RETRIBUTION.—GROG-SELLERS
INTERVIEWED BY WOMEN................. 425

XXXVIII.—PROGRESS OF THE WORK................ 441

XXXIX.—AN HONEST WOMAN....................... 459

XL.—UNDER THE ORANGE-BLOSSOMS........ 473

XLI.—AFTER THE ORANGE-BLOSSOMS......... 492

XLII.—A VISIT TO THE SOCIAL PALACE......... 507

XLIII.—THE INAUGURATION OF THE SOCIAL
PALACE 523

XLIV.—THE BIRTH OF THE HEIR.................. 538

CHAPTER I.

AN OLD LETTER.

✿ ✿ ✿ ✳ I was seven years old when they came—those mysterious little red-faced sisters, which the day before were nowhere in the universe, and the next had sprung up before my bewildered young eyes, full dressed in long white gowns, and looking every way as exactly alike as did the objects I used to see double by "crossing my eyes," as we called it; a habit that brought me many a reprimand.

We lived then, as you know, in L———, Massachusetts, and I looked upon the advent of the little creatures on that fine September morning as the most wonderful stroke of fortune; but I remember that my mother, lying very pale and still among her pillows, watched my delight with sad eyes, and then turned her face wearily to the wall. Aunt Patty, the dear old Goody, long since sleeping in the village churchyard, entered kindly into my childish enthusiasm, turning up the skirts of the white dresses, and then unfolding a mass of soft flannel, finally exposed the velvety little feet, whose pink toes moved incessantly, as if enamored of the air. I very soon grew so boisterous in my delight that I had to be sent ignominiously from the room. I went immediately in search of

my brother Dan, a handsome, rough fellow, whom I found
in the kitchen busily employed with his fishing tackle;
for the unusual excitement in the house afforded him an
opportunity to sly off to the river, where mother had forbidden him to go on pain of severe penalties. I began
eagerly imparting the news.

"O, pshaw! I know all about it," interrupted Dan.
The statement surprised me, but I accepted it as pure
truth, as I generally did all that he said. He was some
years older than I, and I considered him a superior being—
at least everywhere except in school; there, even a partial
sister's eyes had to see that he was a dunce; though a
good-natured one, and a great favorite. He was indefati-
gable in "coasting" the girls and the little boys in winter, and he had a rough humor that pleased them all. I
remember that, at the beginning of one of our winter
terms, the master had offered a prize to the one who
should leave off at the head of the spelling class the
greatest number of times. On the last day of school I
received the prize, flushed with proud delight, standing
at the head of the long line of pupils. Dan was at the
very foot, as usual, and the teacher took occasion to reprove him for his bad lessons and his want of ambition in
trying for the prize.

"Why, I almost got it," said Dan.

"Almost!" echoed the teacher angrily; for we all
knew that Dan had not left off at the head a single day.

"Yes, sir. I should have had it if you had only made
this end the head." A burst of laughter from the teacher
and all the pupils followed this view of the case, and the
echoes, more and more subdued, continued when we were
dismissed to our seats, I hugging the precious prize, which

was a red morocco bound copy of *The Vicar of Wakefield*, and Dan chuckling over the success of his humor. He had consoled and vindicated all the orthographical blockheads, and he was happy. But I am letting my pen run wild, as I like to do when answering your letters.

While I stood watching Dan's manœuvres with his wiggling angle-worms and hooks and sinkers, I asked him if he did not think that the twins were perfectly lovely.

"No, I don't," he replied, impatiently. "I was going to have two months of fun before school commenced, and now I shan't have any. I shall have to run everywhere for them nasty twins; and then the crackers I shall have to pound! Mother didn't have half milk enough for Arthur, and it would take a whole cow for these. Girls, too, both of them!" he added, with great contempt. Here, in fact, was the sore point with Dan. While the baby Arthur lived, he was very fond of him, in his way, and would probably have been gracious over the advent of a new brother; possibly would have pardoned our mother in time for presenting us *one* baby of either sex; but two at a time, and both girls at that! This was too much for Dan's patience, or for his confidence in the discretion of mothers. I was surprised at his cool prediction about the supply of milk, but I deferred to his superior experience and years. He gave me another piece of recondite information just as he started for the river, threatening to kill my pet kitten if I dared to even hint where he had gone. This information was that these particular babies would be "awful cross patches; girls always were."

In time I myself grew to qualify my ecstasy over the

double blessing; for they certainly proved "awful cross patches," and the sacrifices I was obliged to make to them as a child, only a child I think could fully appreciate. ✿ ✿ ✿ ✿

Do you remember the skeleton in the garret—the *memento mori* of our play-house banquets ? ✿ ✿ ✿ ✿

C. F.

"C. F." is my old friend Clara Forest, and I am one of the characters, but it does not matter which one. I shall not appear again in the first person after I have described my first acquaintance with her. It is a long time since I determined to weave the events of her life into a story, and coming across this old letter the other day turned the balance of motives for and against the effort, and I set myself deliberately to work collecting and arranging materials ; for this novel is by no means a structure evolved from the depths of my own consciousness. The groundwork is a simple narration of fact, and even the superstructure is real to a great extent.

In my early days, Clara was my heroine, my princess, but I worshipped her silently, and she never took any special notice of me until years after our first meeting.

I saw her first in a village graveyard one Sunday, between the morning and afternoon services. That was the cheerful spot where the congregations of the different churches walked during the noon recess, discussed funereal subjects, and ate "sweet cake," to use the New England term of that time. Clara was accompanied by her Sunday-school teacher, named Buzzell—a grim and forbidding woman, I thought. Everybody called her "Miss Buzzell," though she was a widow ; but at that time, among the rural people of New England, it was very common to call married ladies Miss; unmarried ones received no title at all. Clara on this day wore a broad-brimmed white straw hat, with wide rose-colored streamers, a white dress and embroidered tunic of the same, and bronzed gaiters, or boots, as we now call them. She was a solid little girl, with a face round and very freckled, a broad, full brow, full pouting rosy lips, radiant blue-grey eyes, with thick, long lashes, and a nose that was pretty, though a little after the *rétroussé* order.

I shall never forget my first sensation. It was a feeling of regret that I had no freckles; for as soon as my eyes rested upon her, there came into my heart a deep desire to be just like her in every particular. Hundreds of times have I recalled her as she appeared to me that day; and I still believe that, upon some secret principle of æsthetics, notwithstanding the general prejudice against freckles, these added to the piquancy of her beauty. As she grew up few called her handsome, except those who could perceive the rich emotional nature that seemed to radiate through every gesture and movement of her supple form, and especially through her bright eyes, whose lids had sometimes a slight quiver or shake from any sudden excitation. This was something instantaneous as to time, and difficult to describe, but it added an extraordinary charm to her soulful beauty. There was always about her an atmosphere of fragrant health, which charmed you like the odors and zephyrs of spring-time. The freckles which, as a child, I had so envied her, disappeared entirely when she reached the nubile age.

On this Sunday in the graveyard I "tagged" after Clara everywhere she went, fascinated by her fresh, full

life, and by her exquisite dress ; but I could find no way
to speak to her, because of her awe-inspiring companion,
though I was often so near to her that her long hat ribbons swept my cheek. After a while my ignorance of
churchyard etiquette came to my aid ; for, finding the
distance between me and this divine vision increasing, I
made a short cut over some intervening graves. Miss
Buzzell turned her awful eyes upon me. I simply noticed that there were many wrinkles converging about her
mouth, and that her breath was redolent of cloves. In a
deep, slow, admonitory voice, she said, "Child! you
should never step on a grave !" It was like a cold leech
dropped suddenly upon the warm, sensitive flesh. I
could do nothing but hang my head in humiliation.
Clara, child-like and human, sympathized with my distress, and told me sweetly that my pantalette was coming
down. It was at the time when girls, in that part of the
country at least, wore this nondescript article fastened on
with the garter, falling down to the foot, and about three
inches below the dress, where it ended with tucks and a
wide hem. Some of us were so extravagant as to add an
edging, which we used to knit of spool cotton. I stooped
down to arrange the rebel pantalette, but when I had
finished, Clara was some graves away from me, and the
church bells were calling back the scattered congregations.

CHAPTER II.

THE SKELETON IN THE GARRET.

ONE beautiful May morning, not long after I first met Clara, I was sent to Dr. Forest's with a basket of eggs. As I opened the little gate leading through the shrubbery and little lawn to the front door, I perceived Clara standing on the wide upper step, with a watering-pot in her hand. She was dressed in white, as usual, and was sprinkling some flowers that grew in a large vase that stood on a pedestal by the steps. She greeted me pleasantly, and led me into the kitchen, where Dinah, the fat black servant, relieved my basket of its contents. Mrs. Forest, a tall, sweet-looking, pale lady, in a white apron, was engaged in making a vast quantity of little cakes, which Clara told me were macaroons for her party—a great event which was to take place that afternoon. I had heard of it, but did not expect an invitation, because I lived quite out of the village, and knew Clara but very slightly. Seeing all these delightful preparations, caused me to break the tenth commandment in my heart, but I was glad that Clara was so happy ; and I lingered in that pleasant kitchen as long as I could, consistently with any degree of propriety. The twins, now some five years old, were the most prominent object in the Forest household, if not in the whole village. At that moment Dinah was picking over raisins, and they kept near her, devouring

all she would give them, and when their importunities
failed they watched their chances, and every now and
then succeeded in grabbing a handful, when they would
disappear, and remain very quiet for a few minutes.
Sometimes Dinah would be quick enough to seize the
little depredatory hand and rob it of its booty. When
she failed, she "clar'd to God" there wouldn't be a raisin
left for Miss Clara's party cake.

The doctor's family were from the South, where Dinah
had formerly been a slave, though her condition was little
better than slavery after the advent of those imps of
twins. The good-natured old servant had loved the other
children very sincerely, and she tried hard to take these
also into her capacious heart, but she never fully succeeded. There was a feud between her and them, born
of their persistent delight in tormenting her. "Hatching
mischief," she said, was their sole occupation during their
waking hours, and their tricks were told by Dinah to
other servants until the whole village laughed over them.

After amusing the twins awhile I rose to go, following
Clara back through the dining-room to the front door.
In the hall she showed me a long table filled with toy
china sets for the amusement, she said, of the "little
girls," Dr. Buzby cards and other games for the older.
I could not repress exclamations of delight at the prospect of so much bliss; but when I informed her that I
had never been invited to a party in my life, I had not the
remotest intention of "fishing" for an invitation to hers.

"You never have been at a party!" she exclaimed,
quite amazed; and looking at me from head to foot, her
heart seemed to be touched at the extent and depth of
my deprivation. Just then Mrs. Forest came into the

dining-room, and Clara said, "Mamma, I should like to invite one other girl to my party, if you are willing. I mean this one." "Certainly, my dear, if you wish it," was the pleasant reply, and thereupon, thanking Clara as well as I could, I left the house, filled with a greater happiness than I had ever known.

On reaching home I readily gained permission to attend Clara's reception, but the question of dress was a serious one, for I well knew how finely her friends would be arrayed ; still I managed as best I could, and three o'clock in the afternoon found me timidly pulling the door-bell at Dr. Forest's. Some other girls arrived before Clara had disposed of my hat and little cape. We were first ushered into the drawing-room, where Mrs. Forest was sewing. She did not rise, but smiled upon us, and addressed to each a few pleasant words.

We soon grew impatient of sitting prim and "behaving" in the sitting-room, and were greatly relieved when we found ourselves playing games among the fragrant lilacs and syringas of the garden. Then followed a game with the innocuous Dr. Buzby cards then in vogue. Clara, more beautiful than ever, I thought, explained the principles of the game to me, in a charming, dogmatic manner. I was the only one ignorant on the subject, and this, with my very plain dress, caused one of the guests to eye me insolently and ask me if I lived in the woods. Clara instantly, and in no measured terms, rebuked her guest's impoliteness, which had the effect to send her off pouting among the lilacs. I remember this because it shows the superior nature of Clara Forest in the most unquestionable way. Children may learn the form of politeness, but the spirit of it is almost invariably absent, and must be from the very nature of human development. Man is first the brute, then the civilizee, and lastly the philosopher ; and the child, in its unfolding, exemplifies these phases just as society does. That Clara was exceptionally fine in her nature I knew well even then, but I was ignorant of the cause until long after.

We were much disturbed in our game of Dr. Buzby by Leila and Linnie, the ubiquitous twins, who vexed and annoyed us in the thousand ways that little ones have at their command. Finally, to escape from the twins, Clara led us up-stairs, through the doctor's study, into his bed-room, and closed the door. This was a plain little room, having a stand, with several books, at the head of the bed, and over it the doctor's night-bell. Clara strictly enjoined us to not so much as touch a single article in her father's rooms, on penalty of being instantly obliged, all of us, to quit our retreat. During our game of cards, Abbie Kendrick asked Clara why this room was called the doctor's exclusively.

"Why, because he sleeps here, to be sure," answered Clara, with a slight *hauteur*, as if unwilling to discuss family matters with her guests. She was a very dignified child, this idol of mine—"proud" was the term girls generally applied to her.

"But does not your mamma sleep here too?" asked Abbie, bold enough to pursue the subject.

"Certainly not," replied Clara. "Papa and mamma do not think it proper to sleep together."

This piece of information surprised us greatly, but we all accepted the fact as showing the immeasurable aristocratic superiority of the Dr. and Mrs. Forest over all the married people we knew. I remember we all approved the system, agreeing that it was quite proper for girls to sleep together, and for no others. How wise we were then ! Some of us have slightly modified our views on the subject since we played that game of cards in the doctor's room ; but we had very fixed and positive opinions then—all except Clara, who listened silently. We decided that if we ever married, which, of course, we never would, we should have two bedrooms, and never, never allow our husbands to enter ours, unless he were a physician and we happened to be ill!

When the Dr. Buzby cards ceased to amuse us, Clara produced her *piece de resistence*, which was her playhouse in the garret, somewhat neglected now, for she was approaching the outposts of young ladyhood. This garret was the one place where the sacrilegious twins had not penetrated. It was the sanctuary in which she had been in the habit of taking refuge when hard pressed by the merciless tyrants, to whom she had always been a patient nurse and victim, for her mother was in delicate health, and Dinah was almost exclusively occupied with the housekeeping. To this sanctuary Clara had removed her broken-nosed dolls, smeared and torn books, and the wrecks generally that she had snatched from time to time from the grip of the vandals.

We approached this large old garret, under the gable roof, by a rickety flight of stairs, and on reaching the landing a hideous spectacle curdled my young blood and riveted my scared, fascinated eyes. It was a grinning skeleton, suspended to the rafter by a cord and a ring attached to the top of the skull. The other girls being already initiated, laughed my terrors to scorn, while one bold miss of ten, Clara's most intimate friend, Louise

Kendrick, went straight up to the horror, made faces at it, and then deliberately set it spinning! I shall never forget the sinking, sickening sensation at my heart as the eyeless sockets and hideous teeth glared through the dim light at me with every revolution. Clara, seeing how frightened I was, hastened to reassure me by saying, as she placed her arm around me—

"It isn't anything but the bones, you know. We all look like that under our flesh." Comforting thought! It required a long time for me to control myself so that I could enter into the doll-dressing with spirit; and every now and then, as we cut, and planned, and sewed, especially as the light grew dimmer, I turned my head over my shoulder, gingerly, just enough to make sure that the "thing" was not striding toward me. Right glad was I when we were called down to our weak tea, and over the honey and hot biscuits I forgot for the time the agony of fear I had endured. That night, however, the skeleton was "after me" all the time; and my ineffectual struggles to get my long yellow hair out of its bony hands woke me many times with agonizing cries. And all this because my young imagination had been poisoned by ghost stories—the ghost always being represented by a skeleton partially covered with white drapery. I believe now in the "inquisition of science";—that one of its most sacred functions is to seize and punish any person found guilty of entertaining the sensitive, unformed brain of the child with the horrors of the grave, of death, of hell, or any of the unverifiable hypotheses of theology and superstition, born of the general ignorance incident to the childhood of the human race.

CHAPTER III.

DR. FOREST AT HOME.

THE doctor was about forty years old, but his hair was beginning to turn gray and his fine head was a little bald upon the top. He was about the medium height, muscular, with handsome broad shoulders, and very slightly inclined to stoutness. He had fine grey eyes, which he was in the habit of half closing when anything puzzled him. It was an exceedingly benevolent and expressive face, which won utter confidence at the first glance. He wore light, steel-bowed spectacles, which he never removed, apparently, from one year's end to another. In repose, his mouth had an expression of severity; and when studying, he had a curious habit of protruding his under-lip; but the moment he spoke this mouth became handsome, expressing the large-heartedness and the ready humor that made him a favorite with all who knew him.

About the old house of the doctor, there was a quaint and dignified air, given by the books and numerous pictures, most of them quite old, and by the heavy antique furniture, relic of a former generation. It was not the air of wealth exactly, yet no one could suspect, from the general appearance of things, that there was a chronic scarcity of money in the family, and that the gentle Mrs. Forest had such sore difficulty in making

ends meet. This, too, when the doctor was the best physician for miles around, and quantities of money were due
him in all directions. The truth was, he could not collect
what was due him. Unless absolutely driven to the wall,
he could not ask any of his patients for money; and when
they wished to return equivalents for his services, in the
shape of corn, and apples, and potatoes, he said not a word
until the cellar became so full that Dinah rebelled. In
the spring, when seed potatoes gave out at planting time,
every farmer knew where to make up his deficit; though
in such cases he never thought of paying the good doctor
money for them, but promised to return them at harvest
time, not being particular at all to consider that a bushel
now was worth five or ten in the autumn. Still, the doctor did not complain, being gentle to a fault, though he
took note of all things. As to his children, he confessed
frankly that he did not know how to bring them up, and
when he was in doubt about any matter of discipline, he
generally let them have their own way. An incident will
illustrate his method: the large room where Mrs. Forest
and the twins slept was directly beside the doctor's, and
as they did not like the darkness a lamp was always kept
burning there. One night when the doctor, having been
up all the previous night, had gone to bed early, he was
prevented from sleeping by a tin-whistle in the mouth of
Leila. He called out to her to stop, as he wished to go
to sleep. Presently there came to the doctor's ears a
faint little "*toot! toot!*" from the whistle. Linnie tried
hard to hush her sister, and reminded her of the voice
from the next room. "Oh, its only papa!" said Leila
impatiently; which, the doctor hearing, caused him to
investigate the motive of the child's remark, and philoso-

phizing upon the subject, he went to sleep finally to the accompaniment of the "*toot! toot! toot!*" which Leila kept up until she was tired of it.

Mrs. Buzzell, Clara's Sunday-school teacher, and an old friend of Mrs. Forest, had a very tender spot in her heart for the doctor, whom she regarded, and rightly too, as one of the best physicians in the world. No one understood her internal perturbations as he did, and she took all the medicines he prescribed with a faith that was somewhat remarkable, considering that she had been under his treatment for twelve years and more, and still required his services more than ever. Probably her sublime faith was based on the conviction of the awful things that *would* have happened but for his medicines. She lived a lonely life by herself, and was very fond of spending an afternoon at the doctor's house, and having long conversations on nothing in particular with Mrs. Forest. Her visits were sometimes almost an infliction to Mrs. Forest, who had a strong housewifely pride in nice teas, which the chronic scarcity of money, before mentioned, rendered difficult to attain in many instances. To be sure there was always bacon and a barrel of fine hominy in the kitchen, which sufficed for Dinah's southern tastes, and the family could always fall back upon these if necessary, and the latter at least was never absent from the family breakfast; but they could hardly serve a respectable tea-table where cake and creamy hot biscuits were a *sine qua non* according to all good housekeepers.

On one occasion, just before breakfast, Mrs. Buzzell sent a note to her friend expressing her intention to spend the afternoon with her, "if agreeable." Now it just was not "agreeable," for the commissariat was at a low ebb—lower, indeed, than it had ever been ; but Mrs. Forest, of course, sent back a polite answer expressing delight at the prospect of the visit, not even dreaming, probably, of the conventional fib that her answer contained.

While she was writing the reply for the messenger to take back to Mrs. Buzzell, Dinah's soul was being tried unusually in the kitchen by the conduct of the twins, which reached a climax when one of them actually threw a kitten into Aunt Dinah's boiling hominy kettle. She was long-suffering, though her threats were severe and frequent ; but this time her patience gave way entirely, and taking off a colossal carpet-slipper she spanked the offending twin right soundly. Mild Mrs. Forest hearing the uproar from the kitchen, sent Dan to bring the children to her room. Both were howling at the top of their voices, for one never cried without the other joining in on principle. Then she went down to the kitchen and reproved Dinah for taking the discipline of the children into her own hands. Dinah was too exasperated to be reasoned with. She burst out—

"I bars eberyting wid dem chil'en, missus ; but *I clar to God, I won't hab dem kittens in de hominy pot!* "

To the outside world, the Forest family was a model of domestic felicity, and not without cause as family life goes ; but Mrs. Forest was very far from a happy woman. This was due partly to her delicate health, which gave her a disposition to "borrow trouble," and to look too much beyond the grave for the happiness a stronger and more philosophical nature would have created out of her really fortunate environment. At times, she still suffered from the loss of the baby Arthur, though he had been dead some eight years. The doctor could hardly understand this as a normal expression, and she often accused him of a lack of sympathy. He himself submitted calmly always to the inevitable, learned the lesson that any misfortune afforded, applied it practically to his daily life, and in no other way remembered a suffering that was in the past. His wife, he said, had a passion for the " luxury of woe," and this was a diseased condition. Dan gave her a world of trouble. She had made an idol of him from his birth, and it was indeed hard to feel that her deep love for him was not sufficient to cure him of a single one of his bad habits. Years of the most loving effort to make him take off his hat on entering the house, had been unavailing ; and he still tramped through her tidy house with dirty shoes every day of his life, and though nearly fourteen years of age, it is questionable whether he had abandoned the charming habit of coming down stairs astride the baluster. He teased the twins, worried Clara whenever an opportunity offered, went and came without asking permission of his mother, and at table he was distressingly awkward. On this particular morning the doctor said to him, a little after sitting down to the breakfast table and while he was serving the hominy—

"Now Dan, my boy, I've been cheated out of my morning sleep by the hubbub in the house, and my nerves are irritated ; so you'll save them a shock and much oblige me if you will give me warning when you are going to upset your glass, or wipe your knife off the table with your sleeve."

Dan had more affection for his father than for any other being in the world. He hung his head, but answered good-naturedly, "I'm not going to do either this morning, sir." During this reply he was vigorously mixing a piece of very hard butter in the hominy which his father had just put into his plate, and the result was the landing of his plate, bottom upwards, on the floor by the way of his legs. Mrs. Forest uttered an exclamation of despair; but Clara quietly rose, removed the *debris*, and brought Dan another plate. This time, Dan was really distressed, and his mortification was increased by the doctor's laughing.

"Never mind, my son," he said, putting his right hand kindly on Dan's shoulder. "This time it was more my fault than yours. I made you nervous by my criticism." The idea of Dan's being nervous was an exquisite compliment from its perfect novelty. The doctor saw that the boy for once was greatly ashamed, and so he immediately changed the subject to Leila, who sat in her high chair on Dan's right. "So Miss Mischief," he said, "you set out to cook a kitten in the hominy this morning did you, eh? I'm very glad you failed, and I advise you to not try it again."

"I sall took ee titten to-maw-yer, I sall."

"You will cook the kitten to-morrow, will you?" he said, repressing a disposition to laugh. "Look here, Leila, if you try that again I hope you'll get a much larger dose of Dinah's slipper, and you shall not have a kiss from papa, nor come to the table with him for a whole week."

"Poor kitty! her toes ache so," said Linnie, who spoke quite plainly compared with her sister, and whose heart also was more tender. The doctor praised Linnie's sympathy with the kitten, and while reading Leila a little lecture on cruelty, the bell rang, and he was called off to see a patient.

During the day Mrs. Forest consulted Clara on the subject of the afternoon tea, for she was sorely perplexed and mortified, as she said, because there was nothing in the house.

"Why, mamma, I don't see why you should bother yourself. We have nice, fresh, Graham bread, some delicious cheese, any quantity of fruit, and Dinah can make some hominy. Mrs. Buzzell don't ever taste hominy, and she'll be delighted with it, I know. Papa would find such food excellent ; and I am sure what is good enough for papa is good enough for anybody in this world."

"Yes, my child, it is *good* enough, no doubt ; but it is such an odd jumble. Who ever heard of such a tea ? You know Mrs. Buzzell's appetite is fastidious, and I like to have something savory for her. Of course the doctor's credit is good at the grocer's, and everywhere, for that matter, but I have never used it, and never intended to ; but I think I shall have to make an exception to-day. We *must* have some butter and some sugar."

"Now, mamma, you know Mrs. Buzzell is always complaining about her digestion. On principle, you should never give her anything but simple food—just like this tea we are going to have ; and I wouldn't put the cheese on the table either. It may destroy the effect of papa's medicines," added Clara, laughing.

Mrs. Forest descanted with much bitterness upon the laxity of the doctor in collecting the money due him. "Well, my child," she said, after a pause, "I must trust to Providence." This intention she always expressed after dwelling upon the doctor's bad management and the exhausted state of the larder; but she evidently thought there was great virtue in such trust, as if Providence ought to be highly complimented by her confidence. This consultation took place in the kitchen pantry, and was finally ended by the entrance of Dinah with a slop-pail from the upper regions, at the same time that a country wagon drove around to the kitchen door.

CHAPTER IV.

ONE OF DR. FOREST'S PATIENTS.

THE doctor used to say that "Trust in Providence and keep your powder dry" was a good injunction, but would be better reversed; and whatever he believed, Clara subscribed to as if by instinct. So when her mother, in the kitchen pantry, expressed her determination to trust to Providence, Clara received it with a little scowl of impatience.

Dinah came into the drawing-room a few minutes later, and Mrs. Forest and Clara followed her back to the kitchen. The wagon which had just driven away contained some grateful patient of the doctor. He had left with Dinah a half dozen nicely-dressed spring chickens, some golden balls of fragrant butter, and two boxes of fresh honey in the comb. Mrs. Forest looked silently at her daughter, every feature expressing, "You see I trusted in Providence." Clara laughed pleasantly, repressing the temptation to remind her mother that the wagon must have been on its way with the welcome treasures long before that decision to trust in Providence was made; but she only said, "Now you can give Mrs. Buzzell a nice attack of indigestion. O mamma! your desire to give her something 'savory,' as you said, is only a deep-laid scheme to increase papa's practice. I see it all now. Mrs. Buzzell is one of his few patients who pay promptly !"

"Why ! what levity !" exclaimed Mrs. Forest, who, now that her anxiety about a respectable tea was removed, felt at peace with the world, and her sense of the fitness of things was answered.

Mrs. Buzzell came in good season. She was a prim lady of sixty or more, dressed in a neat black grenadine dress, open to a point from the throat. This open space was filled in with spotless illusion lace, fastened with a little jet brooch. Her white hair was beautifully rolled in three puffs on either side of her head, and surmounted by a white cap with a border or frill, and lavender-colored strings. She was a very active, industrious person, though a sufferer from her ailments. During the afternoon she spoke of her digestion several times. On these occasions Clara made a knowing, mischievous sign to her mother, who was dignifiedly oblivious, apparently, to what her saucy daughter was thinking.

Clara set the tea-table herself with her mother's choice old china, which seemed to feel its rare importance only when arranged upon a snowy cloth. After all Mrs. Forest's anxiety, the tea was as delightfully respectable as her heart could wish. The twins, however, set up in their high chairs, detracted a good deal from the solemnity of the occasion, for their behavior, always especially bad when "company" was present, was sufficient to make Mrs. Buzzell's cap-border stand up in consternation. They kicked the under side of the table with the toes of their little shoes, setting the cups dancing in their saucers, whenever the supply of honey gave out and was not instantly renewed, or when reproved by their gentle

mother for the quantity of cake they thought proper to
discuss. Whenever their conduct became unbearable, a
kind of semi-yell from Dan distracted their attention for
a few moments, enabling the ladies to continue their mild
comments upon the diseases incident to children, and the
superior taste of the new milliner's bonnets and caps.

Clara silently watched and anticipated the wants of the
twins, wearing a weary, responsible look, for they weighed
upon her young life like the world upon the shoulders of
Atlas. Since they were babies, creeping about, putting
everything animate or inanimate into their mouths, and
calling every man papa who approached them, Clara had
gradually assumed more and more the care of them, being
stronger in mind and body than her mother. Her method
of managing these irrepressibles, was very reprehensible
in one respect, but she had been led into it by the necessity of some method, and the impossibility of moving the
rebellious little tyrants by any reasonable means. She
had taken advantage of their passion for doing anything
they were forbidden to do, even though that in itself were
disagreeable to them. For example, after tea the great
desideratum was to get the twins upstairs to bed, for
there was little possibility of quiet conversation where
they were. The doctor had just come in, and was very
contentedly sipping his rather insipid tea, and gathering up
what remained of the eatables, to the accompaniment of
a somewhat detailed account of Mrs. Buzzell's "wretched
digestion."

"Now, Linnie," said Clara, "you wish to stay down
and play, don't you? but Clara is going upstairs." It
was never necessary to address but one at a time, for whatever one decided to do was certain to be immediately re-

peated by the other. By the time she had reached the stairs, Linnie dropped her toys and started, Leila following closely, both determined to perish rather than stay down-stairs, as they supposed they were expected to do. Once arrived in the sleeping chamber, similar manœuvres inveigled the twins into bed, and when they were finally sleeping, Clara went down to the sitting-room. The doctor noticed her weary look, and said, "My child, you have too much responsibility. Papa must try to send you away to school. I have been thinking of your method in managing those children. Surely you do not think you are right in controlling them by such motives?"

"I suppose not, papa," answered Clara, who had sat down on a stool at her father's side, and was "resting," as she used to call it, in the magnetic caresses of his hand upon her brown hair; "but it saves time."

"Ah! my daughter. How many follies are committed under that plea! See what you do by this course. In the first place, you cultivate obstinacy in the little ones, which is bad enough, and then you dull the fine edge of your conscience by doing what your better sense condemns, I am sure."

"She is not so much to be blamed," said Mrs. Forest. "It is one of Dan's tricks. She learned it from him."

"What does papa's girl think of that as an excuse?" he asked, studying her fine face.

"I don't think it excuses me, papa. I know it does not."

"You are right. Dan should learn of you, not you of him, in matters of conscience. I only wish he had your conscientiousness, and your love of books, too. I never see him reading. I wonder where the young rat is to-night." Clara knew pretty well where Dan was, but for his sake she kept silent. She was always merciful to his delinquencies; probably from the fear that she did not love him as she believed a sister should love her brother. No two children could well be more unlike; and for years he had bullied her unmercifully, though he would not permit others to do so, and his tough little fist was ready to the head of any urchin in school or in the street, who dared to show the least disrespect for his sister. He monopolized that matter himself, and carried teazing to cruel extremes. She was easily irritated by him, especially in her earlier years, and whenever he saw her becoming angry, it was a constant practice of his to seize both her hands and hold them as in a vise, mocking her impotent rage until it grew to murder in her heart. This was a persecution so often repeated that it had completely destroyed all her natural tenderness for him, which the sensitive child reproached herself for, and sought to atone by treating him with great kindness.

Ah! what a nursery of crooked, abnormal motives the family often is! How many really deep wrongs are done to impressible children, to which the parents are utterly blind, because so ignorant of the laws of mental development. When Clara's troubles with Dan were unendurable, she had sometimes gone to her mother. Once she did so, bursting out with, "*I wish I could kill him.*" The mother was horrified; but, alas! only at the language; not seeing beneath the surface what madness had been induced in the child's heart, nor inferring a necessary and adequate cause. She only reproved Clara for such "dreadful words," and sent for Dan. "My son, why do you teaze your sister so? Do you not know it is very wicked, and that if you are wicked you will never go to Heaven ? " In truth, she was utterly incapable of comprehending the difficulty between the children, and as Dan was on his good behavior when his father was present, and as all the family tacitly agreed to never trouble the doctor unnecessarily, knowing that he ought to rest during the short time his practice left him free, he never knew of this peculiar trial of Clara's until long after.

When Mrs. Forest would remind Dan of his danger of losing Heaven, she naturally thought that it should have great weight with him ; though if she could have read his thoughts, she would have quickly seen her mistake. Heaven, to Dan, meant a country

" Where congregations ne'er break up,
And Sabbaths never end ; "

and though he thought such a dull place might do for girls and for people like the widow Buzzell, he knew perfectly well that it was no place for a live boy, who liked fishing and setting snares in the woods much better than any congregation he could imagine.

But to go back to the family circle. When the doctor wondered where the " young rat " was, Clara kept silent. Mrs. Buzzell hazarded the suggestion that he might be off with those low Dykes—the Dykes being a family whom nobody visited, and who were generally set down as "no better than they should be." This was precisely where Dan was at that moment, and the attraction was possibly Susie Dykes, though he took no particular notice of any one but Jim Dykes, who possessed a pair of old battered foils, and with them gave the delighted Dan several desultory lessons in the art of fencing. Jim being a great swaggerer, and a little older than Dan, was mighty in his eyes; especially when he discoursed on the "guards" and "passes," his hat cocked over his left eye, his legs straddled, and an unmanageable end of tobacco in his mouth.

"It is strange," said Mrs. Forest, "what Dan finds so agreeable in that family. I am sure I could not endure the house. Mrs. Dykes is a slattern, and her children have no sort of bringing up, as I am told."

"Why," said the doctor, "I don't see but Susie is a very nice girl. She behaves very well indeed—totally unlike that uncouth brother of hers. I like the pretty way she does her hair."

"For my part, I distrust girls or women who please only men," said Mrs. Buzzell. "I've heard several men praise her looks."

"I'm inclined to think that her charm is not so much in her looks as in her good nature. She always smiles as if she were happy. The signs of happiness rest one so ;"— and the doctor sighed.

"Men," said Mrs. Forest, who seldom generalized, "are unsatisfied unless women are always gay and smiling ; but how can we be ? Household cares so drag us down, and the care of children, especially two at a time, is too much for any one."

"Yet children used to be considered a blessing," remarked the doctor, and added humorously, "but I can see how any woman might be blest to death by a too frequent repetition of this doubling extravagance of your sex."

Mrs. Forest was always annoyed at this suggestion, which the doctor often teazed his wife with, just to see the expression of impatient credulity on her face. She pretended not to notice it this time, but answered, a little spiritedly, " So they are a blessing, of course. I do not mean to deny that, but one may have many trials about them. I'm sure I have my share with Dan. He is almost sixteen, and yet I am quite sure he prefers to be ragged and dirty to looking like a gentleman's son. It does annoy me so to think I have no influence over him in this matter."

" I think, mamma," said Clara, raising her head from her father's knee, " that Susie Dykes will have more influence in that matter than you have. He made a famous toilet to-day before going out. You should see his room. It looks like an old cockatoo cage after the bird has been bathing—only cockatoos can't leave their towels and stockings scattered over the floor."

" Did he really change his stockings ? " asked Mrs. Forest in amazement. Then there's something wrong. It must be the first time in his life he ever did such a thing of his own accord ! "

When Mrs. Buzzell rose to go the doctor rose also, and, as usual, gallantly accompanied her. The conversation on the way was a little tiresome to the doctor, but his heart was far too kind to permit him to show it, for he knew that he was much esteemed by this patient, and he pitied her lonely life. In answer to her complaints about her digestion he said, " And you ate honey and hot bread to-night. You should have eaten only a crust of bread, and chewed it well."

" Oh dear, no—that is, I am never troubled about what I eat at your house. I can digest anything perfectly well there ; but everything disagrees with me at home. I have told you that often, doctor," she added, as if pained that he should not remember.

"Pardon me, I did not forget; but I thought I must take that with a certain margin, as I am compelled to do much that my women patients tell me; but I see I must make you an exception, and the result is that my treatment can do you no good. You need more excitement—a larger life. While you live such a lonely way, medicines are of little use. You see the doctor is a humbug, more or less, and must be until he can prescribe changes in the social conditions as well as of diet and climate. Anyway considered, doctoring with drugs is more the business of the charlatan than of the true scientist. The longer I live the more I see the folly of patching up the stomach and the liver when the true disease is in the soul."

"Soul! why, doctor, I was afraid you did not believe in the soul."

"But I do, only you Christians and spiritualists, so called, have such a beastly material conception of soul that you can scarcely understand the scientific faith. Be sure that I believe in the immortality of soul, but I *know* that structure corresponds to function; that is the first law of nature. Now the soul, as you conceive it, is not a spiritual conception, but some kind of organization—a ghost, in short, having functions, but the Devil himself cannot define its structure."

"Well, I am not a scientific person, doctor, so I will not pretend I know much; but I think I know that the only way to be happy is to keep as near to Christ as we can." After quite a long pause, during which doctor and patient reached the little veranda porch of Mrs. Buzzell's home, she added, "Shall I keep on taking that cardiac mixture, or would you recommend something else?"

"Nothing else," he said, holding her hand a moment,

" only a good-night kiss from your doctor." This he added gravely, and then pressed his grizzly moustache lightly first upon one and then the other of his patient's faded cheeks. The prescription was quite new, though the doctor had often kissed her forehead after sitting by her bed, talking to her while holding her hand.

" Is this a general treatment ? " asked Mrs. Buzzell good-humoredly, " or am I an exception ? "

" This is a special treatment, because specially indicated," he said. " You are thoroughly womanly in your nature, and you really need the magnetism of affection. You suffer more from your secluded life than most people would. Good night ; I will call soon," and with that he left her. To the ordinary observer Mrs. Buzzell passed as a formal prude, cold and unattractive, but in reality, there was in her heart, an under-current of refined sensibility. To be sure it would not have been safe or prudent, at least, for any other man to attempt to kiss her cheek as the doctor had done, but she knew there was no guile in his heart, and she justly held his kindness and his deep sympathy with her as a most precious treasure. Coarse men are wont to scoff at the attraction women find in ministers and physicians, especially women whose social conditions are unfortunate ; but the solution is very simple : physicians, at least, generally know more of human nature than other men do. This is true, of course, only of those of the nobler moral type. No others win the confidence of refined women, though their vanity may blind them to the wide difference there is between ordinary and extraordinary confidence, for every physician, if not every priest, receives a certain amount of confidence from the nature of his office. The physi-

cians of the high type to which Dr. Forest belongs, know
to a certainty the amount of mutual sympathy existing
between their women patients and their husbands, when,
as is often the case, there is no verbal confession of
grievances ; and even when, if such grievances exist, there
is special care taken to conceal them. The kind-hearted
and high-minded physician, especially if he be a man of
the world, as all great physicians have invariably been,
is the priestly confessor among Protestants. He no more
thinks of betraying the confidences of his patients than
the Catholic priest does those of the confessional. He is
not restrained from a feeling of honor—there is no re-
straint in the case, for there is not the slightest temptation to talk of such confidences. It is not in that way
that the physician regards them. He has received them
by the thousand, and they excite no wonder in his mind ;
besides, who could understand them as he does ? He
receives them seriously enough, for whatever the cause,
suffering is positive and demands his sympathy, and the
true physician accords it as by instinct. To the vulgar,
causes seem often very amusing. To the physician, he
who " dies of a rose in aromatic pain," is none the less dead
than if hit by a cannon-ball.

When you see two men walking in the street, and
another in front of them trips and falls on the pavement,
watch the effect of the accident on the two men. If one
guffaws with amusement, and the other rushes to the
victim, helps him up with grave ceremony and sympathetic words, you may draw this conclusion : the first is
an ignoramus, and very likely an American ; the other is
a physician or a Frenchman ; for as a rule the French
are incapable of seeing anything comical in an incident

fraught with danger to a fellow-mortal. Not that American men are less generous and kind-hearted than other people, but they are ashamed of the imputation of effeminacy, and consider it laudable to conceal the signs of delicate sensibility.

Mrs. Buzzell could not probably have explained exactly what it was in the character of Dr. Forest that made him seem so unlike all other men. She would have naturally called it religion, only the doctor was most unquestionably different, in his views of social morality and "saving grace," from all the devout people she had ever known. She thought herself a very strict believer in orthodox dogmas, but in truth she would herself have rejected any "scheme of salvation" that was not some way capable of including him. Perhaps she could not see clearly how, so she prayed for him constantly, and believed that God would never suffer such purity of heart, and such devotion to everything good and true, to go unrewarded. It was clearly "unreasonable." She could understand, she thought, how good works might not count much in themselves, but motives could never go for naught; and the doctor's motives were so nobly superior that they *must* come by the grace of God. So on that rock she rested her fears for the doctor's salvation.

CHAPTER V.

THE TATTOOING.

TWO years are passed, and nothing that very specially affects the doctor's family has happened. The twins go to school, quarrel with each other, as sisters generally do, but they give Aunt Dinah less trouble. They have grown far too considerate to attempt flavoring the hominy with live kitten, an event which, for a very long time, she constantly feared would be repeated. They are "as like as two peas," according to most people outside of the family, though in fact, with the exception of their size and dress, they do not much resemble each other. Leila is a natural egotist, and has everything pretty much her own way, for Linnie has no rights which her more positive sister is inclined to respect. Linnie, who is much more generous and affectionate than Leila, protests loudly against the tyranny of her sister, "yells," as Leila poetically calls weeping, but in the end invariably yields.

Dan is about seventeen, and with Clara attends the village high-school. His educational progress is of the same order as that which distinguished him in the old district-school spelling class, where the head was at the wrong end of the room! To his loving mother he is a vexation of spirit, though he is less awkward at table, and he has learned to take off his hat, and with great effort, and for a short time, to behave "like a gentleman's

son," as she says. Still he finds Jim Dykes as irresistible
as ever, for the two are now endeared by one or two des-
perate encounters, wherein the "science" acquired from
his worthy teacher had enabled Dan to prove himself
master. He was much prouder of this than he would
have been of any honor at the disposal of the high-school,
for the great bully, Jim Dykes, treated him with distinguished respect.

One evening, when Mrs. Forest was sitting up for him,
as she always did, he came in very late. She reproved
him for passing his time in low company, whereupon he
stoutly defended the whole Dykes family on general principles. This he had never done before. She was seriously concerned, and when she spoke of Susie Dykes, he
answered insolently and went upstairs in a huff. When
the doctor entered, a little later, his wife appeared at the
head of the stairs, and asked him to come up to Dan's
room, whither she had followed him, as she had often
done, to offer silent prayers at his bedside, when distrust-
ing all mortal power to guide him safely through the
temptations of youth. He was sleeping, as she expected ;
but she had been diverted from her pious purpose by a sight
that turned all her maternal solicitude into indignation
and refined disgust. The doctor followed Mrs. Forest
into the boy's room, where he lay asleep, as stalwart and
beautiful in form as any rustic Adonis could well be. He
had thrown the covering partially off, for it was warm,
and one of his incurable habits was to sleep entirely nude.
This the doctor said he had inherited from his old Saxon
ancestry, who always slept in that way.

The cause of his mother's perturbation was soon perceived by the doctor. This was a fresh tattooing on his

left arm, extending quite from the elbow to the wrist. It was abominably but clearly done, in blue and scarlet, the design being two hearts spitted with a dart, between the names DAN FOREST and SUSAN DYKES.

"The young donkey!" said the doctor, laughing; and on the way down-stairs he added, "This young America is too fast for you, is he not, Fannie?"

"I must say you take it very coolly, doctor. Such a shocking thing! To think of his disfiguring himself for life in that way." Mrs. Forest looked in despair.

"My dear, there's nothing to be done. You must accept the inevitable. What astonishes me is the precocity of the rascal. See! nothing has ever given that boy any enthusiasm in life. In school he's a perfect laggard, and though now past sixteen, cannot write a decent letter. He has idled away his time, with no real interest in anything. Now, here is born in him suddenly a new life, and it so charms him that he disfigures himself for life, as you say, in order to immortalize the sentiment, not questioning for a moment that Susan Dykes will remain so long as he lives the same divinity in his eyes that she now seems. If we could only utilize such forces when they appear! but under our present subversive social system, they are as unmanageable as the unloosed affrites of the *Arabian Nights*."

Mrs. Forest looked bewildered. The doctor went on:

"Suppose this girl had been in Dan's class and superior to him intellectually (as she is in fact), and he had to recite every day with her eyes upon him. Don't you see what a spur it would be to his learning his lessons? The strongest motive would be to distinguish himself, and so win her admiration. Well. Dan is your idol,

Fannie. I confess I know nothing about him, nor how to help him; but for Clara I am decided. She's a child after my own heart, and, by Heaven! she shall have a chance. She shall not be sacrificed for want of anything in my power to do for her. She must go to school, Fannie. In a month the fall term commences at Stonybrook College. There are no decent schools for girls, but that I believe is about the best we have. Can you get her ready, do you think?"

Mrs. Forest was amazed at this sudden decision, and she answered despondently, "What *am* I to do without Clara? she is so much help to me."

"I know; but we must not spoil the girl's future. This is the beginning of the age of strong women, and Clara is a natural student; besides she has a noble head everyway. Time was when piano-playing, a little mono-chromatic daubing, and an infinitesimal amount of book lore, sufficed for a girl. That time is past. I want Clara to develop her forces all she possibly can under the present social conditions. She must be strong and self-supporting."

"Why! don't you expect her to marry?"

"No; that is, I don't care. I'd as soon she would not. As things go, sensible, educated, and self-poised women are better single than married, even to the best class of men. About every man is conscious that he's a tyrant; but slaves make tyrants. If there were no slaves there would be no tyrants, but a great republic of equals."

"Why, doctor! Have I not always been a good wife to you?" and the tears came to her eyes.

This was so unexpected, that the doctor felt inclined to laugh. He had been looking into vacancy as he talked,

not dreaming that he was uttering words that could by
any possibility be turned into any personal application.
He had forgotten for a moment the fact that Mrs. Forest
was like many women, who never fail to see a personal
reflection in any comment upon woman's culture or condition, or upon anything unusual in household management. Sometimes, for example, the bread bought at the
baker's would prove unusually chippy and innutritious,
but never could the doctor remark the fact without hurt-
ing his wife's feelings, as if she had personally made the
bread and staked her reputation upon its giving perfect
satisfaction. The doctor knew well this weakness, but
had forgotten it for a moment. Had he been looking at
her while he talked, he would have tempered his voice or
words probably.

"A good wife, dear! of course you have," he said,
caressing her, "though I have not quite forgiven you for
doubling my responsibilities."

This was the doctor's one marital teaze, which was so
comically effective that he could not resist repeating it,
occasionally, to hear her defend herself with the ingenuous
concern of one half conscious of being in the wrong, yet
not knowing how. When this subject was exhausted, and
Mrs. Forest's temporary grief also, the subject of sending
Clara to school was resumed. Mrs. Forest asked how it
could be accomplished. "It will cost so much," she
said.

"Why, I am as rich as a Jew, Fannie," he replied.
"Old Kendrick actually paid me to-day all his long
standing bill. You know I've just got him through a
horrid case of peritonitis," he added, with an inward
chuckle, seeing that he had spoken ambiguously, and

knowing that certain people are always anxious to know the name of a disease, which generally satisfies their curiosity in proportion to the incomprehensibility of the term—"a serious case of peritonitis, and feeling very comfortable to-day, but that his life was still in my ;nds, he had an access of gratitude, and promised to pay me every cent as soon as he got out of the house. I joked him and declared that my only sure way to get my fees was to dispatch him speedily, which I seriously thought I would do on reflection, as the settlement would be certain then. That joke did the business ; for he made me ring for the servant, whom he ordered to bring him his writing materials, and then and there he made out a cheque for the amount."

"But, dear, you should first have a nice whole suit of clothes yourself," said Mrs. Forest.

"Oh no ; I'll get on well enough. I should feel too much like a swell in a whole new suit." In truth, the good doctor had not experienced that luxury for years, and his appearance was not a great many removes from the condition known as "seedy ;" but thanks to Mrs. Buzzell's devotion, he was always kept supplied with elegant linen and hand-knit stockings for summer and winter, which he always wore long and gartered above the knee. In gloves he was somewhat extravagant, for he held that a physician's hands should be preserved sensitive and fine to the touch ; especially when he filled the office of surgeon as well as physician, as most country doctors do.

Dr. Forest's medicaments in all ordinary cases were of the most simple kind, and his rival, Dr. Delano, and even old Dr. Gallup, were in much better repute at the druggists than he was, for his heart was always with the poor, and to these he generally furnished most of the medicines himself. He understood well the weakness of uncultivated people, shown nowhere more signally than in their faith in the potency of mysterious drugs ; and when he called for "two glasses, two-thirds filled with fresh water," he did it with an assumption of certainty that convinced his patient that life or death might be in those words, "two-thirds ;" and when he emptied a harmless powder, perhaps of magnesia or carbonate of soda, into one and stirred it carefully, and then some other equally innocuous substance into the other glass, stirring each alternately, it was with an air that said plainly, "Beware how you trifle with the time and the manner of taking these !"

Though it can by no means be proved that the popular and almost adored Dr. Forest gave bread pills and innocuous medicines generally, yet it is exceedingly probable that he did, and his marvelous success goes far by way of corroboration. Apparently, he knew just what to do in all cases. Water he insisted upon so mercilessly that his patients became regularly habituated to taking a warm bath while they waited for his visit. To the questions of the better educated of his patients he used to say, "Lord bless you, how do I know ? Do you think medicine a science whose every problem can be worked out by a formula like those of algebra or geometry ? We knew precious little of the absolute value of medicines when all that is incontrovertible is admitted and all the rest rejected. One thing is certain, there is nowhere on this two-cent planet at present the conditions for perfect health, because there are nowhere the conditions for perfect happiness. Bless your heart! instead of being decrepit and played out at seventy or eighty years, we ought to be teaching boys how to turn double-back somersaults, or making sonnets to fresh and beautiful women who are great-grandmothers. Life, as we know it now, is but a miserable travesty of the real destiny of our race when we become integrally developed, and have brought the planet thoroughly under our united control. If a physician is up with the science of his time and a true man, about all he can say honestly is : keep your lungs, skin, liver, and kidneys in working order, lead an active, temperate life, possess your soul in quiet, and send for the doctor when you know you haven't done these and want to shove the responsibility off upon him."

He was severe to many of his patients, but so popular that he had to manœuvre shrewdly to give the young Dr. Delano a chance to establish himself. Among the poor, the old, and especially the forlorn, like poor Mrs. Buzzell, he made his longest visits ; and where he knew that love and sympathy were "indicated," he gave them freely, as in the case of this lonely woman. He often caressed her thin hand after counting her pulse, held his cool, soft, magnetic hand long upon her forehead ; sometimes closing her eyes thus while he talked gayly, told her comical anecdotes in his life, which made her laugh, and so stimulated some laggard function into working order.

CHAPTER VI.

CLARA AT STONYBROOK COLLEGE.

"STONYBROOK COLLEGE" would have been more appropriately, as well as more modestly, termed Stonybrook School at the time Clara entered it, for it was hardly more than a high-school for girls, though it stood well among institutions for the education of young ladies at a time when the equal education of the sexes was deemed an utopian idea among most people. It ranks much higher now that preparatory schools of a nobler order have furnished a more advanced class of students, and so more truly deserves the name, college. It stands upon the summit of a grand swell of land overlooking a large provincial city. The grounds are beautifully wooded, and laid out in handsome lawns, gardens, and groves. It boasts a really promising botanical garden, and the practical instruction of the young ladies in botany has always been well and systematically conducted. Clara, after a short time, took the first place in the botanical class, and in most of her studies.

There was one thing about this school which rendered it únpopular among the superficial of society, who desire only that their daughters shall secure the honor of graduating, quite independent of the fact of the amount of culture that such honor should presuppose. Very many students who entered Stonybrook College never graduated, and there was for a long time a severe struggle between the president and certain of the board of directors on the question of lowering the standard required for graduation. The latter argued that the first requisite was to make the school popular; while the former, a really learned and progressive spirit, maintained that popularity secured by lowering the grade of requirements would simply result in a primary school, by whatever high-sounding name it might be called, and that this was not the object of the founder, and moreover was the sure method to destroy the nobler popularity that should be aimed at. The president and his friends finally carried the day, and it was this fact that determined Dr. Forest to choose this institution for his favorite child. She had now been a student there two years.

It was June, and a Thursday afternoon holiday Through the groves and lawns the young girls promenaded in twos and threes, conversing with that enthusiasm about nothing which none but girls are capable of. When deeply enough penetrating into the grove to be out of sight of any "stray teacher," as they would somewhat disrespectfully say, they often familiarly twined their arms about each others' slender waists, and so continued their walks, joining other groups from time to time. Their conversation was of that lofty and learned order which girls from twelve to seventeen, in female colleges, naturally assume. It may not be amiss to take up a little time with a sample:

Nettie.—"Still two whole months before vacation! I declare, I shall die before the time comes."

Hattie.—"*I* don't think it seems so long. I do wish,

Nettie, you had taken geometry this term. You've no idea how nice it is."

Nettie.—" Thank you. Algebra is quite enough to drive me distracted. You are one of the strong-minded, you know. You just cram a few of your sines and co-sines into my head, along with the surds and reciprocals already there, if you want to see a raving, incomprehensible ' idgeot,' as you call it."

Hattie.—" I *never* pronounced it so in my life. You are the one to mispronounce words, and to make mistakes too. Why, you've just been talking of sines and cosines of geometry. Those are terms of trigonometry. Don't you know it?"

Nettie.—" No ; and what is more, I don't care. If I had my way, I'd just burn all the algebras in the college.'

Carrie.—" I'm glad you haven't your way, then. I think algebra perfectly splendid."

Hattie.—" I like algebra too, but geometry is more interesting. I think it perfectly lovely."

Nettie.—" I don't believe either of you. Mathematics are a horrid bore anyway."

Hattie.—" *Mathematics are!* O shade of Goold Brown !"

Nettie.—" Well, that ought to be correct. You wouldn't say the ' scissors is,' would you?"

Hattie.—" I would if I wanted to, *carissima mia.*"

Carrie.—" You never call me *Carissima*, Hattie."

Hattie.—" You see, you are Carrie in the positive, not *cara*, so you can't be *carissima* in the superlative. Why don't you laugh at my pun, you owls?"

Nettie.—" You don't give time enough. I was just

bringing my powerful mind to a focus on the punning
point when you interrupted."

Carrie.—" I was thinking of the dear, kind, old Signore
Pozzese."

Hattie.—" Mercy! Spare the adjectives. I had no
idea you were so in love with that precious Italian professor; but you need not set your cap for him. He has
no eyes but for one, and that is Signorina Clara. Everybody can see he's lost his heart to her."

Carrie.—" I can't endure that Clara Forest. She puts
on such airs of dignity and general superiority. Why,
here she comes! I hope she didn't hear me."

Clara approached, reading aloud, but in a low mono-
tone, from a little book. She did not notice the trio until
close upon them. They greeted her kindly; and Carrie,
who a moment before could not "endure" her, was specially sweet in her manner. But we should not be too
severe upon Carrie's hypocrisy. Most of us have been
guilty of the same inconsistency in one or another form.
These were all nice girls, aye, and bright girls too, naturally, despite their opinions upon algebra and geometry.
When we consider the paucity of conditions for high culture that young women may command, we should wonder,
not that they are so frivolous, but that they so often rise
above the petty ambitions of fashionable life.

Clara passed on, after a few pleasant words, and sat
down in a quiet nook to finish her book. It was the
Jaques of George Sand; and as she read on she was
deeply moved by the masterly rendering of the hopeless
passion of the hero, and especially by his heroic sacrifice
to his wife. Being thoroughly absorbed by her reflections and emotions, she did not hear the light step of Miss

Marston, her favorite teacher, who came and sat down beside her.

"My dear, what have you been reading?" she asked. Clara handed her the book frankly, knowing well it would not be approved, for George Sand was one of the tabooed authors in Stonybrook.

"I am grieved to find you reading such books, Miss Forest," said the teacher, looking very gravely at the pupil. Miss Marston's home was in a town near Oakdale, and she had known Dr. Forest by reputation quite well. She knew of his omnivorous literary tastes, and was wondering if his daughter had not possibly inherited them.

Clara answered, looking straight in Miss Marston's clear brown eyes, "I am sorry you are grieved—very sorry; but I cannot see why such a book as this should be classed with those unfit to be read." And she blushed deeply, as girls will from a thousand different emotions.

"See how you blush while you say it," said Miss Marston, in a tone of real severity.

"I blush at everything," replied Clara, angry at the weakness; "but I would not say what I do not think—most certainly I would not to you."

"Where did you obtain this book?"

"One of the students lent it to me."

"Which one?"

"I must not say, because she asked me to not tell, and I promised. I wish I had not, for I do not like to confess this promise to you." Clara was sorely troubled. She knew this teacher had a real affection for her, as, indeed, all her teachers had, for she was frank and straightforward always, never shirked any task, and was the life of all recitations in which she took part. She asked questions and explanations innumerable, and would never quit studying any difficult point until she had thoroughly mastered it. Such pupils are ever the delight and the support of the faithful teacher; and no matter whether personally sympathetic, or charming in other ways, they are sure to be honored and treated with great consideration by any teacher worthy of the name. There is no surer test of a teacher's utter incapacity than that his favorites are the pretty, wheedling shirks of the class-room.

Miss Marston was silent for a little time after Clara's expression of regret, and then she said kindly, "That is well said, Clara. Of course, you must keep your promise; but do you not see that you were wrong to borrow a book which your fellow-student was ashamed to have known she possessed?"

"I cannot say she was ashamed of having this book. I feel certain that if she had read it as carefully as I have, she would not have made the request. I could never be ashamed to own such a book as this."

"That is no argument. You are too young and inexperienced to judge of books, and when your teachers forbid the reading of certain kinds of literature, it is because they know that their influence is baneful. Remember the old adage, 'Touch pitch and be defiled.'"

"But I am sure this is not pitch," Clara answered, spiritedly; "and I do not think there is so much wisdom in that old saying—or at least it is often misapplied. My mother used to make a great effort to keep Dan and me from playing with certain children; but my father always declared that we ought to play with poor, neglected

children, who sought our society ; because, as he said, if
our manners were more gentle than theirs, the result
would be a culture to them which we had no right to
withhold.   When my mother quoted this adage, he used
to say, 'Pitch will not stick to ice,' meaning that the
badness of these children would not hurt us if we loved
the good and the beautiful, and sought it everywhere, as
he had taught us to do."

"Then you wish me to understand, I presume, that
you set your judgment against mine, and will read per-
nicious books if it pleases you to do so ? "

Clara looked hurt by this, and her faith in Miss Marston received a shock.   Why could not this good, wise
teacher understand at once, without so many words ?   By
yielding graciously, Clara was sure of caressing words and
the old mutual trust.   She was tempted to do so, because
her love of approval by those she admired was a strong
passion.   While different motives struggled for control,
she remembered certain words of Dr. Forest, in his last
conversation with her, in his study, the evening before
she left, when he had held her on his knees and talked to
her very seriously upon many matters, some of which he
had never broached before.   "Be magnanimous always to
those who fail," he had said; but Clara had never dreamed
that one of her teachers would be "weighed in the balance
and found wanting."   She had at the time thought only
of her class-mates, who might fail in many ways.   So
when she spoke, as she did after a little pause, she had
determined to rise or fall in her teacher's estimation, as
she must, by the expression only of the best and most
honest sentiments of her heart.

"You have been so good to me, Miss Marston," she

said, and her words came with some difficulty—"you
must know I am anxious to keep your good opinion of
me ; but I must be true to myself, and I will. I *cannot*
think nor feel that this book is not good and moral. It
has wakened my best feelings. In the story the wife,
Fernande, ceases to love her husband, and loves some
one else. The reader must feel the deepest sympathy
for poor Jaques, who dies that he may not stand
in the way of his wife's happiness. I constantly felt, as
I read, that if I were Fernande, I would torture myself
sooner than let myself grow cold to such a grand, noble
creature as Jaques. I am perfectly sure, if I were ever
in a like position, I should be much more careful to take
the wisest course from having read this book."

"You are very different from other girls, Clara. It
will not make you vain to tell you that you are eminently
superior to most of them ; but I fear you lack respect for
your elders. You are self-willed ; but I know you wish
to do right. We will say no more about it ; " and she
took the young girl's hand in both hers and caressed it
softly. Love always won Clara. She was a creature
of tender emotions ; to see Miss Marston yielding
touched her profoundly, and she said quickly, her eyes
full of tears, " I must do just right about this, or I shall
be horridly unhappy. You have known papa many years,
and he spoke of you in the highest praise ; but I have
found you nobler and better than even he could tell me.
You know he is what they call a liberal—a 'free-thinker,'
as some say—and he is so just and noble in all his words
and acts that I believe he must be right in his principles,
though mamma does not think so. I know that you too
are a 'liberal' "—Miss Marston started—"O, I know. I

have often heard you talking to other teachers, and I notice you take the very views that my father does of many things. Now, I will tell you what I will do. Will you promise me one little thing without asking what it is ? "

" That, I should say, is something for me to do instead of you."

" Well, it is preliminary to what I am to do."

" I never do that, Clara—well, yes, I promise you, provided always it is not something absolutely absurd. What do you wish ? "

" You said you had not read *Jaques*. I want you to read it carefully, just as I have done, and then if, in your judgment, it is a bad book for me to have read, I promise while I remain here to read nothing without your permission."

Miss Marston crammed the *brochure* into her dress pocket, saying, " I like your trust in me, but you will be disappointed. I shall be forced to condemn, I know ; but I will be fair ; and now please to be careful how you call me a *liberal*. It is a very equivocal compliment for a lady."

" Are not angels liberals ? " asked Clara, smiling, the little wrinkles gathering about her pretty eyes as she spoke.

" I am not acquainted with the private opinions of that fraternity," said Miss Marston, wondering what next.

" Because if you are, I always call you a liberal." Miss Marston smiled, kissed Clara's cheek, and walked on. She was a good little woman, who had drank rather deeply at the bitter fountains of life. She was in a safe haven now, and being a studious and conscientious teacher, did her work nobly and well.

CHAPTER VII.

OAKDALE some years ago was a very old-fashioned village, built around the traditional "common," facing which were two taverns, one called the "Rising Sun," several country stores, a printing office, many residences, more or less elegant, and the Congregationalist church. The Methodist was on a side street, and the Universalist, which had once occupied a position on the common itself, had been moved off to satisfy the tastes, and possibly the prejudices, of the citizens; for the Universalist was not the popular church of Oakdale, though its preachers generally "drew" well, the doctor said, among the floating population, and those who stubbornly refused to identify themselves with any sect whatever. Dr. Forest went sometimes to this unpopular church, but Mrs. Forest was a staunch member of tho Congregationalist—the only one having any pretence to respectability in her eyes. In time Oakdale changed wonderfully, and some two years after Clara's entrance into Stonybrook College, it had become quite a manufacturing centre, for the railroad had brought new vitality into the old-fashioned town. It was now a city; boasted two rival newspapers, three paved thoroughfares, and several nice brick sidewalks. The doctor's business shared the common prosperity. Mrs. Forest delighted her soul in the multiplying cares incident upon the gratification in some degree of her social ambition. The twins were quite large girls, attending school in the village. Leila, who boasted that she was the elder, as she was by an hour or so, led her sister by the nose, figuratively speaking, being pretty and selfish, and therefore a tyrant. These precious sisters quarreled from their cradle up ; yet they were attached to each other by a bond, not so palpable but hardly less effective, than that uniting the famous Siamese brothers, for they pined if separated for a single day ; though their reunion was often followed by a disagreement that ended in fiery recrimination, if not in uprooted curls. Oh, those twins ! Nature had somehow so exhausted herself in producing their bodies that there was no force left for their souls, which Dinah "clar'd to God" were wholly wanting. This was not true of Linnie, at least, for she was generally sweet in her temper, as well as kind and obliging, when in her best moods.

The Dykes family had broken up—gone no one knew or cared whither, all except Susie, who was left to shift for herself in the old house that had been their home. Here the doctor found her one day, weeping for her good-for-nothing brother, who, if report said truly, had good reasons for not appearing in Oakdale. The doctor at once cheered her heart by bidding her stop crying, and trust him as her friend. His kindness drew from her the fact, that Mrs. Dykes was only her step-mother, and Jim no relation whatever. Her father, a wretched victim of intemperance, had been dead for years, and poor Susie's condition was forlorn in the extreme ; and yet, for some reason which she did not explain, she seemed exceedingly loth to quit the place and go with the doctor to his home. He finally prevailed, however, and Mrs. Forest, who was first shocked at the doctor's step—he "would do such strange things"—soon found Susie very useful, and the temporary asylum, that the doctor had asked his wife to extend to the girl, grew finally permanent. To Susie it was a new and better world; and as she loved Dan with all her lonely little heart, she served his family with devotion. Everything belonging to him was sacred in her eyes.

Dan, meanwhile, had disappeared some weeks from the paternal roof, having given notice to his mother of his intention to leave a few days before that event. Still she did not believe he could do such a thing, and when it occurred, she was sorely troubled, though he was, as he said, old enough to take care of himself. She had long since been compelled to abandon her cherished hopes for her first-born. He could not apply himself in school, and always laid the blame of his low grade upon the teacher, or upon some circumstance for which he, Dan, was wholly irresponsible. In the art of excuses he was perfect, and had been from his earliest years. These he gave in a glib, ready manner, looking up with frank eyes that never failed to deceive a stranger. He had as many projects as there were days in the year. At one time he would be a jeweler, and the doctor secured him a position where he might learn the trade. This he gave up in a week, and so with many other schemes, until his father was utterly discouraged; but he never uttered a word of blame, knowing well that Dan could no more change his nature than could the leopard his spots. When he left home, therefore, the doctor comforted his wife, assuring her that it was a good thing for Dan to strike out for himself, and that he was sure to return some day when she least expected it; and so he did—horror of horrors! He turned up one day on a peddler's cart, and entering the house in his usual unceremonious way, solicited patronage for his unconscionably varied wares. Mrs. Forest came near fainting, but Dan greatly enjoyed horrifying her. He was not so satisfied with the effect upon the doctor, who said kindly, "My son, I would rather see you an honest peddler than a dishonest statesman." These words rang in Dan's ears. It seemed, then, that he could satisfy his father's hopes for him by peddling Yankee notions and tin kettles! Nothing that had ever happened to Dan had really touched his self-conceit like this. He made no answer but a low whistle.

It was a quaint picture, there in the large old sitting-room. The doctor sat by the grate smoking his little Gambier clay pipe, with a goose's wing-bone for a stem. Dan, rosy with health and strength, and long riding in the open air, whip in hand, his pantaloons inside his boot-legs, and Mrs. Forest hanging upon his muscular arm, a little pained that her son seemed so indifferent to her tenderness—a tenderness so great that she had not even noticed yet the disposition of the legs of his trowsers! He got away from his mother's caresses as soon as he could without positive rudeness, for well he knew that there was "metal more attractive" in the house somewhere; having kept up a correspondence with Susie as well as was practicable with his being constantly moving from town to town. His mother would have something brought in for him to eat;—no, he would go into the kitchen and have Dinah give him something. He would much prefer that. Mrs. Forest did not once think of Susie, or perhaps she would have followed him. Certainly she would, had she known that Dinah was making an elaborate search for eggs in the barn. So Dan found Susie alone, and the meeting was very demonstrative, on his side at least. He held her pressed like a vise in his strong arms, making her both happy and wretched at once—happy at the rude proofs of his affection, and wretched lest her love for him should be discovered. Hearing steps he released her, and said he had come for something to eat. Susie, too full of joy at meeting the one being in the world who loved her, to know what she was about, brought Dan a plate of soda-biscuits, and then stopped to look at him. He crunched two or three between his strong white teeth, interspersing the operation with more kisses, and then Dinah was observed approaching the house. Susie disappeared into the pantry, conscious of the tell-tale blushes flushing her whole face.

"Lor bress you honey, I'se glad to see ye. I knowed ye hadn't runned away."

" You knew I'd turn up like a bad penny, Dinah. So I have, but I'm off again directly. I say, Susie," he called, " if I've to eat any more of these crackers, do bring me some coffee, or a ramrod, or something to help get them down."

"Lor sakes ! Massa Dan, who gived ye such trash ? " and bustling about she made him sit down, while she placed before him every delicacy she could lay her hands on. Susie, meanwhile, went on with her work quite unconscious of his presence, Dinah thought ; but Mrs. Forest, coming in soon after, did not fail to notice the flush on Susie's face, and to attribute it to Dan's presence ; so when he would not bring his peddler's cart around to the barn, out of sight of prying eyes, nor stay even an hour longer, she did not press him much. Clearly he was better away, now that Susie Dykes was a fixture in the family, but she insisted upon his giving her a private interview after the doctor had been called away to his patients. She talked to him of religion, of duty, urged him to give up this peddling as unworthy of his talents, and above all things to avoid low connections. Not one word did she utter directly of that which lay nearest her heart, though Dan knew well what she meant by low connections. In brief, he was bored by his mother's "preaching," though he listened passively enough, but felt infinitely relieved when he mounted his cart and drove off, covertly throwing a kiss to Susie, who was watching him by the curtain edge of an upper window.

In fact, Dan had never led so free and easy a life before, and his adventures furnished matter to delight Susie's heart; for under an assumed name he wrote her very constantly for a long time. After a while he gave up peddling, and became a brakeman on a railroad. This for a time filled his ambition, like a goblet, to the brim. But his income was decidedly small, and would never permit him to put enough by to marry Susie and run away with her, a feat he had long desired to accomplish. Clearly New England was a slow place for making money, when a fellow had nothing to commence on. If he only had this something to start with, he would succeed in any kind of mercantile operation. He had a talent for business. He had proved it by a successful enterprise when he was ten years old. This enterprise was the buying of some young ducks with money that the doctor had given him. They grew and flourished on corn and otn‹‹ food that cost Dan nothing, and when they were ready for market, he sold them to his mother at a high price, and ate them himself! This operation had often been quoted by the doctor to dampen Dan's ardor when he wanted money to commence business for himself. The doctor knew the volatile nature of his boy, and that he would not succeed unless conditions were about as favorable as in the duck enterprise. Still the good doctor had done much for Dan, being willing to buy him all the experience he could possibly afford, and he regretted that this was so little; but he must, as he told Dan, look out for his girls; boys could rough it, and learn prudence and forecast by experience. This was on the occasion of Dan's next visit home, when he was wild with the desire to set up a livery stable, with the secret idea of finally doing a "big thing" in fast horses. This part, however, he concealed. The doctor having been able to put by a little sum for his "girls" during the past few years, was almost persuaded to yield and start Dan in his new business scheme; but this time Mrs. Forest's entreaties and tears prevailed, at least for the time; not that she believed wholly that Dan would fail, but keeping a stable was such a disreputable thing in her eyes. It was so closely and inevitably connected with drinking and fast young men, both of which, to her horror, she had found that he had a taste for, though not as yet developed to any alarming extent.

When, therefore, the doctor got ready to give his final answer, Dan was disposed to be quite saucy. He told his father that "other fellows" were not expected to get a start in the world without help, and that if Clara had wanted such assistance it would be forthcoming.

"Well, Dan," replied the doctor, rising and falling softly on his heels, as he stood with his back to the fire, in his little study, "I think you may be right. If Clara wanted to go into the horse business on graduating from Stonybrook, I think I should lay no straw in her way. By Jove! I think she'd succeed, though."

"Succeed!" Dan echoed, in contempt. This irritated the doctor a little.

"Yes, sir, *succeed*. I think she would. She has ten times the brains of any young fellow I know. Women are going into business now-a-days, and considering their want of business experience, their success is marvelous. I can't say I'd prefer the horse business for Clara, but I hope to Heaven she will take up with something beside matrimony. Girls have a poor show as things are, and a father feels bound to look out for them first."

"I don't see it"—answered Dan, somewhat irreverently—"I think girls have a much better show than we have;" and he sat down, with the back of a chair between his legs, and went on: "I don't see anything much easier than to sit in the parlor, drumming on the piano until the richest fellow comes along, then nab him."

"Good God!" exclaimed Dr. Forest. "You envy them that fate, do you? How would you like some rich woman to offer to give you her name, and to keep you during good behavior; that is, as long as you remained devoted to her, faithful, and the rest? What would you say to such an offer?"

Dan laughed aloud at the picture, but said, with some

laudable confusion, "If you want my honest opinion, sir, I shouldn't like to swear I could stand the test."

This answer took the doctor unawares, and he lost his gravity at once. Besides, being a true believer in the absolute equal rights of all human beings, the case had not seemed half so shocking as he would have it appear to Dan. His conscience accused him, and he said, smiling, "Well, my boy, I like your frankness. I heard a witty woman say once that if men, with their present moral standard, were suddenly to be transformed into women, they would all be on the town in a week. The fact is, neither sex should be kept by the other. Independence, honest self-support, by honest, productive industry, is the thing for women as well as men;" and as the doctor turned to empty his pipe into the grate, he asked Dan how much money he wanted to establish his livery business. Dan explained, with minute detail, just how matters stood, how fortunate the opening, how little the investment required, how certain the success. The doctor promised the funds, confessing at the same time that he had little faith, but that he could not endure that his son should think his father lacking in the desire to help him. " I much prefer you should think me a fool, my boy, than that you should believe me cold-blooded and calculating in my dealings with any one."

Now the thing was done, the doctor had to meet his wife and try to convince her, what he did not believe himself, that he had acted wisely. He failed miserably, and she wore an injured, martyr air for days, not at all comforted by his justification, which was the old saw, "Experience keeps a dear school, but fools will learn in no other." Dan would not be persuaded to change his mind and enter some other business. He talked of horses till she was glad to drop the subject; and in three months had lost everything. The doctor paid his debts, but said not one word of reproach, and Dan went back to the railroad, fully persuaded that he would have made money enough could he only have had more to throw away.

CHAPTER VIII.

PHILOSOPHY VANQUISHED.

ONE night, some months before Clara's final return from Stonybrook, the doctor returned home weary and "cross," as he said. To the twins this used to mean that he was not in the humor to enjoy their clambering over him; but they felt themselves young ladies now, and "cross" meant that the doctor hoped they had done their piano practising during the day. Their torturing the piano was something endless and excruciating, but the doctor bore all domestic annoyances with the kind, long-suffering spirit that characterized the good family man—the great man, indeed—that he really was.

Women are beginning to see the folly of allowing their "lords" to write the biographies of great men, and are gradually taking the task upon themselves. When they do their full share of this work, there will be found in history many pigmies that would have swelled to colossi under the pens of their own sex; for their claims to the honor of greatness as moral forces will be judged by the way they treat women, specially and generally. A man may be great in a particular sense, if he is nothing but a military or political leader, or profound as a scientist; but he can never be great integrally as a man, if he lacks tenderness, justice, or faith in humanity. Men who are very tender as lovers, and deeply sensitive to the influence of women, usually have the reputation among brutal men of being "hen-pecked"—a word never found in the vocabulary of refined people.

On this occasion, as the doctor's family sat down to tea, Mrs. Forest enquired after the health of Mrs. Buzzell, whom the doctor had been visiting regularly for many days. She was more comfortable, the doctor said.

"I don't think," remarked Mrs. Forest, "that her illness would endure so long if Dr. Delano attended her."

"Oh, ho! A reflection upon my professional skill," said the doctor, wiping the creamy tea from his grizzly moustache; but he added, laughing, "If there is anything Mrs. Buzzell enjoys, it is a good long serious illness."

"That is because you pet her so. I think she is a ridiculous old thing."

"That is not kind, Fannie. I don't see how you can speak so of a good old friend like that. We ought never to forget that she is somewhat enfeebled by age, and really has no one to care for her."

"I don't see that that is any reason why you should make a martyr of yourself."

"Oh, I do not. It is pleasant to me to see her faded eyes light up when I enter the room. I know I am the medium of a great consolation to her; and giving happiness should make us happy always."

"Really! You are quite tender to your interesting patient."

"Fannie, you disgust me," he said, setting his cup down emphatically. "If this infernal world chooses to be cruel and mean, to laugh at those who are pining for sympathy and love—*you* ought to be capable of better sentiments." The doctor added a more vehement word.

"What! profanity? You do pain me so by your violent way of speaking," complained the doctor's wife.

"There!" said Leila, "papa is really getting cross;" and lancing a confident saucy look at her father, whose crossness had no terrors for her, she seized her gentler-willed sister and waltzed her out of the room to the accompaniment of "Good riddance, you sauce-box," from the doctor, and a stately rebuke from Mrs. Forest. When they were alone, Mrs. Forest repeated in other words her last remark to the doctor, who answered—

"Yes, I know I am always giving you pain when I remind you of your want of sympathy except for those who are a part of you. One's children are not all the world, and to love only them is narrow and selfish. Suffering, wherever we find it, has claims upon us."

"Charity begins at home," said Mrs. Forest, sententiously.

"Yes; *begins*, but it should not end there. I have been wondering every day why you do not go and see Mrs. Buzzell, knowing how lonely she is, with no society but that of her old servant." Now Mrs. Forest was indeed intending to go and sit awhile with her old friend, and carry her some dainties; but she did not feel in a gracious mood, and would not confess it. She said rather, "She has too much of your society to miss mine, I think."

This was exasperating. The doctor rose, and Mrs. Forest touched the spring of the table-bell. "Somehow you will forever dance in a pint-pot; you cannot see anything in a broad light," he said, "and Leila is going to be just like you. She requires nice dresses, a little music, a little flattery, a good deal of sentimental, unchristlike piety, and her cup runneth over. A grand life, a grand emotion, will never come to her. It would burst her like a soap-bubble, as it would you, to do anything not set down as proper by your set."

"I should like to know some of your women who see things in a broad light. Who are they?"

"Well," said the doctor, after a pause, "it is no use to cite examples. Most of them have someway outraged Mrs. Grundy, and you would not believe in them."

"Yes; I suppose, in order to see things in a broad light," said Mrs. Forest, contemptuously pronouncing the words, "one must become disreputable. Thank you; I prefer a good reputation, and what you are pleased to call a pint-pot dance."

"By ——," exclaimed the doctor, excitedly, "I do believe the first condition for the development of broad sympathies for humanity in a woman's heart is the loss of respectability as defined by hypocrites and prudes." Mrs. Forest looked horrified; but the entrance of Susie to remove the tea-things in answer to the bell, prevented her reply. As Susie went on with her work noiselessly, avoiding the slightest clatter of cups and spoons, the doctor continued, watching her movements as he spoke: "We should cultivate a feeling of unity with all nature, of which we are a part. That will force us out of our narrow lives, and make happiness possible to us only when all around us are happy. The inculcation of this sentiment of unity is so important, that we cannot over-estimate it, for it will lead to grand association schemes for the amelioration of mankind. There are people in this town to-day, who labor hard from year to year, and yet want the conditions for a decent life; children who never have the chance of seeing a fine picture, or wearing a pretty suit of clothes."

"I know that is very sad, but your free-thinkers do nothing for them. It is the ladies of our church who carry food and clothing to the children of the poor." Mrs. Forest, as she said this, noticed something in her husband's face which made her add, "You know, my dear, I always except you."

"Why," said the doctor, "here are the Unitarians, all free-thinkers, according to your creed, for they do not accept your orthodox scheme of salvation; but you can't deny they do more for the poor than all the orthodox in the country. Take the firm of Ely & Gherrish, one a Unitarian and the other a Deist, as they call him; they have built a magnificent home for their workmen, whereby they are provided with many of the luxuries of wealth, and at about the cost of ordinary lodgings. How much nobler it is to help people to independence than to inculcate the spirit of begging, by your small charities!"

"We can't all build workingmen's homes, like Ely & Gherrish," said Mrs. Forest, "but that should not hinder us from doing what we can."

"I admit the worthiness of your motives, and the temporary good you do; but it is none the less true that it degrades the being to be the recipient of charity. No; charity don't work, as a social system. The poor-house don't work. The orphan asylum don't work. Now, to one who has the scientific method in his examination of social problems, the moment a system don't work, he knows it is wrong. Then the first duty is to discover why it don't, and substitute a better."

"All of which is very easy—in words," said Mrs. Forest.

"In words!" echoed the doctor. "Why, we are doing it literally every day. Take the steam-engine and the telegraph. When the necessity arose for more rapid transportation, we tried awhile to breed faster and stronger horses, make better wagons and roads, but we found that did not work, and so we substituted the steam-car and the railroad; so with the postal system, the telegraph and the steam printing-press."

Mrs. Forest saw that the doctor held a strong position logically, so she waived the question by giving some final orders to Susie about work for the next morning, and then dismissed her summarily. When she was gone the doctor said, "Do you think you are as kind to that poor child as you ought to be?"

"Dear me! what next?" answered Mrs. Forest, with a sigh. "Yes, I think I am. I give her time to sew for herself, and she has a good home. I must say she behaves remarkably well, considering her bringing up."

"I am greatly interested in her," the doctor said. "I wish Clara was here. That's a girl after my own heart, you know. Clara has the true democratic—that is, the true human spirit. She would pity this lonely Susie, and help her to have some object in life."

"Object in life! Why, what better object can she have than to behave herself, and be happy by doing her duty?" Mrs. Forest, with her "little hoard of maxims," was armed at all points. It was as hard to grapple with her as with a porcupine. She was so utterly different from

the doctor in her way of looking at things, that it is hard
to do her justice. The doctor's radical ideas had always
-alarmed her, and it had troubled her exceedingly to find
that Clara delighted in just those radical notions that
were her horror. It was clear, too, that Clara wrote her
mother from duty—short, dutiful, correct, and very commonplace notes. To her father she scrawled long, rapid,
charmingly frank and interesting letters, signing herself always "*Papa's Own Girl.*" To her mother she
invariably subscribed herself, "Your affectionate daughter," which indeed Mrs. Forest considered in rather
more ladylike taste, but she was a little jealous all the
same.

When Mrs. Forest gave her opinion, in such a decided
manner, about Susie's duty, the doctor paused awhile and
filled his pipe in an absent kind of way, holding his box
of tobacco with some difficulty, so as to not disturb
" Hommie," the cat, who would jump upon his knee whenever he sat down. Mrs. Forest was never troubled with
such familiarity on the part of Hommie, so named by the
twins in honor of his perilous adventure in the hominy
pot when a kitten. " Doing one's duty," the doctor said,
" is not all there is of life. This Susie must feel the need
of friends sadly. I wish you would take more interest in
her, Fannie—talk to her and gain her sympathy."

"I don't care to talk to her much, and she don't care
to hear me."

"That is because you talk to her about saving her
soul—a subject about which she knows just as much as
you do. Of course, it must bore her. Talk to her of
herself; get her to read, and to take interest in some
subject."

"She's not very intellectual," replied Mrs. Forest, laconically.

"What!" said the doctor. "Why, she's as bright as a dollar. See what a fine head she has!"

"Very likely. I don't believe in heads, as you do. Some of the most stupid people I know are all head."

"Ah! quality as well as quantity must be considered. In this case the quality is good."

"I have not much hope for her. To be sure she goes to church, but I think it may be from the fear of displeasing me if she stays at home."

"I am sorry she goes at all from that motive," said the doctor.

"When Dan is here, she stays at home evenings, and I notice how she looks at him. When he is not here she often goes out in the evening. I'm sure I don't know where she goes nor what she does."

"Well, don't be meanly suspicious. I know the girl's heart is right. What can you expect? You treat her like a menial, and she feels it. She does your bidding because it means her daily bread, and because she has lost her heart to Dan. Poor little thing! That's the saddest of all. She's happy if she can only look at him; but otherwise finding no companions, no sympathy here, of course she seeks the few acquaintances she has outside, in the hope of answering this need—a need as imperative as that for food or air. You will some time find that it is a misfortune that you cannot take her into your heart and help her more. Let her think that Dan is the only creature that cares for her, and she will come to depend too much upon his regard, which I doubt not is already on the wane."

"Yes ; I think he would like to erase that abominable tattooing. Silly boy ! "

"I'm not sure but that is the evidence of the best impulse that ever swayed him."

"Mercy ! doctor, how can you talk so ? How would you like your only son to marry such a person ? "

"He might do worse," answered the doctor, decidedly.

This was too much for Mrs. Forest's patience—too much for adequate expression in decorous words ; so she folded her sewing, and left the doctor to the cat and his pipe.

CHAPTER IX.

THE LION'S DEN.

SUSIE DYKES was a little woman even among the rather diminutive. She had pretty soft grey eyes, a slender, well-shaped waist, and a wealth of light yellow hair. The pretty and simple way she arranged it the doctor had often noticed. She combed it straight back, twisted a part of it into a heavy coil, which she passed over the top of her round head, carrying the end back, and braiding it in with the rest to form a knot, fastened low with a comb. It was a very pretty, Quakerish coiffure, but very becoming. Considering the low family from which she came, the quiet and even distinguished air about her was marvelous. Mrs. Forest could not understand it, and so she refused to admit its existence. The doctor always spoke to Susie with great gentleness; but as the twins snubbed her, and his wife's dignified coldness oppressed her heavily, he forebore to be as familiarly kind with her as he wished, lest the contrast should make her dislike his wife and daughters. But he went as far as he thought prudent. Once he told her that her ears were as pretty as Clara's; a compliment that little Susie never ceased to be proud of. Lately, by the doctor's influence, Mrs. Buzzell, now recovered from her illness, had become quite interested in Susie, and had helped her about her wardrobe, which showed

want of means, though not of mending, for Susie was
naturally neat about everything. Mrs. Forest gave her
due credit for this, knowing that the instruction that she
must have received from Mrs. Dykes was none of the best.

Poor Susie's child-life had been a sad one, like the lives
of the children of the poor generally; and she was happier now than she had ever been, despite the cold, unsym-
pathetic relation she bore to Mrs. Forest, whom she
longed to love like a daughter; for whatever belonged to
Dan, was precious in her eyes. She was naturally very
bright, as the doctor said, but what little education she
had received in a neighboring district school had been
painfully gained through the persecutions of more fortunate school-mates, who, with the savage cruelty of
children, made sport of her poverty, not knowing what
they did.

It is a folly, doubtless, to dress up little children like
popinjays, that they may outshine their companions, and
thus cultivate their own vanity at the expense of nobler
feelings; but certainly it is a vital wrong to send a
child among his fellows in a mean and untidy attire. For
not having the philosophy of maturer years to support
him against the ridicule he excites, he is either humiliated
and degraded by it, or else moved to revenge or hate;
and these feelings, if long entertained, crush out the finer
possibilities of his nature, and so in both cases he is
robbed and wronged. The ridicule and persecution that
Susie had endured had the usual effect upon the sensitive
of her sex. She was humiliated, and answered only with
tears. She had never dreamed that she had elements of
real loveliness in mind and person, and when Dan first
began to notice her—he a proud, handsome fellow, be-

longing to the best of Oakdale's choice society—she
was transported with joyful gratitude, and would have
laid down her life for him without counting it much of a
sacrifice.

When Dan failed in his livery-stable enterprise, he
went back to the railroad, and soon rose to the position
of conductor, where he seemed really to have found his
level. He liked the position, gave good satisfaction to
the company, and received a very fair salary for his work.
Susie, meanwhile, loved him more and more, and longed
for, yet dreaded, his bearish caresses. The opportunity
to see her alone did not occur often, for he was home
only on Sundays, and then she went to church with Mrs.
Forest. This annoyed Dan; and the obstacles in the
way of passing an hour alone with Susie were many, and
almost insurmountable. The twins, either one or both,
had still the most remarkable talent for being just where
they were not wanted. He used to send them away from
the garden or orchard when he chanced to find Susie
there; but they were apt to tell of this, which troubled
Susie, and so he desisted. The last time he had tried to
get rid of Leila, endeavoring to show her that she ought
to go and practice her piano studies, he received the pert
answer, "Thank you; I don't play secular music on
Sunday." Dan answered with a long crescendo whistle,
and abandoned tactics in Leila's case. But fate sometimes gave him a few minutes with Susie. On one
occasion she had gone at Dinah's request to bring pears
from the orchard—Dinah having very possibly an ulterior
motive, for Dan had been very gracious to the old servant lately. He followed Susie after a few minutes—a
very few—leisurely smoking a cigar.

As a specimen of a fine animal, Dan was certainly handsome; and this is hardly doing him justice, for it must be admitted that very good women—aye, and very superior women—have adored just such fine animals. There must be some justification, which severe moralists cannot comprehend, for action and reaction are equal. Dan was tall, his back finely curved, broad shoulders, and his head was right regally poised thereon. He had bright dark eyes, curly brown hair, a light, youthful moustache and slight side-whiskers, and what would be called a fine mouth, though not of the nobler type to which Clara's belonged. Hers might be termed sensuous, his sensual; yet perhaps the term is too severe. It was pleasant to look at Dan's mouth when he talked, and it must be confessed that his kisses were found distractingly sweet to some others beside little Susie.

On entering the part of the orchard where Susie was, he leaned against the trunk of an old fruit-tree and called her to him.

"I must not stay long," she said, looking up lovingly into his face, as she stood before him. "Dinah will be waiting for these;" and she blushed and dropped her pretty eyes among the fruit.

"Let her wait," he said. "You don't mind keeping me waiting, I notice;" and throwing away his cigar, he drew her into his arms and kissed her rosy lips again and again, holding her like a vise. Susie wished to remain there forever, though she kept denying him her lips, and hiding her face on his breast. That was at least one feeling; another was a strong impulse to run away, but she dared not show this for fear of displeasing him. When, therefore, Leila came running down the path bareheaded, her hair streaming out on the wind, it was a relief to Susie, though an exasperation to Dan.

As time wore on from Sunday to Sunday—for Susie counted time only by the slow recurrence of these days— she began to be troubled a little about Dan's regard for her. To be sure, he always told her he loved her dearly, and that she was "sweeter than a rose;" but he seemed to talk less of their future, and his new life out in the world had changed his manner to her, which was not so respectful as in the olden time. Ah! the olden time, when Susie had been so ashamed of Jim and his ways, so impatient of her rude surroundings, until Dan appeared and gladdened all her life as the sunshine gladdens the little wayside flower. She had never been troubled about his demonstrations then, and she passed in retrospection the old days when the boyish lover had scarcely dared to press her hand. She recalled continually one particular evening when he had found her alone—the first and last time they had ever been alone for a whole evening. That was the time when he gave her his first kiss—a quick little touch on the cheek, not like the burning kisses he insisted upon now. Where had he learned so much about love-making? He knew little enough about it then, when, blushing even like herself, he had made her promise to be his forever, and sealed the betrothal by that indelible record upon his arm. Clearly there was a change in Dan, but Susie's heart refused to recognize it as a vital change. It was, indeed, the same old drama, played over and over again since the world began—the woman at home, dependent, busied with her little routine of duties, cherishing and nursing her one tender romance; the man mixing with the broader world, yielding to its varied

attractions, taking and giving love, or the mockery of
love, wherever he can find it, and so daily unfitting himself more and more for the rôle in which the home-keep-
ing woman has cast him. Susie waited and trusted, but
life during the week was very dull ; the few acquaintances
of her former life attracted her less and less, and she
ceased altogether to visit them. This time happened to
be a season of revivals, and Oakdale received a large in-
flux of the " spirit." The twins became "serious," much
to the joy of Mrs. Forest and—it must be confessed—the
disgust of the doctor, who entertained very phrenological
views upon the subject of sudden changes of nature. But
under the influence of this seriousness, Leila, who had the
most serious attack, became suddenly gracious to Susie,
and would insist upon her being saved also ; so she
dragged her to prayer-meetings in season and out of
season, the latter being on Sunday evenings, when Dan
was at home. Dan could scarcely believe his senses when
he found that there was in this world anything that could
charm Susie away from him, even for an hour ; so she had
the satisfaction of witnessing another revival, that of
Dan's flickering affection for his first love. He did, indeed, seem to treat her with more softness, though he
distrusted the value of her piety, since it caused her to
hold more strict views on the propriety of vehement
kisses. The twins, after a few months, lost their passion
for prayer-meetings entirely, but Susie kept right on,
with that sincerity and singleness of heart that characterized all that she did. She had found sympathy among
certain people of the church, though of rather a stiff and
at-arms-length kind ; but in her own sincere devotion,
and in the reading of religious books, she found much

consolation. Not that she could understand them or criticise them; but when she came to anything that breathed the loving spirit of Christ, it sank into her lonely heart, and blessed her with something like peace.

One perfect moonlit evening, about a year after the events just narrated, and only a few months before Clara's final return from Stonybrook College, Susie, returning home from some evening "meeting," unexpectedly met Dan. He drew her hand caressingly over his arm, saying, as he turned to walk home with her, "Susie does not care for me any more."

"O, Dan!" she exclaimed, in an imploring tone, for her little heart was full of its best emotions, and this want of faith in her love pained her.

"Fact. She has become a saint, and so cares nothing for my kisses."

"O, you wrong Susie, Dan. She does love you dearly."

"I know. She says she prays for me, and I don't believe in prayers. Kisses are 'indicated,' as doctors say, in my case."

"You do wrong to speak so, Dan. Surely it is good to pray when one is lonely and sad. I try to be good, but I am not, very. I fear I shall never go to Heaven." Dan, for reply, gave his crescendo whistle, and then said, stopping short in the bright moonlight, and looking down into her face, "The idea of a good child like you troubling your little head about Heaven. The domestic economy of that institution must be very shiftlessly managed if such as you are not in great demand."

"O, you must not talk so, Dan! I do so wish you could see religion as it really is."

"Fiddlesticks!" said Dan. "If I must be a spoon, I prefer to be made so by a live woman, not a morbid longing to twang a golden harp."

"Your father does not talk like that," replied Susie, who was always timid before Dan's outbursts of humor, but the belief that she was in the right made her bold. "I know he will not go to church, but he is so good! and he never says anything against others going, if they find spiritual food in what he says are dry husks to him."

"He's a fine old chap, no mistake about that, and he forgets more every day than most people ever know ; but he's soft in spots. If I had only known him when he was a young man, I should have helped him to cut his eye-teeth."

"Ah!" said Susie, "what you call his 'soft spots' are his noblest qualities. What can be more benevolent and sweet than his treatment of poor old Mrs. Buzzell?"

"Is that a conundrum?" Dan asked, in his rollicking way.

"He is so good!" said Susie, taking no notice of Dan's levity ; "and I often think if he would join the church it would influence you——"

"No, it wouldn't," interrupted Dan. "I'm only sensitive to your influence. You could do anything with me if you loved me as you once did." They had just entered the gate and stopped a moment under the lilacs by the path. Susie looked up into Dan's face and said, with a voice that trembled, "It is cruel for you to doubt me. I have not changed, unless"—"to love you more," she would have said, but her words were checked by the depth of her emotion.

"You do not show it, then."

"O Dan! I pray for you always. I think of you every moment. How can I prove it better?" she asked, with despairing tenderness.

"O, much better you can prove it, Susie;" and under the fragrant lilacs, under the dear, bright stars, a thought blacker than mortal night entered Dan's heart.

"How do I know you pray for me?" he asked, caressing her hand very softly. "I do not hear you. Come to my room and pray for me there, and I shall believe you."

"Do you really wish me to?" she asked, with a look that would have softened any heart but that of this sleek young tiger, whose white teeth glistened in the moonlight.

"I will," she said simply, mentally reproaching herself for a momentary suspicion that had entered her mind.

When Susie entered Dan's room on her pious mission, he at once closed the door and locked it. Susie protested earnestly, but the only reply it elicited was a long-continued fit of subdued laughter which Dan indulged himself in, tilting back his chair and holding his fingers interlaced at the back of his head. Then he insisted upon a kiss as a preliminary.

"No, no," cried Susie. "Open the door and let me go. O Dan, you were not serious, after all. I wish I had not believed you;" and the poor girl covered her face and sobbed.

"Serious? Never was so serious in my life, as I can prove to you; but what is the use of praying for me if

my heart is not in the right mood, and nothing can dc
that but a kiss, though a hundred would make it surer.
How Susie must love me. She cries because I ask for
one." ✿ ✿ ✿ ✿

Susie never prayed for Dan that night. Her prayers
were all for herself. Alas! that they should have availed
so little!

CHAPTER X.

THE early days of September had come, and the day of Clara's return. Dinah had scoured every pot and pan until they shone like mirrors, cooked the cakes and "lolly-pops" generally that Clara had liked so well as a child, for she was still a child in Dinah's thought, which took no note of the changes that four years must bring to a young lady. She longed for Clara's final home-coming, for between the twins and her there had always been a kind of feud, and they were, according to her, "no comfort to the house;" and though she liked Susie very much, there was nothing in the world so bright and lovely in her eyes as "Miss Clary."

All was joy and bustle in the doctor's house. The "fatted calf," figuratively speaking, was ready, and the best chamber, newly fitted up for Clara, had received the addition of another bed, for Miss Marston was coming with her, at the cordial invitation of the doctor and Mrs. Forest. They wished to express their gratitude for her kindness to their child during her term at Stonybrook, and as Miss Marston had considerable curiosity to see the eccentric Dr. Forest, it was very pleasant to accept the invitation. The friendship between her and Clara had begun early after their meeting, and had soon ripened into a more tender regard and confidence than either women or men often inspire in each other. The result of Clara's tactics regarding *Jaques* had even added to this mutual esteem, for Miss Marston frankly confessed that the motive of the book was noble, and though she thought it too emotional for young girls as a rule, admitted that it would do no harm to Clara, because she was disposed to be a "philosopher and an observer," as she said. After this, Clara's reading was never criticised. She was allowed full range in the college library, and certain of the alcoves, seldom visited except by one or two of the teachers, were familiar to her. She had graduated with the first honors, and there were not a few tears of real regret when she bade her school friends good-bye.

Clara had been home only once during her long absence, and the meeting with the dear ones at home was a great joy. Miss Marston was introduced, and then came the embraces : first the mother's, then the twins, who were astonished into silence by the queenly carriage and address of Clara. Dr. Forest stood talking with Miss Marston, waiting his turn, and having no eyes but for his daughter. She came presently, and Miss Marston politely moved away. "The sweetest last !" whispered Clara, as her father pressed her to his heart, answering only, "*Papa's own girl.*" Here fat old Dinah was descried in the dining-room, wiping her grinning face with her apron. At a gesture from Clara she came to the drawing-room door, and Clara submitted to be hugged, and kissed, and "bressed," and cried over till she cried anew herself. Miss Marston looked a little surprised at this familiarity with a negro servant, until she recalled the fact that the doctor's family had lived many years in the South, where, there being never a pos-

sible question of equality before the late civil war, the
negro was often petted even like much-loved brutes.

That evening there was a grand reception in the doctor's old-fashioned house, in honor of Clara's return.
Dan came in after all the friends had arrived, and for a
time he saw no one but Clara, who advanced to meet
him, offering him her hand affectionately, but instead of
taking it, he grabbed the whole stately person of his
sister and gave her a most bearish hugging and kissing,
which embarrassed her somewhat, perhaps, because she
knew Dr. Delano's eyes were upon her. She had just
left his side, and the few minutes conversation with him
had given her a taste of feminine power. She had seen
in every look, and word, and movement, that she impressed him deeply. After escaping from Dan's grip, she
glanced back to Dr. Delano. His eyes were averted.
Was it from disgust at Dan's rough way of meeting her,
or from delicacy? At all events he seemed to have
dropped her out of his thoughts, and was apparently
greatly absorbed in conversation with Leila, and as he
talked he occasionally twisted the long ends of a fine dark
moustache. He was a rather distinguished looking man,
perhaps a little too self-conscious, and old in Leila's eyes,
though in the prime of life, being not much over thirty.

Before Dan would let Clara go, he said, glancing
at the piano, where a quiet, graceful lady was just sitting
down to play, "That washed-out virgin is your divinity,
Miss Marston, I presume."

"Hush! brother. You will never speak so of her
when she has once deigned to notice you. No one
escapes the magic of her style, I assure you."

"I wouldn't give a sixpence for one woman's judg-

ment of another, sis ; but I'll try on the magic as soon
as you like. See ! there's my *bête noir* making dead
for me ; " and leaving his sister to entertain Mrs. Buzzell,
he just nodded to her and went to Susie, who was sitting
quite alone in the corner of the room, pretending to be
interested in an album of photographs. He greeted her
with a pleasant word, and her sense of being neglected
vanished instantly. Ah ! is it counted a blessing to love
like this poor child ? Sentimental or emotional people
never count themselves happy except when floundering
in some sea of passionate madness. Do they not deceive
themselves as to the nature of happiness ? Is it well for
any human soul to so depend upon another for every
thrill of pleasure ; aye, to have the very literal beating
of the heart, in its normal way, dependent upon the
smiles, the tender words, of any single creature among all
the good and beautiful beings that the world contains ?
Be it wise or foolish, it is the fate of many people to love
in just this mad way ; though it excites the contempt of
those who can regulate the play of their emotions as
easily as we do the movement of a clock by raising or
lowering the pendulum.

Susie kept on turning the leaves of Clara's album,
though listening intently to every syllable her lover
uttered. Stopping longer over one, he noticed it.
" Clara's tenth wonder, eh ? " he said. " How do you
like it ? "

" I think it very beautiful ; don't you ? "

" Bosh ! she has no color, no life," he answered, glancing toward the original. " Why, you are a thousand
times prettier, Susie." This made the little heart very
happy indeed ; and she looked up into Dan's face with a

loving, trusting pride, that touched him for a moment; the next, he was forced to give his attention to Miss Marston, whose fine voice swelled through the room in the *brindisi* of *La Traviata*, the one bit of Italian music that Dan happened to know well, and as he listened, he was entranced. The voice seemed to upbear him as on wings. How passionately the pale little woman sung. Could such a voice belong to the commonplace lady he had thought Miss Marston to be? A few minutes later, when he was presented to her, and her little white hand lay in his for a moment, he longed to kiss it; and was consciously awkward as he spoke the words of greeting. Miss Marston knew how to put him at his ease at once, he never suspecting that she was exercising a common art among certain refined people of society. She made him thoroughly satisfied with the way he had deported himself, and he left her with a sense of delight, as if he had covered himself with glory. He returned to her as soon as he could, and scarcely noticed Susie for the rest of the evening. Susie waited until sure that Dan had no thought of returning to talk with her any more, and when she could no longer control her emotion from the company, she crept away to her room, and cried bitterly, while the sound of music and joyous laughter from below fell like mockery upon her lonely heart.

Dan's infatuation for Miss Marston was sudden and irresistible, and soon became evident to everybody. To Clara it was an evidence of appreciation which she had thought him incapable of; and having no knowledge of his relation to Susie, she was delighted, though in her eyes Miss Marston was too good for Dan, and that he might win her seemed an absurdity. She thought, how-

ever, with the faith in love that all women cherish, that
his admiration would have a softening and refining influence, which in this case was much needed. Miss Marston was very gracious. She sang for him whenever he
asked her, and without the least effort charmed him in
every way. When he made her a compliment, instead of
saying that she hated flattery, as most country girls
have the bad manners to do, she smiled and thanked
him. In truth, her whole air and manner was a revelation of womanhood to Dan. He received her gracious
politeness as a sign of preference, and before a week had
passed, Susie was a millstone about his neck. She, meanwhile, half dazed with the knowledge of Dan's disaffection, and the fate worse than death that hung over her,
went about the house, pale, silent, brooding over the
thought of death as the only possible escape for such as
she. Mrs. Forest was quite touched by her sad face,
treated her more kindly than usual, and even seemed disposed to talk to her. She asked her one day why she
never went to see her friends, as she used to do.

"I have no friends," Susie answered, with a stony expression that alarmed Mrs. Forest. What could she
mean? "It must be," she said to herself, "Dan's
attention to Miss Marston. Poor thing! I wonder if she
really expected him to marry her?"

By and by the quick eye of Dr. Forest detected Susie's
condition, and his anger at his son was bitter and terrible;
but he said nothing, waiting for the end of the week,
when Dan would come home for the Sunday. Saturday
evening the doctor came in rather late. He first went
into the drawing-room and staid a few minutes. Dan
was basking in the heaven of Miss Marston's smiles. The

parlor casement windows were open on the southern
veranda, where they sat breathing the odor of the honey-
suckles that climbed over the old wooden pillars. Clara
was scarcely less happy than Dan, for Dr. Delano had
been exceedingly agreeable that special evening, and she
had just discovered that he had a certain, as yet ill-de-
fined, but wholly delicious influence upon her. Mrs.
Forest was delighted. Dr. Delano was a " party " after
her own heart ; so she kept discreetly at the further end
of the room, and engaged the twins near her to the best
of her ability, that they might not disturb either the flirtation at the piano or that on the veranda. As the doctor
entered, Leila was teazing Clara about Dr. Delano, who
had just left, and there was no little spite in this teazing,
for Leila had fallen in the doctor's eyes from what appeared to be a first class object to a third class one at
best, since the advent of Clara.

"Don't mind her, sister Clara," said Linnie. "Her nose
is out of joint, that is all." Leila scowled without turning
her head, and continued her bantering, while Clara kept
on improvising pretty variations upon Weber's *Der-
nière Pensée.* "Oh, are you not tired of that gloomy
air?" exclaimed Leila. "You ought to play something
more gay, I should say ; perhaps, though, it is appropri-
ate as a wail."

" Your remarks are very silly, my child," said Mrs.
Forest mildly, " and quite out of taste."

" Well, it's so dull here. One is overpowered by a
great event like the prospect of a marriage. I wouldn't
have Dr. Delano, though, if I was dying to get married.'

" And pray why not, Miss Wisdom ? " asked the doctor.

"Well, he's too old, in the first place," replied Leila.

"Old!" repeated Clara, leaving the piano and approaching the back of her father's chair. "He is not as old as papa, and I always wanted to marry papa," she added, laughing and caressing his head with both her hands.

"Why, Clara!" exclaimed Mrs. Forest. "You make such unaccountably strange speeches."

"My girl flatters her old papa, does she not, by comparing him to her younger slaves?" As he said this he drew one of her hands round to his lips and kissed it.

"Good-night!" said Linnie, going toward the door. "When Clara and papa commence making love, I always leave."

Leila enjoyed this sally immensely, judging by the peal of laughter with which she greeted it. She kissed her mother, as did Linnie, and then the doctor, who took the opportunity to whisper to her, "Don't undress till you hear me go up stairs. Then I wish you to come down and tell Dan to come to my study."

A few minutes later Leila bounced on to the veranda, exclaiming, "Papa wants you, Dan, in his study. Quick!" and with this she disappeared as she came.

The summons was so sudden that Miss Marston started; but Dan, knowing the nature of Leila, did not apprehend that any one had fallen dead in a fit, as he might otherwise be justified in supposing. He assured Miss Marston that it was only Leila's way, said he would be absent but a few minutes, and expressed a hope to find her on his return.

Dan passed into the parlor through the glass door, meeting Clara, who joined Miss Marston. He then remembered for the first time that Susie, despairing probably of seeing him alone, had given him a note when she had opened the front door for him that evening.   He stopped by the parlor door, out of sight of Miss Marston, and ran over it hurriedly.   What it contained was terrible enough ; and the writing was blurred, evidently by tears, but the effort the poor girl had made to cheat her breaking heart into the belief that Dan still loved her, was lost on him.   He was not fine enough to understand it.

As Dan crossed the threshold of his father's study, the doctor wheeled round from his desk. and rose, not offering Dan a seat.   Dan saw with an inward misgiving that a storm was threatening.   It burst upon him without the slightest preliminary.

"Young man," the doctor said, with perfect command of his voice, "I suppose you are aware of the condition of Susie Dykes through your folly."

Dan silently approached the mantle-piece, on which he leaned for support, for he was profoundly agitated.   The doctor, who noticed everything, was moved at the signs of wretchedness his words had caused, and he continued, less severely, "I am sorry for you, my son ; but my greater concern is about this poor girl.   To a man it is nothing ; to a woman it is worse than death."

Dan thought of the gracious being on the veranda, brilliant, refined, unapproachable, but for whose favor he had dared to hope, and he thought the misfortune was worse than death for him also ; and as he waited, chewing the end of his youthful moustache, his heart hardened toward the poor girl who had so tenderly loved, so foolishly trusted him.   But his silence was exasperating the doctor, who, he well knew, would see but one way to pay for his " folly," as he had termed it. He said, therefore, doggedly, without looking up, "What is done is done. I suppose you wish me to marry her."

"*I* wish you to marry her, you young scoundrel !" replied the doctor, livid with indignation at the heartlessness of his son. "If you have lost all affection for her, does not your sense of honor prompt you to make the only reparation possible, when you have done a wrong like this to an innocent girl ? "

"Innocent !" sneered Dan, " I'm not over sure about that, sir."

Hearing loud words proceeding from the doctor's study, and guessing what might be the cause, Susie, pale and trembling, crept down the stairs, which ended just at the doctor's door. She heard distinctly these words from the lips that were so dear to her, and unable to move hand or foot, she sank down on the stairs. Poor girl ! She had obeyed the instinct of her tender heart, meaning, if Dan was suffering under his father's anger for her sake, to go and shield him, woman-like, and take all the blame on herself. Upon this noble impulse Dan's words had fallen like cold steel upon her warm heart. Her wonder was overwhelming when she heard the doctor reply in a clear, distinct tone :

"Great God ! that from a son of mine ! Cowardly, ignobly, seeking to cover your baseness by degrading a weak young girl, whose only fault is loving you a thousand times more than you deserve. You have sought her and courted her favor ever since she was thirteen years old. Even as long ago as that, you promised her marriage, and tattooed yourself with her name as a seal of

the promise.   She never doubted your honesty for years,
and when, through her devotion for you and the Devil
knows not what arts exercised on your part, she sacrifices
everything a woman can sacrifice, you would basely
desert her.   I tell you it is the most damnable act a
man can perpetrate.   Brute force and ignorance have
oppressed woman in all history, making her a slave to
petty cares, denying her the political and social equality
that belongs by right to human beings, and. making her
dependent like a slave.   Of course this has cramped
woman's free growth in every way, and the man who
takes advantage of her weakness, as you have done with
Susie Dykes, deserves the execration of all honorable
men."

"For God's sake, father, don't speak so loud!" cried
Dan, who was in mortal terror lest Miss Marston should
hear.

"I will neither control my voice nor my indignation
at your meanness.   The whole world deserves to know
the base dog who would deceive and betray a woman
through her folly in loving him too well."

"Hold, sir!   I have some feeling as well as you, and
I won't stand any more of this."

The doctor moved toward the door, and Dan knew
well it would not be easy to escape; nor did he feel
much inclined to try it, for he felt the weakness of guilt.
The doctor continued : "You will hear all I have got to
say, and then I have done with you.   There can be no
question in my mind that this girl knows only you.
Whom has she known, or sought, or cared for, except
you ?   But this, in my opinion, is of little importance.
The worst women are about good enough for the best of

us. See how much more generous they are! They, in the freshness and cleanness of youth and health, take husbands who have consorted with the vilest, whose blood is vitiated with foul diseases, though every woman feels that a man's standard of morality should be as high as hers. The sophisms that men take refuge in, in this connection, are beneath the contempt of common sense. Sir, you could in no way have made me despise your character as you have by that one insinuation. Do I not know you, sir? What are you that you should demand spotless innocence in a young woman? In this matter every honest man is bound to believe the woman whose repute is good. Does this girl confess to having been debauched by others?" demanded the doctor, whose rage knew no bounds.

"Of course not. According to her, she is most immaculate; but I know better."

"Do you?" said the doctor, with fine contempt. "No man has a right to make that statement of any girl of good reputation; and let me tell you, for the benefit of your ignorance, that scientific men are not so confident in such cases. You have graduated in the Jim Dykes school, and all blackguards are wise on such subjects."

Dan's respect for his father was greatly tried. His way of showing resentment was of the Jim Dykes order; and during his father's outburst he had been angry enough to have felled any other man to the earth. He felt dimly something of his father's moral force and the secret of his power among men, as he had never done before. He felt abased before the sublime justice of the doctor; but still the doctor, who understood the heart so well, did not know of the new sentiment that Dan

cherished for Miss Marston, as for a superior being. He
wished he could tell his father. It would at least be a
new complication that would interest him as a philosopher,
and perhaps make him less hard upon him. This passed
through Dan's mind as the doctor continued, in a calmer
tone : " But I have said enough ; more, perhaps, than
you will ever understand. The question now is, are you
ready to make this girl the only reparation in your
power ? "

"I am no hero," said Dan, bitterly. "A little while
ago it would not have been so hard. You have wronged
me in some things, though I know I have not done right.
Yes, I am ready to marry Susie Dykes to-morrow, though
I confess I would rather die."

Here the door opened, and Susie, who had heard all,
ashy pale and trembling in every limb, confronted her
lover, more dead than alive, and scarcely able to articulate
the words : " God forgive you, Dan, and make you happy.
You will never marry Susie Dykes ;" and sinking down
exhausted from her emotion, the doctor caught her and
kissed her forehead. "Brave girl!" he said. "Are you
really in earnest ? Would you really refuse, under such
circumstances?" "I would die ten thousand deaths,"
she cried, "rather than permit him to make a sacrifice in
keeping his word to me," and she motioned violently for
Dan to leave her presence.

As he rushed from the room and from the house, covered with shame and self-contempt, Dan was as wretched
as his most murderous enemy could have desired. When
the door closed behind him, Susie sobbed bitterly, and
the doctor lifted her bodily and laid her on the lounge.

"I did not think you had so much character," he said,

laying his hands on her temples. " You are a good girl, though you have thrown away your heart and gone the way of many. You shall never want a friend, my dear child. I shall stand by you. Now cheer up, and we will see what can be done by and by." As he said this, he mixed her a powder, not too innocuous this time, and as he held it to her lips she moaned, " Oh, good, kind, noble one, you would be kinder to me if you would help me end my wretched life. Oh, do, doctor ! Do give me something ; I will never tell that it was you."

" Very likely not. You couldn't very well, if it was an effective dose," said the doctor, trying to be gay for her sake.

" Oh ! I mean when I am suffering—dying. Do you think I would tell ? Oh, you do not know me ! "

" Nonsense, little one. Now, shut your eyes and let me hold my hand over them. This powder will soon take effect. You are young, and the world has need of brave hearts and willing hands like yours. Don't *feel* disgraced, and you will not be so in fact. Cultivate the thought that it is not you, but conventional society that makes it wrong to have a child by one you love, and right by one you loathe, if you happen to be married to him. Remember this: grief does not last forever; and if you are wise, this experience may prove a blessing to you—nothing like it to show a woman the gold from the dross." As he said this, music rang out from happy voices in the parlor, for none but the actors themselves knew of the drama enacted in the doctor's study. Susie thought Dan was there in the parlor, careless of her suffering, and she sobbed aloud in her agony: " What shall I do ? what shall I do ? "

"Put your whole trouble on me. Go straight to bed, now, and take this powder along, but don't take it if you can get to sleep without it. I will go and talk with Mrs. Forest, and see if she will help us."

"*Us*," repeated Susie, covering the doctor's hand with tears and kisses. "You are as good as Christ was, and if I live, I will show you how I thank you for your goodness—how I love you for being so good to me in this awful time."

"Trust me, child. I shall be the same to you tomorrow and every day. Bear up bravely, and all will come out right."

Susie tottered up stairs and sought her little room. She threw herself down by her bed, and wept and prayed, but no peace came to her troubled soul. She forgot the doctor's powder, and when she woke, it was nearly daylight, and she was lying faint and ill on the floor beside her bed. She took the powder then, and with great effort got her clothes off and went to bed.

CHAPTER XI.

FAITH AND WORKS.

THE next morning the doctor found Susie weak and
feverish, and forbade her to leave her bed. He told
her he had not been able to talk with Mrs. Forest, but
should do so the coming evening, and meanwhile Dinah
would be very kind to her and see that she did not want
for anything. He was deeply touched by her condition,
seeing her lie there alone, pale and suffering, with no
woman's sympathy to cheer her, though the house was
full of women; and he dwelt with some bitterness upon
the fact that he could not by a word bring his wife to his
side in kindly, womanly faith that his impulses were
generous and right. Clara he knew he could influence,
but he wished her to act freely, and not through love for
him; therefore he determined to have a talk with Mrs.
Forest first, but meanwhile he had had a word with good
old Dinah, and flattered her exceedingly by saying, "Now,
you know all, Dinah, and I count on your help and discretion. You and I are the only ones in the house who
know this. Help Susie all you can, for my sake, and
mind that you say nothing. Are you sure you can keep
the secret, Dinah?"

"Lor bress you, Massa! Massa knows Dinah can."

"All right, Dinah. I trust you, and I go away feeling

easier now ; ' and he pressed the old servant's hand cordially.

This interview had taken place while Dinah was putting the dining-room in order; and while getting the hominy and coffee ready for breakfast, she found opportunity to prepare Susie some traditional medicament and carry it to her. Her heart was overflowing with real sympathy for Susie, and her pride that the wise and great Dr. Forest had chosen to take her alone into his confidence, made her feel exceedingly important in her own eyes.

" Lor bress you, chile ! " she said, her shining black face beaming as she held the cup to Susie's mouth, " Why didn't ye tell old Dinah long fore dis time ? Dinah could a helped ye, mebbe. Not now. Massa 'd kill me, now you done gone told him ; but cheer up, honey. Dem accidens will happen mos all de time ! "

Susie, weak and suffering as she was, could not resist a smile, and as she drank the decoction Dinah had brought, she thanked her with tears. It was the first woman who had come to her in her sorrow, and she did not think of Dinah's black skin, but silently thanked God for this blessing.

The breakfast in Dr. Forest's family was the pleasantest meal of the day, for it was the only one when he was pretty certain to be present. On this morning, however, there was something like a cloud over the family circle, which seemed to oppress all except Leila, who chatted gayly to, or rather at, Miss Marston. The latter did not respond readily, and Leila turned her batteries upon Linnie, who was rather of a sentimental turn, and fancied that she was a victim of heart disease. Sentimental young ladies perfectly dote on heart disease. Linnie was disgusted with the incredulity of the family about the cause of her ailment. Even old Dinah had said, " Lor, Miss Linnie, you is growing like a potato-vine, and dese pains ain't noffin but de growing pains ! " After that Leila teazed her sister unmercifully about her " growing pains; " but that being frowned down by the family, it was held in reserve for private persecution. By-and-by Leila, finding the want of gayety at the breakfast table quite oppressive, drew a long sigh as she laid down her napkin.

" What is the matter, my child ? " asked the doctor. Leila glanced at her sister mischievously, tilting her head low on the left side, and answered :

" Oh, I have got such a fearful pain in my diaphragm! " Miss Marston laughed, not fully comprehending the malice of the young minx, but the rest were very grave. Leila was impatient over mysteries, and clearly there was something in the air on this particular morning, so she soon began to probe the silence.

" I declare this breakfast is as solemn as a Quaker funeral," she said ; and as no one made any remark, she asked where Susie was.

" She is quite ill this morning, my dear," answered the doctor ; " quite ill. I hope you and Linnie will try to take her place until she is better."

" I will, papa," replied Linnie ; " and I will help nurse her too, for I think Susie is really nice." Then there was silence again until Leila exclaimed, " Dear me ! They say everybody have their skeleton closet. I thought we were an exception, as we keep ours right out fairly in the light. Why, it's an age since I saw him. I must go up

in the garret and give the old darling a ·' gyrate,' as we
used to say. Do you remember, Clara ? "

" I remember many things," replied Clara, with a dignity that was perhaps a little sophomorical.

" O, do we ? How antique we are getting."

" Yes ; I remember, for example, that there is a certain
young lady who will probably go on repeating a certain
grammatical solecism until she is gray," answered Clara,
alluding to Leila's " everybody have." Leila made an
indiscriminate onslaught upon grammars generally, during
which the doctor was called away to his patients, and the
breakfast ended.

During the day Mrs. Forest, and subsequently Clara,
visited Susie's room ; but in both cases Susie seemed disturbed, and disinclined to enter upon the details of her
illness, and declared she wanted nothing. She thanked
them for their kindness, and once, upon some gentle word
from Mrs. Forest, she hid her eyes, which had filled with
tears. Dinah was the only welcome presence to the poor
girl during that long, sad day, and for obvious reasons.

Early in the evening Dr. Delano called, and made himself very agreeable to all the ladies, and especially so to
Clara, a little later, when they had a long tête-a-tête on
the old south-facing veranda. The sunset had been
magnificent, and as Dr. Delano was quite seriously
enamoured with Clara, he was gay, poetic, appreciative—
everything that could charm her—but she could say little
in reply to his fervid eloquence, for she had the disadvan-
tage of being immeasurably in love, and consequently felt
a certain awkwardness, a triumph to Dr. Delano, growing
sweeter and sweeter every hour. It was her first romance.
It was his—well, not his first, certainly. *That* was an

early attachment to Ella Wills, his father's ward, and this
night he told Clara the story of that romance, showing
her, of course, beyond a shadow of doubt, that *that* was
a very insignificant passion—"as water unto wine," was
the way he characterized it—comparing it to his present
deeper and dearer love. Do not lovers, not always, but
very generally, tell this same old fib? The truth was,
he had adored Ella with all a boy's enthusiasm, and she
had flirted with him persistently—"outrageously," Miss
Charlotte Delano, the doctor's sister, declared—and had
escaped heart-free herself. So when he came to tell her
in words that his heart was under her feet, she affected
the most innocent surprise, and hoped she had not led
him to suppose, etc., etc. In the end she somehow won
his respect, for he did not curse her, as rejected lovers do,
at least in most novels. She wept very lavishly, for she
meant to keep him in reserve, and marry him finally, if
no more brilliant offer occurred, or if ever in danger of
becoming an old maid—that terror of women who have
no serious object in life. When Dr. Delano first began
to mention Clara in his letters to his sister Charlotte,
which he did once as "the noblest and sweetest of mortal
women," Ella felt personally affronted, and commenced
at once to speculate on the chances of winning him back,
not once asking herself if this "noblest and sweetest
woman" had not already acquired rights over the heart
once so lightly rejected. She had not seen him since his
return from Europe, where he had spent three years in
completing his medical education.

Ella always played the kitten, though she was no longer
a child, and a very Methuselah, if age could be numbered
by her conquests. She had no heart to speak of, and less

conscience, but she impressed every male creature with a sense of childish, artless innocence. She was a brunette, petite, with dark short ringlets about her small head, a peach bloom on her cheeks, and a babyish, pouting mouth, whose sweetness Albert Delano had found difficult to forget, or even to recall without regret, until he had found in Clara something infinitely superior to the sweetness and prettiness that had so charmed him in earlier days. This something he hardly comprehended, though he owned its power to a certain extent. It was soul, for want of a better name—a moral sweetness, a divine, emotional sensitiveness, and a straightforward honesty of purpose, that made you conscious, last of all, that she was beautiful in person and exceedingly graceful in every movement.

This evening Clara remembered long after, as the happiest in her life. The bright moon shone through the climbing foliage on the veranda, carpeting the floor with soft mosaic patterns, through which the "mated footsteps" of the lovers passed and repassed, talking in low tones of the beauty of the scene, at intervals, when time could be spared from the dearer theme of their perfections in each other's eyes, and the future that, before them,

——" like a fruitful land reposed."

Of course, they took no note of time, and Miss Marston, after talking some time with Mrs. Forest, went quietly to her room. Leila fidgeted about for awhile, and then exclaimed, crossly :

"I *don't* see why they wish to moon out there all night."

"Why, Leila !" said Mrs. Forest, reproachfully. "I

see nothing improper in their enjoying each other's society, and you should not speak in that way."

"She's jealous," remarked Linnie.

"You mean thing! I'm not," Leila answered, in a high key, and then they went to bed to fight it out in the ordinary sisterly way; and I take it that sisters can be as caustic and insolently mean in their treatment of each other as any kindred under the sun. In this case, however, Linnie was really fond of her sister, and would have manifested it quite lavishly by way of petting, but for being discouraged and called "spooney" by Leila whenever she attempted any expression of sentiment.

Mrs. Forest waited awhile after the twins were gone, and then went to the veranda and gave the lovers some friendly caution about the night air. This duty discharged, and hearing her husband enter his sleeping-room, she joined him there. He was very glad to see her, for he wished to broach the subject of Susie's condition, a task requiring considerable diplomacy, for he knew Mrs. Forest would naturally be merciless to one like Susie. But the doctor in his diplomacy, as Clara said, did very well until he came to the diplomatic part, and then he lost the first requisite, patience. He greeted Mrs Forest very pleasantly, and told her she never looked lovelier in her life.

"Ah! dear," she answered, "it is very sweet to hear you say so, but"—and she viewed herself composedly in the mirror of the doctor's wardrobe—"this glass shows me my wrinkles and my gray hair."

"Well, your hair is beautiful, and I like these little crows'-feet at the corners of your eyes; but this is not what makes your beauty in my eyes—" and he came

beside her, and put his arm around her—" it is the softness and tenderness of expression in your face. You did
not have this as a girl." Here was possibly the approach
to the needed diplomacy.

" Yet you used to rave about my beauty ; and how
indifferent I was to it."

" To which ? "

" To your raving, to be sure."

" Ah ! of course."

" See how my color has gone. I think I never was
vain, but who can look at such a reflection with any satisfaction ? You are bronzed by exposure, but that rather
improves you, and I'm sure, as we stand here, you look
ten years younger than I do, instead of five older. That
is because you have had no babies."

" Ah ! Indeed ! " exclaimed the doctor, with Panta-
gruelistic gayety. " I thought they were all mine—all but
that doubling feat. That was entirely your invention."

" For shame ! Have you not teazed me enough with
that. I think you are so absurd. I wish you would
never make such a remark again."

" Well, then, I won't ; but the way you take it is so
amusing. Are you going to stay ? "

" Do you wish me to ? "

" Ah ! That is not to be considered," said the doctor,
with his usual gallantry, which was not gallantry at all
in his case, but the simple expression of his interpretation of woman's most primitive right. " The question
is, do *you* wish to stay ? "

" Yes, dear."

" You don't come too often these days," he said, toying with her ear.

"That is because I know that you are tired, and would rather sleep when you have left your study."

"Too tired, you think, to enjoy your presence?"

"Yes; you know I have not lost the girlish habit of liking to lie awake and talk. You go to sleep the moment you touch the pillow. Ah, me! how we change! I remember how you used to keep me awake with your ineffable words and caresses! and I was so indifferent then. You loved me more than I could possibly appreciate;" and she added, taking the hair-pins from her silvery hair, and with a little sigh, "Ah! if I were only young again!" For answer, the doctor sang the trivial words of Beranger:

> "Combien je regrette
> Mon bras si dodu,
> Ma jambe bien faite
> Et le temps perdu."

"Translate your French. It is something shocking, no doubt."

"No, indeed. But I could not do it justice. I promise to keep you awake to-night though, for I must consult you about a matter of importance."

"What is it about?"

"It is about Susie Dykes."

"She does look ill, I think, and she has been so silent and moody lately. You don't think she has anything serious the matter with her, do you?"

"Yes, serious enough. It is strange you have not guessed."

"What!" exclaimed Mrs. Forest, a sudden light breaking into her mind. "You don't mean to say——"

"Yes, just that," interrupted the doctor, "and the

agony of the poor girl is dreadful. What is worse, Dan has put it out of his power to save her from disgrace."

"Dan!" exclaimed Mrs. Forest, in great disgust. "I don't believe he knows anything about it. The shameless thing! No doubt——"

"Now! now! Don't go off at half-cock. He admits it all—did so in my study last night, where he said he would rather die than marry Susie."

"Oh, Heaven! How dreadful for Dan!"

"And you think only of him."

"Only of him! Is he not my child? Is it not natural that I should think only of him?"

"Many things are natural that are very selfish. Is Susie not somebody's child too as well as Dan? And what is his suffering compared to hers? Will the world howl at him as a sinner, kick him down further into hell, and abandon him with virtuous scorn? No, no; there's plenty of girls here in Oakdale, of good family too, who would marry him to-morrow for all his damnable treachery to this poor girl, while the hypocrites, drawing their immaculate skirts clear of his victim, wink at his act, and distinguish it 'as sowing wild oats.' And you, my wife—you among the number! You would send her out to die in the streets, would you?"

"I am sorry for her, of course. You know I am."

Mrs. Forest was thinking of Clara's prospects; of the aristocratic Delanos, who were soon coming to Oakdale, and the event was important. What would they say at Clara's family supporting and harboring under their roof a girl so disgraced? Mrs. Forest added, "But we cannot be expected to be victimized because of her want of virtue. Of course she cannot stay here."

" Virtue ! " said the doctor, with contempt. " Virtue, in any decent code of morals, must include all the best qualities of the heart. You are one of the soulless Pharisees who would cover it with a fig-leaf. I thought I knew you better, Fannie. Some one says, if you would know a man, divide an inheritance with him; but, by ——, after you have slept in a woman's arms twenty odd years, shared your fortune and all the joys and sorrows of life with her for that time, a simple case like this arises when you expect common human sympathy, and she fails you utterly."

Mrs. Forest began to sob quietly, but finding to her astonishment that this redoubtable weapon had lost its power over the soft-hearted doctor, she was piqued, and hardened her heart like a flint. She began hastily replacing her hair-pins in her hair. This was to punish him by depriving him of her presence for the night, which she had so sweetly promised. The doctor noted this movement, the critical moment, probably, if only his diplomacy had been equal to the situation; but he was " a plain, blunt man," as Mark Antony says of himself, and he had already played his last card. He knew it was hopeless. Mrs. Forest, gentle, mild, pious, as she undoubtedly was, could not understand the doctor's broad love of humanity. She had no power of loving anything that was not distinctly her own ; but she was sure of her own integrity, and when told by the doctor that there was no more virtue in her love than in that of a hen for her chickens when she gathers her own under her wings, but pecks away all others, even though motherless and dying for care, she was not in the least disturbed; she was sure of her own position, and as immovable as a rock. " Do as you like," he said to her, giving up the case, but determined to speak his mind freely; "do as you like, you and the other godly who pretend to be followers of one who said, 'Neither do I condemn thee.' Your respect for Christ is a common farce. It is merely a thing of form and respectability. You don't take the trouble to see what manner of man he really was, or you would see how impossible it is for you to have any sentiments in common with him. Was he not a radical, sitting down with publicans and sinners, shocking all the conventional morality of his time, befriending the needy, supporting the outcasts of society, and a thorough despiser of all cant and hypocrisy?"

"I dislike to hear any one quoting Christ who does not believe in him," said Mrs. Forest very softly, but none the less angry for all that.

"Believe," echoed the doctor. "*You* are the real infidel. Do you believe in the divine nature of Christ? Of course you do not; for if you did, you would have more respect for his morality and magnanimity of character. Do you believe in your heaven? You have no shadow of real faith in it, and you know it in your own heart, for it is a place where this same unhappy girl may be your equal or superior, according to your own scheme of salvation; and you know you would prefer annihilation to any such democratic mixing of saint and sinner. Do you think you can make me think you believe in hell, when you coolly run the risk of its terrors by turning against the suffering wretches whom Christ helped and befriended? Oh, Fannie! you have no religion in your heart, for you have no love for humanity; or, call it religion if you like, and say you have no honest human sympathy, and no faith that can triumph over the little expedients and conventional proprieties of the day."

" I do not wish to manifest levity, but it does seem to me amusing to hear *you* talk of faith."

At another time the doctor would have ceased in despair ; but it is so hard to believe absolutely that those allied to us by many tender ties, can never respect our most sacred convictions ; besides, the doctor's sense of human justice was outraged, and he had not yet given full vent to his righteous indignation.

" I will not try to show you that I have a faith which you can never comprehend. It would be useless," he said, " but I can tell you, though you could never persuade me to cant and howl among your pious herd, that I respect Christ and his example as I respect the dignity of all sympathy for human misery ; and I shall prove it by standing by this unhappy girl. I am none the less ready to do so because her suffering is caused by a knave whom I had the misfortune to beget."

" Why, I never heard any one utter such language !" exclaimed Mrs. Forest; " but it is useless to reason with you, when you are in a passion. For my part, I think ' charity begins at home.' "

" Yes, I know you do ; and according to your creed, it not only begins but ends there also."

" Would you sacrifice the prospects of your children to protect a shameless girl ? "

" I'd sacrifice anything and everything on earth to show my faith in the triumph of justice. Besides, this girl is not shameless. She has a noble nature. She told Dan to his face that he would never marry Susie Dykes—this when she found he would marry her, but only as a duty.

Yes, madam, you can now measure my faith, which you despise, and see what it is worth beside yours. Let what will come, I shall stand by this girl. Life, with the consciousness that I have acted like a cur, is not worth having. Now you had better go and pray for grace to do unto others as you would have others do unto you;" and the doctor burst into a bitter laugh, as the door closed behind her who had come with wifely tenderness to sleep by his side.

CHAPTER XII.

MRS. FOREST had often had rather severe con-
flicts with her husband on questions of morality
and justice, upon which, in her mind, he held very lax
notions. This, however, was the first time they had been
diametrically opposed in a matter of actual practice, and
she was considerably disturbed, though she carried away
the gratification of having preserved that serenity of soul
that naturally belongs to those who are in the right;
moreover she was somewhat piqued in her womanly
vanity, because the doctor had not desired her to stay
sufficiently to yield the point. But there was one deep
satisfaction for her that atoned for everything : Lan was
in no danger of being compelled to marry Susie Dykes.
During all the first part of her conversation with the
doctor, she had mortally feared that he would insist on
bringing this about.

As she descended the stairs, she found Clara bolting
the front door. She had just let Dr. Delano out, after
bidding him good-night as many times as lovers usually
do, and was in a blissful state of mind. Her beautiful,
limpid eyes shone brilliantly through her long lashes,
her lips were crimson and dewy, and her whole being
expressed the happiness of the young, poetic enthusiast.

"Come and sleep with me, daughter. I wish to talk

with you," she said, embracing Clara with more effusion than was her wont, and Clara saw that some grief disturbed her mother. What could it be? Surely not disapproval of her attachment to Dr. Delano, for had not her mother smiled upon the happy lovers not an hour ago? This settled, in Clara's thought, there could be nothing serious in what her mother had to say, and this special night she wished to be alone. There seemed lately no time to think, to enjoy the delicious creations of a vivid imagination, stimulated by a passion as real and sweet as it was dreamy and ideal. The longing to be alone with her thoughts made her say, " Come into the parlor, mamma dear, and tell me there."

" No," said Mrs. Forest, with the persistence of a child, " I want you with me," and she added, reproachfully, " Is it a sacrifice ? " thus forcing Clara to say what was not strictly true—" Certainly not, mamma dear. I will go with you."

Long into the night Mrs. Forest talked earnestly to her daughter. Clara was shocked, as any romantic young girl would be, having the case presented in its worst light—disgusted, indeed—but she was much too severe upon Dan to please her mother. Clara was her father's own girl, as Mrs. Forest knew, and her heart was naturally inclined to pity Susie, and she said to her mother in extenuation, " She is so young, you know, and without any education, or she would know she could never win a lover in that way." This was a sign of wisdom that pleased Mrs. Forest.

" My daughter, I am sure," she said, " would never be in danger of forwardness and immodesty with gentlemen ; and I will say here, my dear, that much being alone with gentlemen before marriage, is very injudicious, for the most honorable of them will take advantage of such confidence."

Clara was rather inclined to believe this, recalling certain passages on the veranda that evening, but she was very silent on that subject. Mrs. Forest returned to the subject of Susie, and labored to show the importance of having her out of the house as soon as possible. " Your father is so unreasonable. I really believe he thinks it our duty to have her here. Why, I should die of shame to have the Delanos know it. What would they think ? "

" We must do right, mamma, whatever people think."

" Yes, yes ; but we can do right in a prudent way, and there is so much at stake. Dr. Delano asked your father's permission to address you only to-day." Clara knew this fact, but it was very agreeable to have a second account of it. " Your father is so unlike the rest of the world. I was shocked at his answer. Instead of thanking Dr. Delano for the honor, as would have been the proper way, he answeied brusquely, ' Bless my soul ! Delano, it's none of my business. I don't see what the girl can want with your ridiculous addresses, but that is her affair. You know I advocate woman's rights, and that includes her right to make a fool of herself ; ' and he actually laughed." Clara asked anxiously how Dr. Delano received it—that was the all-important part to her.

" Oh, he took it exceedingly well, I am glad to say. He held out his hand to your father, and thanked him in a very gentlemanly style."

" Did papa say any more ? "

"Such a lot of nonsense! He said he. had brought you up to be independent. For my part, I think an independent girl dreadful. He said he had told you what rascally dogs men were, and if this was the result of his warning, why he must submit. You cannot imagine how mortified I was. Your father was called away then, and I apologized to Dr. Delano for his manner."

"Why, mamma! the idea of apologizing for papa's manner. I should not think of doing Dr. Delano the injustice of supposing he could not understand and appreciate my father. He speaks of him in a way that charms me."

Mrs. Forest kept on talking, making a mountain of the importance of getting rid of Susie. She would, of course, be kind to her; all the ladies of the church would do something for her; but Dr. Delano's august father and Miss Charlotte were coming, and they must never hear of this terrible disgrace.

Clara was bewildered. Her education at Stonybrook had inculcated the conventional respect for the proprieties; but now face to face with a practical trouble like this, she did not feel like trusting entirely her mother, who was the very soul of conventionality. She would see her father, and then judge for herself; and with this decision she dropped asleep.

In the morning Clara slept rather late, and when she went down-stairs her father was gone. During breakfast Mrs. Forest had hardly addressed a word to him. In her mind, there was a kind of lovers' quarrel between her and the doctor. There had been many of these in her married life; but feeling conscious of her power when she chose to be gracious, it did not trouble her much. She felt he ought to be punished, and rather enjoyed his perturbation, not being sufficiently discriminating to perceive how deeply he was disappointed in her want of sympathy with his desire to help Susie in her strait. If Clara should fail him also, it would go hard with poor Susie. He determined, however, to say very little to Clara until he found how she would be disposed to act. This was a most interesting point to him. How would his Clara face a thing like this? Of course he might influence her through her love for him, but he scorned to do that—she must act freely. If he saw her, he would simply state the case and leave her to her own decision. The opportunity occurred unexpectedly, for in his drive across the common, in the middle of the forenoon, he overtook his daughter, who was out for a walk. He drew up beside her and talked a few minutes, being careful to avoid any expression as to how a woman ought to act to any sister woman in such a case. He expressed simply his own feeling for Susie, and his determination to stand by her. Clara listened silently, and walked home turning the matter over in her own mind. She found herself unconsciously calculating effects, after the manner of her mother, and was disgusted with this evidence of meanness. When she reached home, Miss Marston and her mother were in the drawing-room, where the latter had just informed her guest of the scandal, regretting that anything so unpleasant should occur during Miss Marston's visit. Mrs. Forest was careful to avoid mentioning her son as in any way implicated, but she was pleased to have some one with whom she could talk of her troubles and cares—one, too, who had sound notions upon moral questions. Miss Marston indeed was a rigid moralist of the conventional school, not, indeed, from any narrowness of heart, but through logical conclusions from premises which, if not sound in principle, were at least well considered. Mrs. Forest knew that the influence of her guest was very great over Clara, because of her affection and admiration for Miss Marston, and so Mrs. Forest continued the conversation about Susie after Clara entered. One thing troubled her, however. Clara was ignorant of her mother's intention to shield Dan from Miss Marston's censure; and she might, by some ill-timed remark, let out the cat that her mother would so carefully tie up. Tact was necessary, and she soon found a pretext to send Clara to her room for something, and another pretext to follow her and implore her to not mention Dan. What was the use? It could do no good, and it was her duty to be kind to Dan as well as to Susie. Clara said nothing, but pondered deeply over her mother's ways of securing her ends.

When the conversation was resumed, Mrs. Forest showed a remarkable clemency toward Susie, especially after discovering that Clara had been talking with her father during her walk. This was tact again. Clara had somehow inherited her father's tendency to radicalism, and might be easily shocked into a heroic course toward her brother's victim.

"I do not think," said Mrs. Forest, "that we can do better than to get her a place where she can be quiet; and as she is so very deft with her needle, and can make herself useful in many ways, I do not think this will be difficult."

"This will be to fail her in what she most needs—sympathy," Clara remarked.

"My dear Clara," said Miss Marston, "we cannot sym-pathize with folly unless we are foolish ourselves. You know the meaning of the word sympathy."

There was a little too much of the dogmatism of the teacher in this to please Clara, but she showed no dis-pleasure in her very calm reply : "But we can sympa-thize with suffering in all cases."

"Yet even for her good," replied Mrs. Forest, "we should show disapprobation of her conduct. By being too lenient, it would lead her to hold her act lightly, and open the way for its repetition."

"Well, I think, mamma, with all proper deference, that your reasoning is exceedingly weak. Will not one terrible lesson like this be enough for any girl like Susie ? Besides, you forget how many years it must be before she can outlive her love for——" Mrs. Forest trembled ; but Clara saw the danger her mother dreaded, and con-tinued, "for her betrayer, and by that time she will be-come staid and prudent."

"I think myself," said Miss Marston, "that there is little danger of her repeating her folly. She seems really a very modest young person. She has undoubtedly fallen through an ill-directed affection. What sort of a man is her lover, and where is he ? "

Mrs. Forest did not dare meet Clara's eyes during her quick answer, "Oh, it is a young man in town. He does not seem to care anything for her."

"I consider him an unprincipled wretch," replied Clara, indignantly. Her mother's determination to screen Dan looked very ugly in her eyes. "Papa says he offered to marry her," she continued, addressing Miss Marston, "but in a way that showed he considered it a great sacrifice ; and she was proud enough and womanly enough to throw his insulting offer back in his teeth. I like her for that, and I think we ought to protect her right generously. I mean to help her, at all events."

" My child ! " cried Mrs. Forest, in alarm. " You are so impulsive, so imprudent. You will certainly be talked about."

" I don't think, mamma, that should make any difference when we know we are in the right. I believe the right way is to find out what our duty is, and then, to do it openly and fairly."

" My dear," said Miss Marston, " there are very Quixotic ways of doing our duty." She said this in a cool, decided way, that chafed Clara's growing heroic mood, and she replied, bitterly : " I could avoid these ways, I suppose, by making bibs and baby things in secret, and sending them to her anonymously, but I think that would be contemptible. I know if such an awful thing should happen to any one of my dear friends, my equals, or to my own sister, I should go to her and comfort her with my sympathy ; and if there is any goodness or nobility in doing so for a dear friend, there must be still more virtue in such a course when the object is a poor, friendless girl, deprived of all advantages of education and social culture until she came here."

" Very well reasoned," said Miss Marston, ironically ; " but I am sorry to see that you forget how this young person has profited by the advantages for social culture that she has already had in this family."

Clara's eyes fairly flashed, and Mrs. Forest saw that she was sorely tempted to show Miss Marston what social and moral influence Susie had been under through one

member of the family at least; so she made haste to answer soothingly, almost before the words were out of Miss
Marston's mouth, " You are so young, my daughter, that
it hardly becomes you to seem to know so much more
than your elders about what is right and proper. I know
your motives are generous, but you must not trust yourself wholly in such a case as this. You are wrong in
supposing that showing open sympathy with a girl who
has fallen from virtue, can do her any good ; and it certainly may injure you irreparably."

" Your whole tone, mamma, is cold and calculating.
This poor girl is alone, and in an agony of grief such as
we have never dreamed of. If helping her bear up under
her burden, must injure me, even irreparably, as you say,
let it do so. I do not want the favor nor the admiration
of the Priest and the Levite who pass by on the other
side. Besides, I do not act alone. I have had the counsel
of the clearest head I know, and as noble a heart as ever
beat." Here Clara paused and sighed heavily, almost
overcome with a feeling of disappointment that Miss
Marston should manifest so little generosity, and one of
sorrow also that she had been compelled to express sentiments that must wound her much-loved teacher and
friend. As she expected, Miss Marston took refuge in
dignified silence, understanding herself, of course, as
included among the Priests and Levites. Mrs. Forest
remarked that all experience showed the feelings to be
dangerous guides ; as also were what were loosely called
principles ; that the only thing that upheld pure morals
was religion, and therefore it was the only sure guide.

Clara had often seen this making religious duty an
excuse for selfishness, and she had a contempt for it as

natural as was her repulsion to everything dark and ugly. She replied boldly, " I hear much about principles and religion, and I am compelled to judge them by their fruits. My father, you say, has no religion. Surely principles are better than religion, if one leads to helpful sympathy with all misfortune, and the other to cold calculation of the effect of evil tongues. I have thought over all the possible results, mamma, and I have decided. I know one who will help Susie openly, and without either calculation or shame ; and I shall certainly follow his example, for I will trust my father's sense of right against the world ! " and with this, delivered very dramatically and rapidly, Clara left the room.

6

CHAPTER XIII.

PAPA'S OWN GIRL.

NOT long after Clara left her mother and Miss Marston, she rapped very softly on Susie's door, not wishing to wake her if sleeping, and thus oblivious for the time, to her misery. Thinking it was Dinah, Susie bade the knocker come in. She was trying to dress herself, and sat by her glass brushing her long light hair. Perceiving the happy sister of Dan, resplendent in her youth and beauty, Susie buried her face with her pretty round arms, and wept softly. Clara approached her, and patted her white shoulder, saying, "Poor Susie! I have come to comfort you in your trouble. I know all about it, and I am so sorry, but I blame my brother far more than I do you;" at the mention of Dan, Susie sobbed aloud. "He is so cruel to you after all your loving him."

"Don't blame him too much," sobbed Susie. "He could not help it. If I were handsome and educated like Miss Marston, he would love me always; but it is so hard. I wonder why I cannot die. Every hour is harder and harder to bear."

Clara's tender heart was profoundly touched. This was the first time she had ever been brought face to face with real anguish, and she found it more terrible than any romance had ever pictured it. She reproached herself for ever thinking even for one moment of consequences.

in view of so plain a question of duty as trying to comfort this poor girl in every possible way. Yet she hardly knew what to say or do in the presence of such agony. She felt the necessity, however, of saying something, and inspiration and hope came as soon as she saw her words had any effect. "Don't give way so, dear child, I beg you. Remember what papa says, 'Grief cannot last forever.' Time will soften it all away, and if you live a noble life after this, as I am confident you will, you will have good and true friends. See how papa is going to stand by you; and I am also, if you will let me."

"If I will let you!" repeated Susie, raising her head. "What a good angel you are! I am not good enough to deserve so much kindness."

"Why, do you know, I think you are. I don't think any of the family but papa appreciate your sweetness and goodness. Now I want to tell you that Miss Marston will never marry Dan. She would never dream of such a thing. There is an idol in her heart enshrined, which no common man could displace; but that is a little secret, and I only tell it to reassure you. You are not going to sink down under this misfortune like a common-spirited girl. Do you know I admire you so much for refusing to be saved by Dan as a charity on his part? I've been thinking of it all day. You can win him back if you will; I'm sure of it, and the way to do it is to show him that he is not important enough for a woman to die for —not important enough to destroy your happiness for all time either. I tell you there is nothing so sure to win the love of men as to force them to admire our strength and independence. The clinging vines become very disagreeable and burdensome to the oaks after a time."

Clara said all this smiling cheerfully, and not in a patronizing "I am holier than thou" way at all. This won Susie's heart, and gave her a first impulse of hope.

"Oh, how good you are, Miss Forest. You come like warm sunlight into a cold dungeon, and I bless you with all my soul. And how selfish I am to let you stand all this time." And Susie rose and begged Clara to be seated, and excuse her while she finished dressing. Clara was struck with the delicacy of feeling in this poor girl, and especially by her good manners; and every minute in her presence increased her faith in her natural worth. "If I had only been here," she said to herself, "I would have helped her to study and be interested in something in the universe besides Dan, and this would never have happened." Then a new thought struck her suddenly, and she said, "What you want now is distraction from the one subject that worries you. What do you say to commencing to study seriously, and making me your teacher?"

"Oh, I will do anything in the world, and you shall never regret—" she said, but broke down before she could finish, after a moment adding, "never regret helping poor Susie. No one ever cared for me but Dan, and it was natural that I should love him too well——"

"Don't think of him just now any more," said Clara. "Of course it was natural. It is too bad that you have had so little chance for education, but we will make up for lost time." Clara remembered the delight she had often experienced when, finding a pot-flower drooping, she had given it water, and waited to see it slowly lift up its limp foliage, as if in gratitude to the beneficent hand that came to its relief. How much grander the pleasure in raising up a sorrow-burdened human soul, she thought ; and life seemed to have more scope and meaning to her from that hour. She entered enthusiastically into her plan of teaching Susie, and was delighted at the quick response it met.

"I have so longed to learn. I have tried to study grammar alone, but it is very difficult to get on. I fear you will find me so ignorant that you will give up in despair. I know so little of books ; but I can read, and write too, but I am a dreadful poor speller though. Dan used to laugh at me so."

"Did he ? Why he was a perfect blockhead himself in school, and forever at the foot of the spelling-class."

"Why, Miss Forest ! I thought he was a beautiful writer and speller," said Susie, wondering if this could be so.

"Have you any of his letters ? " asked Clara, laughing and thinking it would be a good stroke of policy to show Susie that her tyrant was not quite omnipotent in wisdom.

Susie produced from the bottom of a well-worn paper box, whose corners, both of box and cover, had been carefully sewed together, a package of letters, and handed it confidently to Clara, who took out one at random, which was written while Dan was in the peddling business. It ran thus:

"MY DARLING SUSIE: I have gone all over this one horse town of Boilston to-day, and have sold a peice of red coton velvit for a sofer covering and some pins and matches and that is all. To-morrow I shall be in Marlboro and expect to do a big buisness. I have not written to the governer yet becaus I want to show him I can live and succede to, away from home, so dont tell whear I am til I come back whitch will be next weak. Thear is a pretty little house here for sail and I mean to buy it as soon as I get money enough. How would you like it as a preasent? Only I shall expect you to take me as a purmanent border and I may be a very dispeptick one and hard to pleas."

There was much more about the cottage, and many expressions of tenderness and anxiety because he thought Susie did not fully return his love. Clara sighed as she refolded the letter, to think that one of her sex should be so deficient in culture as to take this effusion as a masterpiece of composition ; but it revealed the fact that Dan had loved Susie sincerely in his way, and made her look very leniently upon Susie's inordinate faith in him.

"Are there any mistakes in that ? " asked Susie, seeing that Clara was silent.

"Yes, dear; plenty of them," she answered, regretting her determination to destroy any of the poor child's illusions ; but she had committed herself to it, and so she pointed out the errors consecutively, beginning with "peice" in the first line, and then she said, "You see, if he had any serious education himself, he would not laugh at your mistakes in spelling. Only ignoramuses are vain about small accomplishments. I do not doubt in the least that your own letters were superior to this."

"Oh, I think not; but you can see for yourself. He gave them to me to keep, because he is always going about. He always keeps my last till I write again, and then returns it for me to keep—I mean he always did do so—but he will never write me again," she said, struggling with her emotion, as she gave Clara one of her letters to Dan. Clara read with quiet interest, forgetting all thought of the orthography in the simple eloquence expressed in every sentence. Tears came into her eyes as she read the closing paragraphs, "but I must not sit up later though I could never wish to stop. It is so sweet to know where you are and to send you words of love and then so much more sweet to know that you care for them. I must be up early to help your mother who is so kind to me. I keep thinking all the day that some-time she may come to like me and be willing that I should be your wife though I know I am not worthy of so high an honor. Your family would be ashamed of mine, Dan. This is a hard thought, but it is not my fault, and I mean to be good and true always. I read all the time I can get, and try to improve all I can. Do not laugh at my spelling, dearest. Remember I never went to school steadily but two months in my life. When we are together you will teach me, and I shall show you how seriously I can study. Good-night, dearest one. I kiss you in my thoughts and all my love and all my life are yours forever."

"Oh, how blind your love has made you, Susie. Why, this letter is eloquent. If my brother had been capable of understanding your generous sensibility, he would rather have sought to learn of you, than to have presumed to be your teacher. There are errors in orthography, but not half so many as there are in his; besides the senti-ment of yours is noble, and that of his is not. You spell beautiful with two ll's, and there are one or two other errors; but I believe they are all from studying Dan's ridiculous style. You write a pretty hand, and your head, as papa says, is an excellent one. There is nothing to hinder your getting a fair education. I will teach you the Latin and Greek words from which ours are made up, also rhetoric, and history, and geography, and we will study botany together. You will be charmed with botany. I have all the text-books, and I want you to commence even to-morrow, so that you can have no time to brood over your miseries. I know you won't do as silly girls do who, when persecuted for falling one step, think they may as well go quite down to perdition. Remember, you are not really degraded in my eyes, and I want you to take me into your heart as a true friend."

Susie at this knelt down beside Clara, and burying her head in her lap sobbed anew, but quickly raised her head, saying, "I am only crying now for joy, because God is so good in sending you to me. Never in this world shall I forget the blessed help and comfort you bring to me. You will go to a home of your own some day, and if you will have me, I will come and take all your cares. I will keep your house. I will learn to do everything; and oh! I shall love you to my dying day."

" Dear, dear Susie!" said Clara, her own eyes full of tears as she bent down and kissed Susie tenderly. "You would pay me too generously for what gives me so much pleasure. I ask only that you will be happy and make the best of everything. Do not kneel before me."

"Oh, let me, do! It is natural for me, when I see anything so good and beautiful as you are; but have you thought that others will not think of me as you do? I am afraid you will pay dearly for your goodness to poor Susie."

"Have no fear. I despise cold, shallow-hearted people, and shall lose the love of none but them. Papa will love me better, and that is compensation enough for that which merits no compensation at all. His approbation is worth more than that of all the world without it." Clara found Susie quite capable of appreciating the character of Dr. Forest, and that raised her at once higher in her estimation. She talked with her some time longer, and then rose to go ; but just then she saw Susie's face blanch and her limbs shake. She had forgotten how great a strain this long interview must have been to Susie in her weak condition, and quickly atoned for her oversight, first by bringing her a cordial, and then helping her to undress and put her to bed like a child. Susie submitted like a tired baby. Her eyes were greatly swollen with weeping, and for these Clara brought hot water, and laid a compress upon them, saying, " Hot water, you know, is better for inflammation. That's what the new school says, and we belong to the new school. Papa is a radical, they say ; so are we. We believe in love, not in hate ; in happiness, not in misery ;" and Clara kissed Susie and bade her good-bye, saying, " Now go to sleep, if you can. Rest perfectly quiet. Trust to me and papa, and all will be well. No, don't say a word. I won't be thanked and called an angel, for I am only a girl like you, and in your place you would be just as kind to me."

Clara left Susie's chamber in a most enviable frame of mind. She had experienced a new pleasure from her course toward Susie, and in her heart she wondered why all the world was not loving and kind, when to be so created such deep satisfaction. "I think I did right too," she said to herself, "in instilling a little healthy poison into Susie's mind about Dan. If she can see a few of his meannesses, perhaps she will suffer less from the 'pangs of despised love.'" Still Clara was not quite sure that she was right in lowering Dan in Susie's estimation. On general principles, she would have naturally opposed anything of the kind; but Susie's restoration to peace of mind and usefulness was the one object to be gained. To this end her self-respect must be roused, which could hardly be effected while she considered herself Dan's inferior intellectually. Clara determined to prove to Susie her own innate strength, and humble Dan by showing him what a pearl he had thrown away. This was a labor worthy of Clara, and she left Susie's room feeling that she loved all the world better for the course she had taken, and her heart was so full of human sweetness that she poured it out on everybody; on Dinah, whom she helped for an hour or two in her household work; on her twin sisters, who were not inclined much, especially Leila, to sentiment. Clara helped them both with their piano practice, petted them, called them her darlings, and encouraged them in every way. Linnie was touched by Clara's kindness, and when she left said to Leila:

"How sweet Clara is, isn't she?"

"As honey and nectar," replied Leila; "all of a sudden, too. I guess she's experienced religion," she added, with her clear, metallic laugh. Leila was like Dan in many ways. The spirit of devotion was apparently wholly wanting in her nature. She was one of those whose doubting was an offence to freedom of thought, and whom you would rather see canting bigots than supporters of any principle dear to you. The doctor came in some time before tea, and went directly to Susie's room, where he remained a full half hour. The change that he perceived in Susie was a revelation to him of his daughter's character that brought an infinite relief, and more than justified all his hopes of her. As he went down the family were going into the dining-room. Clara stood at the foot of the stairs, waiting for him. He drew her head down on his breast and caressed it fondly; then held it away with both hands, and looked searchingly into her splendid eyes. This scrutiny evidently revealed what he sought, for he said softly and slowly, dwelling fondly on each word, "*Papa's own girl;*" and then they joined the family in the dining-room.

CHAPTER XIV.

DAN'S MONEY RETURNED—THE DOCTOR CONQUERED.

THE twins, who were now about thirteen years of age, had great difficulty in fathoming the secret regarding Susie, for, being the youngest of the children, they were still babies in the eyes of the family. They were not long in "nosing out," as Leila called it, the real difficulty, and they discussed the subject together in a naive way that would have been amusing but for the heartlessness they displayed ; still it was the heartlessness of the kitten over the agonies of a captive mouse, and perhaps implied no real cruelty of purpose beyond a certain spitefulness that they were not considered of sufficient importance to be taken into anybody's confidence. Even Dinah snubbed them in a supercilious way when they attempted to obtain information from her, and they revenged themselves in a thousand nameless ways. Susie meanwhile had recovered from her illness occasioned by the shock she had received, and made superhuman efforts to win some little show of sympathy from Mrs. Forest. Clara had talked Miss Marston over to her side in a measure, so that she manifested a good deal of kindness to poor Susie, whose position was very difficult to endure. The twins, taking their cue from their mother, ignored Susie's existence completely, more especially Leila, who, though in the habit of shirking every duty upon the willing hands of Susie, informed "Miss Dykes," as she called her one day for the first time, that she need not come into her room any more to do the chamber-work. Susie looked at her with mild, sorrowful eyes, set down the water she had brought, and left the room without a word. Linnie, being softer in her feelings, said, "I think you are too bad, Leila. Did you see how she looked at you?"

"No, nor I don't care. She's a nasty thing."

"I don't see much difference between her now and a week ago, when you used to kiss her when you wanted her to do anything for you." Leila flared up, and a very sisterly fight ensued. Linnie was no match for the hard-headed Leila in a contest of words, but in revenge, later in the day, she told Clara how Susie had been treated. This happened to be a good policy, though not intended as such. Clara drew her arm about Linnie, saying, "I am glad, sister dear, that you show some feeling. I knew you would, and I have wanted to take you into my confidence, for you are more mature for your age than Leila is; but mamma thought it not best. I think she is wrong, and I am going to tell you the truth. You have guessed it already. Susie, you know, has loved Dan since she was your age, and she has been foolish of course; but I want you to remember that she was a poor, ignorant, neglected child, and Dan was engaged to marry her. I blame him infinitely more than I do her. He was very selfish and unprincipled."

"So I think, sissy. I thought it must be Dan—the mean thing. I'm real sorry for Susie; but what a goose she must be to care so for *him*." And so another friend was won over to Susie. Linnie grew immensely important in her own eyes after this confidence of Clara, who told her, among other pretty compliments, that she was "right womanly" in her sentiments.

On one of those weary days, when Susie felt like destroying her life despite the kindness and sympathy of Clara and her father, she received a note from Dan. It was written in a cold, heartless style that she could scarcely believe him capable of after all she knew of him, and ended: "I don't want you to be disgraced through me, and I am willing to marry you. Name the time and place, and I will be on hand. It is no use to palaver and swear I shall be supremely happy, and all that; but you are 'ruined,' of course, if I don't, and I'm willing to do it, and ought to for the prospective brat's sake, at least." The letter enclosed a cheque for fifty dollars. Susie regarded the money greedily. She had never had half as much in her whole life, and this would buy so many things she needed, and then she read Dan's heartless letter again, crying bitterly. Not one word of tenderness; nothing of the old love was left, only pity and an offer to sacrifice himself to save her. Disgust with her weakness, self-reproach, indignation, possessed her by turns, and the result was sending back the letter and the cheque, with only these words: "I can beg in the streets for myself or for your child much easier than I can accept charity from you. O my God! that I should come to this—to have money thrown at me like a bone to a dog, from one, too, whom I have so loved and trusted. Believe me, the only favor I ask, is that you may forget that I ever cared for you, for—

'I am shamed through all my being
To have loved so weak a thing.' "

When Dan received this, he was surprised, to say the

least, and chewed his moustache viciously. Beyond all
his pique at the way his offer was received, there was
a dawning respect for the girl he had ruined, as he
thought; but Susie was not quite ruined yet, thanks to
the generous sympathy of Dr. Forest and his daughter;
and losing her respect for Dan, through finding out
how soulless and unworthy he was, her heart-aches on
account of his faithlessness gradually began to sub-
side. Pretty soon another letter came, containing one
hundred dollars in greenbacks. This time he confessed admiration for her "pluck," as he called it, but
swore that if she sent back this money he would burn it,
leaving enough of the notes to show her he had kept
his word. This was why he had sent greenbacks, which,
if destroyed, could not be made good like a bank
cheque.

Susie resolved to show this letter to Clara, and ask
her advice, apologizing for not doing so with the first
one. In fact Susie had enjoyed, in a bitter way, her answer, knowing it would wound Dan's vanity, and she had
feared that Clara's advice would interfere with this satisfaction. The letter was written in a moment of exaltation, and was the wisest thing Susie could have done;
but yet after it was in the post-office and beyond recall,
the poor girl suffered new tortures lest her words should
alienate him still further from her; for she had to own
that, after all, she had not utterly given up the hope that
he was only temporarily under some new influence, that
made him act so dishonorably toward her. Love is not
only blind, but absolutely idiotic, in its faith. When
once we are even partially free from his gilded toils, how

wide our eyes are opened ! How microscopic their power to detect and measure infinitesimal quantities of meanness in the lover.

Clara was away when the second letter came, and Mrs. Forest and her visitor were out riding. Just as she had folded and put away Dan's second letter, the doctor came in. He greeted her pleasantly, and threw himself wearily on the lounge in the dining-room. Upon his inquiring for Clara, Susie told him she was out. " But cannot I take her place, just for once ? " she asked. " You want your bath, I know, for you always say that nothing rests you so much ; " and not waiting for any verbal assent, Susie ran and pumped the water from the rain-cistern into the bath-tub, and added a pail of hot water from Dinah's range. The bath refreshed him, as it always did, and when he came back Susie had his pipe filled for him, and a cup of fresh coffee beside it.

" What a grand sachem I am, to be so coddled by nice women. Now come and talk to me, Susie," he said, stretching himself on the lounge. Susie sat down beside him on a low stool, and showed him Dan's first letter and a copy of her answer.

" Good for your answer, Susie. I rather like it, though it is a little romantic. Yes, I like it; but your sending back the money—ah! that was too romantic by far. He's a spendthrift, and the best possible use he can make of his money is to give it to you. Don't you do it again—hear ?—if he sends you any more."

Susie listened to the doctor, but could not tell him just then that Dan had sent more, having stubbornly determined to refuse it, as she had the first; but she would consult Clara first. Seeing her silent, the doctor said :

> " ' Is there confusion in the little isle?
> Let what is broken so remain.'

"See! I am romantic, too. I also quote Tennyson. You've borne up bravely, Susie, these last days, and by and by all will be right. I am going to find you a place with some patient of mine, as near here as possible." Susie's face beamed at this. She felt that she could not possibly stay much longer in the doctor's house, for she knew how Mrs. Forest felt toward her. He left her no time to thank him before he added, "I trust you are cultivating a healthy contempt for your rascally lover? "

"Do you think he will never, never care for Susie any more? " she asked. "See! he commences even this letter ' *Dear Susie,*' " and she looked up inquiringly to the doctor, who answered, after a long pause:

"What dry husks a hungry heart will feed upon! Pitiful, pitiful!" and the doctor uttered a heavy sigh. "Why, no; he cares nothing for you beyond a feeling of pity, which no one could possibly withhold who had any natural feeling. I say this because the sooner you give up all hope that his disaffection is an accident, the better it will be for you."

"Yet only so little while ago he told me I was all the world to him."

"And he wrote you often, didn't he? "

"Yes. Sometimes twice a day," said Susie, smiling through her tears.

"Well, when he did that he was in love. There is no sign of that delectable state, so constant. You may lay it down as a law, *if a man loves he writes,* and simply because he cannot avoid doing so. He *must* be governed by the strongest impulse. When he is writing he does not know when to stop, for being away from an object that strongly attracts him, writing is the most effective solace. In fact, the amount a lover writes is a very good barometer of the pressure he is under from his passion."

" But might he not be so busy he could not write?"

" He would take the hours for sleeping, because writing would be far pleasanter than sleeping. Of course there are accidents, serious illness, and so forth. I speak of natural, happy, passional attraction."

" Why, I have not written myself sometimes because, indeed, I loved him so much," said Susie.

"Ah! I was calculating the motives of my own sex. I doubt if the Devil himself could fathom all a woman's motives."

" I am sorry you think so, sir," said the serious little Susie. " I mean I could not write because I wanted so to keep his love, and feared to reproach him, feared to be too loving, feared and distrusted my power every way; and so I often tore up letter after letter—often brought them back from the post-office door, and did not write perhaps for days; and yet I loved him so, all the time, that I could not sleep."

" Poor child!" said the doctor, taking her hand. " Don't you see you were but proving my rule, for in the first place you *did* write continually, according to your own confession; and then you remember I said *happy* passional attraction."

" Oh, yes. I see you are right. You are always right; but do you not think love may sometimes return when once it goes out of the heart?"

"That's a deep question, little woman—the rehabilitation of love. In romances, it happens often enough; but I am an old fellow, and I never knew a case in actual life. It is like small-pox, I suspect, and never breaks out the second time.

"But people do love deeply the second time."

"Yes. I see my comparison is not well chosen; well, like the water of a river which never passes over its bed but once."

While the doctor was conversing with Susie, Mrs. Forest was also engaged in her service, though with motives wholly different from those actuating the doctor, who talked to her to give her strength and self-confidence. He had never taken the trouble to have her sit by him, before the discovery of her sad condition, and seeing how deeply she appreciated his attention to her, made the giving of it very pleasant to him. Mrs. Forest, during her ride, called on old Mrs. Buzzell, who lived a very solitary life with her one old servant, to see if she would not receive Susie in her disgrace. Mrs. Forest was careful to mention all Susie's good qualities, and Mrs. Buzzell at first felt inclined to assent because she was lonely, and had observed Susie with much interest whenever she had visited at the doctor's house, and felt quite attracted to her; but some way she sniffed in the air that Mrs. Forest's society notions were at the bottom of this move of hers, and so her reply was rather galling to one of Mrs. Forest's refinement.

"Well, I will try to help her, and, as you say, no doubt the other ladies of our church will do the same; but if your house is too highly respectable to shelter her, of course mine is, and so there's an end of that."

This was Mrs. Forest's last call upon Mrs. Buzzell. Their friendship, such as it was, had lasted twenty years, and thus it was brought to a sudden end, by wounding each other's vanity. While they confined their mutual interests to gossip, and to superficial considerations of things generally, they met as on a bridge; but when deeper questions arose the bridge fell through, and they found themselves separated as by an impassable torrent. When Mrs. Forest had gone, Mrs. Buzzell questioned whether she herself had acted in a Christian spirit, and she was forced to confess that she had not. She thought, indeed, that she was very sorry, and anxious to apologize; but in fact her regret amounted to very little, for she would have been drawn and quartered in her present mood before she would have taken Susie in, after Mrs. Forest's presumption.

This same day, in the early evening, after Clara was dressed for receiving Dr. Delano, she sat awhile with Susie in the room of the latter, and helped her in her first lesson; but they continually wandered from the subject of nouns and articles to those lying nearer the hearts of both. Still Susie's recitation was very successful. She concealed from her friend the painful effort it had cost to concentrate her attention upon study, even for one minute, and hours had been consumed in preparing herself so that she might not disappoint Clara.

"Now you are going to do splendidly," said Clara, assigning her a certain portion of history for the next day, to be read over and recited in Susie's own language, and a very short task in a text-book of etymology. Clara had the true instinct of the teacher, and knew better than to give long tasks to a beginner, lest they should dis-

courage. After this, Susie showed her Dan's first letter
and its answer, and before there was any time for Clara
to reprove her for returning the money, she gave her Dan's
second letter, telling her at the same time that she was
resolved to refuse the money. Clara held the money very
closely, and said, " I shall not let you send this back.
He is just pig-headed enough to burn it as he threatens
I will write him that I have seized it to prevent your returning it, and that I shall use it as I think best." This
she did, and Susie was forced to yield, not being sorry to
have the responsibility thus completely removed from her
own shoulders. She then consulted Clara about going
away, and this Clara confessed was to be considered. " I
do not wonder that you cannot endure mamma's coldness," she said, "but do not think of it to-night. Dr.
Delano is anxious for our marriage to take place immediately, and *entre nous*—that is, between ourselves—I am
myself going to manifest what mamma calls 'indecent
haste' to get married, so that I may have a home for
you ;" and Clara laughed gayly, to prevent Susie's taking
it seriously, though in reality it was not wholly a pleasantry on her part. The ring of the door-bell interrupted
Clara's speech, and she bade Susie good night tenderly,
urging her to con over her lessons, and then go to bed
and sleep. Susie clung to her friend a moment, crying
silently ; indeed, she cried so often that Clara found the
best way was to not notice it too much ; but she said,
" Would you like me to come back after my friend has
gone ? " " Oh, do ! " replied Susie. "Come and hear my
lessons. I must have something to do, or I shall go crazy.
If I can only get away from here——" " Yes, yes, I
know just how you feel," said Clara; " but it will not be

long. I am going to talk with papa, if I am up when he comes home, and then I'll come and tell you about it." Susie begged Clara to understand how deeply she regretted leaving her and the doctor, but he would call on her, she knew. "And so shall I, every day of my life. Why, of course I shall, to hear your lessons. But I must go now;" and with another hasty kiss, after the manner of girls, Clara ran down-stairs.

Clara had thought to give Susie her sympathy and moral support in her trouble, but she had not dreamed of ever really loving her as a friend. And yet a week had not passed before she discovered qualities and sensibilities in Susie that not only surprised her, but made her compare most favorably with all the young friends Clara had known. The doctor was delighted with the growing regard of his daughter for Susie, in whom he had full faith. "Depend upon it, Clara," he said, "Susie is a real gem, and under your polishing, you will see how she will shine out by-and-by. I think she will prove your best friend among women."

The next morning the doctor had a long talk with his wife, who had "pouted" him, as the French say, ever since their last stormy interview; but he found it useless to try to move her. She was still as firm as a rock, though manifesting it in a way that seemed very gentle; and by appealing to his affection for her, by recalling the tenderness on his part that had endured all through their married life, the happiness that reigned in their home until he became "estranged" from her, as she said, and especially by her tears, which he called cowardly weapons, because she knew beforehand that he could not resist them— by all this she succeeded in making the good doctor *feel* that he was a brute, though he knew perfectly well that he had acted only justly and honorably in protecting a good girl in a disgrace caused by his own son. In the end he petted and caressed her, and turned her tears into smiles that were a triumph, but he saw in them only delight at his caresses.

That night Mrs. Forest appeared in the doctor's room in a ravishing night toilet that had been packed away in lavender since the days of their honeymoon.

Is it possible that even virtuous married men are sometimes the victims of artful women?

CHAPTER XV.

AS Mrs. Buzzell was watering her house plants, a few days after the visit of the doctor's wife, a letter arrived for her, and her eyes brightened, seeing the doctor's handwriting in the superscription. She was very familiar with this handwriting, not from letters, indeed—nothing so romantic, but from his manifold medical prescriptions for her dyspepsia. There was no person in the world she esteemed so highly as she did Dr. Forest, and receiving a letter from him was a rare delight; yet she did not open it at once, but kept on tending her plants, which occupied a large table before the south window of her sitting-room. She did not open it hastily, probably for the same reason that has led many of us on receiving several letters, to leave the specially coveted one until the last, or perhaps until we were quite at ease and alone. At all events, Mrs. Buzzell waited until the flowers were all watered, and the stray drops of water fallen on the square of oiled cloth beneath the table carefully wiped up. Then she sat down, put on her gold-bowed spectacles, opened her letter, and read:

"MY DEAR MRS. BUZZELL: I have wormed out of my wife this evening the object and the result of her late visit to you. I can quite understand, as I told her, why you should have refused her request.

"Now, you two women have danced in pint-pots all your lives, but with this difference : you, because the tether of your education and surroundings never permitted you to examine principles and motives of action outside of a given circumference ; she, because the pint-pot fits her like a glove, and she measures the harmony of the spheres by this beautiful fit. She has never tried to breathe the broader, freer atmosphere outside, because her theory is, the pint-pot first and the universe afterward.

"By the pint-pot you know I mean society. Mrs. Forest sees plainly that no devotee of conventional morality can stand by a girl, especially one who is poor and humble in social position, and give her moral support through disgrace, without being 'talked about'—that bugbear of little souls. Fools will say it is countenancing vice. I appeal to you because, from many sentiments I have heard you utter, I believe you capable of defying shallow criticism when you know you are right. I know you have broad and generous impulses, and you are young enough in soul and in body [this was a Bismarckian stroke of diplomacy, but the honest doctor never knew it] to obey them. You are the mother of no human child, but childless women should be the mothers of the world—sad for all its sorrows, glad for all its joys.

"Susie Dykes has more heart and brain than nine-tenths of the women I know, and if we treat her right fraternally—as I intend to do even if every one else abandons her—she will come out all right. She has not fallen yet ; for she respects herself, despite this misfortune. I can say truly that I take pleasure in keeping this victim's head above the muddy swash of conventional virtue that would wash her under.

" Will you be my real friend, and stand by me in this work ? There is nothing like a good woman's heart where such help is needed."

The letter was well calculated to effect its purpose. There is nothing like faith in the justice and generosity of human nature, to call these qualities into action, even in the narrowest hearts. The doctor's faith in Mrs. Buzzell made her feel equal to facing martyrdom; and then she was very proud of his appealing to her to stand by him when his own wife failed him ; so without delay she put on her old gloves and her antique bonnet, shut her cat out of the house lest he should worry her canaries, and marched straight over to Dr. Forest's, and called for Susie Dykes, without the slightest mention of the mistress of the family. Susie came down to meet her with wondering eyes. What could it mean that the staid and dignified Mrs. Buzzell should so honor her? She soon learned the object of Mrs. Buzzell's call, and that very night, having packed all her worldly goods in two paper boxes and a bundle, she slept under the roof of her new friend.

The fact of Susie's condition soon leaked out, and the "muddy swash," as the doctor termed it, began to rise threateningly. Clara nobly sustained her, went every day and heard her lessons, as she had resolved to do, for having once decided upon the right course, she was indeed her father's own girl, and there was no thought of turning back. Susie's prompt response to Clara's kindness, touched her heart, and gradually the friendship for her *protégée* grew into a deep and sincere affection, nourished by the best feelings of both.

In the plants of Mrs. Buzzell's sitting-room, in her garden, and in the woods behind her house, there was ample means for botanizing, though at first it was a hard task for Susie to study. The mental effort required to distinguish the monocotyledonous and the dicotyledonous in the specimens she and Clara gathered, seemed a mockery to her over-burdened soul; but the struggle paid well. In a few weeks she became deeply interested in all her studies, and her rapid progress astonished her little circle of friends. Meanwhile, she carefully tended Mrs. Buzzell's plants, which after a time began to respond to the knowledge she had acquired of their nature and different wants, and day by day she took some new responsibility of household cares from Mrs. Buzzell, who, after a month, could not have been induced to part with Susie. She took the whole charge of the wardrobe of the coming waif, and the hard lines about her mouth softened with the new, strange pleasure in the work that awakened memories of nearly forty years before, when, as a young wife, she had once, with loving care, prepared numerous tiny articles for a baby that never wore them. They had lain ever since, packed away in camphor, and no one had ever known the secret but her husband, now dead many years. Many times she had been tempted to give them to this or that friend, but her generosity could not quite overcome a sense of shame that women always experience over a useless work of this kind; yet she dreaded to have them found after her death, and there was a soft spot somewhere in her old heart, that would not let her destroy them. One day, therefore, with many misgivings, she unpacked with Susie the antique, camphor-scented trunk, and told the little history of her early married years, delighted only that Susie did not laugh at her. The idea of the serious little Susie laughing at any human disappointment, was simply absurd. She only said:

"It was too bad, when you were married to one you loved, and the baby would have been so welcome."

"Well," said Mrs. Buzzell, kindly, "we'll make this baby welcome in spite of everything. We can't understand all God's ways; and who knows but this may be a trial that will lead you nearer to Him who judges hearts not as men judge, but as one who made them, and knows all their secret springs?"

This little experience, which to Mrs. Buzzell seemed a most important confidence, tended to develop all the dormant softness and tenderness of her nature; and one day the little, old baby-wardrobe was brought down, and her own wrinkled hands washed out the odor of camphor and the yellow of forty years.

As Susie's fate had been so well provided for, and especially as Miss Marston's visit was drawing to its close, Dan again appeared on the scene. In fact he could no longer keep away from this woman who had captured him, body and soul. He thought of her all the time, and the fear that she might not return his love, made his days and nights wretched. It was a new experience for Dan. Grief did not sit gracefully upon him at all. It was an enemy whose blows his "science" could

not parry, and it made him furious, without leading him
to reflect that he had caused a thousand-fold keener
heart-aches to poor Susie (even apart from the special
wrong he had done her by deserting her at a time when
no man of sensibility ever shows that his heart is growing cold), for we can never suffer from failing to win love,
as from the loss of it when it has become necessary, not
only to our happiness, but even to the rendering of life
tolerable. In his selfishness, Dan thought no suffering
could equal his, and he determined to know his fate
before Miss Marston left Oakdale.

One evening, therefore, he dressed himself with extraordinary care, and sallied forth in the direction of his
father's house. As he drew near, he heard Miss Marston's adorable voice in the parlor, and instead of ringing
at the front door, he went around to the veranda, and
waited until the song ceased. Even then he had not
the courage to approach her—she might come out, he
thought, and be pleased by finding him there. Meanwhile he drank in greedily the sweet half-melodies, half-
harmonies, evoked by her beautiful fingers, as they
strayed over the keyboard of the piano without any
special aim, for she was evidently alone and "fancy
free." Pretty soon he recognized a kind of phantasy
upon an old Scotch ballad, and then her voice swelled
out in the first two lines of "Comin' thro' the Rye," and
then stopped. Again she commenced:

> "Amang the train there is a swain,
>   I dearly love mysel';
> But what's his name and where's his hame,
>   I dinna choose to tell."

This verse she sang entire. "Why this special verse?"

asked Dan's heart, for it was in the state when clinging
to straws is perfectly natural. At this juncture he made
bold to enter by the French window, which was open,
and stood beside her. She attempted to rise, but he
prevented it, begging her to keep on playing—he had
something to say to her, which could be fittest said to
music.

"So it is coming," thought Miss Marston. "How
shall I stave it off?"

If Dan had only read her thoughts as easily as she
read his, he would not have made the headlong plunge
into a declaration of love, as he did, without a moment's
pause. Miss Marston quickly interrupted him.

"You do me honor, Mr. Forest," she said, rising and
looking him calmly in the face; "but——"

Dan was half mad. He thought he detected contempt
in the way she pronounced the word "honor." He
thought some one had been "poisoning her mind"
against him—by the truth in his case—and scarcely
knowing what he was saying, he blurted out this fear
—thus, by a stroke of poetic justice, revealing what the
prudent Mrs. Forest had taken such infinite pains to
conceal.

"Indeed!" exclaimed Miss Marston, coldly. "I never
dreamed that, young as you are, you could be so old in
iniquity. I should much like to be able to respect you for
the sake of your estimable family; but if this is so, and I
see the truth of it in your face, let me give you a word of
advice: I am some years older than you are, and I think
I know human nature well enough to assure you that
you will never win the love of any true woman while

basely deserting another, whose happiness"—and she
added in a low, withering tone, as she turned to leave
the room—"and whose honor you have placed in your
hands." The door closed behind her, and Dan, in
speaking of his sensations years after, remarked that you
could have "knocked him down with a feather."

CHAPTER XVI

DR. DELANO winced a little at the scandals circulating in the village, for he heard the name of his betrothed constantly coupled with that of the "fallen" Susie Dykes. Once he expressed a kind of gentle remonstrance that she should visit Susie so often, but she replied with such frank confidence, as if he could not possibly look at the matter except as one of the very highest and best of earth's creatures, that he felt little in his own eyes, and dropped the subject. Still, he was a good deal disturbed when his father and the stately Miss Charlotte Delano appeared on the scene, coming from the centre of the *élite* of Beacon Hill, in Boston. While in Oakdale they were the guests of the Kendricks, old friends of the Delanos, and the richest people in the county. He knew that the Kendrick girls had cut Clara's acquaintance from the beginning of these scandals. One of these, Louise Kendrick, had been Clara's most intimate friend since their girlhood, when they used to play with the skeleton in the doctor's garret. Clara herself was really distressed over her friend's disaffection, and Mrs. Forest regarded it almost as a calamity, and tortured Clara about it in season and out of season. "I'm sure you might have expected it," she would say, in an injured tone. "Girls, who have a proper regard for their reputation,

shrink instinctively from those who have not." These
speeches roused Clara one day, and she flashed defiance
in a very shocking way. "I begin to hate the very word
reputation," she said. "I wouldn't have it at the cost of
being mean and heartless, like Louise Kendrick." Mrs.
Forest was amazed, and asked her daughter what Dr.
Delano would say if he could hear her utter such sentiments. The answer was very unexpected, and silenced
Mrs. Forest effectually. It came like thunder from a
clear sky :

"I don't know what he would say. I only know it
wouldn't require any extraordinary amount of temptation
to make *him* fall, reputation or not."

This speech sounded very ugly to Clara when once it
was uttered, but she was very angry, and it could not be
recalled, though her heart, if not her head, accused her
of a certain injustice.

The Delanos were not over-pleased that the male representative of the family name and wealth, should marry
out of their "set;" but they were too well bred to not
do honor, at least outwardly, to any wife he saw fit to
choose, provided she was of irreproachable character.
They had a natural contempt for country village scandals, and they saw there was nothing really improper
in Miss Forest's befriending the "unfortunate young
woman." It only showed an ill-directed enthusiasm, excusable in a young lady educated quite irregularly, as
they understood she had been. Mrs. Forest, however,
trembled for fear that what Mr. Delano and his daughter
would hear at the Kendricks about Clara's late course,
would make them think unfavorably of the marriage;
but her soul was at rest when the grave old gentleman,

with his daughter, called formally, and thus recognized
Clara as the son's choice. After this formal call they graciously accepted an invitation to spend the evening at the
doctor's, one inducement being that he was absent in the
first instance, and they had not seen him. Mrs. Forest
was in her element receiving these elegant people. She
had made the evening reception the study of days. On
the occasion she looked very handsome in a pearl-gray silk
with white lace, and her gray hair, in three rolls on each
side of her face, surmounted by a pretty cap. Clara wore
a pretty evening dress of white, with sleeves of illusion,
puffed with narrow green velvet. As a finishing touch,
Mrs. Forest fastened a string of pearls around her daughter's neck, saying, "These, you know, are to be your
wedding present from me. You look exceedingly well,
my daughter, and I want you to talk very little this evening, and especially to avoid any of your father's radical
expressions. I don't want them to think you are——"

"Strong-minded," said Clara, finishing the sentence.
"I know you were not going to say that, but you meant
it. O dear! How different you are from papa. I
wonder how you two ever came to marry. Now *he* would
say to me, 'Be yourself.' *You* never said such a thing
to me in your life. I am not namby-pamby, and I cannot speak with the affected voice of Louise Kendrick,
who is your ideal ; and I must say I am glad of it.
However, mamma dear, I will try to please you, and if
papa don't inspire me, I shall be inane enough to gratify
your taste."

Dr. Delano came early, and had a *tête-à-tête* with
Clara before his people arrived. He had never seen her
neck and arms before, and his expressions of admiration

at their exquisite moulding were perhaps intemperate, after the manner of lovers, but altogether delightful to Clara's ear.   He was proud of her, he said, and wanted his father and sister to see her looking as she did then; and certainly they must have been lacking in appreciation, if they could fail to admire a girl so beautiful as Clara was made by her charming toilet, the grace that was incarnate in every movement, and by every feature of her face, enhanced and glorified by the power of Love's spell.

The evening passed very pleasantly until the subject of the late civil war was mentioned, and then Mrs. Forest fidgeted, expecting every moment some horrid radicalism from the doctor, who would not think like other people! Clara, too, she feared would "talk," and, according to her creed, not only children, but young ladies, should be seen, not heard.

"Under all possible aspects," the doctor said, on this occasion, in reply to some opinion of Mr. Delano, "under all possible aspects, war is a stupendous imbecility."

"Then, sir," replied Mr. Delano, "you would not justify defensive war."

Mr. Delano was a retired cotton speculator.   He was rather slight in build, with small, keen eyes, set deep and near together ; a high, thin, Roman nose, thin lips, teeth of the very best manufacture, his face clean-shaven, and his dress faultless in its elegance.

"No, sir, I should not," the doctor answered.

"Yet it seems to me that the principle of giving your cloak also, to the rascal who takes your coat, works very ill in practice, at least in these degenerate days."

"Ah! that may be.   I certainly never attempted to

carry it into practice. If we have a barbarian people for a neighbor, and they organize an army to destroy us, we must, of course, defend ourselves. We should have the *esprit de corps* which would rouse men, women, and children even, to help crush the invaders in a single day; but this would not be organized war, as generally understood. Moreover, if we had barbarian enemies, it would be the wiser policy to conquer them by making them our friends; and that is by no means an impractical policy, as has been proved by history. Between civilized nations, this method of settling difficulties, is an insult to the dignity of civilization. In the first place, it never settles anything, any more than the duel does."

No one seemed ready to defend dueling; and seeing a pause, Clara said, "I think the history of horrid wars might end with this generation, if only women could be inspired with a normal disgust for all kinds of murdering."

Mrs. Forest thought that was not so bad, if only Clara would say nothing more radical. She herself believed that women would be the most effective instruments, under divine will, of ending human butchery.

Miss Delano regarded Clara as if astonished at opinions in a young lady. The old gentleman was evidently struck, for he deigned to reply to her directly.

"Yet the fair hands of your sex, Miss Forest, even to-day, are engaged buckling on the armor of their male friends."

"I am sorry, sir, that this is true."

"Your daughter seems to have opinions"—said Miss Delano to Mrs. Forest, with whom she had been keeping up a separate conversation—"not common to young *l*adies of her age." This was really intended as a compliment, but was not taken as such at the time.

"I hope I am not unpatriotic," said Clara, looking straight at Miss Delano with a frank, sweet expression. "I love my country ; but I love other countries also, and I have been taught to look upon the human race as one, and not simply to confine my sympathies to the place where I happened to be born. It seems to me clearly a duty to cultivate this feeling of unity."

"These sentiments do you honor," replied Mr. Delano, anxious to draw out this girl, who was not like any he had ever met; "but it seems to me singular that you should have arrived at such conclusions at your time of life."

"It ought not to be singular, I think. I have heard the doctrines of peace and the brotherhood of man presented by my father ever since I can remember. It is perfectly impossible for me to see anything in military glory worthy of admiration. To me, any honest laboring man is more noble than the military hero, and I consider the sword a badge of disgrace. If I were a man, I should be so ashamed to be seen with such a thing at my side ! Think what it suggests !" said Clara, with disgust in every feature of her beautiful face.

"It is true, father," said the son, "that this spirit in women would soon put an end to war. We should hardly fight, if we thereby made ourselves despicable in the eyes of those we love."

"But this spirit among women, my son, would make cowards of us all."

"That, I think, is a great mistake," said Dr. Forest. "It might in time make us forget how to use the sword and the bayonet dexterously—a 'consummation devoutly to be wished,' in my opinion ; but, good Heaven ! sir, is the courage and manliness of men to be measured by their skill in killing each other, as the valor of the savage by the number of scalps he can show ? He can brave death, if that be the test, in nobler ways than at the hands of some mad, misguided brother."

"Yet, in all examination of such questions, we must not forget that human passions remain the same. In all ages mankind has shown a decided tendency towards conquest."

"Certainly," replied the doctor, "human passions remain the same : that is, no new faculties are created, and none destroyed ; but their relative activity differs with degrees and stages of development. You and I have the same faculties that in the Apache express themselves in pow-wow-ing and scalping, yet we neither pow-wow nor scalp : we have outgrown that kind of gratification for the passion, but we still express it in fighting. The time will come when we shall have outgrown that kind of expression as well. The desire to triumph over obstacles, to succeed, as well as the passion for organizing great enterprises, will always find ample avenues of expression and gratification." The doctor paused, fearing to monopolize the conversation.

"I should much like to hear your views as to the way those passions can be gratified," said Mr. Delano.

"In many ways," replied the doctor. "Suppose, instead of going into the South to subdue and kill our fellow-men, we had organized our vast army for the purpose of draining and reclaiming the Dismal Swamp. That would have been a noble work. Where now that miserable tract is exhaling poisonous vapors, it might be to-day yielding fruits and grains to feed the children starving in our cities."

"Why, this is constructive radicalism!" said Mr. Delano. "But while our army were reclaiming the Dismal Swamp, the Southern army would have been marching into our Northern towns and laying them waste!"

"No; I think," said Miss Delano, "they would have been astounded into very good humor, and would have at once set about adjusting our quarrel amicably."

"It is difficult to say," said the doctor, "how our Southern citizens would have taken the invasion of a non-fighting army. The slavery system is a fearful drag upon the growth of the higher faculties. If we had gone down there to build them railroads and school-houses, they might have considered it very patronizing on our part. Slavery made white men despise labor; so they would not have felt like joining in, perhaps, like good fellows, though they were 'spoiling' for action, and their chivalry, as they called it, dreamed only of military glory, as the sole gentlemanly expression of their bottled-up forces. If they had respected labor, they would have met us right fraternally; but then, if they had understood the dignity of labor, slavery would have never been, and consequently our civil war would have been avoided; so our speculation is useless."

"It is very interesting, at all events," said Dr. Delano. "I confess that the idea of a grand army to drain the Dismal Swamp inspires me. I would join such an expedition with enthusiasm."

Miss Delano suggested that such an army need not become demoralized for the want of woman's influence, because they could take women along with them ; and Clara drew a glowing picture of camp-life under such conditions, with music and fancy-dress balls to inspire the workers after the day's labor, which, with an army of fifty thousand or more perfectly organized, need not become drudgery, for each division could be constantly relieved after three or four hours, which would constitute a day's work. "And then when all was over," Clara continued, "when all the glory was gained, you would have, in place of murders on your conscience, the satisfaction of having created only pleasure, and benefited all coming generations."

"It would be a very economical campaign," said Mr. Delano. "Your war debt would be reduced to zero; for as the work would require several years, you could carry on at the same time all the agricultural and manufacturing operations necessary to support your army."

"But the greatest economy," said Dr. Delano, "would be the economy of men. Citizens being the most valuable part of the body politic."

"That is the best part of it," said Clara. "You would have no bones bleaching on some terrible field of glory ; no mothers and wives and orphans mourning for their dead. I think that 'glory' is a gilded snare that catches only fools. There can be no true glory in a work that shames humanity."

"For my part, I should like to see war ended forever," said Miss Charlotte ; "but I think preaching a crusade against glory will not do any good."

"If preached by women, it certainly will," said the doctor. "As soon as the rank and file, without which there could be no army, and consequently no war, come to realize the contemptible position they occupy as puppets in the hands of an ambitious glory-seeking few, they will say No ; and when, by general culture, they come to respect labor and human rights, they will say, 'We will do no murder ; we believe in labor—in building up, not in tearing down.' Depend upon it, the solution is simpler than politicians and demagogues have ever dreamed, and nearer, too, for the growing moral sense of the age points directly to a time when international disputes will all be settled by arbitration ; and when, if two nations are about to grip each other's throats, all the other nations, as by instinct, will unite and separate them."

"How could they do that without fighting also?" asked Mr. Delano.

"Why, by mere remonstrance. Is there any person insensible to public opinion? A nation is only a body of individuals. It could not stand against the moral convictions of the majority of nations. It would be simply impossible. If one man is foolish enough to fight a wind-mill, like Don Quixote, you cannot suppose any nation of men would be."

"I admit that," replied Mr. Delano; "yet I am not convinced that we shall ever arrive at that reign of reason ; and your constructive army does not seem to me to meet all the wants supplied by the destructive one. There must be far more excitement in the latter."

"But we must not forget that, as man reaches a higher state of culture, he shuns violent excitement of all kinds—it has no charm for him. Natural attractions constantly demand better and finer food for their gratifications. To deny this, is like saying that because man loves conviviality and exhilaration, he must always continue to gratify them by the rum shop and a free-fight."

At this point in the conversation Miss Marston, who had been out of town on a visit, came in, and entertained the company by her exquisite singing, and soon after Dinah brought in a tray of dainties, and a decanter of California wine. While the company were sipping the wine, she reappeared with fruit. Her black face always beamed with delight on "massa's company." The doctor made some kindly remark to her, as he always did, and poured her out a glass of wine. Mrs. Forest was unspeakably shocked. On this special occasion why could he not behave himself properly? Dinah took the glass with thanks, and said, raising it to her sable lips, "I hopes massa'l lib forebber." This was her toast; and grinning upon the amused guests, she courtesyed to them and left. The doctor thoroughly enjoyed this shock to conventional propriety. Clara was not disturbed in the least, for whatever her father did was right in her eyes. Mrs. Forest made some excuse to Miss Delano for what she called the doctor's "eccentricity."

"Your family is Southern, I believe," said Mr. Delano.

"I am," said Mrs. Forest, a little proudly, "but my husband is not."

"No," said the doctor, "I am of the good old New England, witch-burning stock; though I lived South many years." Mr. Delano asked him if he did not find his sympathies in this war rather on the side of the South. "No more than with the North," he answered. "I deplore it for the injury it must do to the whole country and to the world at large. The moral sense of the civilized world has a natural right to forbid anything so imbecile as an appeal to arms."

"Do you suppose, sir," asked Miss Delano, "if you had taken the vote of all the people of this country on the question of war or secession, the majority would have decided for secession?"

"Most certainly I do, if you mean the people, madame, and not simply the fighting portion. Men would not vote for war if it involved the destruction of their mothers and sisters, daughters, wives, and sweethearts, and women are said to be more tender towards those they love, than men are."

"I must say," said Mrs. Forest, "I do not think any nation has a right to declare war without consulting women—those who must be the greatest sufferers in the end." This was very bold for Mrs. Forest, who seldom expressed opinions on such questions. This was just after the emancipation proclamation, and the doctor remarked that the abolition of slavery was a grand result, but even that was purchased too dearly.

"I never identified myself with the abolition movement," said Mr. Delano, not mentioning the fact that, as a cotton-broker, his policy did not lie in that direction; "but slavery is a relic of barbarism, and therefore out of place in the nineteenth century. Still you are right, perhaps, that war does really never settle vexed questions. I foresee confusion worse confounded in our future political relations with the South."

Mr. Delano and his daughter stayed quite late, and evidently enjoyed their visit, and were more pleased with

the family of Albert's future wife than they had expected.
When they were gone, Mrs. Forest inwardly thanked
God that the conversation had been providentially prevented from drifting into religion or woman's rights, and
went to bed in a very serene state of mind

CHAPTER XVII

COSTLY GRAPES.

WHEN Dan left his father's house after his rejection by Miss Marston, he was really wretched for the first time in his life; yet the experience did not soften him as fine natures are softened by unhappy love. Between his set teeth he called her hard names, and cursed himself for giving her the opportunity to reject his offer. He passed Susie during this walk, who, being surprised, looked up into his face with the old light in her eyes. He met her eyes as we meet a stranger's, without a sign of recognition; whereat the poor girl's limbs trembled, and putting down her veil after passing him, she walked on blinded by her tears.

In his frame of mind, Dan looked upon all women as his enemies, and especially Susie, but for whom he might have won the queenly Miss Marston. But for the recentness of his rebuff, he would have spoken kindly enough to Susie, for he was capable of pity, and he had considerable affection in his nature, though it was of the bearish kind, wholly divested of that sensitive, tender element which, when a woman has once known it, makes valueless all other love of men. It is not found in common men, however, who are mostly capable of violent demonstration, without any of that high sentiment which seeks only to learn the real desire of the loved one, and then studies to gratify it, finding keen delight in that, and that alone. It is true, also, that few women are capable of inspiring such a sentiment, and so the world knows little of the highest phase of the passion of love. Susie had never known any love but Dan's, and though it had occurred to her that there might be kisses, for example, not so much like the pounce of a hawk upon a pigeon, as his were, still she had loved him with all her heart, and it was terrible, even when she knew he had ceased to love her, to think that he could pass her in the street without a sign of recognition. But Susie had out-lived that experience, and with the certainty that he was lost to her forever, and with time and the accession of new thoughts and cares, and especially with the interest Clara had succeeded in awakening in regular daily study, her grief lessened. There were, first hours, and then whole days, when there were no heart-aches on his account. Over the thought of this she would invariably rejoice, as over a great triumph, until some treacherous retrospection of happier days quickened the old tender-ness into life—renewed agonies that she thought were quieted forever, and revealed her situation as dreadful beyond mortal endurance.

After Miss Marston left Oakdale, Dan went home once or twice, but it was like a strange place to him. His father, to be sure, treated him much the same, and never alluded to Susie by any accident. Mrs. Forest pitied him more than ever, and Clara was at least polite to him on all occasions. He could see and feel, however, that his conduct was detestable in her eyes, and as for Leila and Linnie, he considered them of slight importance. One day he discovered that Clara knew of his offering himself to Miss Marston, and of the galling manner with which he had been refused, and this made him furious. Miss Marston, then, had despised him too much to keep his humiliation a secret, as any honorable woman would do under ordinary circumstances.

Miss Marston would indeed have been the last person to reveal such a thing, but the day before her departure, in a long talk with Clara, she expressed the desire that Clara would make it certain to Susie that Dan was nothing to her. " You know," she said, " how a person in her abandoned condition would naturally feel toward one she supposed the cause of her being abandoned. Do convince her that there has never been the slightest encouragement on my part—no intimacy whatever between me and your brother, no thought of correspondence, or anything of the kind;" and then she told Clara of the last meeting with Dan, and expressed unqualified disapproval of him altogether ; at the same time sending kind messages to Susie, and a present of a microscope for her botanical studies.

"There is one thing I have wished to ask you, Miss Marston," said Clara, " but I have never dared to. Will you tell me just your true impressions of Albert ? " Miss Marston did not reply satisfactorily, and Clara, putting her arm around her rather timidly, for the teacher that expressed itself in every word and manner, still continued to awe Clara, as it had done in Stonybrook, urged a reply. She had often noticed Miss Marston studying Albert. The two were very polite to each other, but it was easy to see that there was little true sympathy between them. Thus urged, Miss Marston answered : " I have studied him carefully, because he has your happiness in his hands.

I confess I fear greatly that you are not just the kind of wife he should select." Clara was grieved, not understanding Miss Marston, and she said quickly, "I have often wondered that he should think so highly of me."

"No, no. It is not a question of your worthiness. You are worthy, I think, of any one—certainly of Dr. Delano ; but there is a self-sufficiency, well concealed by his culture, that will some time be very apt to run counter to your ideas of justice and devotion. I only say I fear, understand. I may be wrong ; but I would urge you to avoid the first misunderstanding. It would be hard, I think, for him to examine himself with merciless justice. You have that power, which I see you inherit from your father, who is a wonderfully superior man."

"Liberally translated," said Clara, smiling, "you think Albert a tyrant. You do not understand him fully, I think, but I am glad of your frank opinion. I shall be careful to be good and just to him, and I think I shall never have cause to admire him less than I do now;" and Clara went on revealing, little by little, to Miss Marston a sentiment so near adoration that it almost appalled her, and convinced her still further that such an exalted passion could never find full response, nor be even comprehended by Albert Delano ; but she said no more. The next day she left Oakdale. Her trunk had been sent to the station, which was but a short distance, and she and Clara were to walk. They passed Mrs. Buzzell's cottage, and Miss Marston gratified Clara greatly by calling on Susie, and being really kind and friendly to her, a proceeding that quite astonished Mrs. Forest when she heard of it.

As the weeks passed Mrs. Buzzell bravely stemmed the

current of popular disapprobation at her act of " countenancing vice;" for the consciousness of doing right was enhanced by the good qualities she was constantly discovering in Susie. Mrs. Buzzell's temper, never very sweet, had not improved by years of loneliness, and when criticised by her female friends, she gave them back "as good as they sent," to use her own words; and so it came to pass that the piously-disposed ladies of the congregation to which Mrs. Buzzell belonged, and which had barely escaped receiving Susie as a member, had not the opportunity to patronize Susie, and to extend charity to her in that condescending way too well known to many an unfortunate. The continuance of such patronage depends upon the utter humility of the recipient. She must confess herself a vile sinner, be willing to take thankfully the position of the lowest scrub, and express in every act that her patronizers are above her as the stars above the earth. Let the victim dare to show any ambition to regain her self-respect, any dissatisfaction because the daughters of her patronizers treat her with contempt, while they smile graciously upon the author of her degradation, and the patronage ceases at once.

"This is the way society protects itself," said Mrs. Buzzell to Mrs. Kendrick, the banker's wife, one of the would-be patronizers; "but is there not something wrong in the system that blasts and destroys the woman, while it winks at the sin of the man? I have come to see that in most cases, as in this, for example, her fault is much less than his. Man is taught self-dependence from the cradle; woman to depend upon man; and when she does so to the utmost limit, trusting every hope of happiness in his honor, this is a common result. We have called the doctor a radical, and graciously excused his eccentricities because he is so good a physician and so kind a man; but face to face with such facts, I see he is nearer right than we are."

"Your judgment is misled by your sympathies, Mrs. Buzzell," said the banker's lady. "Do you not see that if unmarried mothers and their children are to be respected, there is no safety for legal wives and legitimate children? If society comes to recognize the position of mistress as respectable, to be a wife will be a very questionable honor."

"Well, I sometimes think it is," said Mrs. Buzzell, turning over in her mind this new and practical view of the case, and forgetting, in a kind of dreamy retrospection, that a moment before she had intended to smite Mrs. Kendrick "hip and thigh."

"They think we lose our youth when we begin to fade a little," said Mrs. Kendrick, "when in fact we are then more sensitive than ever to the better part of love; and having a baby makes a very baby of a woman in this respect. Do what we will, though, we cannot keep the very element in a man's love without which we don't care for his love at all; and children hardly prove the consolation we expect, except, indeed, when they are babies. When they grow older they go from us, they wound us, and seem to spend half their lives fighting against our desires. After all, it is better to keep our thoughts beyond this world. I find, myself, very little pleasure in it."

It was very seldom that Mrs. Kendrick gave any expression to the dark under-current of her life. She passed for a very happy woman, and Mrs. Forest considered her position every way enviable. Her husband

was rich, as all husbands should be in her opinion, as a
duty they owe to society, and he was never known to be
eccentric in anything. Mrs. Forest would have found him
perfect. As a young man he had been enthusiastic, loved
art and poetry, and talked of high purposes in life. He
had even written very fair verses himself, and his wife,
before marriage and some time after, had adored him ;
but he had in time so changed the diet of his soul, that
whereas it once seemed wholly to feed upon grand aspirations, and upon the beautiful in all things, it now gorged
itself upon bonds and stocks, and assimilated vast quantities of the nutriment. His romantic wife became
practical too, but she was bitter over the loss of her
illusions, and turned the whole current of her life into
social ambition. She had the finest establishment in the
county, and she seemed to study day and night to show
her husband how dependent she was upon society—how
little upon him—for her sum of happiness. For years
they had ceased to wound each other's vanity, as married
people do after the romance is outlived and the conjugal
yoke begins to gall them. It was not worth the trouble.
Society held them up as shining examples of conjugal
felicity. They always spoke of each other before the
world in a tone of reserve, as if the nature of their mutual
relations was too sacred to be questioned or discussed.
And yet, with all this outside homage and interior luxury,
with all her fine carriages and horses, elegant toilettes,
splendid gardens and green-houses, Mrs. Kendrick really
found life a burden, as thousands of women do in her
position, not knowing that their trouble is the want of
a wider sphere of action.

Mr. Kendrick must have been enormously rich. It

was the wonder of all the country round that so much money could be squandered without the least effect upon the supply. Wise heads declared that Kendrick's farms and grounds were badly managed, and it was well known that, notwithstanding the extent and cost of keeping his gardens and green-houses, flowers had to be ordered from professional florists on every occasion of a grand reception. Kendrick himself tried to take interest in his winter-gardens. In one there was a large black Hamburg grape-vine, bearing one magnificent bunch of fruit. He had watched this from day to day, but he knew nothing of the art of cultivation under glass, and was made to feel himself a very second-rate object when in the presence of the head-gardener, who was a pompous and important functionary. During the last winter Mr. Kendrick, in paying the coal bill, took the trouble to glance over it. The winter was not yet ended, and there were seventy-five tons of coal consumed for the hot-houses! On this occasion Mr. Kendrick ventured to go to the head-gardener and suggest mildly his astonishment at the consumption of coal. The functionary pointed reproachfully to that bunch of black Hamburgs, and Mr. Kendrick was silent.

On the occasion of Mrs. Kendrick's call, she asked Mrs. Buzzell, as she rose to go, if she could do anything to help her in the responsibility she had assumed. "I want your sympathy of course," replied Mrs. Buzzell. "It is not pleasant to feel that you are condemned for doing what you know to be your duty."

"I certainly do not condemn you," said Mrs. Kendrick; "but I could never do myself what you are doing; and I think you would see your duty in a different light if you were the mother of a marriageable daughter."

"What then are we to do, as Christians, in cases like this?"

"Oh, I suppose there ought to be a respectable institution for them, where they could find protection and work to do, and some provision made for the education of their children. I would give something towards the establishment of such an institution; but I could not afford to defend openly a girl like this, as you are doing."

"But don't you see, that the religion of Christ plainly teaches us to forgive the erring, and so help them to a higher life."

"My dear Mrs. Buzzell, the Christian religion, as interpreted to-day, adapts itself to the exigencies of society. That religion, as taught by Christ and his apostles, would be as much out of place in our present social system as a monk would be in a modern ball-room."

When Dr. Forest called, a day or two after, Mrs. Buzzell told him of Mrs. Kendrick's speech. "She is more of a philosopher than I thought," he said.

"But don't you think that a very shocking way to look at religion, doctor?"

"Ah! my dear friend; it should never shock us to hear a truth. The only real Christians, according to the original type, to be found to-day, are among certain orders of the Catholic church, who literally 'take no heed of the morrow,' never have 'scrip in their purse,' or a second suit of clothes. They literally crucify the flesh, and study to be just like Christ. Mrs. Kendrick is perfectly right. You see, in helping and befriending one like Susie, whom modern society despises and neglects, you are a very old-fashioned kind of Christian, though not necessarily of the primitive type."

"Well, if I can only be a Christian in the *true* sense, whatever that may be, it is all I ask for myself," said Mrs. Buzzell, earnestly.

"And by that you mean pure in all your thoughts, and upright in all your dealings, and nothing else."

"Certainly I do."

"Well, that is what I call true morality. You call it by a different name. We don't differ so much. For bigot and infidel, we stand very comfortably near together, I should say," said the doctor, smiling. Mrs. Buzzell saw she had admitted too much by that "nothing else," but she did not feel like arguing, and so turned the subject.

CHAPTER XVIII.

WITH October, came busy days for Clara. Her mother was in a fever from the fear that the wedding *trousseau* would not be ready by the middle of November, when the wedding was to take place. The twins sewed very cleverly when the fit was on; but the fits were very uncertain, and Dr. Delano very imprudently, as Mrs. Forest thought, would call every evening of his life; but then, men were always so very inconsiderate, she said. Little bundles of linen exquisitely made up, kept constantly coming home from some mysterious laboratory. Mrs. Forest was silent, though she recognized at a glance the deft fingers of Susie; but Clara said they were made by her good fairy. One day, to facilitate the sewing operations, Mrs. Forest offered the twins money if they would do certain work. It had not the least effect. Leila explained shrewdly:

"You know, mamma, you will tell us just how to spend the money—so it would be just like having you buy things for us"

"It would be nice," said Linnie, "to have just a little money to squander."

"And what do you do, pray, with all the immense sums you have wheedled out of your father?" asked the doctor, laughing.

"I hope you are not so spooney, papa"—(spooney was a pet word of Leila's)—"as to think we squander it. Why, mamma always directs just what we shall do with our money. She admits it is our money, and we can do as we like with it; but you see, papa," continued Leila, with a sly little wink at her mother's expense, "we don't ever like, you know!"

The doctor laughed, and said: "Now, then, we'll change the venue. How much will you sew for by the yard—measuring every inch fairly with your tape measure—provided you can do just what you like with your money?"

"Will five cents be too much, mamma?" asked both the girls in a breath.

"Not if you pay your board out of it, I think," said Mrs. Forest, smiling sweetly.

"No, no," said the doctor, "we owe you board, and comfortable clothing and education, from the fact that you were not consulted in the unimportant matter of being born or not born. I assure you, it is folly to squander money; but that is one of the things you must learn by experience. I make you both this offer: five cents for every yard well done and measured by your mother; and no one shall question what you do with your earnings; five cents for every yard well done, and for every dollar earned I will add fifty cents, because this is not shop-work, but what would come under the head of 'fine sewing,' I believe."

The effect was astounding. Mrs. Forest, before a week ended, had positively to scold both girls for their assiduity, and Clara's sewing went on like magic.

On one of the Sundays between these busy days, Dan

came home. He looked worn and sad, Clara thought, and this was enough to move her gentle heart. She sang to him a new song, and when she found a moment alone with him, began to probe him in regard to his sentiments for Susie. She thought the best thing in the world that could happen, would be the marriage of him and Susie, being in a condition of mind herself to consider marriage a panacea and the divinest of all blessings. Dan expressed a desire to "do the right thing." Clara snapped at this like a hungry little fish at a bait. "Why not marry her at once, then?" Dan's reply was not wholly satisfactory, but sufficient to induce her to keep Dr. Delano waiting for her that evening a full half hour, while she was away, no one knew where, but in fact closeted with Mrs. Buzzell. The next Sunday, finding home a little more pleasant, Dan appeared again, and Clara was not long in bringing about a private talk. She repeated her question, "Why not marry Susie?" Dan had, in fact, been thinking of Susie with less hard feelings for her crime of loving him too well, and standing between him and Miss Marston, as he thought. But Susie was the only woman who had ever loved him, and he was tempted to do the "right thing" if only to have some one to adore him! Generous man! But then it must be admitted that he was under a spell he had no power to shake off. Miss Marston had inspired a stronger passion in him than any one else ever had, or perhaps could. He could not appreciate the latent qualities in Susie's character, and if he could, love does not deal with qualities, as such. It is mind that does this, and Dan was a creature of feeling, impulse, rather than of reason. Susie had loved him too fondly, and only with very superior natures does excess of fondness make the subject dearer. The great charm in Miss Marston was the impassable barrier of her total indifference to him; but he could not see the cause. She was superior to him, and that he knew; so, indeed, was Susie, and just as far out of his reach by the superiority of her nature, though not by circumstances.

Dan said this time, in answer to his sister's question, half in fun, half in earnest, that Susie didn't care much for him, and that he had "had about enough snubbing lately from women."

"Oh, how little you know of women!" was Clara's response.

Dan defended himself, and a lively discussion ensued, in which Clara illustrated her position by an allusion to his old habit of holding her hands and laughing at her helpless rage. "If you had known the nature of girls you would never have done such a thing," she said, "for it made me hate you, and to this day I cannot think of it without indignation, though we should not remember wrongs done us by children."

"You were pert and saucy," said Dan, "and put on airs of superiority, because you got your lessons and were petted by the teachers."

"And you wished to show your superiority in something, I suppose. Well, we will not think of disagreeable things. You are my only brother, and are going to be just and kind to Susie, so we shall never quarrel any more;" and Clara, putting down all hard feelings caused by Dan's betrayal and desertion of Susie, passed her hand affectionately through his arm, and then submitted to being hugged, though she could not forbear a little

resentment at his roughness. " No woman of refinement
will ever love such a bear," she said.

" Nonsense ! women like to be handled roughly."

" That shows how much you know about it—about refined women, at least. Do you think Miss Marston—"

" D—n Miss Marston ! "

" I am ashamed of you."

" Of course : you always were. Your big snob, Delano,
would not say ' mill-dam,' I suppose. You'll get enough
of him, or I'm greatly mistaken. *He* is one of the kind
that understands women, no doubt."

Clara was very angry, but for Susie's sake and the object she had set her heart upon, she controlled the expression of it. She had succeeded in making Dan promise to call on Susie that very evening, and both she and
Mrs. Buzzell had urged Susie to marry Dan if he proposed it, and he had already assented. Clara went over
to Mrs. Buzzell's with Dan, and, leaving him in the parlor, sent Susie to him, kissing her, and saying, " You
know it is not wholly for your own sake, dear, or we
would not have urged it."

As Susie entered, he rose and took her hand. She
gave his the faintest little pressure, and left him no time
for preliminaries, but said at once, " You know the one
cause that has made me yield, against my better judgment, to the desire of your sister and my good friend,
Mrs. Buzzell. Understand well, I do so on this condition, which I imagine," she added, a little bitterly, " you
will have no objection to—that you never recognize me as
your wife in any way. I, on my part, shall never claim
any legal rights any more than if you were actually
dead."

"That seems to me all bosh. We are not to live together, and that is enough. Of course, I marry you because I wish to save you from bearing all the brunt of the battle."

"The worst is over. All that I can suffer from disgrace I have already suffered; but I have not lost my self-respect, low as I may be in your esteem; and I shall not, thanks to the noble hearts that came to me when I thought God had forsaken me as well as you."

When Susie said, "low as I am in your esteem," she had had a sudden hope that it might reveal his unnatural conduct toward her in so terrible a light that he would hate himself, and exhibit some sorrow for the misery he had caused, if not a desire to atone by trying to call back to her his wandering heart—love is so blind, so foolish, in its way of hoping against hope! She had decided that the marriage should be only a legal act, to make her child what society calls legitimate; but oh! it would have been so sweet to her to be forced to change that decision through a tender appeal from Dan—through anything that showed he held her love precious, and would not lose it after all; but no such sign came. He only said, in a way that wounded her deeply, "I don't see the use of harping on what is past, nor in getting married, if you are not to have the advantage of being known as a wife."

It cost Susie a terrible effort to not spurn him and his offer with contempt, for her mood was rapidly passing from the negative to the positive; but she was in a peculiar position. Clara and Mrs. Buzzell expected her to take a certain course, and she could make any sacrifice rather than disappoint them. She said, therefore, very calmly, " I have said that it is not for myself that I assent to your marrying me ; the child might not live ; and then I should regret that you were obliged to be known as the husband of Susie Dykes. Unless it lives, this ceremony will never be made known by my consent."

" No danger of its not living. That is not the kind that has a weak hold on life. Well, have it all your own way," he added, cowardly letting every responsibility fall upon her.

Susie was sick at heart, and longed to end the meeting. She had heard enough. She rose, to signify the fact. Dan took his hat, and, as he did so, said, " There's no use crying over spilled milk. We will be friends, at least. Kiss me, Susie."

" Why should I kiss the lover of Miss Marston ? I confess I had rather not. But do not think me angry, or that I have any desire to reproach you. I know you could not resist a powerful attraction like that, and from my very soul, Dan, I wish I were dead and you her husband ;" and controlling her emotion, she smiled and gave him her hand cordially. He was tempted greatly to draw her towards him and kiss her, whether she desired it or not ; but something in her face he had never seen there before—something of firmness and womanly dignity that awed him—prevented him, and, pressing her hand hurriedly, he left the house. When he was gone, of course Susie gave way utterly to her sorrow. She had thought lately, that in her reading and study, in her work and in present and prospective cares, she had finally escaped most of her suffering ; but this evening had revealed more clinging to straws, more feeding the hungry heart upon dry husks, to use the doctor's words. The process of robbing the heart of its illusions is long and tedious. Let us have patience with Susie. There is something rare and fine in her nature that begins to show itself through all her hard conditions; and despite the low surroundings of her childhood, she has grown already above that, like the sacred lotus above the mud; and as the mud nourishes and develops the beautiful lily under the sunbeam, so the sad memories of Susie's early life, aided by the vivifying influence of the kindly human sympathy she has won, will nourish and develop a grace and beauty of soul that will fit her for the work she has to do.

Passively, Susie submitted to the judgment of Clara and Mrs. Buzzell, and a day or two later the marriage was to take place, in a distant town at the terminus of Dan's railroad route, where he had "six hours off," he said, and that was "time enough to do considerable damage." Clara was to accompany her friend, and to see her safely home again. She arrived at Mrs. Buzzell's some time before the train left, but found Susie ready, even to her hat and gloves, but looking, as she declared, a picture of gloom. She was dressed entirely in black.

"Well, then," said Susie, trying to smile, "my looks do not belie my feelings. I feel a presentiment that something bad is going to happen."

"I begin to think," remarked Mrs. Buzzell, as she insisted upon Susie's swallowing a glass of her currant wine, "that we have done wrong to urge the poor child to this step. I'm afraid no good will come of it."

"Come! let us be off at once," said Clara, gayly. "I don't like this aspect of indecision in Mrs. Buzzell. It means anything but business."

Dan came occasionally and sat near them during the journey. He said he had "seen the parson and arranged everything all right." Susie kept her veil down all the time. On arriving at the terminus, Dan sent them to the ladies' room in the station, having some matter of business to attend to, and then joined them and conducted them in a carriage to a hotel, though the distance was exceedingly short, and into a fine private room, where an elegant dinner for three was already waiting. Clara tried to be gay, and really could have been so but for Susie, who trembled like a leaf and looked very pale. Clara removed Susie's hat and shawl, and said a thousand reassuring words. Susie tried hard to respond. Clara saw with pain the effort, and pitied Susie more than ever. Here the waiter appeared, his napkin over his arm, and asked if he should serve the dinner. Clara whispered to Dan to put it off, if he could, a few minutes, and for mercy's sake to say something comforting to Susie.

"You may wait ten minutes," said Dan to the waiter; "but bring the wine at once."

"Gay wedding, sis. Don't you think so?"

"Oh, don't mind my feeling a little ill," said Susie, with an effort. "I feel a little better already." Dan expressed himself as being "hungry as a wolf," and no doubt he was. He had, in the simple ignorance of his nature, thought a nice dinner would please Clara and Susie, and felt a little savage to have it put off; therefore, more perhaps from hunger than anything else, he went and sat down by Susie, and took her hand in his. Tears, tears forever! What could the poor child do but cry? Dan was a little touched, and made a very praiseworthy attempt to soothe her.

"Oh, I wish I could cry them all out," said Susie, wiping her eyes. "You are so good, both of you, to have so much patience with me. There!" she said, laughing dismally, "I believe there are no more."

When the champagne came—of course Dan had provided that—he poured it out copiously and dismissed the waiter. He insisted upon both Susie and Clara drinking, and, fearing to displease him, they assented. No sooner were their glasses half empty than he refilled them; and then the soup was served. With the second course the waiter brought more champagne, and when he left Clara exclaimed, good naturedly, "Mercy! Dan, you are not expecting us to drink any more?"

"Why not? It seems we need something to keep our courage screwed up to the sticking point."

Oh, our courage is in no danger of failing, is it, Susie? Think of it! In an hour or so you will be a lawful and wedded wife; and oh! you don't know how much more *I* shall respect you! Only a nice little bit of juggling, and honor will come out of dishonor, like Jack out of his box." After awhile Susie talked a little, though she could eat nothing after the soup. Dan's spirits rose mightily with the second bottle of champagne, and he began to be even sentimental to Susie, who took the liberty, after a while, to beg him to not drink any more champagne.

"What's two bottles of champagne on your wedding-day?" he roared. "Did you ever hear how they drink whisky in Texas? A friend of mine was traveling out there last winter, and he stopped at a half-way house, and found they had not a drop; but they told him the widow Smith, living a mile further on, had a barrel the

Saturday before. He would get plenty there. So he rode on, and driving up to the door, sung out. A woman poked her head out of the door and asked what he wanted. He told her he wanted something to drink. She told him she had not a thing to drink in the house. 'Why,' said he, 'they told me back here that you had a barrel of whisky last Saturday.'

"'Well, so I did; but what's one barrel of whisky with five little children and the cow dry?'" Dan laughed vociferously at his story, and his guests laughed also, but more to please him, for they were both a little serious over his drinking. They kept him, however, from ordering a third bottle; but in revenge he visited the barroom on their way to the carriage, which was waiting at the door. On the way to the minister's house Susie whispered to Clara, without Dan's perceiving it, "I should have heeded my presentiment, and stayed at home."

At the minister's house they were shown into the parlor, where they were kept waiting some time, Susie growing more and more agitated every moment; but Dan seemed to be quite sober, and behaved very well until the minister came. He was a tall, fat, pompous man, with a face that repelled Clara instinctively. He noticed Susie's agitation, and asked some questions that Dan took offence at, but he really only remonstrated, Clara thought, in quite proper terms, under the circumstances; but the functionary grew very red in the face, and said: "Your conduct, sir, allow me to say, is exceedingly improper. Allow me to say, sir, I doubt if you are a fit subject for this solemn service."

" I know my own business, and don't want any palavering. You do your own business, and I'll do mine, without your preaching."

"My business, as you call it, is not at your service to-day," he said, rising. "I order you to leave the house. I have nothing to do with low ruffians."

"You shall have something to do with a gentleman though, once in your life," said Dan, approaching him threateningly. Clara and Susie were already in the hall. Clara called Dan imperatively, and proceeded to the door, supporting Susie, who was ready to faint. They heard the minister say a very insulting thing in reply to Dan's threat, and the next moment a fall like a sack of wheat was easily interpreted. Dan had applied his "science," and the fat man was sprawling on the carpet. Before any of the family appeared, the carriage drove off. Dan raved and swore, though he was sober enough so far as the effects of his drinking went. To Clara's utter astonishment, Susie seemed perfectly recovered from all her anxiety, and even smiled.

"We can get the four o'clock train," said Clara, looking at her watch. "We will not wait for yours, as we intended." Dan savagely changed the order to the coachman. At the station Clara would not speak nor look at her brother, with whom she was infinitely disgusted ; but Susie shook hands with him, and said, "I was ashamed of you for being so violent, Dan, but I am happier than I have been since I saw you last."

"I think you are a fool," he said, sullenly.

"May be I am, dear, but I am not your wife." She said this without the slightest anger, and smiled on him like a seraph, as she entered the car which was just moving.

Thus ended Dan's marriage.

CHAPTER XIX.

THE BABY.—LOVERS' ADIEUX.

THE effort Clara had made to do a great service for Susie, had failed dismally, and her mortification was intense, and for the first time she was a little disappointed with Susie, that she could be so serene, and evidently glad even, that the movement had failed. Clara's refinement of nature and purpose was shocked beyond expression by the coarse conduct of her brother, and not until the doctor came home, late in the evening, and after she had had a long talk with him, did she begin to feel the least return of comfort. "My dear," he said, "depend upon it, you ought not to feel so mortified. Why, the dignity and real elevation of character that this has revealed in Susie is a compensation for almost anything that could happen. Don't you see how this shows, beyond a shadow of doubt, that she is no common girl?"

"I've known that a long time, papa. She surprises me every day. I shall not be able to help her much more in her botany; nor in anything, indeed. It is well I am going away, to save my credit. The dear girl thinks me so proficient, that it makes me ashamed of myself. Oh, papa! I passed at Stonybrook for a very satisfactory student; but if I had had this experience with Susie before going there, I should have done better. Susie has taught me what application means."

Clara had not gone into the house on returning with Susie, but left her at Mrs. Buzzell's door. Susie, on entering, threw her arms around Mrs. Buzzell, and laughed and cried together, and it was some time before she could tell the whole story to her friend. The good old lady was horrified at Dan's treatment of the parson, but she was quite content at the result of the expedition.

"God, who numbers the very hairs of our heads, Susie, is directing all things for the best. If you bear your yoke bravely, you will be raised up for some good work in the world. I wonder now, how I could have entered into the scheme so confidently; but it was Clara's enthusiasm. I felt all the time that we might be just whipping the Devil around the stump, and so we were."

"I could have interfered," said Susie, "between Dan and the minister, and my appeal would have been heard; but something stronger than my motive to do so, controlled me. I felt ashamed to marry Dan. It seemed to me so unholy a thing, when he does not love me, but is thinking all the time of another and dearer woman."

"That shame was a noble feeling, dear; and shows me what your nature really is, better than I ever knew it."

The next day Clara went over as usual to hear Susie's lessons. She found her alone, by the table in the sitting-room, tearing apart and analyzing flowers with her new microscope. As Clara entered she rose, and as their eyes met, the owlish gravity of Clara struck Susie comically, and this, in conjunction with the memory of yesterday's proceedings, made her burst out into a low, musical laugh, which Clara's gravity could not resist.

"Well, you are a study, Susie. I came over here from habit simply. I had no idea you would have any

lessons, and here you have already been out botanizing
alone."

"Why, Clara, I have not felt so well in weeks and
weeks. A great weight is lifted from my heart. Dan is
gone out of my hopes forever, and henceforth I shall
stand alone so far as he is concerned. He is free—and
oh, it relieves me so to think of that!"

"Well, dear, I guess you are nearer right than any
of us. I felt a little hard at you, coming home yesterday,
for the triumph that I detected in your eyes every time
I looked at them. You are a strange little being, but I
am reconciled after a long talk with papa. He applauds
you to the skies; but let us get through with our lessons,
for he will be here by and by. Of course, he will keep
the secret, and I think there is no danger from Dan," she
added, laughing.

After the lessons were finished, Susie, obeying a strong
impulse, poured out her grateful heart to Clara for all
her care and kindness. During the conversation, Clara
said: "When I am a married woman I shall be so much
more independent. No tongue will dare wag against me
because I am your friend."

"It pains me more than anything else," said Susie,
"to think that being my friend must injure you."

"It cannot. It cannot injure any one to do what is
decent and right. Knowing you, dear, and befriending
you in your trouble, has shown me more of the world
than I could have learned otherwise in an age. To be
sure it has destroyed some illusions. I shall not have
Louise Kendrick for bride's-maid, but I've found her out,
and that is something. Why, you ought to see the
letters she sent me constantly during the four years I was

at Stonybrook. Such protestations of unalterable friendship! You, Susie, though you are no spoiled pet of fortune, like her, have a heart that is worth ten thousand of hers. She is a mere fair-weather friend, though I did not suspect it; but you, I know, would never fail me."

"How I should hate myself if I thought that were possible; but it cannot be. My only trouble is, that I may never be able to be of any real service to you. Do you remember the fable we read of the lion and the mouse? How the mouse gnawed the meshes of the net, 'and left the noble lion to go where he pleased?' Remember this, you precious girl, if you are ever in trouble: *real, deep affection is capable of creating a will that may work wonders even with the poorest means.*" Clara was struck with Susie's enthusiasm of sentiment, which at times found expression in the most eloquent way; and she remembered these words and the manner of their utterance in after years.

Not many days before the time set for Clara's wedding, Dr. Delano received a telegram from home. His father was dangerously ill and sent for his son; so the marriage could not take place till January. Meanwhile, and during the very last days of the year, Susie's baby was born. Mrs. Buzzell virtually adopted it at once. This little helpless one, so charming in all its movements, Susie thought, lifted the last burden from her heart caused by Dan's unworthiness. She felt strong enough to brave anything for its sake, and before it was a week old her mind was busy with schemes for making money, that she might give it all the advantages of education and culture. She held its tiny, tightly-clinging fingers in hers, looked into its uncertain colored eyes, and marveled, as mothers are wont to marvel, over a mystery as old as nature, and yet ever charming, ever new. The desire to have Dan see the baby often recurred to Susie. She felt more kindly towards him since she had definitely abandoned all hope of his ever loving her again, and since a new and infinitely tender, infinitely absorbing love had been born in her own heart. She could not wholly share Clara's intense disgust for Dan's conduct when they had last met, though she by no means approved of it. She spoke to Mrs. Buzzell of her desire that Dan should see the baby, and Mrs. Buzzell admitted that the wish was natural; but even while they were considering the propriety of writing a note to Dan the doctor called, bringing the news that his son had started for California the day before. In a letter to his mother he had said that he should not "come back in a hurry." Susie was very silent. He had not cared, then, to wait until his child was born—not even cared really whether she or it, or both, lived or died. The next moment there came a new feeling, and this was shame that she had loved so coarse a being. To be sure, she had expressed the same thing to Dan in returning his money; but this was partly real and partly the effect of exaltation of mood. This time, the feeling was the result of pure reason, and it was permanent.

If letters are Love's barometer, as Dr. Forest once expressed it, Clara must have been well satisfied with the fervency and sincerity of her lover's devotion, for he wrote continually. The letters were delivered at eight o'clock in the morning—the hour when the doctor's family were always at breakfast—and though the postman's ring was a very common occurrence during this family reunion, it had never been so constant before. Leila and Linnie, on sitting down to the table, used to amuse themselves speculating whether it would occur before the hominy was served all around, or during the second cup of coffee. When the ring came, and Dinah marched through the dining-room to open the door, it was a perennial joke with Leila to pass the honey or the sugar-bowl to Clara, and when she good-naturedly refused them, apologizing for their deficiency in sweetness. As Clara could not be teazed in the least, so long as nothing disrespectful was said of her idol, it was wonderful that the sisters could find so much pleasure in an endless repetition of a child-ish pleasantry. On one of these occasions, when Dinah brought in the regulation letter to Clara, Leila said:

"Papa, do you know how Dr. Delano commences all his letters to Clara?" Clara looked a little annoyed as she put her precious missive in her pocket for future delectation. Could it be possible that her privacy had been invaded by her saucy sisters?

"Why, yes," the doctor answered, humoring Leila. "I think I could guess; that is, if it were any of my business."

"Well, guess then," said Leila, nothing daunted by the implied rebuke; but seeing he did not try, she declared boldly that they all commenced, "Essence of Violet and Consummate Sweetness." This time there was a general laugh, and Leila was satisfied over the suc-cess of a joke that had been concocted hours before. On another occasion when the letter came, Leila expressed the pious hope that Mr. Delano's case was in the hands of some physician less distracted and harassed for time than Dr. Delano must be. "I'm sure his literary labors must weigh heavily upon him, though perhaps he employs a stenographic amanuensis."

One day, when the letter was brought in as usual, Clara said, " Why, this is not for me ! "

" What ! " exclaimed Leila, " you don't mean to say it isn't from *consummate sweetness*, do you ? "

" No ; but this seems to be addressed to you." And she handed the letter across the table to Leila, preserving the utmost gravity. Leila's eyes shone with delight, but she concealed that part of her sensation, and only gave vent to her surprise. " Is it possible," she said, " that there are two persons in the universe that can command a letter from Dr. Delano ? "

" Let us hear what he says, my daughter," said Mrs. Forest, gravely.

" Yes, do read it, Leila. No doubt it commences ' Essence of Violet.' "

" No ; I don't receive love letters, Miss Linnie."

" You receive only such, I trust, as are proper to be read in the bosom of the family. Are you very sure of it ? " asked the doctor, who, from a glance at Clara, suspected some practical joke upon Leila. Thus badgered, Leila reluctantly unfolded her letter. The first word, which she did not read out, caused the most rosy blush imaginable. The laugh was at Leila's expense this time, and the next day Clara's letter came to the breakfast-table without comment.

Once, during his father's illness, Dr. Delano passed a night at Oakdale. It was just cold enough to render the wood fire in the grate, pleasant ; for though midwinter, the weather was unusually mild, and the lovers lingered in the parlor long after the family had retired. Every

9

moment was a delight to Clara, and everything the doctor could say possessed a vital interest. He was pleased to commend the old parlor; no room in the world, he said, had so great a charm for him. It was indeed a pleasant old room, permeated and invested by a spirit of comfort and ease that even the new carpet and heavy curtains, lately added by Mrs. Forest, could not destroy. The tall, old-fashioned clock stood diagonally across one of the corners, placidly marking the time and showing the phases of the moon as it had done at least ever since Clara could remember. During the evening's conversation, Miss Ella Wills was mentioned, and, at Clara's request, Dr. Delano gave a minute description of all her "points," as he humorously called them.

"Why, she must be very beautiful!" exclaimed Clara.

"Not beautiful," he said, "but very pretty. Clara alone, is really beautiful. She is less than 'moonlight unto sunlight,' compared to you, dearest." And he spoke sincerely, though Ella had revived a little of her old charm for him, and not without design on her part, for flirting was her element; she had reduced it to a science; and then she saw in Albert a very different object from the one she had once made her victim. She had been at Newport on the occasion of his return from Europe, and having a rich lion in tow—even the distinguished and very elegant Count Frauenstein—she did not go home with the rest of the family to meet him, it being the first of the season. She contented herself by sending him kind messages, and soon after he established himself for preliminary practice, in Oakdale, a town where the family name had prestige and influence.

The affair with the count at Newport had not terminated to the satisfaction of Miss Mills, he having soon transferred his attentions to a New York belle, not rich, compared to Ella, and a "perfect fright," in the judgment of her rival. But even the new attraction was but a very temporary affair. Ella was approaching the dreaded state which even friends may designate as that of old maid, and she had just begun to make up her mind to marry Albert when she heard of his engagement. This was unexpected, but she said to herself, "Engagement is one thing, and marriage another." When he came home at the summons of his father, he was so greatly changed, so infinitely improved, that flirting with him had all the charm of novelty, beside the greater charm involved in the fact of his indifference to the battery of wiles that had once been so potent. She looked very young still. Her mind was youthful enough in its character, and she had preserved all the innocent, kittenish ways that are so irresistible to a certain class of men.

While Albert talked of his old flame, on the evening in question, Clara listened intently, looking all the time straight into his eyes. At length he asked her why she studied his eyes so earnestly.

"Do you not like me to study them?"

"What a question! But I wish to know what you are thinking. You told me once you were afraid of my eyes."

"That is what I am thinking to-night, Albert. They are surely the brightest eyes in the world, as you know they are the dearest to me. I can find no fault with them; and yet I have an indefinable fear sometimes, when I look into them, as if they could be cold and cruel. I reproach myself, but I tell you every thought. Ought I to tell you this?"

"Yes, for I would hear all the voices of the sea, darling mine; but this voice is a delusion. Albert can never be cold to you. You are his very soul. He could die for you, and count it no sacrifice; and he only cares for life that he may make yours beautiful."

"Forgive me, beautiful eyes!" Clara said, tenderly caressing their lids. "Can *you* forgive me, Albert?"

"There is no such thing as forgiveness between lovers, for they can do each other no wrong."

"I dare not think how perfect my happiness is," said Clara, fervently, "and yet I can think of nothing else. I am constantly studying love. It seems to me that all married people lose their illusions. Papa and mamma were once romantic lovers. I have lately found a number of his old letters. I could not resist reading some of them. They are the most fervent and tender letters I ever read in my life—except yours, dearest—and yet they are flung away

'amid the old lumber of the garret,'

like the oaken chest where Ginevra found a grave. It is strange! After all that divine passion, they could be separated for weeks and months without any suffering for the need of each other!"

"That change will never come to us, precious one. Love shall be tenderly nursed; it will not flourish under coldness or inconstancy. It is too tender a plant; only the ruder, coarser vegetation can outlive the cold atmosphere of the frigid zones. With our love, precious one, there shall be no winter. Can you not trust me?"

"Trust you? With all my heart, with all my soul I trust you. You know everything about love and the mysteries of life; but one thing I want to say. I want you to know all about me, dear one. I care nothing about love except as we know it and feel it to-night. If Fate ever cheats us of this, let us not live together and play that the dream still remains. It would be a mockery that would kill me. I am strangely moved to-night. With all my happiness, the thought *will* come that you will change—that I shall not have the power to keep the freshness of your love."

"I defy augury, precious one. You are not quite well to-night. I am sure of this, or I should be pained. If I change, it will not be your fault. You are perfect. No one could love with so much infinite tenderness as my darling. If I ever love you less, it will be because I have grown unworthy of you, which the gods forbid. In a week—one short week—and you will be mine, not more surely than you are now, but openly in the eyes of the world."

Dr. Delano was to leave in the early train, and it was decided to bid good-bye in the old parlor, where the fire was burning low, for they had sat late, forgetting how cold the room had become. Albert wrapped her tenderly in her shawl, and the parting ceremonies commenced. It is a very long process, as lovers of the Romeo and Juliet type are well aware. They separated a few steps and said good night, and then rushed together for "one more kiss," which was only the prelude to one more, and that not the last. To the cold-blooded writers of romance, such a parting calls up the vision of the two polite Chinamen, host and guest, who could not allow themselves to out-do each other in etiquette. At the garden gates of the host, they advanced and saluted, and retreated and advanced again, until night came on, when their friends interfered and dragged them apart !

CHAPTER XX.

MRS. FOREST was in her element preparing for the "show," as the doctor called the marriage ceremonies ; but Albert won her heart by agreeing with her in everything, orange blossoms, church, and all. Discussing the matter over for the twentieth time, she reproached her husband for his imbuing Clara with his odd notions, and contrasted them with the love of proper and conventional proceedings, which characterized the future son-in-law.

"I wonder at him," said the doctor, with some impatience. "He is the only sensible man I ever knew who liked that sort of vulgar show. Men generally submit because it pleases women ; but to my eyes a young woman conventionally gotten up as a bride, simply suggests a victim tricked out for sacrifice."

"How dreadful you are, doctor ! You have such monstrous ideas ; but I did hope Clara would be sensible."

"Oh, I'm going to be sensible, mamma dear. Albert is satisfied, and I shall offer no further resistance. I submit even to the orange blossoms, though I can't bear their oppressing odor. Papa has had his way about the Unitarian minister, who has no church here, and so I shall escape that part of the show, as papa calls it. There'll be no kissing the bride either, for that is a

vulgar custom, no longer tolerated among refined people.
I wonder where the custom came from ? "

"It is not easy to say where any custom originated.
This one can be traced back to feudal times, when the
lord of the manor had the first-fruits of everything, and
took the brides home to himself for a time, and the bridegroom was forced to submit."

"Of course, they did not consult the bride at all," said
Clara.

"No," replied the doctor. "That slaves have no rights
which their masters are bound to respect, is a logical de-
duction from the doctrine that slavery is right. Women
are beginning to see that they are slaves in one sense.
They are not permitted, legally or morally, to dispose of
their affections according to their tastes. When a man
assassinates one whom his wife regards too favorably to
please him, he is generally acquitted by the courts.
Common-sense would show that the wife had sufficient
interest in the matter to be consulted ; but *honor* does
not admit her rights."

"That is perfectly right," said Mrs. Forest. "If a
married woman so far forgets the duty she owes to society
as to fall in love with any one, she deserves no voice in
anything."

"That is simply the spirit of the inquisition, Fannie,
and nothing else. I have always admitted the importance
of facts, in my reasoning. Now, some of the best women
in the world, and I believe the majority of all that ever
lived, have been attracted, in a greater or less degree, by
other men than their husbands. What will you do with
the facts ? "

"If any sensible woman is so unfortunate," said Mrs.

Forest, "she never acknowledges it—never admits it, even to herself, that she loves in any improper way. She can do this at least."

"There you go again, Fannie! measuring the world with your six-inch rule. If the world don't square with your measurements, so much the worse for the world. Women and men do not create themselves, nor the motives that govern them. A motive does not determine human action because it is weak, or ought to be weak, according to your measuring; it controls from the mathematical law that the strongest *must* prevail. Suppose the attracting power to be two and the resisting force one; you can tell beforehand what the result will be; therefore the folly of blaming in such a case."

"I might pity a woman who listens to the promptings of an illegal affection, but I certainly should never admire her. How could I admire one so weak as not to know that by the very fact of listening to improper declarations of love, she always wins contempt, even from the man himself."

"Not always—not by any means always. If I should love a married woman, and she should listen to my telling her of it, I should by no means despise her. I should despise her if she insulted me by supposing I wished her to do anything base or unwomanly."

"Oh, you! You are an anomaly. You know I always count you out, when speaking of general principles. The Lord only knows how far a woman might go without being 'unwomanly' in your eyes."

"Ah!" responded the doctor, with a peculiar accent, which was his way of declaring that there was no more to be said upon the subject.

On the day preceding the important event, Leila and Linnie were running here and there in a state of great excitement. They were for once thoroughly interested in everything, and especially in their own toilettes, if not in the bride's, for they were to be two of the four bride's-maids. Mrs. Forest had determined that everything relating to this event should be "respectable," and she always pronounced the word with severe certainty of what it meant. To be sure, to some persons the term is vague and even unpleasant; but these were all ill-regulated minds, according to Mrs. Forest, and she pitied them. After breakfast, Clara made a long visit to Susie, cheered her by earnest protestations of continued friendship, and by promises to write often. The pretty baby was duly petted and caressed, and invited to "kiss auntie"—words of recognition always infinitely sweet to Susie's ear. The kissing consisted in the baby's smobbing its uneasy little wet mouth over Clara's face; not a very satisfactory operation, one would think; but all the tender grace of the woman that had been developed by Clara's brave friendship for poor Susie, and by the deep love she cherished for Albert, shone through the halo of happiness surrounding the brow of the morrow's bride.

The wedding-day dawned auspiciously, and the sun shone bright and warm, though it was the middle of January. A full hour before the ceremony, the twins had the bride dressed and paraded duly before the mirrors, to see that her drapery fell with the proper grace, and that nothing was wanting. Mrs. Kendrick had sent quantities of flowers for the decoration of the parlor, and was herself to be present. Louise, finding

that the affair was going to be so "nice," cried with
vexation that she had behaved so meanly to Clara.

Mrs. Forest came in just as the bride was dressed.

"Does she not look sweet, mamma," asked Linnie.

"Yes," said Mrs. Forest, hesitatingly; "but you are
too flushed, my daughter. Let me see if your corset is
not too tight. No? Well, Linnie, get her some lemonade
—that is cooling."

"Oh don't, mamma! you distract me!" exclaimed
Clara, scowling under her orange blossoms. "I do wish
no one could look at me for the next ten years. I feel so
like a theatre-queen—so utterly ridiculous."

Mrs. Forest was distressed. The twins uttered exclamations. "Why, she has not said such a word
before!" said Linnie.

"No; I meant to be very good, and what mamma
calls sensible, but I am so horridly nervous."

"You are such an incomprehensible child," remarked
Mrs. Forest, severely. "You are veritably *sauvage*, as
the French say. This, the supreme hour to all well-
regulated young ladies, you seem to regard as a misfortune."

"Well, I do. I suppose I am not a well-regulated
young lady, for I hate the hot-house odor of these flowers.
I hate myself, that I have submitted to make a spectacle
of myself. This is the supreme hour for girls, is it?
Well, I wonder that they have no more refinement."

"What on earth do you set out to marry Dr. Delano
for, I should like to know," said Leila, concealing her
crossness with difficulty.

"Because I love him, you goosey! but it don't follow, therefore, that I like to make a guy of myself."

"A guy! oh! oh!" exclaimed the much-tried sisters. "You never began to look anything like half so sweet before." Mrs. Forest stood in mute bewilderment, and Clara began to relent.

"There," she said. "It's all over. I am sensible now, mamma—a perfect stoic. There's papa coming!" and opening the door herself, she threw herself into his arms, and sobbed a little, though laughing at the same time. "Oh, I can't enjoy crying one bit, papa. I'm thinking all the time of my orange blossoms. Look, papa, and see if you haven't crushed one of the things."

"Well, I *never* saw anybody behave so!" exclaimed Leila, in disgust. "If I ever get married——"

"Your conduct will be perfectly exemplary," interrupted the doctor, and then giving all his attention to Clara, he said, tenderly: "My poor darling! They would have it so. They don't understand papa's girl. Her poetry is inside, and this paraphernalia don't fitly express it."

"Now, doctor, you should not encourage Clara's strange notions. There's a carriage. I must go. Do calm the child. She is not fit to be seen."

"That's just true, mamma. It's exactly what I feel."

"All this nonsense, besides being in bad taste, is against common sense," the doctor said, not noticing his wife's flurry. "Marriage festivals should take place after marriage, if at all, when the union has proved a success, and there is something to rejoice over. *This* is like celebrating the purchase of a lottery-ticket." Mrs. Forest left in despair. The twins bore the "coddling," as they called the father's tender manifestations to his favorite child, as long as they could, and then they begged him to go, as they had "only a half hour to dress"; by which they meant but a very small part of the operation, being bathed, and coiffed, and dressed already, except for the robes and veils.

"Well, go on with your dressing," the doctor said, provokingly. "*I* don't mind girls' dressing, or undressing, for that matter. On the whole, I rather like this flummery, and I think I won't go without a consideration."

"I'll give you two kisses, papa, if you'll go this minute."

"Oh, fie! You were always too mercenary with your favors, Leila. I'll take the kisses, though; but not for going."

The doctor on leaving, went to his wife's room, where she was fuming because of his want of sense on such an occasion. "There is not ten minutes," she said. "and you have not done one thing toward dressing

"Bless my soul! I never once thought of it," he answered. "Why, I'm to put on that new claw-hammer. If I should fail to wear that, the earth's inclination to the ecliptic would be disturbed."

"Do, for mercy's sake, go, if you have any regard for me." Thus appealed to, the doctor sought his room. Once there, he surveyed the scene. Every article was carefully laid out in the most perfect order. He had only thought of the new claw-hammer, and here was evidently the preconceived design for a perfect change of every rag. Every article was placed where it should naturally come in the order of dressing. New toilet articles, scented soaps, hot water—everything silently commanding him to fall into line. First there escaped from the good doctor a smothered laugh; then a protest, and then—submission to the letter. He set about the work of rejuvenation with a perfect fury of dispatch, and when he found he should be ready in time, the spirit of fun seized him. He kept opening his door and bawling to his wife his distress at a thousand imaginary oversights and delinquencies. Once he declared she had forgotten his "pouncet box," then his "hoops," his "chignon," his "chemisette," his "gored waistcoat," and lastly, in an agony, he called for tweezers, pretending he had discovered one hair too many in his "back hair." But finally he emerged radiant, and sought Clara at once. "Behold me, my daughter!" he said in a tragic voice, applying a delicate, scented pocket handkerchief to his lips. "Are you resigned to your fate now?"

"Why, we thought you were crazy, papa," said Clara; "but how quickly you have performed all this change. I must say you are looking magnificent. You are one of the very few men I ever saw, who look well in a dress-coat."

"Well, I came to you for sympathy. Is this my reward?"

"I can't pity you in the least, papa; you are too sweet."

"Yes, I am," he said, sniffing the perfume of his fine handkerchief. "Here, take this, Linnie. I must go and see if I can't find a handkerchief that will not make me smell so much like a lady's maid."

Leila and Linnie both laughed. "You'll have to smell sweet to-day, papa," they said, "for mamma has kept all your clothes in a drawer with a perfume sachet, these two weeks!" He left the room to a perfect chorus of laughter, and a few minutes later might have been seen in his study, diligently puffing at his pipe, first for his own comfort, and then to do what he could, at that late hour, to render negative the effect of Mrs. Forest's sachets.

Notwithstanding all the perturbation of Mrs. Forest, the whole " show " went off in the most perfect order, and without the slightest " impropriety " of any kind. Clara was not flushed, like a hoydenish country bride, but looked very pale and " interesting; " while the bridegroom, in every word and motion, was perfection itself in her eyes, no less than in Clara's, though judged from a very different standpoint.

CHAPTER XXI.

IT is early in Summer. Mrs. Buzzell and Susie, now her trusted and much-loved friend, are sitting on the little vine-shaded porch of her cottage—not really a cottage, for it is at least an ordinary-sized country house, strong and well built; but she herself always so designates it. The baby, Minnie, is creeping over the porch floor, crowing with infantine glee, and now and then climbing up by the knees of Mrs. Buzzell, or by the railing which has been constructed to keep her within bounds. The lower leaves and buds of the roses and morning-glories, have suffered at her little hands, but she has learned by this time that they are not good to eat, and so pulls them off and scatters them in pure wantonness. The two women have been discussing a letter just received from Clara.

For a time Clara's letters were constantly arriving, not only to Susie, to Dr. Forest, to her mother, but alternately to the twins. These letters breathed the happiness that surrounded Clara like an atmosphere, and was rather implied than directly expressed, except to Susie. Mrs. Forest rejoiced that her eldest daughter was well established, and secretly she was greatly relieved to have Clara's fate off her mind. There was no knowing, in her opinion, what Clara would have come to, with her inherited tendency to freedom, so unlike other girls, if she had not fortunately married young. Why, she might have become a frequenter of conventions, an agitator of woman's rights—that was indeed what Mrs. Forest feared most—but, thanks to Providence, she had made an excellent match, and the mother's soul was at rest, or free to plan and scheme for the respectable establishment of her two remaining daughters.

On this summer day, in the little shaded porch, Susie had read to her friend, some portions of Clara's last letter. Mrs. Buzzell sighed, and said, "It is too exalted for this commonplace world. It will not last."

"Oh, do not say that!" exclaimed Susie.

"I know it sounds like croaking, Susie, but you will see I am right. It is always so. Clara worships that man, and we should worship nothing but the Creator. When we do, we lose it. When mothers make idols of their children, as her mother did of Dan, they die, or turn out like him. I am glad you do not love yours unreasonably. It is auntie who is in danger here," said the good old lady, taking up the child and caressing it fondly.

"I cannot believe it a crime to love—even to love inordinately, as Clara does," said Susie. "Her nature is peculiarly fervent. She told me once that the look, the touch of Albert's hand, made her tremulous with emotion. If he should fail her, she would suffer more than most of us could, I think."

"Of course he will fail her," said Mrs. Buzzell, with unusual feeling. "Men never meet the demands of a nature like that. They think it adorable at first, and then they grow indifferent. It is much better to love in a calm way, and, like Mrs. Kendrick, to show their husbands that heaven is not wholly confined to their smiles, nor hell to their frowns."

Susie was astonished at the fervency displayed by Mrs. Buzzell. "Could this faded, gray old lady, have had her romance also?." Susie's reflections were interrupted by the doctor's gig, which came almost noiselessly around the corner, over the smooth, sandy road. He sprang upon the porch with the supple nerve of a boy, and astonished Mrs. Buzzell by kissing her right in the face of the village. "You two women are as grave as owls," he said. "What have you been talking about? Out with it, Susie!"

"We were talking of love," Susie answered, not intending to be specially definite.

"Do ever two women talk of anything else, I wonder? Abusing us dogs of men, I suppose. Can't you furnish me with a cup of water and a little piece of soap?" he asked, addressing Mrs. Buzzell. "I want to amuse the baby."

"We were regretting," continued Susie, "that we are not able to love sensibly and moderately. When we love with all our hearts, are we ever fully met?—after the first, I mean."

"With that first, you are satisfied, then," said the doctor, taking a piece of India-rubber tubing from his pocket, and blowing his first bubble. For a time, all the attention was concentrated on the doctor's bubbles, some of which, by certain movements of his hands, he managed to keep in the air a long time, while the baby crowed with mad delight. For days after, the little thing amused everybody by her attempts to blow bubbles with every stick or pencil she could get, and even labored very hard to accomplish the feat with her teaspoon. When the doctor grew tired of blowing, he resumed the conversation ; but Minnie was insatiable : no sooner was one bubble burst, than she cried for another, but was finally pacified by having the tube and cup all to herself. After sucking some of the soapy water into her mouth, and making a very wry face, she succeeded in blowing some little ones on the top of the water, and got very angry after the twentieth attempt to pick them out with her fingers. Susie was scarcely less excited than the baby, over the exquisite beauty of the soap-bubbles, and listened eagerly to the doctor's explanation of their colors and construction.

Seeing Susie so interested, he said, "It is a pity your studying was interrupted. You have the spirit of the scientific investigator. I wonder if I can't manage to take Clara's place ? " he said, after a pause.

"Oh, your time is too precious, doctor," said Susie.

"I couldn't be regular, but I tell you what I'll do. If you'll have some recitation ready whenever I come, I'll give you a few minutes." That was enough for Susie, and from that time the doctor became her tutor, taking up, first, chemistry and natural philosophy, and then other branches. But this is wandering from the subject of conversation interrupted by the blowing of bubbles.

"The truth is," said the doctor, "women, in their love, do not fully meet men. According to my experience, few women ever comprehend the ardor with which men are capable of loving them. Now, the question is, is it when they do, or do not, so respond perfectly, that women meet the fate of Semele ? "

"The fate of Semele ? " queried Mrs. Buzzell.

"Yes; she loved Jove, and was utterly consumed for her daring."

"I remember now," said Mrs. Buzzell, smiling. "Why, her fate was not so bad, for her suffering was but momentary. Her lover was a god. That must be quite an advantage; and then he loved perfectly, and she also, I suppose." Mrs. Buzzell was in a complaisant mood, or she would not have treated any heathen mythology so considerately. "I never thought of it before in that light," replied the doctor. "She must have been the only woman whom any lover ever satisfied. Your sex is very exacting. You expect men to keep up to concert-pitch all the time; but, you see, we have to go out into the world and purvey for bread-and-butter. *Sine Cerere et Baccho friget Venus*, you know."

"*Sine Cerere*," repeated Susie, laboring with the Latin, of which she knew a little.

"'Without corn and wine love freezes' will do," said the doctor.

"True," said Mrs. Buzzell; "but it is just where corn and wine are abundant, that you feed us on dry husks—not to mention that you seek pastures new, for yourselves."

"I see I must defend my sex," said the doctor, with mock gravity, "Now we do not feed you on dry husks, but we assume to know what is best for you. Are we not your heaven-appointed keepers? You would live forever on ambrosia, and that is not good for the constitution as a regular diet; besides the supply is limited, I am sorry to say. The truth is, dear ladies—I am serious now—you women have not yet found the secret of your power. What we call the material forces, in the beginning rule the world. Man gains his freedom first,

then women, then children. Women are not free yet.
They should be independent, should travel, mix with the
world, conduct enterprises, and never be forced to marry
from any pecuniary motives. That is the way the 'state-
lier Eden' is coming back to man. Man cannot be
happy, and morally strong, until women have worked out
their social salvation. No one should stake everything
on the throw of a die. Women do that; and are taught
that it is wise. They keep their interests narrowed to a
point, and what with petty household cares and 'tying
baby sashes,' as Mrs. Browning says, they cease to grow,
except in one direction. They live as though they had
but one organ, and that the heart; figuratively speaking, I mean," added the anatomist. "This is their fate
when they are sensitive and emotional. When they are
colder in temperament, they gangrene with social ambition; spend their lives in scheming to out-do their
neighbors in fashion and display. This would not be
possible if they had other resources, but they have not;
because at the start, they have no education to speak of,
and few are interested in any literature but that of novels
and romances, which they waste time over without much
discrimination. Good Lord! what an amount of trash
they wade through! But then, very few people have the
culture implied in the art of getting the nuts out of a
book without swallowing husk and all. It is one of the
last things learned by the student, and women are rarely
students."

"So, in the end," said Mrs. Buzzell, "man, mixing
with the world and interesting his mind with politics and
science, finds his intellectual needs supplied outside of
home. Well, he has *other* needs."

" Yes, certainly. Home is the nucleus of all his affections; and because it is the nucleus or centre, it should include the possibilities of answering to the greater part of his needs. The woman who responds most fully to a man's various attractions, will keep his love fresh the longest; but when she can respond to little else except his desire to be petted and caressed, she is in danger of responding too fully to that, and so clogs his appetite with her very sweetness."

" Women learn this," said Susie, " and that is why so many become heartless flirts. Who can wonder ? "

" That is true of some very lovely women ; but not of the finest, Susie. It would not be possible to you, nor to Clara."

To be compared in any way to the superb Clara, was a compliment that Susie was keenly sensitive to ; and her love and gratitude grew with the self-respect and womanly dignity that the nobler course of her few friends, insensibly and continually stimulated into action.

When the doctor rose to go, Mrs. Buzzell detained him to look at her flowers—" or rather Susie's," she said. The large table by the south window was full of plants and flowers in flourishing condition. Two orange shrubs, about three feet high, were loaded with young fruit ; and in another room, less warm, by an east window, were boxes of violets and mignonette.

" I never saw any one succeed, as she does, with flowers. I never could get violets or mignonette to blossom in winter. I see now, I kept them too warm. Last winter, Susie sent bouquets of these to the new hotel, and sold them at high prices." " She must apply what she has learned of botany," said the doctor. " I see here, the result of what can be nothing else than a scientific method."

"And yet I confess my patience used to be tried a little last summer and fall, over her persistence in dissecting plants and poring over books about them. I think I was foolish, and am anxious to do a little penance. I've been thinking seriously of building a conservatory on this south side ; using the window as a door. The village has grown so, there must be quite a demand for flowers and plants in pots, and we are only a few miles from the city, you know."

"It is the best impulse you ever had, Mrs. Buzzell," the doctor said, very earnestly. "Susie has practical ideas, and this is the door to her independence. Go ahead without any delay. I will put in some money with pleasure, if you need it, besides giving twenty-five dollars out and out. It is June now. By next winter she could have plenty of violets, and that alone would pay well. I see she has a bed of them outside. Where does she get her stock ? I never knew violets so fragrant as these are. The *Marie Louise* violet, I see."

"Oh, a root, a slip here and there. Everything she touches succeeds. She is constantly bringing leaf mold from the woods. That is one of her secrets. Her fragrant violets she ordered in January from Anderson. They came in square pieces of turf."

The doctor encouraged Mrs. Buzzell to such good effect, that in two days the carpenters were at work, and in less than a month a nice flower-room, twenty feet by twelve, heated by a little furnace in the cellar, was in working order ; only the furnace, of course, was not yet needed. Susie had written to one of the great florists near the city, and ordered some stock ; and somehow her letter had elicited an offer of any advice she might need. Besides this, the florist sent her a manual on hot-house culture. This manual was a godsend to Susie. She wrote back her thanks, and, probably, recognizing a soul in the business man, she told him of herself and her hopes. After this there ensued quite a correspondence. In November Susie's violets were ready in masses, and she sent him specimens, packed nicely in moss. To this he replied :

" Your success greatly surprises me, but your bouquets are awkwardly put up—that is, wastefully, for ten violets are a generous number for a small winter bouquet. You need a few lessons, and if you desire them enough to come here, you can receive them in my establishment gratis. I will admit frankly that your white Neapolitans are better than mine. This is very remarkable, for it is a shy bloomer. I will sell all your violets for you this winter, if you wish it."

Susie's heart leaped at the offer of instruction ; and packing up all her violets and many other flowers, that the florist might see them, she set out on her journey, leaving many and oft-repeated directions about the care of the conservatory, and very few about the baby ; for Mrs. Buzzell was not likely to neglect Minnie, as Susie well knew.

Arrived at the florist's, Susie set herself at work as if her life depended upon it. The florist was unusually interested in Susie, who talked with him freely and with confidence. He gave her numerous suggestions about her flower culture, and took her home with him to his family, instead of letting her go to a hotel, as she intended, for

she had determined to stay a week. In the florist's family
Susie made more friends; but there was a kind of incu-
bus upon her all the while. How could she know if they
would be as kind to her as they were, if they knew her
history? At the end of the week, however, she felt that
she had made good use of her time. She had not contented herself with learning the theories of flower culture,
but had put her own hands to everything, and familiar-
ized them with operations destined to be of great service
to her. The florist had noticed that there was something
peculiar about this young woman, and shrewdly guessed
that there was some secret trouble in her life; but her
earnestness and gentleness of demeanor were greatly in her
favor, and he was not sorry for the offer he had made her,
to dispose of all the violets she should produce the ensuing
winter, though that act would be of little service to him.
It was, in fact, a generous impulse to help the praiseworthy ambition of the young florist, and Susie felt,
rather than knew, this to be the fact, and acknowledged it
indirectly. When she shook hands with the florist on
leaving, she looked searchingly into his eyes and said, " I
shall not forget your goodness to me, an utter stranger to
you. Your help means more than you know."

If we could read Susie's busy thoughts, as she rode home
communing with her own soul, to use a trite expression,
we should find them running something in this wise:
" This visit is a great step gained. I find I need not be
modest. I know a thousand times more of flowers than
does this great florist who has built up an immense and
successful business; and what he knows of practical
details more than I do, I can learn without the hard
experience he has had. If I am prudent, I need not make

10

any ruinous failures. Oh, to be rich! To own my own house, my own fortune, and never more be a dependent even upon the dearest and noblest people in the world! I may; I *must* accomplish this. I must! I must! Minnie is bright and pretty. Better that she died than grow up poor and ignorant, to do the bidding of others. I wonder if she will be really intellectual—capable of being highly educated, capable of lofty sentiments and principles. Ah! I am not proud that one like Dan is her father, but not in all the world could she have better blood than that of Dr. Forest. Great, noble, generous man! He knows I am grateful, but he does not know I could kiss his feet, and not then express how I adore his character. In his eyes, I am just as good, just as virtuous, as if baby had never been born. In Mrs. Buzzell's I am very dear, I know, but still a Magdalen. She would stand by me during good behavior; he would follow me with tender, helpful sympathy, if I should suffer any degradation. He would never lose hope that I could rise and atone for every folly. What a power there is in such trust. It must give the basest nature a very passion to justify it. So will I justify it, or I will die in the attempt. I could die any death much easier than I could take any course that would make him feel he had been mistaken in me. Yet they say he is not a Christian. He is irreverent. Mrs. Buzzell asked him if he had never suffered gloomy, despairing moods, and he assured her he had; but to her question, had he not, under such circumstances, felt the instinct to pray to God, he looked her calmly, seriously in the face, and said he should as soon think of finding relief in turning double-back somersaults. That was just what he said, and she knew he was perfectly truthful. He said, however, it was wise to pray, or go through any innocent manœuvre that would insure relief; and then he showed how the real method was distraction, as he called it—calling into action new faculties of the mind, and thus resting the overwrought ones. I don't find it much use to pray. Praying cannot remove disgrace, and shame, and suffering; but I trust in the unknown power that underlies all things. That power must be God. Obeying our highest impulses is the only thing we are sure is right. My highest impulse is to work for baby—to make her life all that life can be to her. Yet I have one awful fear, whenever I think of the future. When she goes out among children, in the streets or at school, they will no doubt tell her she is a bastard! She may come to me crying, and ask me what it means. Sometimes I think I would rather she should die than grow up to find her mother —— Oh! no, no! That is cowardly. I will make her respect me. I can read and study and educate myself, so that she will be forced to respect me, whatever others say. If I can only make money enough, I will take her abroad and educate her there; but I will tell her all, just as soon as she can reason, and if she inherits any of the soul of Dr. Forest, all will be well; but if she should not be like him! If she should be like Mrs. Forest, or coarse in soul like Dan——"

Thus thinking and foreshadowing, Susie reached home.

CHAPTER XXII.

THE FIRST CLOUD.

DR. DELANO, on taking his bride home, was somewhat surprised that Ella had left—accepted suddenly an invitation to spend the winter in Maryland, among some old friends of the family. Clara was hurt by this evident desire to avoid Albert's wife, but his vanity was secretly well satisfied by the act. Ella could not stay and witness a happiness that should have been hers. He excused her going, therefore, with a good grace, and made Clara do so also, though the effort revealed a flaw in the diamond, a touch of vanity she had not dreamed could exist in her idol.

Mr. Delano received his daughter-in-law with a quiet, courteous pleasure, that was evidently felt. Miss Charlotte's manner was stately, and just what it should be according to etiquette, though a good deal out of harmony with Clara's exalted happiness, which made her a little impatient to see people so calm and self-possessed.

Mr. Delano, after his illness, yielded to the advice of friends and retired from business. It had proved a very unwise step. He had given all the best years of his life to acquiring wealth—in fact, to preparing for the enjoyment of life ; and lo ! when the wealth was gained, the enjoyment he had promised himself fled before him like the horizon " whose margin fades forever and forever " as we move. He had been rich enough all his life had he only known it, and the increase of luxurious surroundings in his stately residence on Beacon street were no more than Dead Sea apples in his mouth. During his active business life he had constantly purchased books and extended his library. These also he was to enjoy by-and-by, when he got leisure to read anything beyond the daily papers. He had not counted the fact that there are many things wealth cannot purchase, and among them is the capacity for ease.

On the wide and elegant balcony upon which his library opened, commanding a view of a beautiful garden at the rear of the mansion, there had been swung an elegant Mexican grass hammock for Mr. Delano's special ease when reading. The house was on a corner lot, and the balcony was protected from the gaze of passers on the side street by screens of fawn-colored gauze. The old gentleman often took a book and lay down in his luxurious hammock, to see if he could not accustom himself to enjoyment, but he never succeeded. His brain was a vast cotton mart and exchange in full blast, and he longed every day to go back to that business which he had spent his life preparing to escape.

The old adage that "habit is second nature" is a very true one, and was illustrated perfectly in the case of Mr. Delano. His nature had come to relish nothing in the world so much as the cares, schemes, responsibilities, and the general excitement incident to money-making by speculation. It had all the charm of gambling, without the moral obloquy attached to it; though, to be sure, certain "crazy radicals" call it all gambling, and to them, one appears as immoral as the other. It is certain that any old gambler at *rouge et noir*, in Mr. Delano's situation, would have found the days drag on just in the same weary way. The evenings, which Mr. Delano used to enjoy as a relaxation from business, were now more wearisome than the days, and the coming of his son and daughter-in-law was the signal for throwing the house open for the reception of people that he dreaded. During these receptions he moved uneasily through the drawing-rooms, principally occupied in avoiding stepping on the trains of the ladies, and never knowing what to say to their stereotyped, "How exceedingly well you are looking, Mr. Delano." The only compensation was to get some old broker or stock gambler, who was bored to death like himself, into a corner, and talk of "the trifling of adults," which, according to St. Augustine, "is called business."

During the winter after Clara's marriage, she saw a great deal of Boston's choice society, and to please Albert who was very proud of her, she accepted many an invitation when she would have enjoyed herself much more alone with him, or, in his absence, a quiet hour with the old gentleman, reading to him or talking, as his mood directed. As time passed, Albert was less and less at home evenings, and seemed to find attractions at his club, which secretly troubled Clara, but she uttered no word of complaint, and only sought to make up for those attractions, as best she could, when he spent his evenings at home.

In March, Ella came home. She was full of her pretty ways, and delighted Albert by her multiform flattering attentions to Clara. "I was afraid—you can't tell how afraid I was—that you would never forgive me for running off like a *sauvage;* but you have, have you not?

I have heard so much of your goodness from Albert. When he came home last November he could talk of nothing but you—your grace, your beauty, generosity, accomplishments. I declare I was quite bewildered. Will you forgive me if I say I did not believe quite all he said ? but I do now. I believe every word since I have seen you." Clara had her doubts about the sincerity of Ella, but she would give no expression to them for fear of being unjust; and as Miss Delano had never attracted her especially—indeed, had never shown any tendency to real intimacy, though she was polite and graciously kind—it was rather pleasant, therefore, to Clara, who had been nearly frozen by a winter of Boston society, to be thawed into spontaneous gayety, even by a gushing, superficial creature like Ella. It was the first time since Clara's school days that she had given herself up to pure nonsense—to volumes of talk without meaning—and it pleased at first simply by its novelty ; and besides this, nothing delighted Albert so much as the good understanding between his wife and Ella. He encouraged every sign of intimacy between them, and this of itself was motive strong enough to induce Clara to be exceedingly gracious to his old friend. To please Albert in all ways constituted the joy of her life, though the halo investing him was dimmed slightly, from time to time, as she discovered little traces of ill-temper and impatience at the smallest and most insignificant disappointments. Once, for example, not long after Ella's return, he complained of the coffee at breakfast, saying pettishly, " I don't see how any cook, with good coffee and boiling water, can manage to make such a flavorless mess as this ! "

"It is one of your articles of faith, you know," said Miss Charlotte," "that a perfect cup of coffee is not possible on the Western Continent."

Albert made no reply, which Clara noted as a signal manifestation of self-control, for this was not certainly "pouring oil upon the troubled waters." In Paris, Albert had greatly appreciated the excellent quality of the coffee, and had brought home with him a French *cafétière*, which ever after appeared on the Delano breakfast-table.

"Why, my son," said Mr. Delano, "I consider this coffee very good ;" and he sipped his with gusto.

"But it is not perfect ; and there is no excuse for it, that I can see. However, the toast is so infinitely worse. that I suppose the coffee ought to escape comment. Ella had the bad taste to laugh.

Miss Delano replied satirically, and in the same breath asked for more toast.

"I should like to find one woman," said Albert, "who could hear the least criticism on any housekeeping detail without immediately taking it as a personal matter. You did not make the toast, Charlotte, and why try to make it out good when it is not, and force yourself to eat more than you want, by way of argument ? You must know that it is made of stale bread."

"I was not aware that toast is usually made of fresh bread," said Miss Charlotte.

"As a chemist, I can assure you that it makes the best, though stale bread will do ; but it does not follow that the older it is, the better. If it did, then the loaves lately excavated at Pompeii would be just the thing."

"I think a chemist at the breakfast-table," rejoined

Miss Delano, "is about as comfortable as the *memento mori* of the ancients."

"The Pompeian loaves," said Clara, anxious to avoid any more unpleasant words between Albert and Charlotte, "having been toasted to a cinder, some two thousand years ago, would make a sorry toast, even if stale bread is better than fresh."

"So you find a flaw in my logic, do you? I forgot the original toasting. It takes a woman to keep hold of all the intricate threads of the logical web." Clara looked at Albert, to satisfy herself that he was not laughing at her, or at women in general, which was much the same thing in effect.

"I always wanted to study logic, but I suppose I could not understand it. I am a little ignoramus," said Ella, with a pretty *moue*.

"I am sure you could learn logic or anything else," said Albert, looking very sweetly upon Ella. "If you could not, so much the worse for logic;" and for the rest of the breakfast Albert devoted himself to conversation with Ella. He seemed to be charmed with every insignificant thing she said—laughed at jokes which were certainly totally innocent of any spirit of wit. This did not escape Clara, and after the family rose from the breakfast-table, she followed Mr. Delano to his private library, where her presence was always a delight.

That afternoon Albert returned earlier than usual. Ella's bright eyes beamed upon him as he opened the hall door with the latch-key. She held out both her hands to him. He pressed them gently, and as he released them, asked where Clara was. He was thinking how gratifying it was to have his coming always anticipated with pleasure. It flattered him that Ella was always so glad to meet him; it was such a contrast to the old times, when he hung upon every word and motion of hers. He remembered her indifference to him then; and comparing it with her present behavior, he could come to but one conclusion; and in that conclusion there lay hidden a sense of triumph.

When he asked for Clara, Ella's eyes fell with such a pretty gesture of despair, that he regretted his question. Quickly regaining a pretended lost self-possession, she replied, "She is in Mr. Delano's library. She reads there almost every day, and has for ever so long. I can hardly get a sight of her."

Albert knew that Clara liked to sit with his father, and that her presence cheered and delighted him; and for this he was glad; but he did not like her to neglect him, her husband, and on this special day too, when he had left the house without bidding her good-bye. Clearly, she was very remiss in not being in the parlor waiting for him, after he had treated her to so much indifference! That is masculine logic. No?

Albert hung up his hat and light overcoat in the hall, and went with Ella into the sitting-room, and begged her to excuse him for lying down on the lounge, as he was tired and had a slight headache.

"I am so sorry! Can I not cure your head?" and sitting down beside him, she laid her hand on his forehead, and passed her fingers through his hair for some minutes. During the process Miss Charlotte entered noiselessly. Ella started violently. "Don't stop!" he said, aloud. "You do my head good!" Miss Charlotte left the room.

" Why did you start so, Ella ? I was surprised. It was bad, too, for Charlotte is the first of prudes."

" Oh, she will think me awful ! I will go now; there is a step on the stairs."

" Sit still ! " he said very positively, but in a low tone. " I hope it is Clara. No, it is not," he said, after a moment's listening. " Well, go if you must, and tell Clara that I am here; but I must pay this pretty hand for charming away my headache ; " and saying this, he opened it with both hands, and placing its rosy palm upon his lips, he held it there for some seconds with his eyes closed. Ella drew it away gently, and left the room. He lay there still, with his eyes closed, enjoying sensuously the magnetic thrill that Ella's touch awakened, and wondering if, after all, this were not the woman whom he should have married. It was a dangerous speculation, as his own thought admitted ; and then he thought of Clara's tender trust in him, and reproached himself as if he had been guilty of betraying it. When he opened his eyes Clara stood beside him, her eyes full of gentle concern.

" Why did you not come to me or send for me at once, Albert ? " she asked reproachfully. " I have just met Ella, who says she has been trying to soothe your head. She looked flushed. Oh, Albert ! can any one take the place of Clara when you are ill ? "

" No, dear one. How absurd."

" Why did she look so flushed ? What had you been saying to her ? Forgive me. I should not catechise you in this way." Upon this, Albert rose and took her very tenderly in his arms.

" What would become of me, dearest, if I should lose

you ? " she said, raising her head from his shoulder and looking into his eyes almost wildly.

" My child, what a question ! "

" But answer me, Albert," she said imperatively.

" I hope you would be sensible enough to forget that you ever cared for one so unworthy of you," he replied.

" Sweet words ! Do you know, Albert, I could never be jealous of you ? "

" Are you sure ? They say if you can love you can be jealous," he said, bending his head on one side and searching her eyes.

" I am sure. Jealousy implies anger with the loved one, or hatred of the rival. I could never feel either. I could only suffer; " and with a deep, long sigh, she laid her head back upon his shoulder. Presently raising it, she continued, " You said you learned abroad the meaning of the term ' illusions,' as applied to love. Except you, my father is the only person whom I ever heard use it in the same sense. There is no word that can supply its place. It implies the distinction between the love of lovers and all other kinds of love, and more than that, it implies all that is divine in loving. I think it hard to preserve these precious illusions, but without them love would have no charm for me. I should become a wretched wife."

" But we will not lose our illusions, precious. What should come between us ? Are we not irrevocably bound to each other by the very act of marriage ? "

" No," Clara said decidedly and with emotion. " We are only bound by those very illusions. The divine spirit of Love makes and justifies marriage. The body is nothing to me, when the soul is gone. You are a very elegant man, Albert—elegant and beautiful in all eyes, but in mine you are beauty and strength and tenderness in one. You are everything to me; but your dear eyes, your lips, your eloquent tongue, would lose all their charm, with the loss of the soul of all."

" Why, child, you are trembling like a leaf. Are you quite well ? "

" Albert, why did she look flushed ? " and she looked appealingly, searchingly into his eyes.

"I—I believe you are jealous after all," he said.

Clara turned slowly and left the room without a word.

" Jealous, by Jove ! " he said to himself when she was gone, and the idea flattered his vanity as it would that of the commonest soul. Clara had told him she could not be jealous, as the word is generally understood. That she could only suffer; but the words meant little to him. She had spoken the exact truth. In her venture, she had staked everything, and believed, as all women do under the same circumstances, that notwithstanding the coldness and indifference of married people, visible everywhere to the most superficial observer, that it was the result of a lack of wisdom—that love in all its divine freshness, could be preserved. Albert had held the same opinion, and had often said the danger lay in the first withholding of perfect trust. "Love should be cultivated like the most tender plant," he had said.

He mused over the matter for a half hour, and then went to Clara's room, where he found her, not " drowned in tears," as he had anticipated, but very calmly dressing for dinner.

" I was afraid my Clara was going to be silly," he said, smoothing her fine hair the wrong way, as men will, for it was rolled back at the sides over a heavy twist, and, of course, his caresses endangered the elegant finish of her coiffure, which had cost Clara more effort than he knew.

"Smooth my hair back, dear," she said. "Don't you see the way it is brushed?" and taking his fine hand, she passed it over her hair in the right way.

"You mean I had better keep my hands away. Don't you?" he asked, pleasantly.

"No, no; only that you should not endanger the structure, or I shall have it to do over again. You may pull my curls, baby. You can't hurt them."

"Don't call me baby. You know I hate it."

"Excuse me. I am sorry you dislike it. There is no pet word that seems so tender to me. I wonder what possible word could offend me. if you found it a real medium of fondness?"

"Suppose I should call you ducky?"

"That sounds common and trivial; but if it served to express the tenderness that the word 'baby' does to me, I should soon find it adorable. Albert," she said, after a pause, and with great enthusiasm, twining her bare arms about his neck, "Clara loves you as you have never dreamed of loving. Her love is greater than you need— greater than you can possibly respond to—and one day you will find it a millstone around your neck!"

"Well, that is pleasant. How long since you arrived at that astute conclusion?" he asked, laughing, as if greatly amused. "I thought my love satisfied you."

"Do not speak in that tone. Do not make me regret wearing my heart upon my sleeve. Your love satisfied me when I had not understood the depth of my own;

now, when a crisis comes, and you see me shaken like a reed, you do not answer seriousness with seriousness, intensity with intensity. You call me jealous, and treat me like a pretty butterfly woman, who must be managed by her husband."

"A crisis! I like that. You find me alone a moment with an old friend, who happens to be a charming woman, and you call it a crisis!"

"I think a physician should reason more nicely than that; he should look at effects. Was the princess in the story, who was made all black and blue by sleeping on a crumpled rose-leaf, any the less black and blue because it *was* a rose-petal, and not a brush-heap?"

"There are some princesses who are morbidly sensitive. I would have them harden their *epidermdes* a little."

"I understand," Clara said, deeply hurt, but controlling her emotion through a sense of pride never before experienced in Albert's presence, for she had been as frank and trusting as a little child, not dreaming that he could ever fail her in sympathy. "Perhaps," she added, forcing herself to smile, "I shall think best to commence the hardening process. Go now, or I shall keep the dinner waiting." Then followed a wealth of cheap endearments and caresses on Albert's part, which Clara responded to mechanically. She was positively relieved when he was gone. She knew well she had not exaggerated the importance of this first jar in the harmony of her life with Albert, but just now there was no time to think—no time to give way to tears that would have been a relief. She bit her lips to bring the color into them, and felt, as she took her seat at the table, that she bore well the scrutiny of Albert's and Ella's eyes. Miss Delano was very grave, and rather more attentive to Clara than usual.

Ella felt certain that there had been a "scene," as she would have called it, between Clara and Albert. She had betrayed her confusion to Clara an hour ago on leaving him; but here was Clara all smiles and self-possession. "Evidently she thinks me too insignificant to ruffle the current of her bliss," was Ella's thought, and had been for some time. It piqued her as it would any flirt; and the devil had possessed her from the first to try if her old influence upon Albert was entirely lost. This was the secret of her going from home when the happy couple were to arrive. "Let him have enough of his village beauty," she had said. "By the time the spring comes he will find her society rather tame." To do Ella justice, she had not intended to create any serious disturbance between Albert and his wife, though she could not forgive him for marrying any one until he had made certain that his old love was forever beyond his reach, and there was a secret spite in her heart when she found the "village beauty" superior in culture and manners, as well as in personal charms, to most of the women she had met. It was a dangerous experiment, as it proved, her effort to discover the state of Albert's feeling towards her, for she had found herself thinking and dreaming of him constantly, while he seemed still wholly absorbed with his devotion to Clara. That day, however, had brought a little triumph to the flirt.

Any disinterested observer would have pronounced the family dinner-party a very happy one, and much interested in the various topics that were discussed. How much we talk of candor and frankness, as if any one of us ever admitted either, among the virtues of society. The frankness that passes current as such, is but a base counterfeit, as any one may find by circulating an infinitesimal quantity of the genuine metal. He will be set down instantly as an uncomfortable Marplot. Little children alone exemplify real candor, and how we adore it in them! But it don't do for grown people, any more than the religion of Christ, as taught by him and his Apostles, will do, according to Mrs. Kendrick, for the exigencies of modern times. There was Miss Delano presiding at the table with suave good-breeding, while under the smile with which she served the dessert to Ella, there lurked a deep contempt of that young lady's "ways" with Albert; Clara, apparently without a care and conversing easily upon various subjects, was in fact suffering and longing to get away; Albert's light laugh and animated chit-chat, mostly with Ella, concealed a dismal dissatisfaction with fate, that had made him appear something less than absolute perfection in his wife's eyes; Ella appeared as gay as a bird and as transparent as crystal, yet she would have cut off her little finger sooner than have her real thoughts and feelings engrafted on the consciousness of those present. Mr. Delano, indeed, had not much feeling of any kind except that of general weariness, which he carefully concealed, and so was in some degree masked like the rest.

After dinner Albert played backgammon with Ella, who affected to be very fond of the game. Clara knew well that it was an affectation, for whenever Mr. Delano proposed playing, Ella was very slow to respond. To the old gentleman, this game was almost his only evening amusement, and though Clara disliked it, she often played out of

pure kindness to him. Clara was by no means displeased
that her husband's society was agreeable to Ella. It was
natural and right; but this special evening she would have
been flattered by some devotion of Albert's time to herself.
She was all gentleness and kindness, and feared, above
all things, being unjust or seemingly selfish, through her
exceeding fondness for her husband. "He will not play
long," she said to herself, and sat down by Miss Charlotte
with her sewing. When the game or games were finished, Albert left the house, saying only that he was to
meet some board of medical men. Clara's heart sank.
She looked at him, and his eyes met hers with the most
ordinary indifferent smile, such as he might bestow upon
his father or Charlotte. She went to her rooms earlier
than usual, and sat for a long time musing before the fire
of their pleasant, private sitting-room. The reflection
would come that, since Ella's return, Albert had cared
less and less for that room. Until very lately, he had
always sought it immediately after dinner, whether Clara
was there or not, knowing well she would not wait long
before seeking him there. As she recalled every incident
of the past month, little events that had meant nothing
at the time, were full of significance, and her heart cried
out in anguish with the fear that Albert was changing.
When he had left her before dinner, she had suffered a
moment of intense pain. He had not seemed to understand her, and for the first time she felt that something
had gone out of her life ; and now, as she sat waiting for
him, she almost dreaded his coming. She did not wish
to conceal any little heart-ache from Albert : it was torture to think it necessary. Why could he not soothe it
away ? Why should it not seem important to him, what-

ever its cause? Was she indeed too sensitive? Yet he had adored her for that very sensitiveness! She repeated his words "morbidly sensitive," and out of the fear to do injustice to him, tried to believe that she was suffering some indisposition—that she was nervous, and had exaggerated a very slight misunderstanding. Clearly she *was* nervous, and ought not to meet Albert until sleep and rest had restored her. "I should not see him in this mood," she said to herself, as she entered her bedroom. "Oh, if I might have one right the Turkish woman has!—if I might put my slippers outside my door, with the certainty that it would protect me from all intrusion, even from that of my husband!"

CHAPTER XXIII.

THE INVITATION TO THE WHITE MOUNTAINS.

THE first cloud obscuring the heaven of Clara's perfect happiness as a wife, had passed. The sun shone again, but never with its ineffable brightness. Love's perfect Eden was forever lost.

Dr. Delano and his wife had been keeping house a little over a year. Clara performed all wifely duties with perfect care. She had been apparently satisfied with Albert's course to Ella. She made no complaints, was cheerful always, received all his friends with a cordial grace that pleased him well, and if her caresses had lost their old tenderness, he had not wondered at the change—alas! he had not even noticed it;—and yet Clara believed that the trusting, childlike happiness that had been theirs at first, would, by some miracle, return. She cherished this hope as the drowning cling to straws. Ardent and romantic in her nature, feeling certain that her love was perfect and could meet all the needs of Albert, she was terribly shaken by the discovery that the petting, the flattery, the languishing ways of Ella, charmed him more than anything else in the world. She did not blame him nor Ella. It was inevitable that they should like each other, but there were times when her life seemed unendurable.

Ella was often at the house, and Clara received her as

she did many of Albert's friends, with whom she had no
special sympathy; but when one day Albert reproached
her for showing no affection to Ella, and dwelt upon
Ella's virtues, among which were her simplicity, her
affection, her child-like innocence, Clara's patience
gave way: "I do not love her," she said, "and you know
it well. Why should I play the hypocrite? I will treat
her well, because she is your friend. We pretend that
we have a higher guide than mere conventional rules,
which would forbid your ever asking me to receive a
woman who stands between me and your love. Ask no
more of me, Albert," she said, with an expression he but
partly comprehended. "Ask no more of me, Albert, or
I shall fail you, not only in this but in all things."

Sometimes the temptation was great to open Albert's
eyes as to Ella's childlike innocence, but Clara was really
above using such a weapon against her rival; besides,
she doubted that they could be opened. Ella was, apparently, without a single flaw in his eyes.

With the summer came the discussion of passing the
heated term at the White Mountains. Albert declared
that Clara was looking a little fatigued, and the change
would give her tone and color. She received this evidence of anxiety about her health with great pleasure.
The prospect of several weeks, in a delightful country,
alone with Albert, was in itself sufficient to bring color to
her cheeks, and to re-awaken her fondest hopes. Mr.
Delano, with Charlotte and Ella, were to spend the summer as usual at Newport; but it happened that just
before Miss Charlotte announced to her father that her
preparations were completed, Ella decided to wait and

join Clara and Albert in their trip to the White Mountains. Miss Delano expressed unqualified surprise.

"I don't know why you should be surprised. Am I not old enough to choose for myself?"

"You are *old* enough to be discreet," said Miss Delano, severely; "but, I can assure you, you are not."

"I know. It is always indiscreet to do what you wish to."

"No, Miss Wills; it is indiscreet to wish to do what good sense condemns."

"I'm sure I cannot see that good sense condemns my wish to go to the White Mountains with Clara and Albert."

"You mean with Albert and Clara. I would ask you if you have been invited by Albert's wife?"

Ella winced. She saw but one escape, and that was through a falsehood.

"Certainly I have," she said, with effrontery.

"What is this?" asked Mr. Delano, slow, like most men, to understand the disputes of women. Miss Delano having the issue clearly thrust upon her, explained very succinctly.

"My dear Ella," said the mild old gentleman, mildly, and as if a sudden thought had struck him, "you know you were an old flame of Albert's, and you know he is a very hot-headed fellow. I think you *are* playing with the fire."

The very mildness of the old gentleman was like tinder to flames, in its effect. Ella answered insolently, and flirted out of the room. Under such circumstances, she thought the best way to convince Mr. Delano and his daughter that they had wronged her, was to show them that they had made her ill. She stayed in her room two whole days, and by great effort, refusing all food during that time, she succeeded pretty well. During the second day she wrote the following letter to Albert:

"DEAREST FRIEND:—I am ill and suffering. It is useless to struggle against fate. No one cares for Ella but you—no one understands her—and they would have me think it wicked to see you. What does it matter that we know our love is pure? They will not believe it. Let us submit to fate, dear, dearest Albert. We had better not meet again, since we cannot be understood. Though it breaks my heart to say it, *farewell forever!*

"Your unhappy
"ELLA."

Whether Ella guessed what would be the result of this epistle or not, she felt she had done a sublime stroke of duty. She had bade him an eternal farewell, and if he did not abide by it, the fault was not hers. Albert, of course, flew to the rescue gallantly, and that no time should be lost, ordered the carriage for the purpose. He called for Ella, who refused to see him; whereupon he called for his sister, and expended considerable brotherly fury upon that staid maiden. She, on her side, told him some very unpalatable truths, and gave him some advice, which was yet more distasteful, and to which he replied angrily:

"You know no more of my wife than you do of Ella, whom you never understood." Miss Delano gave her views of Ella's character and general motives of conduct in most well-bred but unmistakable terms, and ended by saying, "If Clara Forest is a woman to be deceived by

Ella Wills, to 'love' her as you say, then I am fearfully mistaken in the woman. The truth is, you are using her love for you, to abuse her good sense."

Albert did not fail to show that he had a profound contempt for such ideas of love as might be entertained by prudes and old maids, though he was too polite to use the latter term to any lady. People who are married are apt to think that only they have any understanding of love, just as parents presume that they are better qualified to bring up children from the fact of their maternity or paternity, than others who have no children; though all experience shows that the capacity to bear children, by no means implies the capacity to rear them properly.

In this encounter of brother and sister, Miss Charlotte manifested the calm dignity of one sure of her position, while Albert showed all the blustering, virtuous indignation of the guilty man; however, in the end he succeeded, not only in seeing Ella, but in bearing her away in triumph.

Clara was sufficiently surprised when he arrived with his charge, and supported her upstairs in an apparently dying condition, though she had contrived to look exceedingly interesting in a white cashmere wrapper, fastened at the throat by a huge scarlet ribbon, which made her pallor more noticeable by contrast. The old family physician, Dr. Hanaford, had been called in, but when he came the patient was gone. Mr. Delano advised him to follow her. This Dr. Hanaford was much inclined to do on learning that Albert was unaware that the family physician had been sent for; and further, he did not wish to trust his patient in the hands of young Dr. Delano, which proved that he did not understand the nature of her case. Arrived at Ella's bedside, he examined her tongue, her pulse, and asked all the usual impertinent questions which doctors seldom omit, even when summoned to prescribe for a sty on the eyelid. Ella, who had never in her life been seriously ill, and knew well that she was not now, winced under the doctor's examination into her case, the gravity of which he measured by his inability to comprehend it. By dint of nasty medicaments, a low diet, and close confinement, he succeeded in a few days in making Ella very comfortably ill, and she enjoyed greatly the care and anxiety of her friends. Clara was wholly deceived, and nursed Ella with the greatest care, but said nothing about her joining their summer excursion. This vexed Ella, who was determined that Clara should extend the invitation voluntarily. On the occasion of Dr. Hanaford's next visit, he recommended change of air. "Oh, doctor, I can't go anywhere," she replied, languidly. "I don't wish to move."

"But, my dear Miss Wills, I advise it. It is the only thing for you in your present condition."

"Well, then, don't send me to the sea-side. I hate the sea, and am always made ill by being near it. Now, you will not, will you, dear doctor?" she added, in her most caressing manner. "If you do, I will die just to spite you."

"No, my dear Miss Wills, I am rather inclined to think a mountain region ——"

"No, no; don't advise anything to-day, doctor dear. Wait till to-morrow. I have such a horrid pain in my side."

"In your right side? That is a favorable symptom. The bile ——"

11

"Oh, don't. I haven't any such horrid thing!" she said, insinuating her little jeweled hand into his large palm by way of mollifying him. "What hour will you come to-morrow?"

"At two o'clock."

"Precisely? I cannot bear to wait for you a minute. It makes me *so* nervous." The doctor declared his intention to be punctual, which was all Ella cared to know, and she was glad when he was gone. The next day, a few minutes before two, she sent for Clara, pretending to need greatly her soothing presence; and when the doctor came she insisted upon Clara's remaining. This was a part of her plot. Pretty soon she managed to lead up to the subject of the proposed change of air by saying,

"Oh, I am such a trouble to you, Clara dear! but it will not be long. The doctor is going to send me to the sea-side."

"On the contrary," replied the unsuspecting old doctor. "I wish you to have the bracing atmosphere of the mountains." Ella turned her head to the wall with a weary sigh. The doctor expressed regret at recommending anything contrary to the young lady's inclinations. Clara herself had not the slightest suspicion of Ella's scheme, and from the goodness of her heart said, "We are going to the White Mountains, doctor, and can take her with us. I have no doubt that the mountain air will be better for her than anything else." This was a pure, generous self-sacrifice on Clara's part, costing more effort than any one could guess.

When Albert heard of the gracious offer of his wife, he was exuberant in his thanks—called her his sensible, generous love, and was so demonstrative in his tenderness, that Clara forgot to reflect that it was all due to her making a sacrifice to Ella.

As the days passed, Ella grew tired of being desperately ill; so she secretly threw away Dr. Hanaford's medicines and ate everything that was offered her. She wished to be ill enough to alarm Albert, and yet she must contrive to look charming in his eyes, and the work required a good deal of study. Pretty soon she left her bed, and spent her time in planning ravishing convalescent *toilettes*, complaining to Albert all the time of the dire condition of her health. On one occasion he found her reclining on a lounge in a pretty white-and-blue gown, her hair exquisitely dressed, and looking a picture of health. She complained of "utter weariness"—would not talk further than to say she cared for nothing in the world but to die and be out of everybody's way. Of course he called her endearing names, and begged her to live for his sake; he could not endure life without her. Finally he persuaded her to eat some delicious hot-house grapes he had brought her, and to consent to endure existence a little longer!

During Ella's illness Mr. Delano called upon her, and the day following Miss Charlotte also. She was a very kind person at heart, though her manner was a little of the forbidding style. She urged Ella to go home, and talked to her of the danger and the impropriety also of courting the affections of married men. Ella could not be angry, for Miss Delano's manner and accent on this occasion were really sympathetic and friendly. Ella could now declare with a good grace that she was engaged to accompany Albert and Clara to the White Mountains —that Clara had urged it and desired it. Miss Delano was nonplussed, and soon after took her leave.

CHAPTER XXIV.

A FEW days later, and when nearly all the preparations for the White Mountain trip were finished,
Clara expressed a desire to run home to Oakdale for three
or four days. It was a lovely morning in the last days
of June, and the scene was at the breakfast-table. Ella
floated languidly in at the last moment, in a lovely
morning-dress of white lawn, puffed and flounced, and
with wide flowing sleeves that exposed well her pretty
arms. At her breast she wore a knot of narrow blue ribbons and a little bouquet of fresh rosebuds. Her hair,
which curled naturally, she had brushed out and passed
her fingers through and through it, until it lay in innumerable fluffy ringlets and curls kept back from her face
by a wide blue ribbon, fringed at the ends and tied in an
elegant bow at the top of her head. "How pretty she
is!" said the eyes of Albert. Ella seated herself in her
place languidly, as if life were the very burden she pretended it was. "How pretty you look, Ella!" said Clara,
generously. "It does not seem as if you could ever grow
old."

"Like you, for example," said Albert, smiling.

"I know I am young enough," replied Clara, "but I
do not think I ever looked as fresh as Ella does."

"I am sure I would exchange all the freshness that

you seem to admire so much," said Ella, "for a nose as elegant as yours."

"Yes, I believe my nose is irreproachable," replied Clara, smiling ; "but as a child, it was certainly a pug."

"Like mine."

"No, yours is not that by any means. I think you should be quite satisfied with your person."

Albert looked from one woman to the other. He knew Clara was several years younger than Ella, and yet she looked older—an effect heightened by her dress, a plain light gray with plain cuffs, and collar fastened by a bow of rich black ribbon. Albert wondered why she would wear black, when she knew he hated it. Clearly she did not study to please him, as Ella did. He did not reflect, possibly he did not know, that Clara's little dower from her father had been exhausted, though managed with the greatest care, and that it would scarcely have permitted her to dress like Ella for a single year. Clara had never yet asked Albert for any of the money that he spent freely upon his own dress, on his friends in wines and cigars, at his club, and in many ways ; and as he had several times expressed surprise at the extent of the household expenses, she had endeavored, in ways he never suspected, to reduce them. She may be blamed, but she simply could not bring herself to ask him for any money for herself. The old, perfect, child-like confidence was gone. She thought, moreover, that a husband's duty was to set aside for the mistress of the house, a certain generous allowance for her personal and household expenses ; and not dole money out week by week, to meet current expenses. It seemed to her very undignified, to say the least, and not what her father would have done, as he had proved ever since the growth of Oakdale and the increase of his practice enabled him to count on a steady income. She did not, however, attribute Albert's course to penuriousness or selfishness, but simply to ignorance of the ideas of a wife on this subject. Time would harmonize all this, she thought, if ever the old Eden came back, with that divine mutual confidence that makes it wise to express every thought freely and frankly. So she went on from day to day managing Albert's house with a rare skill, improved by constant experience and a quick practical intelligence, receiving his friends, gracing his table and his drawing-rooms with her sweet presence, and in return receiving such attentions from him as his nature suggested, when not absorbed by Ella's charms, or by the claims of other friends. She learned to be a hypocrite, as many a wife has done. If she expressed the grief that was in her heart, even by a tone, a word, Albert's pleasure was affected by it. To be sure, his course was much like that of a person holding your head under water, and then feeling injured because you are so inconsiderate as to look strangled! At times Clara felt as if she could go mad at Albert's persistence in declaring that his love had in no way changed. A thousand words and acts and movements, proved his protestations utterly false; and between her struggle to please him by liking Ella, whom any other woman of spirit would have felt justified in hating, to attend to all the household responsibilities, to show a smiling face when her heart was breaking, to do strict justice to Albert and Ella in all her thoughts—between all these trials, no wonder she looked old beside the rosy freshness of triumphant love, that shone unclouded in Ella's pretty face. No wonder she desired to go home to her father—to one who never misunderstood her, who never required her to conceal any thought or emotion—one whom she could please wholly, by being herself in all things. Sometimes it seemed that she could not wait one moment; that she must fly to him, whatever the result. But when she mentioned this desire on the morning in question, Albert was astounded. His gesture and words made her indignant. She compared him mentally to her father. The expression of a strong desire for anything, created in Dr. Forest an instinctive impulse to help gratify it.

"I wish much to go," she said simply, as if that alone should be enough.

"But at this time, my dear."

"I will return in less than a week."

"Indeed! You would go alone! Do you suppose I can permit my wife to go home for the first visit after our marriage, without her husband? I shall go with you, of course."

Ella winced. Here was an evidence of the husband's pride in his position. Why, he was not fully hers, after all; and for the first time she felt jealous of the wife. Very soon after she left the room.

Later, in Clara's room, Albert came to her, evidently to talk over the matter. She put her arms about him, and tried the little coquettish arts that used to charm him, only to find for the twentieth time, with secret mortification, that they had lost their power. Ella had the monopoly of all pretty arts now. Clara knew it, and despised herself for the foolish persistency of hoping against hope, lowering her dignity by seeking to regain anything that such a kitten as Ella Wills could win; but it would be worse than useless to show her feelings. Unhappiness was a crime in Albert's eyes, and he had not seen a tear in hers for many a month. In answer to his question, what had given her such a sudden desire to go home, she answered, " It is not sudden. I have been thinking of it a very long time. I don't think I am over well, and I so wish to see papa. I cannot tell you how strong the desire is."

" You have not mentioned being ill, Clara ; " and with the fatality of many people who wish to avoid a scene, he took the surest means to produce one, for he added, " but you have no faith in me as a physician."

" That is very unjust, Albert."

" If you had any faith in me, you would tell me if you had symptoms of illness."

" Perhaps I should be more flattered if it were not necessary to tell them."

" I do not profess to be a magician, like your father," he said, ironically.

" This is a reflection upon my father," replied Clara, indignantly. " It is not necessary for me to tell you what I think of it. I am not alone in the opinion that he is a very superior physician."

" I did not mean it in the light of a reflection. I know he is a fine French scholar, and keeps himself *au courant* with the methods and discoveries of modern science ; but of course he is a graduate of the old school."

" The subject is painful to me, Albert. I am deeply mortified that you should institute any comparison between yourself and my father in this respect."

" You seem pleased to treat me like a sophomore," he said, angrily, assuming an air of superiority that could not deceive Clara. "You will pardon me for saying, that if this is good taste, it is at least unwise."

"Unwise?" echoed Clara, with disgust. "I deny that I even dreamed of treating you with the slightest disrespect; but tell me, please, what result I ought to fear."

"Oh, nothing; my respect, my admiration, amount to nothing, of course;" and Albert took out his cigar-case, and selecting a Havana, was about to strike a match.

"Put away your match!" said Clara. "You have not my permission to smoke in my room to-day."

"Madame is obeyed," he said, bowing and putting away his cigar. The tone and manner of Clara were so strangely unlike all he knew of her, that he was astonished into good-humored admiration.

"Respect is due to me from you, and all the world, until I forfeit it by ignoble conduct. Your admiration I have thought and hoped I could never lose, for no true man or woman can really love when that is gone;" and as Clara said this, she glanced at her reflection in the glass.

"I think you are right, my dear," he said, coldly.

"It is sad for a woman to lose what little beauty she has, for I think the admiration of most men depends wholly on personal beauty."

"No, Clara. It is happiness that most charms the lover."

"Then, indeed, I have no chance, for I am not happy."

"I was fool enough to think my wife ought to be happy."

"No; the woman you love should be happy. I am proud of being your wife, as you well know, but I would gladly change my state to that of your mistress, could I regain what I feel that I have lost forever. Oh, Albert! the world seems vanishing under my feet, when I think we have come to this."

There was something in the whole attitude of Clara, and especially in the evidence of emotions long repressed, that filled not only the husband, but the physician, with alarm and self-reproach, and he did what all men do when unusually conscious that they are murdering by inches the women who love them. He took her in his arms, covered her with kisses, wept over her, called himself unworthy of a love so divinely tender as hers, and when in some sentence Clara alluded to Ella, he begged she would not mention the name of any other woman to him. What were all the women in the world to him? He had been a brute to even seem to put any other woman before her, or to do anything to cause her the slightest pain. Clara nestled close to his heart, and sobbed herself into a blissful state of trust and hope, as Albert went on. He would never pay any marked attention to Ella since it displeased Clara.

Clara, too happy in being restored to her husband's confidence, answered generously, and through happy tears:

"No, dear one, you must not make her unhappy by an inexplicable change of manner. Do you not think she is really in love with you?"

"There is no doubt of that," he said, with a touch of vanity, for he was but human, and to see this woman, who had caused him so many "pangs of despiséd love," now wholly and helplessly enamored of him, was a triumph bearing in it a poetic justice, a healing sweetness, impossible to resist. He had not desired that any one should occupy his heart but his wife ; for theirs had been a love worth preserving in its freshness. He really desired so to preserve it; and therefore he would have been consistent if, upon the first signs of Ella's passion for him, he had shown her something of his devotion to his wife. It might not have been gallant, according to the creed of men, but it would at least have been profoundly wise. Women instinctively yield to any securely enthroned rival ; perhaps men know this, and hence they so rarely show one woman that they love any object specially, or even act in a manner that will let such fact pass for granted. This is generally true of men in whose temper there is a latent melancholy. They are passionately attracted to their opposites, to those who are gay and happy, and therefore they would fly from suffering, even when they themselves are the cause of it.

Clara found in the bliss caused by Albert's spasmodic return to his old tenderness, an adequate compensation for deferring her visit to Oakdale. She expressed earnestly the wish to please Albert in all things.

"My darling," he said, "you can please me always if you will remain in this sweet mood. Only be happy, and there will be no more clouds."

"But my moods, dear one, depend upon you. How can a dethroned queen be happy ? No: I mean," she added quickly, "when her throne is in danger. You *know* I am not jealous and selfish. I would have all women love you, and I would stay by myself without a murmur, if you wish to ride, or walk, or flirt with them, for nature has made you very gallant and fond of the incense of admiration. I only would feel certain that I hold my old place—mine by right of loving you more than

any other can, as you have always admitted. There
is something in the confident air of Ella when she speaks
to you in my presence, that distresses me ; makes me feel
that you have not shown her my true place in your heart.
Have you, dearest ? ”

Albert knew he had not. To have said yes, would
certainly have been false, and he had a repugnance to
direct falsehood. The position was awkward, but he
managed to satisfy Clara, and in a most heavenly frame
of mind she sent him to tell Ella that she had decided
to put off going to Oakdale for the present.

CHAPTER XXV.

" OAKDALE, *June* 25, 18—.

" MY DEAR GIRL : I have just come from Mrs. Buzzell's. It is about the happiest family I ever knew.
The baby flourishes like a weed, and is as pretty a child
as you would wish to see, and actually resembles your
mother so much that everybody remarks it. This is a
piece of poetic justice that makes me grin with delight.
She ignores still the existence of Susie, the child, and
good Mrs. Buzzell; but she is the only one who hears
anything from Dan. He is in San Francisco, and wears
a huge diamond. That is all I know of my only son.

" Susie's new establishment for flower culture is a
perennial delight. She has written you, so you are
doubtless posted as to the money she made last winter.
Everything promises well for the next. She is bound to
succeed, and if she had capital, could build up a fine
business ; but what is better than all, is the fact that
she has outgrown all her heart-aches, and is really and
truly happy. See, my girl, what we have done for her !
When we remember how ignorant she was, how deficient
in any moral or other training, and therefore how certain
to be guided by her emotions, if we had ' passed by on
the other side,' like the rest, she might have been
damned beyond salvation; yet still I doubt it after all

She reads a great deal, and is the best patron of the new circulating library. 'Give me a list of books,' she said to me, 'that you know are good. If I select for myself I shall waste time, and I want to make up for what I have lost.' Some people would call this lack of individuality, but the fact is, it is real wisdom. Life is too short to read all the books of unknown and new authors. Let them sift through the ten million general readers of the country. If anything is too big to go through the sieve, there will be a noise about it, and then it is time for the discriminate to take it up. Susie devours history, biography, travels, and entertains me greatly by her fresh comments upon them. She has not yet complained of my selection being too serious for her. You see, I keep a copy of my lists, and when I think the pabulum too nutritious, I throw in a few lollypops in the shape of novels, though I don't mean to include all novels under that head. Have you read George Eliot's last? I ask, because I would have you not only read, but read very carefully, everything she writes. In my opinion she is the closest observer and the profoundest thinker among women to-day. Susie has an appreciation of her that is delightful to me. You know, of course, that I am teaching Susie French and natural philosophy. Upon my word, I think I missed my calling. I should have been a teacher of girls—women I should say, for girls are only interesting because they are women *in posse*.

"The great event in Oakdale is the arrival of the Count Von Frauenstein. I met him at the Kendrick's last night, and I like him more than any man I ever met. That is saying a good deal, but I know when a man has the ring of the true metal. He is a Prussian by birth,

but no more belongs to that country than I do to this
10 × 12 study. In fact, he is a genuine cosmopolitan. He
graduated at Cambridge, for his family took up their
residence in England when he was a boy; then he took a
degree in Philosophy in Heidelberg (which don't count
for much in my opinion), then lived some years in France,
where he was sent on some government business. Some
years ago he came into his inheritance, when he made for
this country for the purpose of investing it. Kendrick
says he is worth two millions to his knowledge, and much
more in all probability. Kendrick is laying pipe to
interest him in the new insurance company, but so far
has only succeeded in getting him to help on the new
railroad.

"It was a very stylish affair, the Kendrick reception
last night; music, *chef d'œuvres* of confectionery, ladies
in *undress*, and all that. Your mother was furious about
the display of charms, and of course I defended it—not
on principle, but because she was too savage. Leila and
Linnie were invited, and they would have rejoiced in a
state of *décollété* extending to their boots, I think. Your
mother compromised the matter with black lace, and so
they still live. Frauenstein has a fine voice, and Linnie
was in the seventh heaven when she got a chance to
play him an accompaniment to a song from *Der Frei-
schutz.*

"I never met a real lion in society before, and I studied both with interest. This fashionable society is nothing, after all, but a kind of licensed policy-shop. They
want Frauenstein's money, and Kendrick thinks he has
the best right to it because his cousin was Frauenstein's
mother—an American woman; so you see he has blood !

The Delanos are related to him in about the same degree;
so of course you have heard of him. I like the count for
one reason, and this is, that notwithstanding the display
and cajolery of the women, and the flattery of most of the
men, he had the good taste to talk with your old doctor
more than to any one there; so the race is not wholly
degenerate! In politics he is soundly radical, and hates
war like a Quaker. He sees in it the degradation of the
people. It was refreshing to hear him talk. He says the
wealth-producers of the world are not dependent upon
capital so much as capital upon them, if they only knew
it; for they have everything in their own hands, and are
slowly coming to realize the fact, and to see how they can
organize and accomplish great things. He was very eloquent when the subject of education came up, and presented the whole matter in a clear and new light to most
of those who heard him. He said it was a disgrace to
the age that we have no text-book of morals for the public
schools; and as the various systems of religion have
monopolized the teaching of codes of morals, by shutting
out all religious instruction, we have shut out moral
training as well. It is right to exclude all creeds from
schools supported by the people, but it is a great and
vital error to deprive the young of constant and unremitting instruction in the laws that should govern human
beings in their mutual relations. He would have a text-
book on morals compiled from the writings of all the great
teachers, whether pagan or Christian, excluding every
myth and unverifiable hypothesis. Such a book could be
made as acceptable to all religious sects, as works on arith-
metic or chemistry now are. He talked also of woman's
coming position as that of perfect social and political

equality. It is astonishing how radical Kendrick, old priest Cooke, and many other out-of-her-sphere noodles, have suddenly become. Kendrick actually assented to the very propositions he has repeatedly pooh-pooed when presented by me. I made him feel a little uncomfortable by saying, 'Mind, Kendrick! I shall see that you stick to that.'

"I come now to the important part of your letter. The old Serpent has got into your Eden. Two things I would say to you as a preliminary : first, don't go off at half-cock. This is a common weakness of women. Second, don't expect better bread than can be made of wheat. Your Albert is not so fine in nature as you supposed, or the fact of your being unhappy, even disturbed in your mind about his affection, would be the very strongest motive to self-examination. For myself, I don't much believe in marriage, any way : it don't seem to work. If it could be prevented until the age of forty or so, it would work better. If you were an ordinary woman, I should recommend flirting ; but that would be useless in your case. So, my girl, I cannot help you as I would. I need not dwell on my feelings in the matter. In such cases there is only one physician, and he is the old mower with the hour-glass. Do not forget, that although a woman, you are really a philosopher. Love is not all there is of life ; and as you depend less on its intoxication for your happiness, the more smoothly will work the machinery of destiny, just as the circulation of the blood is effected more normally when we trust to Nature, instead of trying to aid her by counting the beating of our hearts.

"The truth is, I am at a sad loss what to write you on this matter. I feel sure that you will act wisely, and be unjust to no one. The best I can do is to trust to your finer instincts. Action and reaction are equal : so the doctrine of eternal rewards and punishments is true in principle, though we look for heaven and hell in the wrong places. Be sure that Nature always restores the equilibrium. This is always the thought that I comfort myself with. It answers the place that praying does to the devotee. Nature's laws are immutable, and cannot fail us. Be patient, dear girl, and know that there is one old fellow on whom you can rely, no matter what may happen.

"Yours, as you know,

"G. F."

To the ordinary observer, there might not seem to be anything in the doctor's letter to his daughter that should move her deeply ; yet she read all the latter part of it through blinding tears. She received it a few days after her reconciliation with Albert, and answered it immediately as follows :

"DEAR, DEAR PAPA : Your letter consoles and blesses me, but I almost regret mentioning my troubles to you. I *feel* how they sink into your heart, and as I read I was filled with gratitude by the thought that you are still strong and hale and may live as long as I do, which I fervently desire. The very thought of losing you, is terrible. No one can ever understand me like my good, my precious father. Your character is my ideal of all that is noble in manhood, and it was not wise, perhaps, for me to marry, because I must measure all men by your standard, and then be disappointed when they fall below it. I am unreasonable. I should never expect to find any one with your sense of justice, or with your delicate appreciation of everything fine in human motives. I could never deceive you: you see below the surface. I can deceive Albert, and do constantly, and hate myself for it. I can make him happy by wearing a smiling face when my heart is as heavy as lead. About a week ago we had an explanation. He confessed he had been wrong, had neglected my love, and we cried together, and *played* that all our clouds had passed forever. I thought it was possible; but there is something false and forced about our re-established happiness, that mocks our once proud state like a beggar's rags upon a king. Still, I am much happier. I try to dress more showily. Albert likes the lilies-of-the-field style of Ella. Think of your Clara's pride! She enters the lists in a toilet display to regain the admiration of her husband. Is it not pitiful?

"O papa, what am I saying? I meant to write you such a happy letter, but I fear the iron has entered my soul; yet I would not try, even for your sake, to deceive you, and believe me, I am suffering very little now, and I really think I shall recover my lost state. It is this hope that sustains me; but if I am disappointed, I shall rise above it and live. I am papa's own girl, and more proud of being the daughter of such a man than I should be in being the queen of the grandest monarch that ever lived. If for no other reason than for your sake, I would bear up philosophically.

> "'What matters it if I be loved or not?
> And what if he who works shall be forgot?
> The work of Love is no less surely wrought,
> And the great world shall answer me.'

"Are not those grand words? They have just come

to the surface of my memory, like the artist's negative under the developing solution. I mean to keep them before me henceforth, like the *mene tekel* on Belshazzar's wall.

"Good-bye, dearest father, mine. I have written myself into a horrid mood. I have written to Susie, mamma, and others. Trust me, and believe in the good sense of
"PAPA'S OWN GIRL.

"P. S.—I *can* write a letter without a *post scriptum*. You will bear me witness; but I must say just this: *do not be worried about me so long as I am silent*.
"C. F. D."

The next day the White Mountains party set out on their journey, where we will leave them for the present and go back to Oakdale.

The time is sunset, and it is summer. A little child, whose flesh seems moulded from its mother's milk, is playing on the little green lawn before Mrs. Buzzell's porch. It is a creature of exuberant life, of movement incessant, of inexhaustible joy. She has pure blue eyes, and her hair is long, straight, and fine like spun gold. It dances and streams out in the sunlight with the movements of her little frame, as she dances, and laughs, and sings. At first, being carefully and very coquettishly dressed by "Auntie," and let loose upon the lawn, it was joy enough to simply dance and carol in the sunlight, but soon this ceased to suffice her. Her active brain and fingers must have more positive occupation; and a few minutes later "Auntie," coming out on the porch, discovered the sprite pirouetting around her beautiful calladium, a huge leaf-tip in each dimpled hand.

"Min! Min! what *are* you doing?" The electric current of joy was cut off instantly, and the child pouted:—
"I'm only dancing with auntie's *cladium.*"

"Will you let my *cladium,* as you call it, alone? I won't have its leaves twisted to rags." But further admonition was unnecessary, for Minnie descried a well-known horse and "sulky," and she ran toward the gate, crowing at the top of her voice. The doctor jumped out of the vehicle and took the child in his arms, saying, "Well, how is my little Min to-day?"

"Auntie's cwoss," was the somewhat irrelevant response.

"Cross, is she?" he repeated, taking Mrs. Buzzell's hand; "then Minnie must have been a naughty girl."

"No, se wasn't naughty; an auntie nee'n't be so *wough*" (rough).

She was one of those elfin creatures whose accents and gestures, and charming self-asserting confidence that the machinery of the universe is run for their special amusement, make it difficult to resist indulging them in every way. Minnie made you laugh at her, and then she felt sure of her victory over you. The only dispute Mrs. Buzzell and Susie had ever had, was on Min's account; the former declaring that Susie was not quite tender enough to the child. Susie replied, "I think I love her as much as any mother should. I shall devote my life principally to her care and education; but I cannot spend so much time in amusing her as you do, unless I neglect what is of far more consequence."

Susie was reading when the doctor entered. She rose, and greeting him, as she always did, with frank cordiality, held out her book. It was a copy of *Roderick Random.*

"Doctor, you choose my serious reading, I believe with exemplary discretion ; but shall I waste my precious time and peril my immortal soul over such trash as this? Trash is too flattering a name for it. I must borrow yours. I call it, unqualifiedly, *rot*." The doctor laughed, and said :

"Why, you must have some light reading."

"Thank you ; but the levity of this is too great altogether."

"You see, I don't know much about modern novels ; so after George Sand, George Eliot, Thackeray, Balzac, and Dickens, I've reached the end of my tether, and fall back upon the old standard stock."

"Standard !" repeated Susie. "If this is a standard, I pity the dwarf varieties."

"You borrow your rhetorical figure from your business. It smells of the shop," said the doctor smiling.

"Listen ! 'O Jesus ! the very features of Mr. Random ! So saying, Narcissus kissed it with surprising ardor, sheds a flood of tears, and then deposited the lifeless image in her lovely bosom.' Then," said Susie, explaining, "Mr. Random broke from his concealment, when Narcissus 'uttered a fearful shriek, and fainted in the arms of her companion.' Then Roderick, telling his story, says : 'Oh that I were endowed with the expression of a Raphael, the graces of a Guido, the magic touches of a Titian, that I might represent the fond concern, the chastened rapture and ingenuous blush, that mingled on her beauteous face when she opened her eyes upon me, and pronounced, *O heavens! is it you ?*'"

The doctor laughed like a boy. "Why," said he, "I

know any quantity of young women who would read that with rapture."

"And would they this?" asked Susie, reading the last sentence of the book.

"Ah? I confess that is utter nastiness. Smollet! rot!"

"We have just finished Richardson's *Pamela*, taking turns reading it to each other while sewing," said Mrs. Buzzell. "I can scarcely believe that it is the same story that, in my mother's time, was read aloud in the best family circles. Why, I consider it positively indecent."

"You musn't think, doctor, that I am not glad to have read these books," said Susie; "they are very interesting, as showing the taste of a century ago. It must be that we are now much more refined than people were then."

"Certainly we are," said the doctor. "With the invention of the steam-engine and the telegraph, our means of communication with each other all over the world are immeasurably greater, and this is the proximate cause of modern culture. Isolation of the community, the family or the individual favors the savage state, while aggregation tends to stimulate urbanity, generosity, and all our higher faculties. See, therefore, how false the religious teaching that exalted hermits and ascetics of all kinds. Self-torture the church considered praiseworthy, and even to-day we hear of the 'mortification of the flesh,' for God is still a being to be propitiated by the agonies of his creatures. Wherever that conception of Nature or God prevails, we may recognize the traces of the savage, and the absence of any real vitalizing faith. The only living

faith to-day you will find among those called unbelievers
or infidels—men devoted to the discovery of scientific
methods. To them Nature is never inimical to man."

"*Is* Nature never inimical to man?" queried Susie.
"Does not the cold freeze him, the sun scorch him, the
water drown him, wild beasts devour him, the earth-
quake and the lightning destroy him, as well as disease
and accident?"

"Ah!" said the doctor. "What do we mean by
man? Do we mean the savage who has command of a
few of his forces, or the integrally-developed human being,
commanding all his forces, and through this command,
setting himself in harmony with Nature,

"'Like perfect music unto noble words?'

Man has not accomplished this, hence the use of faith.
The best thinkers to-day have the strongest faith that
we are to obtain further and more complete control
over the elements ; that we are to control the weather,
the climate, and make the planet a stately Eden, fit for
the emancipated human race. Is not that a sublime
faith?"

"A much more difficult faith," said Mrs. Buzzell,
"than any I know of."

"To me it is very simple ; simpler far than all others,"
said the doctor. "No one can deny that the whole
history of human beings on this planet is a history of
extending and harmonizing their mutual relations and
interests. See the savage. He is at war with all his
kind, like the beast, except, perhaps, a chosen female of
his species ; then, when he has risen a little higher, he
establishes a harmony of interest in the family, the tribe,

then throughout the race constituting the different tribes, and so a nation is developed—at war, of course, with all other nations, and calling all foreigners barbarians. Then nations recognize each other, and evolve codes of international law, and cease preying upon each other. Have we reached the acme of human progress? So doubtless the savage thought when he had invented a stone knife to scalp his neighbor. When the steam-engine was utilized, who was not satisfied when news could fly over the country at the rate of thirty miles an hour? Who then, except the scientist, would have believed that we should literally 'put a girdle round the earth in forty minutes?' To me, and many others, this increase of harmony among different peoples, points unerringly to the time when the higher nature of man will rule, when his intelligence will come to comprehend the harmony of all human interests, and his affections embrace all mankind as brothers. This is our millennium, Mrs. Buzzell—the reign of peace, harmony, and love."

"Amen!" said Mrs. Buzzell, who was holding the sleeping Minnie in her arms.

"We cannot really disagree," said Susie, "whatever our different creeds, if we only love God in the right way, and that is through faith in humanity. It is because we have not sufficient faith in humanity, that we are so selfish and dishonest."

"That is very true, Susie; but we have not yet the conditions for showing our faith. We shall finally, in the general, concerted action of the world toward great ends. Our forces now are 'like sweet bells jangled.' Melodies are first created, then harmonies, and lastly, grand symphonies."

12

CHAPTER XXVI.

THE CRISIS.

DURING all this summer, so fraught with wretchedness for Clara, Susie was working with untiring energy, extending her arrangements for the future. As an experiment, she set out, in an unused part of Mrs. Buzzell's kitchen-garden, a hundred young shade-trees of new and rare varieties, among them the broad-leaved, rapidly-growing *Paulonia imperialis*. She wisely foresaw that the taste for ornamental trees would increase with the growth of Oakdale and surrounding towns; and then in her thoughts she often saw Clara, her bright hopes wrecked, and weary of life, returning to be helped and blessed by the very one who owed her so much. Then Susie would lose herself in dreams of a vast, successful business, built up all by their own hands, out of which there would come health, and work, and interest in life, independent of the cheating intoxication of love. It was in the midst of reveries like this, that she received the following letter from Clara, dated at North Conway, New Hampshire:

"MY DEAR FRIEND: Do you remember what you once told me about the fable of the lion and the mouse? Oh, child! you are no longer the mouse as compared to me, for you are strong while I am weak. Your wounds are healed, but mine will never heal, for in my madness I am always tearing them open afresh.

"I write you, dear Susie, because there is no one else on earth before whom I can cast off all pride, except my father, and I would spare him a little longer at least, because from my last letters he thinks matters are improving. Judge for yourself. We are still here, though many of the visitors are gone, because Albert and his friend are perfectly happy, and I cannot possibly care whether I go or stay. I keep in my room much of the day, while they ride, or walk, or dance, or play games, all the day and evening, their bliss only marred by the sight of my thin, pale face. Do you know the very hardest thing I have to bear is Albert's telling me that he has not changed, but loves me just as fondly as ever? There is something like murder in my heart when he does this, essaying by argument to show that it cannot be otherwise. Oh, Susie! how well a woman knows that love needs no logic to prove its existence. Long ago he reproached me for saying 'where there is doubt of love, there must be cause for doubt.' When love is perfect, we can no more doubt its existence than we can the presence of the sun at noonday.

"My old friend and teacher, Miss Marston, passed through here with some friends, and stopped several days. I begged Albert to let me play while she was here, the rôle of the happy wife. I think he regrets the change in him, though he cannot resist the power that is leading him from me. He seemed impressed by my stony, tearless face. In answer to Miss Marston's anxiety about my changed looks, I said I had been quite ill, which, heaven knows, is true enough. I manœuvred in every

way to prevent her seeing the state of things. We
actually rode and walked several times without Ella.
This made her pout and flirt with Colonel Murdock, one
of her admirers, which so alarmed Albert that he completely unmasked all my beautiful acting. Miss Marston
soon penetrated beneath the surface. ' Who is this Miss
Wills ? ' she asked. I told her the ward of Mr. Delano,
and an old and dear friend of my husband. ' Is it possible,' she asked, ' that you do not see the nature of the
attachment between your husband and her ? ' Still I
played my part. I was the proud, happy wife, confident
of my husband's affection. I know I made a pitiful
figure. Miss Marston divined the truth, and I expected
every moment she would burst out upon me, as she used
to do upon her pupils, when guilty of deceiving—an
unpardonable offence in her eyes; but I think something in my face alarmed her, and kept her silent. She
was very tender to me, and it was good to have her here.
She was struck with the beauty of Albert. He impresses
every one the same way. His lithe, fine form, his handsome, regular face, and long, dark moustaches, make him
greatly admired by women."

Under a later date, Clara wrote in the same letter:
" This morning Albert received a telegram from Boston,
demanding his presence immediately, for his father is
again very ill. I wished to go with him. There was not
time for Ella to get her half dozen ' Saratogas ' ready.
That was the secret cause of his objection. She would not
like him to take his wife and not her ! I cannot tell you
how keenly I felt his willingness to leave me behind—me,
his once adored Clara, whose absence he could not endure.

" Sometimes I think I am selfish, to burden you with

my sufferings, but I know you would have me do so, and you are right in saying it lightens them to have them shared by sympathetic hearts. I have so much to bear! Long since I have given up the idea of making Albert understand that my trials are greater than I can bear. I gave it up when he came to me and told me of Ella's *unhappiness* because of my coldness to her. Think of it! I, with my breaking heart, must comfort the rosy, happy Ella, when her little finger aches! I must do this or Albert is afflicted. I did not do it. I treat her kindly, but I cannot love her, and never should, under any circumstances. She is little, and soulless, and selfish. How can such a woman touch my heart, when I have seen and appreciated the noble generosity, the soulful delicacy of Susie? Of course Albert thinks I am jealous without knowing it. Can you understand how he wrongs me? I like him to flatter and caress women. It is his nature to be very gallant, only I would know that I hold my old place in his heart, and knowing I have lost it, I would not have him place another before me in the eyes of the world. This he does constantly. For weeks I have suffered a dull pain in the centre of my brain, and at times I fear I shall go mad. I am relieved, actually, by Albert's absence; for a time, at least, I shall be spared the sight of his blissful expression when Ella comes into his presence. Oh, Susie! grief like mine dries up the fountains of my gladness at the happiness of others, and. I long for death as I have sometimes longed for Albert's loving words and kisses, as I knew them in our happy days. How often I think of poor La Vallière's words, referring to the king and Montespan—'When I wish to do penance at the convent of the Carmelites, I will think of what these people have made me suffer.'

"Write me often, dear Susie. Your letters are my one comfort. The thought haunts me that some crisis is approaching. It may be that there is; that I have seen Albert for the last time ; but I am so weary, so anxious for rest, that I would pay for it with this or any sacrifice. Do not afflict yourself too much on my account. Remember I still appear regularly at table. I walk every day, and I am young, and can endure to the end. With love to Mrs. B. and kisses to 'Min,

"Lovingly yours,

"Clara Delano."

Dr. Delano found his father very ill, and his few days of absence lengthened into two weeks. He wrote occasionally to his wife, but every day brought a letter, or a book or magazine, to Ella, which she never read, being engaged in a flirtation that demanded too much dressing and general attention to leave any time for reading. Clara sometimes thought her husband must be crazy. He knew how fond she was of reading. As a school-girl, he had constantly sent her magazines and periodicals, with passages or articles marked which he wished her to notice particularly, and he had told her afterward that he had loved her even then, and thought of her as his future wife.

She often watched Ella in her display of feminine wiles, but could not discover what there was to fascinate men. The subtle mystery escaped all analysis in that case, as it ever does ; but Clara, in her generosity, believed there must be something beneath the surface—

some hidden wealth of sensibility, perhaps—which women could not discover. If Albert had only trusted her as a perfect friend, and had not tried in any way to deceive her when he became absorbed in his passion for Ella, she would have met him nobly and suffered far less ; but her pain had been tenfold increased by his want of confidence in her sympathy. He did not and could not understand her, and this discovery of his weakness was a blow to her self-pride hardly less endurable than his submitting her to the mortifying position of the neglected wife.

One evening, when he had been gone two weeks, Clara sat in her room watching the rosy sunset haze on the old mountains, and thinking over the events of her life. She had just re-read Albert's last letter. The words were there, but the soul was lacking. Later in the evening she recognized Ella's voice proceeding from a balcony beneath. A gentleman was with her, and there could be no doubt that Ella was drawing him on to make the greatest possible fool of himself. Clara heard her own name mentioned by Ella in no flattering terms. Her companion opposed her criticism quite generously, considering his position with regard to Ella. Clara could not sit there without hearing everything, and there was a temptation to do so, as any one can believe who has ever been placed in a similar position. She, however, closed her window with a little noise, and when she opened it again, all was silent. What she had heard Ella say, was, that Dr. Delano's marriage was a " veritable _mésalliance_ "—that there could " never be any real sympathy between them." Once Clara would have written all her thoughts freely to Albert ; now a seal was on her lips. Whatever she might say of Ella would be attributed at once to her inability to comprehend Ella's "childlike" nature. Oh, it was hard to be forced to brood in silence over thoughts and feelings that he, of all the world, should share with her.

That day Clara had received one of Susie's long, nicely-written letters, detailing little village events, the mild flirtations of the twin sisters, the doctor's sayings and doings, the ways and speeches of "little Min," and her own schemes and hopes for the future. "Dear Susie!" thought Clara; "she knows I am unhappy, and so writes me every day, hoping to bring some little sunshine into my life. Why, even Susie shows more love for me than Albert. What is there in his letter? Only the cool assurance that he has not changed—the stupid persistence that the sun is shining, when all the world is wrapped in Cimmerian gloom. My father would never consider me weak enough to be deceived by such shallow pretence."

Clara had gone to her room to answer Albert's letter. For this purpose she had given up joining a moonlight excursion to *Diana's Baths*, a wonderful freak of Nature where, in the solid granite, the trickling water-drops of ages have smoothly carved out vessels of all imaginable shapes, not a few greatly resembling the common bathing-tub. All these vessels were overflowing with the crystal water of a mountain-spring.

Clara sat until far into the night, trying to write to Albert, and knowing all the while that it would be just as well to be silent. And yet she did write a long letter—a cry from an overladen soul that ought to have moved a heart of stone. "I know not why I write," she said, toward the last of the letter. "My reason rebels against these frantic attempts to patch together the fragments of the golden bowl. Love wants its perfect illusions—wants and will have nothing else, these failing. No wonder you try to deceive me when you see how my health and strength, and all the little beauty I ever had, are failing under the griefs I have borne so long. Believe me, dearest, I *do* know I am wrong to write you when I must burden you with sorrow you are powerless to alleviate. I cannot blame you in my heart. It is not your fault that Clara's love has ceased to be the most precious thing in the world to you."

To this there soon came the following reply:

"My Dear Clara :—I wish you would give up studying the death of love, and study its life. You brood over imaginary troubles too much. I wish you could have children, but that will never happen, because you are too unquiet in your temperament. You have no real cause for unhappiness. My regard for Ella in no way interferes with that for my wife. You ought to know that all real love ennobles. Albert never takes back any love that he once freely gives, and my love for you has never suffered the slightest change. Love is not a suffocating warmth, or at least, it should not be.

"I send you some valerian powders. Take one every night at bed-time. I am obliged to go out of town for a day or two on pressing business, and then, dearest, I shall be with you in the flesh, as I am ever in spirit.

"Always and ever yours,

"Albert."

"Never suffered the slightest change!" repeated Clara, bitterly. "What must he think of my common sense?"

His words about children cut her to the heart. She did not believe him, and she despised the whole heartless tone of the letter.

The next morning Ella rapped at her door. She was in a very jaunty traveling dress. She was in very high spirits, and made Clara think she was going away "for good," but finally stated that she was only going down to Wolfboro', on Lake Winnepiseogee, for a day's visit. She would return the next evening. The next morning a letter came. Clara did not notice the postmark, and her heart leaped as she read, in Albert's own hand, "My precious one,"—the old words he had always applied to her. It went on for three pages, in the lover's most impassioned strain. The first few lines revealed the fact that it had been written to Ella, but Clara's eyes were fascinated, and she read every word. He dwelt continually upon Ella's beauty, upon her lips, her "glorious eyes," everything, showing clearly and most unmistakably, that he was wholly, desperately enamored. It was dated the same day and hour as her last letter from Albert, which added, if possible, to the heartlessness of his deception. It had perhaps been purloined from Miss Wills' room, or possibly Ella had dropped it, and one of the boarders, from some justifiable motive, had sent it through the Conway post-office to Mrs. Delano.

Clara sat for a long time with this letter before her, her hands and feet icy cold. Shouts of gay laughter came up from the veranda. Were they discussing the effects this letter would have upon the forlorn wife? Clara did not believe human nature capable of heartlessness like that. Doubtless the person who had found that letter and sent it to her, had been disgusted at her blind faith, her submission to gross neglect that would have roused any woman of spirit to open rebellion. Some woman had sent this letter. The superscription revealed that fact. Poor Clara's thoughts were bitter indeed. She was not lacking in spirit, but it was not her way to bluster and remind her husband of her rights as a wife. He had failed to respect her position before the world, and for this she could not forgive him. She knew well that we cannot command the inward devotion of the heart; that this must be won by charm; and here Clara felt that she was powerless. Still this could not excuse him for deceiving or trying to deceive her. It was so like a common, coarse man's treatment of his peer. Though Clara felt like sinking utterly beneath this blow, her native dignity supported her. After a while she dressed carefully, and joined the groups below. Towards evening, gossip was busy with the story that Dr. Delano and Miss Wills were stopping at a hotel together at Dover. Clara traced the report to Colonel Murdock, who had been absent for a few days, and had returned by the afternoon stage. Clara found an opportunity to speak to him alone.

"I am told," she said, "that this story about my husband is stated as a fact in your possession." Colonel Murdock bowed.

"Will you be kind enough to repeat it to me, if it is true? I charge you, by everything you hold sacred, to tell me only what you know to be *positive fact.*"

Clara was very calm, but there was something in her tone and manner that would have exacted the truth even from the most untruthful. Colonel Murdock had no disposition to deceive, and moreover, he was a very honest man.

"Madam," he said, "I am sorry to afflict you, but it is perfectly true."

"*What* is perfectly true? Do not mind afflicting me."

"That I saw Dr. Delano and Miss Wills in Dover yesterday, at four o'clock in the afternoon, riding together in an open carriage."

"Might you not possibly have been deceived?"

"No, madam, it was your husband; and as for Miss Wills, she recognized me. I may add that she told me distinctly, a few days ago, that she was going to Wolfboro' yesterday, which was a falsehood."

"I thank you, Colonel Murdock, and beg you to excuse me for troubling you," and with a smile upon her lips, and a manner perfectly calm, she left him, and soon after went to her room. It is folly to try to describe the long horrors of that night. They had to be lived through, and Clara counted the hours one by one, for she never touched her bed nor dreamed of sleeping. Early in the evening she had packed her trunk, carefully putting away in Albert's, everything that belonged to him. Some time during the night, she wrote a note to him. The stage was to leave early in the morning. A little while before it started, she ordered a cup of coffee and sent for the landlord. He came in bland and smiling, and asked what he could do to serve her.

"Mr. Hammond," she said, with the air of one confident of carrying all points. "I must leave this morning, and I wish you to loan me, fifty dollars."

"Well, madam, doubtless your husband ——"

"No, no," she said, cutting him short. "I must have it on my own responsibility. Take my watch as security, and understand that my husband is not to pay this under any circumstances. I shall return you the money without delay."

The polite landlord refused the security, and furnished the money. This, with what Clara had in her purse, enabled her to just meet her traveling expenses, and to pay the hotel bill of herself and her guest, Miss Wills, which had been running since Albert left. A few minutes later, after running the gauntlet of a few curious boarders lounging on the veranda, the smiling landlord handed Clara into the coach with great deference.

CHAPTER XXVII.

THE SANCTITY OF MARRIAGE.

THERE was great excitement for the rest of the day in the Kearsarge House, and when the evening coach brought Ella from the railroad station, she was surprised at the coldness with which everybody greeted her; but she was a rich heiress, and scandal handled her with gloves. She explained to one or two, whose lead others would be likely to follow, that her meeting with Dr. Delano in Dover was the purest accident. "Why!" she exclaimed, "what else *could* it have been?" and this passed current, for Colonel Murdock had said nothing, except to Clara, of his knowledge of Ella's pretence that she was going to Wolfboro'. Still, there were some who knew the secret of the letter, and these avoided all further recognition of her, except a few fawners who pretended that that part of the scandal was a pure fabrication. The next day Albert returned, having waited over only for appearance' sake, for he might just as well have come with Ella. He went immediately up to his rooms, and seeing no one, concluded his wife must be out riding or walking; still it was strange, for he had written, informing her of his intended return, and naturally she would have met him at the veranda. Very soon he went to the office and asked the clerk where Mrs. Delano was, but the answer being very indefinite, Colonel Murdock, who had just bought a cigar, volunteered the following:

"Your wife, Dr. Delano? You have killed her, I think; but you'll find your sweetheart in the bowling-alley."

Like lightning it flashed upon the doctor that Murdock had blabbed the Dover affair. This explained the exceedingly cool air with which one or two had returned his greeting on alighting from the coach.

"Insolent coxcomb!" growled Dr. Delano, ready to fly at the colonel's throat; but at the critical moment the clerk thrust a letter into his face, and as he took it, the other left the office. The thought flashed upon the doctor, at the sight of the superscription, that his wife had left the hotel. He returned to his rooms, and shutting himself in, opened Clara's letter. At the sight of the enclosed one which he had written to Ella, he bit his lip and turned pale. Clara had written him the following:

"I enclose you a letter which was found, I suppose, by some one here. I received it through the post-office yesterday. I enclose, also, the hotel bill, which I have paid in full. As to the letter I do not blame you, since it is the expression of a passion that controls you, and I have not lost my faith in manhood because you have proved unworthy. I believe there are men too honorable to call two women '*dearest*' in the same breath. If I did not, I should not be my father's daughter.

"Surely, if there is crime in falseness, you stand accused before all courts of Love; yet you well know that the greatest crime is robbing me of the power to respect you. Love has conquered pride and even self-respect, up to this time, and I have submitted to being made a spectacle of pity and derision—I, the once adored, once honored Clara, forced by you to play the rôle of the hoodwinked wife! When married people desire to live together after they have outlived their illusions, I think they ought to guard each other's honor before the world.

"No matter now. I am going to one who never fails me; one who always loves and caresses me, even when I commit the enormity of daring to suffer. I shall never meet you again, if I can avoid it. Please have my wardrobe, household linen, and whatever belongs specially to me, sent to my father.

"You can get a divorce on the ground of desertion, if you wish to marry. I am willing, and you need not fear that any one can persuade me into opposing you. I sincerely wish you a long and happy life with one who can always be happy, and not brood so much over imaginary troubles as to prevent her being a mother—whose love will not be a 'suffocating warmth,' but one to please you in every way.

"I thank you for sending the valerian powders. I think they were not indicated in my case.

"I write with calmness, after many hours of self-examination and cool reflection as to my best course. Rest assured that I shall not regret the step that gives you cause for a formal divorce, for you have been really divorced from me since the time when you took another to your heart. The letter is very little to me—the spirit everything.

"With kindly feeling,
"CLARA FOREST."

Every word of this letter cut like a two-edged sword, and at the moment, Dr. Delano felt that he could give his life to recall his acts for the last few months. He had never dreamed that there was that in Clara which would impel her to such a step. Truly she must have suffered, before bringing herself to give up even the pleasure of ever meeting him again. He did not accept the letter, however, as a true expression of the Clara he had known. Of course she would long for his presence as days passed, and then would be the time for him to write her to return. A little scandal in a small country place could not injure him materially, but a scandal in Boston such as would be caused by a wife leaving her husband, would affect him very seriously—at this time, too, when his father, who was very fond of Clara, was very feeble. He might do something foolish.

Finally, though Albert was much troubled in mind, he comforted himself with hope ; and when the first impulse of pity for Clara's trials had passed, he began to blame her for taking such a rash step and endangering his good name before the world. This mood remained, fortifying itself, until he became convinced that he had been treated in a very shocking, even insulting manner. She would come back to him of course, but he would dictate the conditions. This settled, he went to find Ella. It was early evening, and she was walking in the maple avenue. She was almost icy in her manner, and reproached him for writing her to come to Dover.

"Why did you come, unless you wished to ? "

"It was very unkind of you," she said, not heeding his remark, "and it has caused such a horrid scandal. I don't believe I shall ever live through it. Where is Clara ?" He was silent, being a little disgusted that at such a time, Ella should think only of herself. "Oh, you need not tell me, if you don't choose to. Oh, I wish I had never come to this horrid place! and now, to make everything worse, you are all changed to me."

The ruling passion was still strong in Albert. He denied the assertion. It was against his principles to change; and as their conduct had shut them out from sympathy with all their surroundings, they naturally needed each other, and parted for the night on the best of terms, after deciding on the wisest plan to pursue. This was, for Ella to pass a month with some friends in Rhode Island, until matters were settled, while Albert was to go at once to Boston, and, by properly representing the case, forestall criticism. Here we will leave them, and go to Oakdale, to see what is passing in Dr. Forest's home at precisely the same hour.

The doctor's family were assembled in the sitting-room, where the wood-fire had just been lighted in the grate, for the evening promised to be chilly. Mrs. Forest and Leila were busily engaged with some needle-work. Linnie was deeply absorbed in *The Woman in White*, and the doctor sat silently watching the fire, forgetting to light his pipe, which had been filled for some time. Upon this quiet tableau the door opened, and Clara, pale as death and travel-stained, entered, and with one great sob threw herself into her father's arms. Mrs. Forest sprang to her feet, exclaiming, "*Clara Forest! You come home like this, and alone! Where is your husband?*"

Clara raised her head from her father's shoulder, and, turning to her mother, said, just above a whisper, and with great effort, "I have no husband. I have left Albert Delano forever!"

Mrs. Forest, forgetting everything in her horror of a woman who has the audacity to leave her husband, and such a model husband too, could not control her indignation, and burst forth in cruel reproaches. The doctor said nothing for a minute or so, but kept on soothing Clara. His patience, however, could not endure his wife's injustice. "Stop, Fannie!" he cried. "You offend me beyond endurance. Our poor girl comes to us ill and faint and weary of the world, and you receive her like this! Good God! Where is your common sense? You should think of the shock this tearing-away must cause her, and reserve your reproaches until you know the circumstances." Clara, who had been clinging to her father, sobbing convulsively, now raised her head and commenced to explain as well as she could, for speaking was almost impossible.

"My daughter," interrupted the doctor, "you need not justify yourself to me. Do I not know that it is natural for a wife to stick to her husband through thick and thin? You are a warm-hearted, honest girl, and the fact that you have left him, is enough for me. I know he has acted like a brute."

"Goodness me!" whispered Leila to her sister. "It's papa's own girl, you see, and of course she can't do anything wrong."

"Hush!" answered Linnie. "I think he's right this time, any way. See those awful black rings around her eyes!" and Linnie, obeying a kind, sisterly instinct, went to her sister and kissed her, saying, "I'm right glad to see you, sissy; but you do look *so* tired. Dinah shall make you a cup of tea, while I go and get you a warm bath ready."

"There's a good heart, Linnie," said the doctor, caressing Linnie's cheek. "The bath is just the thing. We'll try to make your sister forget her troubles, won't we?" Mrs. Forest sank into a chair and began to cry; then she got up and embraced Clara, saying, in a stricken voice, "It is dreadful! but God knows best why afflictions are sent upon me." Leila came last, and pressed her hard little mouth to her sister's cheek, thinking all the time what a dreadful fool Clara was, to leave such a splendid fellow as Dr. Delano, and so rich, too!

That night Clara was in a high fever, and seemed to want no one near her but her father; so at least he interpreted it, and sent all the rest away. He did not enjoin her to keep quiet, as so many people do under any similar circumstances. He knew there could be no greater harm done by talking of her griefs than by silently brooding over them; and as it would be folly to ask her to cease thinking of them, he allowed her to talk on until far into the night, when the quieting medicine he had given her commenced to act, and she sank into a heavy slumber, somewhat comforted by the ever-ready sympathy that she knew could never fail her. She was always as sure of it as that the day will follow the night. From her earliest years she had been in the habit of going to him, instead of her mother, with all her childish troubles. When these resulted from her own wrong-doing, his tenderness was even greater. He never scolded, never blamed her in these cases, but he did what was far wiser: he showed her his own grief that she had been guided by her lower, instead of her higher motives, and this, more than anything else could have done, inspired her to resist temptation. Another principle was continually impressed upon his children by the doctor : that yielding to base feelings made the face ugly, and that constantly being guided by kindness, love and charity, moulded all the features into beauty. Mrs. Forest always doubted the efficacy of such teaching, and did not wait longer than the next morning before telling him that Clara had never sufficiently cared for public opinion, and that this had been constantly fostered and strengthened by her father's principles.

"When you remember," said the doctor, "that I am seldom at home, that you have had ten hours to my one to instil *your* principles, you ought not to complain. Fannie, dear," he said, after a pause, and suddenly changing his defiant mood, "let us do the best we can with life. Heaven knows it is anything but a blessing to most of us." This is what he actually said, but there had been quite a different train of thought in his mind. It had just escaped utterance, through one of those mysteries of brain-action that control our motives. He had been about to say that it had been better for her, and him also, if they had separated twenty years ago ; that nothing cramps the growth of all that is best in manhood and womanhood like the forced intimacy of the marriage tie, when no deep sympathy or mutual trust exists ; that it is like preserving year after year a corpse in your drawing-room with spices and perfumes, pretending that it is only sleeping. He was glad he had not said it, for no power of his could make her enter, even for a moment, the world in which he lived ; and it was useless, and worse than useless, to attempt it. He left soon after on his round of daily visits to his patients, taking with him a note from Clara to Susie, and a little later Mrs. Forest went to Clara's room. This was an interview that Clara dreaded, for her mother would neither comprehend nor excuse her motives for the step she had taken. Clara commenced by saying she was sorry that she had been compelled to do anything that grieved her mother. As she said this she rose and begged her mother to take the arm-chair in which she had been sitting by the fire, wrapped in her mother's "double gown." Mrs. Forest refused kindly, and brought a shawl for Clara's shoulders, as the morning was cold. Clara was touched by this kindness, which she expressed by kissing her mother's hand. Mrs. Forest wanted the whole story. Clara commenced, but broke down after a few sentences. Mrs. Forest soothed her a little, and then sat down quietly and commenced to sew. One of her soothing remarks was that no doubt Albert would forgive her for leaving him, and write for her to return.

"That will only show how little he knows of my father's girl."

"Your father's girl," said Mrs. Forest, with some heat, "was always a Quixotic enthusiast, always holding notions and whims that no sober-minded person ever heard of."

"I don't know that my ambition is to be sober-minded. Heads are very good in their way, but as for me, I believe in hearts."

"And no doubt you worried Albert to death with your romantic nonsense."

"Did I?" said Clara, as if her thoughts were far away. "I wished him to love me, mother dear. If that is being romantic, I am certainly guilty."

"Of course he did love you, but you should not expect

him to go into transports every five minutes. It is foolish
to expect that, after marriage, and I think very bad taste
to desire it. If you had a child to occupy your attention,
you would think less of continual demonstration on the
part of your husband." Clara shrank lower into the folds
of her shawl. She was tired of the mention of this impossible baby.

"I am sure I would rather have my husband's love
than a thousand babies."

"A thousand! Very likely."

"Well, one then. I am glad that I found out his indifference before any such event happened; but Albert
says I shall never have any children because I am too
nervous."

"Does he? Well, I am sure that is very unkind
indeed, when you have been married so short a time. He
had no right to say such a cruel thing." Clara wondered
that her mother should give this such prominence. *She*
had been wounded by it, because of Albert's coldness;
otherwise it would not have affected her, for it could not
sound like a reproach. Mrs. Forest did not seem to comprehend the distinction. She urged Clara, by all the eloquence and argument in her power, to make up the quarrel with her husband. She urged her to consider the disgrace of her step, the wealth and standing of the Delanos,
and the social advantages of such an alliance. This failed
to move Clara, for she had not a particle of social ambition. Wealth sufficient to secure a pleasant home, with
books and flowers and ordinary luxuries, was all she wanted for herself personally; but had misfortune deprived
her of these, she would have met it without a murmur,
and worked night and day to make the deprivations less

hard for Albert to bear. This she expressed to her mother.

"Of course, any good wife would do that; but how much better," said Mrs. Forest, "to have wealth and the position that insures your reception in the highest society."

"The highest society, mother dear, I hold to be that of people of thought and solid culture, and these are always approachable without being heralded by the *fanfari* of wealth and social position."

"I presume you even regret the wealth of your husband, and dream of love in a cottage," said Mrs. Forest, with ill humor.

"How you do misunderstand me, mother dear," said Clara, wearily. "When I express the thoughts and convictions dearest and most sacred to me, you take no notice of them. It was always so with Albert; but I would not have asked even that he should understand me, if he had not grown so cold. And then his persistent solicitude about Ella, his delight in her conversation, which was like the chattering of a monkey, compared to that of any serious person—"

"You mean, compared to yours."

"Why, yes: what is the use of sham modesty in the presence of the truth? She was *not* my equal in anything. If she had been, I should wonder less at his infatuation." Here Mrs. Forest questioned Clara, and extracted the Dover affair.

"Why, Clara!" exclaimed Mrs. Forest. "Why did you not tell me this before? Why, child, I have been too severe. Of course you could not endure such dishonor. Why did you not tell me at first of this?"

"Oh, I did not think that so important. Of course he did not intend it should disgrace me. He did not mean it to be known, of course." Mrs. Forest was shocked beyond measure, and ran on for some minutes giving vent to her indignation against Miss Wills. Clara assured her that Miss Wills was guilty of no further impropriety than meeting Albert, and added, "though that makes little difference to me; when Albert's love was gone, all was gone."

Mrs. Forest was glad to have the assurance that Albert had not been guilty of "absolute infidelity," and saw the way clearly to a speedy reconciliation. "Oh, mother," said Clara, "you do not understand what separates us at all. We are talking to each other in Greek and Sanscrit. Do you not see, I cannot care so much for the body, because I care so much more for the soul? The fidelity that came from love, would be a compliment to me; but ought I to be flattered by a chastity that was merely forced by a promise? Forgive me; you are too material to comprehend that. No infidelity but one, could send me from Albert, and that he has committed a thousand times. What should I go back to? I have no husband, as I told you last night. To live with him, when he longs only for the presence of another woman, shocks my sense of morality."

"But you are married to him. You have a legal right to his property. The law does not hold you as free, nor excuse him for not taking care of you."

"Then the law is a fool. I don't care a straw for it. What right have I to his property? I did not bring any of it to him. If he were my husband in soul, there would be no degradation to my sharing it all with him; but now

13

to go back to his cold heart because simply he is obliged to take care of me, or to avoid scandal ! I beg your pardon. I would die first. If I am to be kept, simply—for mercy's sake let there be the justification of mutual love."

"Mercy !" exclaimed Mrs. Forest. "I never heard such words from a lady's mouth. Why, one would think you had no conception of the sanctity of marriage."

"Oh, mother dear, just now I called your views material, and reproached myself inwardly for the rudeness," said Clara, speaking with great difficulty, "but, honestly, you do take a view of marriage that horrifies me. There is no marriage when love is dead. I could not live through such a solemn farce;" and Clara sank back quite exhausted, and Mrs. Forest, trusting she would listen to reason when she grew calmer, left the room.

CHAPTER XXVIII.

THE EFFECT OF DR. DELANO'S FORGIVENESS.

AS soon as Clara recovered her strength somewhat, she visited Susie daily, and spent a great deal too much time with her, to please Mrs. Forest. One day she found her in her conservatory, where the sashes were all raised, busily planting young tube-rose plants in pots. "These," said Susie, "*must* not flower until December;" and she spoke as though the fate of worlds depended upon her success. "If you never go back, Clara, we will build up a great florist business. We will not only sell flowers, but shrubs, and shade-trees, and evergreens. See these little junipers and spruces," she added, leading Clara to the garden; "they grow just perfectly. Oh, if I only had a thousand dollars! but I shall make quite a little sum this winter;" and so she ran on detailing her hopes and plans, and as she talked, she stooped among brilliant beds of verbenas, and with her scissors commenced the most merciless onslaught, cutting off every flower, and even all the stalks for some inches. Clara uttered an exclamation at the devastation.

"You see I *may* fail with my tube-roses, but I am sure of these. By cutting back the plants, and making the earth soft and rich about them, I force splendid cutting that will root easily, and make nice plants for winter flowering. I have a cooler spot in my conservatory for verbenas."

" Why, Susie, how much you know about the subject !" said Clara, admiringly, as Susie went on with her work.

" I know a little about botany, you see, and I learned a great many practical details at Anderson's. You've no idea how kind he was and is to me. He has engaged to buy every tube-rose, orange-blossom, camellia, violet, and white-rose I can produce from October to April. I shall send my first orange-blossoms in a few days. At Christmas every camellia will bring fifty cents. I shall get forty-five if he retails them at fifty. I only had thirty last winter, but I ought to have at least fifty this coming winter, and the next winter, oh, Clara ! I can have ten times that number easily ; but I want some one to help me. Mrs. Buzzell is growing old, and cannot do as much of the house-work as she did, and I *must* not neglect my flowers."

" Why should I not come with you ? " asked Clara, enthusiastically. " Susie, I have an ' impression,' as the spiritualists say, that this is a heaven-appointed way for you and me to work out our salvation together. I can sell my watch, if necessary, though I would hate to do it. It is an elegant chronometer, given me by father Delano. I am crazy to work, Susie. Can I not do something now ? Why should these fine verbenas lie here to rot, and here you have sweet-mignonette by the yard, all in blossom ! "

" If I only had a place in the city for little bouquets, not the conventional style, but sweet little ones for the hair and to wear at the breast ; " and while she was speaking, she took a spray of scarlet-verbena, set it around with mignonette and a bordering of apple-geranium leaves. "They ought to bring ten cents at this season—at least five."

"Why, Susie, they could be sold by the thousand. I believe Miss Galway, my dresssmaker, could dispose of any number. Let us set to work at once and make up a hundred of them, and you take them to her to-morrow, with a letter from me. I have her confidence, and can count on her assent. Nothing will be lost anyway, if we fail." Susie seized the opportunity, and the work commenced. A layer of thirty just covered the bottom of the basket Susie provided—a very ugly basket, that came from the florist's with Neapolitan violet roots. Five layers, one hundred and fifty bouquets, were ready before Clara left, and the next morning, at ten o'clock, were actually on sale in Miss Galway's window, labeled "ten cents each." Susie returned in high spirits. She had found Miss Galway charming. Two of the bouquets had been sold in five minutes. "Oh, Clara!" she exclaimed, "if I had only known, I could have kept her supplied all summer." At the end of three days, Miss Galway wrote, enclosing twelve dollars, the balance after deducting commission. "The last of the flowers, Miss Galway said, had been sold toward evening, on the Common, by her little sister, who was anxious to sell more." They had pleased Miss Galway's customers, especially because of the rare fragrance of the geranium. Susie sent more, but the stock soon diminished, for she had not counted on this new market. The apple-geranium became precious, and new plans commenced to mature in Susie's ever-active brain.

Meanwhile Mrs. Forest was anxious. Clara's attention

was being called away from the one string her mother constantly kept harping on—the reconciliation. Dr. Forest, however, encouraged the firm of "Dykes and Delano," as he called it, and promised to put some money into the "concern." He was delighted at Clara's first successful idea. "What a thoroughly woman's way of doing things," he said. "No man would ever have had the cheek to impress a dressmaker into the flower business. Go on; you two women have good business notions, and you are sure of success." Mrs. Forest heard these encouragements with inward pain, and finally, when she could not endure the silence of Clara's husband any longer, she wrote to him herself. Her letter was a masterpiece of shallow tact. What he read very plainly "between the lines," was, that he had only to whistle for Clara, and she would fly to him like a submissive spaniel; though Mrs. Forest had by no means intended to make him too confident. She had dwelt long upon the duty to society devolving upon married people, and upon the necessity of circumspect conduct in husbands. The answer came immediately, and was a triumph to Mrs. Forest, who lost no time in bringing the matter up before the doctor and Clara. That day Clara had felt wretched, and had kept her room. She had suffered one of those inevitable relapses, which all those who have "loved and lost" can perfectly understand. It is one of the tricks Love plays us, to leave an impress of his own divine beauty in the heart, through whatever form he has gained entrance there. Clara had been mourning her dead for months, and the agony had only returned on that day, as it had often returned before. The worst of it had been endured, when her father came in in the afternoon. "To-day is a bad day for you, darling, I see. Life is a grasshopper, isn't it ? " This was one of his distortions of the text, " The grasshopper shall be a burden, and desire shall fail."

When Mrs. Forest came in, an hour later, Clara was lying on the lounge and the doctor was reading to her. Mrs. Forest, feeling in a very complaisant mood, and not wishing to present immediately the subject of Albert's letter, sat down to her sewing, and begged the doctor to go on reading. He finished some ten pages of a critique on *Heat as a Mode of Motion*, by Professor Tyndall.

" Well, I call that ponderous," said Mrs. Forest, greatly relieved when the reading ended. " Do *you* really find anything interesting in that, Clara ? "

" Certainly I do, mamma dear. Why do you ask ? "

" Well, it seems to me positive affectation. I can't believe you understand that explanation of expansion by heat."

" But I do. I have read the original carefully. See ! " and taking a lot of spools from her mother's work-basket, she piled them up compactly, their sides all parallel. " Now imagine these spools the atoms of iron, for example, as they lie when the iron is cold. Now a motion is set up among these atoms. That motion is heat, and it changes the relative position of the atoms in this way, or something like it, only I can't make them stand; but don't you see, if I pile them so that their corners only touch, they will occupy more space ? "

" Well, yes. I think I see it somewhat mistily ; but where did you read this and other ponderous books like it ? I think I remember you devoting your time to novels, quite as naturally as other girls."

"Oh, I read a great deal at Stonybrook. We had a blue-stocking society, only we called it *The Bas Bleu Club*. We met every Saturday morning, and darned our stockings to the accompaniment of such reading as this, and the girl who read, got her own stockings darned that day for nothing. One of our obligations was to let nothing pass until we thoroughly comprehended it, and sometimes the matter would be so ponderous, as you say, and our interruptions so numerous, that we got over scarcely a page at a sitting; but we learned a great deal in that way; even our crude guesses at the author's meaning often led to the truth, and our circuitous wandering had a comical charm about it."

"And how many young ladies could be induced to spend their time so seriously?"

"We commenced with over sixty, dwindled down to about twenty, and kept that number very steadily. Miss Marston was the only teacher whom we ever invited to join us. One of her tricks deceived us for a long time. This was to pretend ignorance, and get the other *Bas Bleus* to enlighten her. When we found her out, we revenged ourselves by assuming that she knew nothing, and so explained everything elaborately."

"A secret society, no doubt," said the doctor.

"Oh, yes. We were sworn to the deepest secrecy. We were required to swear by the '*unholeyness* of our stockings;' and when any candidate blushed and hesitated, there was a roar, and we mercifully changed the oath to the 'un-hole-y-ness of our future stockings.'"

"And pray, which way did you swear, my dear?"

"Now, mamma dear, that is personal," said Clara, laughing. "When the session was over, the stockings all nicely mended, and our heads well crammed with scientific nuts for future digestion, the *Bas Bleus* gave way to the most unrestrained jollity. Miss Marston was perfectly charming, and the greatest romp among us. Often, the next Monday in class, listening to her demonstration of problems in trigonometry, we could hardly believe that this grave personage was the *Bas Bleu* who had actually rolled on the carpet with us in the exciting exercise known as *cat's cradle*. But I'm sure no one ever peached, and I don't think she would have cared if any one had."

"No," said the doctor. "Those who have real dignity are never afraid of losing it."

"Young ladies' schools of to-day are very different, I think, from those of my time," said Mrs. Forest. "The teachers I used to know never descended from their dignity pedestal, and if they had I don't think they would have been able to get back again with the grace of Miss Marston." Here Mrs. Forest inquired particularly about the late visit of that lady to the White Mountains, and this lead easily to the object Mrs. Forest had nearest at heart. The doctor sat very quiet while she urged Clara in the most earnest way, to make up her mind to be reconciled to her husband. "You do not feel as I do in this matter," she said, appealing to the doctor. "I do so wish you did."

"If I could feel it to be for the best, Fannie, I would use every effort in my power to bring about a reconciliation."

"Then why do you not do it?" Mrs. Forest asked, brightening up suddenly.

"Because, simply, I can't believe it for the best."

Mrs. Forest's countenance fell. Clara sighed but said nothing while her mother talked of Dr. Delano, wondering why she spoke so confidently of his sentiments toward his wife. Mrs. Forest urged the natural goodness and uprightness of Albert, his anxiety for his wife's return, the blessedness of forgiveness, and then the terrible evils that would result if idle tongues were not made to cease their gossiping.

"Have I not been taught," replied Clara, wearily, "to avoid doing wrong, not from fear of punishment, but from the love of right, and faith in the beneficent results of a wise course—to defy all scandal, if only I was sure of being guided by my best feelings?"

"Our feelings are a blind guide," said Mrs. Forest, reproachfully. "That is your father's teaching, and I must confess I don't see the good effects of it."

"One good effect was going contrary to your advice, mother dear, and befriending Susie Dykes."

"The end is not yet," said Mrs. Forest, sententiously, and apparently much occupied with her sewing. "I believe such latitudinarian sentiments weakened your chances of gaining the permanent respect of your husband. Had you firmly insisted at first that you would not have that ill-regulated Miss Wills in your house, your husband would have honored you all the more for it."

"I never should have dreamed of such a policy," said Clara, very earnestly. "If we had gone and settled in the Desert of Sahara immediately after marriage, where Albert had never seen any woman but me, to be sure, he might not have changed; but I am not proud of a love that I cannot hold against all the flirts in the world

Miss Wills has certainly a greater charm for Albert than I have, and I wish her joy of her conquest. I've cried out about all the tears there are, as Susie said of Dan, and I mean to be sensible, and see if I cannot live without a husband who is the lover of another woman. I mean to go into the flower business with good, true-hearted Susie Dykes."

Mrs. Forest let her sewing drop, but seeing it was not wise to oppose Clara on two points at once, she returned to Albert. He was, she said, very anxious to atone for the past. He could never be happy as he was. He had no deep regard for any one but his wife. Here Mrs. Forest unfolded a letter. Clara's heart beat violently. "Oh, if he does really want me! if he does really love me!" cried she. "Convince me only of that, and I will fly to him. I will humbly ask his forgiveness, and devote every hour of my life to making him happy."

"Well, well, do let us hear what he says," said the doctor, impatiently, seeing with alarm the excited condition of Clara. Amid the most perfect silence, Mrs. Forest smoothed out her letter and commenced :

"MY DEAR MRS. FOREST :—You cannot doubt that I regret as much as you do, the step my wife has taken, and I appreciate the sympathy you kindly offer.

"In my opinion, Mrs. Delano is entirely unjustifiable in so rash a movement. A wife should trust her husband until she has absolute proof of his infidelity. Mrs. Delano will not pretend that she has any such proof, though I admit indiscretion on my part. Tell her, if she will return at once, before any more mischief is wrought by idle tongues, I shall forgive her leaving me, and endeavor hereafter to avoid causes of trouble between us. Until she returns there is nothing more for me to say or do in the premises.

"Accept, dear madam, assurances of my profound respect.

"ALBERT DELANO, M.D."

When Mrs. Forest ended, Clara was lying with her face to the wall, her hand pressed tightly over her heart. Dr. Forest, looking intently into vacancy, was whistling a low melancholy air. Clara turned her head, and as their eyes met, gravity sat on both faces like a pall ; but only for an instant, and then both simultaneously burst into laughter; but Clara's tears flowed at the same time, and her whole frame was convulsed hysterically.

"Fannie," said the doctor, alarmed at Clara's condition, "your letter is too tragic, by far. Go quick and get me some brandy, and have Dinah bring a hot foot-bath."

CHAPTER XXIX.

THE COUNT VON FRAUENSTEIN.

THE fragments of the golden bowl, to use Clara's figure, could not be patched together, and at last Mrs. Forest gave up all hope, and took refuge in the consolations of religion, in a saintly, aggravating way that was hard to witness. Whenever Clara proposed any change in her own life, or even suggested anything for the comfort of the family, the answer was invariably and with a martyr-like sigh of resignation, " Do anything you like. I have no preference." Therefore, as the autumn advanced, Clara spent more and more time with Mrs. Buzzell and Susie. One day the old lady said to Clara, " You had better come here and live. Leila and Linnie are with your mother, and she does not need you. I am really beginning to fear, now I am getting so old, that Min will be neglected. Susie is perfectly absorbed with her potting, and rooting, and slipping, and re-potting, and really she ought not to have any other responsibilities. She used to help Mary a great deal, but now Mary herself is bewitched, and likes nothing so well as ' flower-work,' as she calls it. I expect nothing but that she will abandon the cooking and washing, and take permanently to potting and rooting. If you were here, you could keep Mary out of the clutches of that conservatory. Min will be the next victim," said Mrs. Buzzell, laughing.

"This morning I found her 'helping mamma,' as she said, and Susie declared she was doing good service. This consisted in filling up small pots with soil. The implement used, I noticed, was my big iron kitchen spoon ; but I said nothing. When I see a woman seriously working to gain an independent position, I am always delighted. I never spent any money in my life that brought me such pleasure as that which I invested in that hot-house ; and I'm going to do more, Clara, but, you understand, that is a secret."

"You have already proved yourself a noble friend to Susie," said Clara, warmly.

"Oh, she's done more for me than I ever did for her. I have not had a moment's loneliness since she came, and my health has been better. Min, too, is a great pleasure to me. Though the little rat will pull my work-basket about, I notice she never touches a leaf or flower of Susie's plants, and it wouldn't be healthy for her to do so, I suspect," Mrs. Buzzell added, smiling.

"It is wonderful," said Clara, "that Susie has acquired such a knowledge of flower culture. I don't even now understand the secret of her success."

"The secret, my dear Clara, is the secret of all honest success—eternal vigilance. She failed in several things at first. Her tube-roses, for example, grew all stalks and no flowers. Then the insects troubled her. She fought them by main force at first, but now she has made a discovery—a vase of carbolic soap-suds did not quite meet her expectations, so she added laudanum to it—pure empirical experiment, you see. That was an improvement; then she put in the vase one of the doctor's nastiest old pipe-bowls, and really, I think that was a great discovery. With a little mop she washes the bark of her plants with this mixture; every day some plant is treated, and so she keeps all insects at bay. She actually cried with joy when I promised to build the hot-house. She had not dared to hope for so much, though she often asked me how far I thought one hundred dollars would go towards building a little one, ten feet square. You know I never spent the hundred from Dan, which you gave into my keeping. She thinks it went into the conservatory, but I put something with it and put it by for Min's education; but that, also, is one of my secrets."

But the movement of our story is too slow. We will therefore make a rapid dash over just one year. During this time, Clara, who had taken up her residence with Mrs. Buzzell, suffered many a sleepless night, thinking over her buried hopes, and sometimes feeling as if her life was an utter failure; but the gloom was always dissipated with the hour or so of pleasant morning work with Susie among the flowers, and with the pleasant reunion afterward at the breakfast-table. Mrs. Buzzell, though quite feeble, was always present in her arm-chair, wrapped in her shawl, and Min, also seated in her high-chair, joyous as a bird and as full of animal spirits as a kitten, and of mischief as a young monkey. Her special duty was to arrange a bouquet for the centre of the breakfast table, having *carte blanche* to use her own taste on the flowers and leaves that her mother gave her for the purpose. Mrs. Buzzell used to praise their arrangement without much discretion, but Min had learned by this time to separate her scarlet and blue flowers by white ones, or green leaves, and when she won a compliment from her mother she was always delighted. On one of these occasions, Min sat pouting and would not touch her food.

" What is the matter with my little pet? " asked Clara, twisting one of the child's long, golden tresses.

" I shan't tell."

Mrs. Buzzell looked at Min, praised the toast and the excellence of the coffee, and then, as if suddenly noticing the bouquet, added, " and those pretty flowers! How nicely Minnie has arranged them. Her taste grows better every day." Min's appetite suddenly appeared; but Susie said, " I do not much admire that character which manifests happiness only when praised, and when the temper is not tried. Do you, Clara? I think that is the strongest and best nature which finds its pleasure in making others happy, and that temper is the sweetest which is sweet under vexations." Min knew this was aimed at her, and she suddenly turned the subject of conversation.

" I used to fear," said Mrs. Buzzell, " that my old age would be lonely and cheerless; but God has been infinitely good to me. See what a pleasant family I have about me, when I am weak and need so much care. And with Min to bother me by asking questions I can't answer, surely my life lacks nothing. What do you think of it, Min ? " she asked, addressing the spoiled pet.

" I should think God *might* be good to auntie, 'cause auntie is so good to Min."

" I think you had better not consult Min on points of faith and doctrine," said Clara. " She seems to inherit some of her grandpapa's heresies."

" Auntie Clara, who is my grandpapa ? "

" Why, your doctor, as you call him."

"Is he? honest and true, Auntie Clara? Then I shall call him grandpapa."

"No, no," said Susie, with a faint flush on her face. "Call him just as you do now." She was wondering for the thousandth time how it would be when Minnie commenced to go to school, for example. Children would tell her of her father, and perhaps say ill things of her mother. Already the child's resemblance to Mrs. Forest was remarkable, and grew more marked every day. The likeness consisted particularly in a kind of droop to the eyelids toward the outer corners, giving a dreamy, refined expression. Only a short time before, when Min was playing at the gate, a little girl, one of Mrs. Kendrick's guests, came and made her acquaintance, and asked her to walk with her. Min ran and got permission of "auntie," and started off. They turned up shortly after on the doctor's broad door-steps, and Mrs. Forest, recognizing one of Mrs. Kendrick's visitors, made the children go in, and treated them to cake. She was greatly struck by the rare beauty of the little blonde, and asked her her name. "Sha'n't tell," was the reply, of course. The doctor came in a few minutes later. At the sight of Min seated on her grandmother's knees, eating jelly-cake with great gusto, he burst out laughing. This evidently displeased Min, and kept her from obeying her first impulse, which was to run to "my doctor," as she always called him. "How very maternal you are, Fannie! Whose child is that?"

"She won't tell me her name," said Mrs. Forest, "but she is one of Mrs. Kendrick's friends. Is she not lovely?" she added, toying with Min's rich, sunny hair. The doctor took the child and asked his wife to follow him.

Standing before the mirror in the drawing-room, he held the child's face beside his wife's, saying, "Look at that child's eyes, and then at yours."

"Good heavens, doctor ! You don't mean—"

"That it is your only grandchild !"

Mrs. Forest tied on Min's hat, and suggested to the older girl that she had better not bring the little one so far from home again.

"I sha'n't come to see you again," said Minnie, feeling her dignity offended, "and I sha'n't let my doctor come, either. My Auntie Clara don't send Minnie away." And the child's eyes filled, but she would not cry. The doctor tried to pet her, but she drew away pouting. The doctor looked out of the window as the little ones toddled down the street, and then turning to his wife, tried to waken kindly feelings for Dan's child ; but the seed fell on stony ground. While he was talking, a carriage drove up to the gate and left the Count von Frauenstein. Mrs. Forest was in a flutter. To be so honored by a rich and titled person was a great event. Finding the doctor free, the count stayed to lunch, and talked over great plans that were maturing in his mind. He had just returned from Guise, in France, where he had visited the grand social palace founded by a great French capitalist for his workmen. "I tell you, Dr. Forest," he said, with enthusiasm, "the age is ripe for a grand spring toward social organization, and the sight of that palace of workers inspires me with new hope. There are over a thousand people, honest wealth-producers, surrounded by a sum of conveniences and luxuries to be found nowhere else on the planet, even among the rich."

"Why, I never heard of it !" said Mrs. Forest, pouring

the count a glass of wine, produced freely on this occasion in honor of the distinguished gentleman. " I am greatly interested. What are some of these luxuries ? Do those workmen actually live in a palace ? "

" Aye, madam. A magnificent structure it is, too, I assure you. It is surrounded by groves and gardens and rich fields, through which winds the River Oise. There are nurseries and schools on a magnificent scale, for the children. There are swimming and hot and cold baths for all, medical service of the best, a restaurant, a billiard saloon, a café, a charming theatre, a library and reading-room, societies for various objects, such as music and the drama, beside the board, composed of men and women, who manage the internal affairs of the palace. All the courts of the palace are covered with glass, and the various suites of apartments open on corridors in these courts." The doctor inquired about the water supply, and the ventilation. The latter, the count said, was effected by gigantic underground galleries, opening into the courts, connected by tubes passing up through the walls and opening into each apartment, where they were used mostly in winter, as every suite of rooms was well supplied with windows on the courts, and also on the exterior of the building.

" I am sure it must be a wonderful charity," said Mrs. Forest.

" No, madam," said the count ; " every one of the advantages I have named, and many more, are included in the rents, and Monsieur Godin, the founder, makes six per cent. on the capital invested. It has been in successful operation some twelve years."

Further conversation developed the fact that the count

was to leave the next day to look after business investments in the South and West, which might detain him
some weeks, or even months, after which, he was determined to see what he could do by way of a social palace
for workmen and their families. "Oakdale," he said, "is
not a bad field to commence in. Your industries are
growing, the population rapidly increasing, it is a very
healthy location, pure water, and a nice light soil. I
don't believe in heavy soils. Scientific culture finds more
scope and success with a light one. The doctor was eager
for the experiment. "Before I die, Frauenstein," he
said, "I hope to see a few children, at least, surrounded
by conditions for integral culture. Count on me for
everything in my power to aid the work." Mrs. Forest was a little shocked at the doctor's addressing the
count as simply, "Frauenstein." "It would seem to me,
count," she said, in her suavest tone, "that you, with
your wealth and social position, would find more pleasure
in building yourself a palace, where you could surround
yourself with all that wealth can procure."

"My dear madam, what should I do for society?"

"Goodness gracious!" thought Mrs. Forest, "he is as
crazy as the doctor;" but she asked him to please explain.

"I am very familiar, madam," he replied, "with what
is known as the best society, and of course there is much
real refinement and much honorable sentiment among its
various members; but real nobility of sentiment, by
which I mean devotion to the broad interests of mankind, is very rarely met, and least of all at the courts of
rulers. They are all cramped and degraded by petty
aims, petty intrigues for personal advancement; and

above all, they are lacking the first element of wisdom—
a belief in the people. What is the aristocracy of birth,
name, inherited wealth robbed from generations of wages-
slaves, compared to the grander aristocracy of labor,
which is as old as the evolution of man himself? My
mother, Kendrick's cousin, you know, was the grand-
daughter of a day-laborer. Kendrick wouldn't mention
it for his best span of horses, but I am proud of it. So
far as I know he is the only ancestor I have, who had an
honest right to the bread he ate. So you see, madam, I
would do something to atone for the sins of all the robber
crew to which I belong, and so shorten my prospective
hours in purgatory. To be serious, there is no congenial
society for me anywhere, as life is ordered at present. I
must help to build up a society of men and women who
can be honest and free, because sure of the present and
of the future for themselves and their children. I found
more intelligence, more faith in humanity, and more freedom of expression among those workingmen at Guise,
than I ever met among any set of people in my life ; and
the children, madam ! O, the children ! I can give you no
idea of their rosy health, their frank expression of advanced opinions, and their courteous manners." Mrs.
Forest said that what she understood as "advanced
opinions" would be a very equivocal attraction in a child
according to her way of seeing things.

"But, madam, your way of seeing things," said the
count, courteously, "would be different, if you had been
trained to positive methods of thought. I assure you, in
any case, you would be charmed by the ease, and grace of
address of many of those children. Why it would make
you regret that you were not the mother of the whole

three hundred of them ! There are prizes given them for politeness and grace of bearing.—Think of it ! There is the commencement of stirpiculture, and yet the stupid, lunk-head scientists of the world, are giving *all* their attention to the fossils of a dead past. Depend upon it, madam, this world need not be the vale of tears we have been taught to think. Life is what we should study. Life is what we should love, and as a general rule, the present is the best time to live ; " and the count, praising Mrs. Forest's wine, and apologizing for making a monologue of what should have been a conversation, bade her good-bye and left, taking the doctor with him.

The next day the doctor spent a full hour at Mrs. Buzzell's talking to Clara of Frauenstein and his grand social-palace scheme. Clara expressed regret that she had not seen him. " Regret ! " said the doctor, " you may well regret, for you have lost a rare pleasure. When you see him you will love him, and at first sight too. I am sure of it, for he is the only man I ever met whom I thought worthy of you. He is coming back, though, and then you shall see him. He's a man after my own heart in everything. He's perfect ; he's without a flaw. I know him just as well as if I had been intimate with him for years. Every thought and feeling of the man is honest and true, and what is better than all, he has faith in human nature." Clara was interested, but the count was no vital part of her thoughts as he was of her father's, and besides her heart was filled that day with its old pain. Albert had written, saying simply that, as a year had passed, he thought he had a right to expect she would have had time to reflect upon their mutual position, and that he hoped she had decided to return. It was a very cold letter, but it moved her deeply, and under the first impulse she wrote, sinking every thought of pride, hoping only, blindly, that he would, by an impulse as simple, and as frankly expressed as hers, prove that he loved her despite all that had happened. She wrote:

"DEAR ALBERT:—Your letter moves me deeply, but it does not show me that you have any tender thought of me, any motive of real love in saying you expect me to return. Do you know so little of me after all, as to suppose that I can be influenced by the wealth you speak of? Can you doubt that I would rather be your wife were you poor and unknown, if you only loved me as once you did, than to be your queen were you master of the world, if I must see you seek in other women that which I alone would give?

"Oh, Albert! why can I never make you see me as I am? I have no pride, as you think; willingly would I prove myself the very queen of fools in the eyes of the world—would kneel in the dust and kiss your feet, could I thereby find that you love me with the divine tenderness that once made my life. Dear one, what shall I say? What shall I do? I long, with all my being, for the tender words you used to breathe so eloquently, for the sight of your beautiful eyes, for your kisses and caresses. If you do really want me—me, not your legal mate, but Clara—you will show me this beyond the shadow of a doubt.

"I cannot tell you how I have suffered, and do suffer still, at times. I pray only that I may wake from this long cold night of misery, and find myself in the blessed warmth and light of that love which made me once your proud and happy   CLARA."

To this letter he wrote, among other things not touching the subject nearest Clara's heart: "If you love me so ineffably as you would have me think you do, I should like you to show it in the only possible way—by coming home at once. As for me, I do not pretend to sentiment. We should not trouble ourselves with riddles, dear Clara, but love where we may beneficently, and as much as we can."

To this Clara replied as promptly as to the other: "At last, Albert, I fully understand you. You are true to yourself in this letter, and I respect you for it. You might as well have told me in so many words, 'I do not want my love, but the mistress of my house.' Well, Albert, receive my final, eternal answer: *I shall never go back to you while I live.* Again I assure you, I have no pride. I confess that my eyes are red with weeping, for I have shed the first tears of absolute despair that I ever knew. Until now there has been hope, however faint, but now, every trace is gone. Hereafter, we will study the problems of life as if we had never met."

When Dr. Delano received this letter he knew that all was over, and regretted that he had not played his cards better. He did not love Clara, but he was proud of her, and knew that, as a wife, she was an honor to him. He had not doubted seriously that she would return, and he had intended to humble her by his forgiveness, and in the future make her, through this lesson, a patient, dependent, and wholly exemplary wife. Now there was no hope of

this, and, to make matters worse, Charlotte utterly refused
to see Miss Wills. Mr. Delano died soon after, leaving
all his property to his son, except his daughter's portion.
He had been kept in ignorance, on account of his illness
and his very nervous condition, of the breach between
Clara and his son. He left her his kindest wishes, and
the hope that through her, the family name might be preserved. After his death his daughter wrote a very kind
letter to Clara, manifesting a depth of womanly feeling
which Clara had never suspected could exist under the
austere manners of Miss Delano. From this there arose
a correspondence between them, and the utter frankness
and sweetness of Clara's nature, as it developed in this
new relation, had a great charm for Miss Charlotte. At
first she tried to persuade Clara to return to her husband;
but having the whole case presented to her in a simple
and clear light, she finally approved Clara's course. She
expressed herself strongly on the want of delicacy in men's
treatment of women, and her own satisfaction that she
herself had never given any one of them the power over
her happiness that Clara had. "Come and see me," she
wrote, "whenever you are in the city. I like you and
trust you ; and if you think a sour-tempered old maid
worth cultivating, it will be a great consolation to me."

CHAPTER XXX.

EVENTS which could not be foreseen, were destined to work great changes in the circumstances of several of our characters. One of these—the death of good Mrs. Buzzell—we will pass over quickly, for it is not specially profitable to linger over such scenes of bereavement as the loss of a dear and true friend.

The rich Buzzells in Oakdale had never recognized her existence except in a purely conventional way, and as they were only relatives of her husband, she felt perfectly justified in disposing of her property as she saw fit. She gave all her real estate in trust with "the firm of Dykes, Delano & Company, florists, for Minnie, daughter of Dan Forest and Susie Dykes." "It is the best thing I can do for her," she said, a day or two before she died, while caressing the child, who stood by the arm of "auntie's" big chair. "It will make her independent, in a modest way; so if she chooses to enjoy the luxury of living an old maid, she can do so."

"I sha'n't be a ole maid," said the young lady, replying to the first intelligible words of Mrs. Buzzell.

"I suppose not, dear. You'll give some man the chance to break your heart. I only say you can if you wish," said Mrs. Buzzell. Her furniture and personal property she gave to Susie, and to the firm, a present of one thousand dollars; and so, having set her "house in order," as she said, leaving a kind message for Mrs. Forest, who had so long neglected her, and holding the hand of her well-beloved Dr. Forest, she dropped into her rest, apparently without a shadow of pain.

Some two months after this event, Dr. Forest was roused from his warm bed by a policeman, requesting him to go quickly to the station-house to see if he could revive an unfortunate, who had just been dragged from the icy river.

"Don't wait for me," said the doctor, coming to the head of the stairs in his night-gown. "Go back, and have her stripped and put into warm blankets. Lay her on her stomach and rub her till I come."

The doctor found the rough functionaries at the police-station working over the patient as he had directed, their sympathies being more active from the fact that she was young, and evidently pretty; though not much beauty could be recognized in the deathly pallor, the half-closed eyelids, and the drenched and matted hair that clung to her face and neck. The men pronounced her dead. "I hope not," said the doctor, hastily relieving himself of his overcoat and coming forward. "I think we may revive her," he said, after pinching her flesh and watching intently for signs of circulation. He gave his orders quickly, and then commenced the slow and difficult process of discharging the water from the lungs and inflating them. To the squeamish, and to the unscientific, the operations of the doctor with this ghastly, limp subject, would have seemed unsightly; but no careful observer could have failed to admire Dr. Forest, seeing him thus professionally absorbed. He was excited, as you could see by the intense expression of his whole face but commanding every muscle perfectly, never hesitating, never making a false or awkward motion, he continued his work for about forty minutes, though it would have seemed much longer to a mere spectator. One of these, the officer in charge, seeing no sign of life and becoming impatient with so much apparently useless effort, said in a low tone, " Oh, what is the use, doctor ? Anybody can see she is dead."

" My dear sir," said the doctor, without looking up, " your opinion don't amount to much in this instance. See ! the color is coming ; we have saved her ! " None but the quick, well-trained eye of the doctor could see any change yet, however ; but in a few minutes it was apparent to all. One of the men recognized the young girl as one he had seen at " old mother Torbit's," who was well known as the keeper of a disreputable house. " Poor little woman ! " said the officer. " It's questionable whether we've done her a favor. I think any very unhappy wretch has a right to seek a short cut out of his misery."

" Suppose the short cut don't get you out of the misery," said another policeman, who was placing fresh bottles of hot water at the patient's feet.

" The world has a right to our lives," said the doctor. " We have scarcely a moral right to destroy ourselves, and certainly not while we are free from hideous and certainly mortal diseases."

There was little to be done after respiration had been restored to the patient. In a few minutes she opened her eyes and drew the blankets higher over her breast. One of the officers was struck by this movement, and called the doctor's attention to it, saying, "She has some modesty left. She can't be wholly lost."

"Of course not, or she would not have attempted suicide," said the doctor ; "but shame at exposing the person is no evidence of purity in itself. It is a higher sense of purity that keeps men and women from courses that degrade the moral nature." After a while the doctor asked if there were no better beds in the station than the one on which the girl lay—a miserable old mattress, stretched on a rickety iron bedstead. Being informed that there were not, except in the rooms of the officers, the doctor made up his mind suddenly, and sent one of the men for a hack. As he was wrapping another blanket around the girl, preparatory to her removal, she looked around wildly, and exclaimed, "Oh, why did you take me from the river ? "

"My dear," said the doctor, kindly, "I'm going to take you where you will find sympathy and love, if you are only a sensible girl."

"Oh, I was dead. I know I was dead, and it was all over ; " and she sobbed and moaned in a low tone that touched the tender heart of the doctor. He said : "Well, my dear child, just consider yourself resurrected into a new life. Shut the past all out. You have a good face, and a nice round head. I shall expect great things of you ; " and he smoothed back her wet hair, in a gentle, fatherly fashion, that made her sobs break out anew.

Of course the doctor drove to the home of Clara and Susie. Where else could he take a poor, abandoned woman for womanly sympathy and help ? Hearing the carriage drive up to the gate, and then the loud ring at the door, Clara was alarmed. Throwing on her dressing-gown and putting her bare feet in slippers, she ran down before the servant was out of bed. Her first thought was that something had happened to her father. She was quickly reassured when she opened the door. He had already dismissed the hackman, and stood on the porch with his burden in his arms.

"Papa, dear! What is it? But come in quickly, out of the cold. I was afraid something had happened to you." The doctor laid the partially unconscious girl down, as he said, "It is a poor girl, dragged from the river to-night. The police-station is such a beastly place I couldn't leave her there."

"We must get her into bed at once," said Clara, opening the blankets timidly to see the face. What bed? she was thinking. The one guest-room was too immaculate for such uses—"too cold, too," she said aloud. "I think we must carry her to my bed. Is she —nice, papa?"

"She must, at least, be well washed *outside*," said the doctor, with grim humor, amused at the feminine scruple of his daughter.

"Well, papa, we'll put her right into my warm bed. Won't that be best?"

"Yes, dear. The warmth is what she needs, and your bed must be warmed by a magnetism that should be good for a Magdalen." Here the new servant, Ellen, came in. Mary, Mrs. Buzzell's old servant, had taken a vacation, and was visiting her friends in a distant State. Ellen stared at the muffled figure, but her amazement was intense when, in Clara's room, the partial removal of the blankets revealed a perfectly limp, nude form.

"Mother of God, doctor! Where are the craythur's

clothes?" Clara soon produced a bed-gown, and wrapping her in this, placed her in bed and revived her with stimulants. At this juncture Susie entered, and dismissed Ellen. Then followed an amiable dispute between Susie and Clara, as to which should watch with the patient.

"Well, my girls," the doctor said, holding an arm about each and kissing their foreheads alternately, "I will go home and get some sleep. You will take good care of this poor child, and make her forgive us for bringing her back to life. She came to, once, at the station, and reproached us for taking her from the river. Keep giving her this wine, a teaspoonful at a time, and by-and-by something more nourishing. I'll come over after breakfast. I'm afraid she may have a fever, and give you a great deal of trouble; but I couldn't—well, I couldn't do anything but bring her here."

"You did perfectly right, papa, as you always do. Of course, this will prove another blessing in disguise. Do you think she is conscious now?"

"Yes; she hears all we say, in a dreamy kind of way, I think."

The two women sat by the patient until daylight. She had opened her eyes many times, looking around as if wondering whether she was awake or dreaming. At last, she looked at Susie earnestly for a long time, and then began to cry. Susie comforted her in the kindest way, telling her she was among friends, where she would find plenty to do, and need never go back to her old life. Later in the morning she woke much refreshed, after a long sleep. At first she thought she was alone; but hearing a soft, low singing, she rose up in bed and saw a golden-haired angel, as she almost believed, sitting on the carpet, turning over the leaves of a picture-book. Seeing the stranger awake, the child climbed upon the foot of the bed, folded her hands demurely, and looked into the new face.

"What is your name, little girl?"

"My name is Minnie, and I am my doctor's pet."

"Who is your doctor?"

"My doctor! Don't you know? Why, he brought you here in his arms last night. Mamma said so. Don't you want to go down and see our conservatory?" Min asked, after a pause, anxious to be quite hospitable.

"I fear I am too weak, you sweet little pet, but I should like some water very much."

"Well, my dear, I will bring you some," said the little lady, patronizingly, sliding down from the bed. Susie came back with Minnie, bringing some wine gruel; and as she gave it, she asked the girl's name. "My name is Annie Gilder. I will tell you all about myself. I am not so bad as you think I am. I will tell you all. Shall I?"

"Yes, if you like," answered Susie; "as much as you like, or nothing. I do not think you are bad. I am sure you love truth and honesty better than falsehood and dishonor. Your face shows me that. This evening, if you like, we will come and sit by you." Annie expressed her gratitude in a simple, touching way, said she was much better, and would soon be able to work and be of some use in return for all the kindness she had received. She expressed the greatest admiration for Minnie. She had never in her life, she said, seen so lovely a child. "She will not tell me her name," continued Annie, "but she says she is her doctor's pet."

"She will be called Minnie Forest," said Susie. "You may as well know now as at any time, that her father is the doctor's only son, and that I was never married to him. You see I also have had my troubles, but I have lived through them."

"Oh, how you must have suffered!" exclaimed Annie. "I was not so brave as you, was I? But oh! I felt that I must die, and be where I could forget my awful suffering."

"Don't think of them any more," said Susie, with feeling. "You can live with us, and work with us in our flower business. Who knows what happiness may be in store for you?"

In the evening the doctor called, having been unable in the morning to do more than call at the door, when Clara told him that the patient was doing well. At the sight of him, Annie seized his hand and kissed it with tears. "I am glad already that you saved me," she said; "and oh! I feel that I am among blessed angels. I never met such dear, noble women before. I wonder if there are any others in the whole world like them. To-night I am going to tell them my history. Will you stay and hear it? I should like to have you." The doctor stayed, and that evening the three friends heard a most pitiful story, which was very nearly as follows:

"I was born in ———, about twenty miles from here. My father is a farmer, and a deacon in the church. I am the oldest of six children. All my early years were very sad. I had to work hard all the time, and went to school only in winter, for I had to take care of the younger children. I loved to go to school, but it was hard to keep up with my class, because I had to stay home Mondays and

Tuesdays to help about the washing and ironing, and often other days also. I don't know how I ever learned anything, for my father would never let me have a lamp in my room when I wished to study my lessons. It was very cruel in him, for I loved to read and study, and during the day I never had a moment. He used to whip me when I disobeyed him about borrowing books and papers to read. A girl who lived near, used to lend me her *Waverly Magazines*. That was six years ago, when I was ten years old. One day my mother told him; and he came to my room in an awful rage, and burned them all, though I cried and begged him on my knees to spare them, because they were not mine. It was no use, and my friend was much distressed, for she used to keep them all. I cried over it for days, and my mother was very angry with what she called my silliness. She thought I ought to be a very happy girl, but I was not. I could not be happy. Everything I wished to do was discouraged in every way. They thought me wicked because I was dissatisfied with the poor, cheap clothes my father allowed me; and I was dissatisfied, for my father was not poor. He always had money in the bank. I was never allowed a single pretty dress, like other girls, nor to go to any of their parties. My father called them all kissing parties, and both he and mother said they were ashamed of me because I wished to go. Mother cared for nothing but work, and I could not take the same pleasure in scrubbing and cooking that she did, though I did it all the time, and would have willingly, if I could have been allowed to read or to have any pleasures.

"In our school there was one scholar named George Storrs—the brightest and handsomest of all. I think I always loved him since I was a very little girl; but he never noticed me much until one year ago last August, when one day, on my way to the village, he joined me, and we walked together. The road lay through a beautiful wood, where there was a pond close by the road, full of water-lilies. We stopped, and George took off his shoes and waded in to get me some. Just as he came out with them, I saw my father coming from the village, and only a little distance from us. I screamed with fright, and flew into the bushes. George followed me, and I told him my fears. He told me my father should not hurt me, and I clung to him in an agony of dread. My father passed as though he had not seen me; but oh, how I dreaded to go home that day. I feared he would actually kill me in his anger. The state I was in, and George's kindness, made me tell him of my life at home. He pitied me, and spoke tender words to me—the first I had ever heard. You cannot wonder that I clung to his words, and loved him with all my heart. I told him so. I could not help it. He said I was a good girl, and he had always loved me, and some time he would help me to get away from home. In a month he was to come to this place and work in the *Oakdale Republican* office as compositor. Three times after that I met him in the same place, for my fears had been groundless—my father had not seen me. George promised to write me, and he kept his word, and during a whole year I was happy, in spite of everything. Of course, I had to have him write me under a false name, and I had much trouble to get my letters. There was no one I could trust, and a hundred questions were asked whenever I wished to go to the village. I knew that my love for George was the highest and noblest thing in my soul, and yet I had to conceal it like a crime. Oh, it was so hard! My mother loves her children, I know. She works hard for them; but when she gives them food enough, keeps their clothes decent, and prays for them every day, she feels that she has done all. I do not blame her in the least; but oh! I should have worshipped her, if she had made me trust her like a friend. She never told me of myself—of the changes that happen to girls at a certain age; and when I passed that period I was horrified. I wondered if it were not some dreadful divine punishment sent to me because I did my hair prettily, and tried to manage, with my scanty materials, to make my dress more becoming. For this I was considered bad and perverse by my father. You may wonder at what I am telling you, but it is the solemn truth. In my distress I went to Laura Eliot, a girl much older than myself, who had for three years loaned me books whenever I went to the village. I had never been intimate with her, for she had considered me a mere child, I suppose, and loaned me the books because she was interested in my passion for them. She told me very kindly many things I ought to have learned from my mother, and after that, treated me more like a friend. She lived alone with her father, who was a drunkard, but a man of education, and she had been talked about. I think it was all false. My father never found out about the books she loaned me, but when he learned that I had called on Laura he was angry, and threatened to cowhide me if I ever set foot in her house again; but I did not obey him. I had made a large pocket that I used to tie on under my dress so I could secrete the books. I read in this way a great many works of Scott, Goldsmith, the poems of

Shelley, Burns and Tennyson, and ever so many novels. Laura gave me a little tin oil lamp, which I kept supplied with oil out of money that I kept back cent by cent when I sold butter or eggs for my mother. It was wrong, I know, but mother used to cheat father in the same way. He never allowed her to sell butter or cheese for herself, but it was the only way she could get any money. I kept her secret, of course, for there was no sympathy between me and my father.

"One day, only two weeks ago, I went to the village against my mother's wish. I had urged her to let me go for a month in vain, and I could not resist, for I knew there must be a letter from George. To my great disappointment, there was only one, and it had been lying there over three weeks. That night, after I went to bed, while I was reading George's old letters to make up my loss— they were all the joy I had—" Here poor Annie broke down and cried bitterly. "Poor girl!" said Clara, soothing her. "I am ashamed, papa, that I have ever been unhappy myself, when there is so much misery in the world. Did you ever hear such inhumanity, papa?"

"Yes," he said, "I have heard many similar confessions in my life. For crueltry, bigotry, tyranny to wives and children, commend me to your ignorant, skinflint New England farmer." Clara told Annie she was exhausted, and had better rest. Susie had been crying half the time.

"Oh, let me finish, I beg you. There is little more to tell."

"While I was reading my letters, my father, armed with his cowhide, came in. I suppose he had seen my light shining through my window, though I always curtained it carefully ; and no doubt mother had told him of my going to the village. He seized my letters, and read enough to know they were from a lover. He commanded me to tell him who wrote them, but I was angry at the idea of his coming to whip me like a child, when I was almost sixteen years old. At my refusal, he dragged me from my bed in my chemise and whipped me cruelly. It is two weeks ago, and you can see the marks on me yet. My little sister, who slept with me, woke and screamed, ' Don't kill Annie ! Father, father, don't kill Annie !' At which he laid the whip over her and forced her into silence. I was so outraged that I boldly told him I wished he were burning in the hell he always told me I should go to. I told him to kill me—that it was all I asked of such an inhuman father. This only made him more angry and his blows the harder. Finding I would not tell him who wrote my letters, he left me, commending me to the mercy of God. I told him I despised the God that could be pleased with such as he. He said it was his duty to punish me until he ' broke my will,' and that the next morning he should come again.

" When the house was silent—I suppose two hours or so after he left—I rose, and taking some matches, for he had carried my lamp away, I groped my way down into the parlor, where my mother kept her purse hidden in a chest of drawers. I stole two dollars, half of all poor mother had secreted from my father."

For some time Annie could not go on. The doctor felt her pulse, and giving her some wine, allowed her to finish.

" I then went back, packed up some things in a paper bundle, and waited until I thought it must be near dawn; and then I kissed my little sister and stole out of the house. I walked five miles to the next town, where the stage to this place passes through. The stage fare was just two dollars, and that was all I had. At noon the stage stopped at a hotel, and all the passengers, except a woman and her child, got out. She asked me some questions, and gave me some bread and meat from her basket. When I got here, and found the printing-office, George was gone, and there was no one but a boy, who was washing the ink from his hands at a sink. He could not tell me where George lived, and I was ashamed to go anywhere to inquire for him. I was ashamed of my bundle, of my clothes, of everything, and I was ready to sink with my misery. I knew not what to do; but I could not stand in the street; so I walked away from the village, crying bitterly under my old green vail all the time. I went into a grove, which I have found since was Mr. Kendrick's, and sat down in a little summer-house and cried. I stayed there all night, and slept a good deal, for it was not a very cold night; but in the morning I felt cold and faint. Then I reflected that I could not tell George I had stayed all night in the woods, like a vagabond, and the stage, by which only I could have come, did not arrive except at night; so I wandered to and from this grove all day. Oh, the long, wretched hours! You can imagine them, but I cannot describe them by words.

"I found George. He was greatly surprised to see me, but not glad, I knew. He walked across the Common with me, and I told him my story, or some of it; told him I would find work. He took me to a hotel, the cheapest, as I wished him to, and there left me to another night of misery. The next evening he called, and there was something of his old manner, in his words to me. He thought I could not get work, and that I had better go home. That was dreadful—from him too. The next day, and for over a week, I tried to get work. I asked the landlord to take me as a chamber-maid—everything failed, and as I could not pay my board, one evening, on going to my room, I found my few things at the door, and the door locked. I knew not what to do, and not caring if I died or lived, I walked out to the Common and sat down in the cold. While I was there, a well-dressed girl spoke to me kindly, and asked me why I cried. I told her in a few words, and she took me home with her, and was very kind to me. I did not know what kind of a house it was. Old Mrs. Torbit was a horrid woman, and laughed at me when I wished to work for her. I will not say what she told me, but I did not listen to her. I was there only one night and the next day. The second evening, as I was walking down the stairs, George Storrs came out of the parlor. He looked at me with horror, and then rushed out of the house. I flew to my room, and throwing on my shawl and hat, rushed out and followed him, and overtook him as he was crossing the bridge. I seized his arm in despair, but he flung me off with reproaches, because I had not gone home as he advised me. He would not believe I was innocent of bad acts in that house, and while I was talking to him even, he left me without one word. Then I knew beyond a doubt that he did not love me. He could be cold and cruel too. My suffering, my tears, could not affect him, and then I determined to go out of this terrible world. I stood there on the bridge, saying I know not what, but loud enough I thought for the whole village to hear me.

O God! how I pitied myself. 'Poor Annie! Poor Annie!' I cried many times, and then I threw myself into the cold river. I remember the icy chill, the awful strangling, which seemed to last so long, and then a terrible ringing in my ears, and I thought I was dying without pain. ° ° That is all, dear good friends. The rest you know."

The "dear good friends" then comforted her in every way they knew. Susie and Clara, with tears, kissed her tenderly, and assured her they would not fail her.

"Oh! if some good angel had sent me here to you!" said Annie. "If I had only known anybody could help poor Annie, and feel for her as you do, I should have been spared so much! See, I am worn to a skeleton, almost, and when I left home I was not thin at all. Thank God! for the friends he has sent me."

"Dear girl," said the doctor, with emotion, "I trust all your sorrows are over. To-morrow I shall have something to tell you." And with this the doctor left her.

CHAPTER XXXI.

INTO A BETTER WORLD.

THE next morning, after hearing Annie Gilder's story, the doctor sent a written message to George Storrs, at his boarding-place. As it was Sunday, the young man was free, waited on the doctor immediately, and was shown into his sanctum. Dr. Forest was pleased to see a fresh-complexioned, naissant-moustached, handsome young fellow, very diffident in the presence of the popular physican. The doctor was in his dressing-gown, and put the young man at ease, by asking permission to continue smoking his pipe.

Young Storrs had not yet heard the name of the young woman who had been rescued from the river; no one seemed to know where she was, and the report was current that she had since died. He had a vague dread that the victim would turn out to be one he well knew, and his conscience was troubling him sorely. The doctor commenced by making inquiries about the Gilder family in ——. The replies of the young man satisfied the doctor that old Gilder was just such a man as he had inferred from Annie's statements; that she had been badly treated, and had good cause to be dissatisfied with her hard life at home. Then the doctor told George that this unhappy girl, still bearing on her flesh the marks of her father's cruelty, driven to seek refuge among strangers, and finding the only friend she had in the world, him whom she had loved with all her heart, turning from her in her homeless, penniless condition—that this girl was the one who had tried to end her miseries by drowning herself.

George, on hearing the doctor's words, turned away his face, overcome by his feelings. As soon as he could command his voice, he expressed deep sorrow for the unkindness he had shown to Annie, and declared he would marry her at once, and atone for his conduct, notwithstanding that her reputation was tarnished by the fact of being at such a place as old Mother Torbit's.

"Hold! young man," said the doctor, who, knowing the habits of men, was always impatient and disgusted at their complaining, in any way, of woman's frailty. "You cannot look me in the face, and tell me she is not as chaste as you are, even if she has helped to build up Mother Torbit's business by the same acts that you have; but you have not heard all. She was there only one night and the next day, and took no stock in the business; but even if she had, do you not see that her soul is as white as snow compared to yours? She was found destitute, homeless, abandoned, weeping, on the Common. A girl spoke pityingly to her, and took her home, out of charity. Annie Gilder, a mere child in years, was ignorant of the nature of the house, and begged the old woman to give her work, whereby she might earn her bread. That is why *she* was there in that house. Now what were *you* there for? Were *you* ignorant of the nature of the house also? Had *you* been turned out of doors on a cold winter's night because you had no money and nowhere to lay your head? Ah, Christ! the inhumanity of men to women is enough to make fiends hide their heads in shame. If the whole sex should go mad with vengeance, and murder us all in our sleep, it would scarcely be an injustice to us. Your tears do you credit, young man. I am glad to see them. This pretty, innocent young girl, has won my heart. I have placed her with the two women in this world whom I most honor, and hereafter her life, I trust, will be happy."

George begged the doctor to let him see her. He wished to go to her at once and ask her forgiveness; and then he confessed to the doctor that he had been ashamed of her poor attire; and carrying her awkward bundle for her across the Common, he had met several of his friends, who afterward quizzed and mortified him. The doctor saw how natural this was in a handsome young fellow, just beginning an independent career for himself, dressing like a swell, and feeling immensely important; but he had not done with him yet. "You think, of course, that this poor child is as ready as ever to fall into your arms; but perhaps you are mistaken. She is among those who will teach her the worth of her beauty and goodness, and open to her the way to earning an honest livelihood. She is already deeply attached to her new friends, and has learned the difference between the love that depends upon outside appearances, and that which looks deeper. I trust that terrible struggle between life and death in the icy river, has frozen out of her heart its old warmth for one who could treat her as you have done; but I don't like preaching, young man. I'm no saint myself, and I see clearly that you were controlled by motives which you did not create. You are young, and, with your fine constitution, ought to live to old age. It remains to be seen what you will do with the forces at your command."

George saw that the interview was drawing to a close. Never in his life had he so desired to stand well in the opinion of any one, as in that of this frank, out-spoken, humane old man. Since he had been in Oakdale he had heard innumerable anecdotes of the doctor, all showing the deep admiration with which the populace regarded him ; so in a moment of enthusiasm, possible rarely except in youth, George laid his heart open to the doctor ; confessed his faults, his desire to follow the promptings of his higher nature, and to do some good in the world. The doctor, always sensitive to such moods, laid his hand kindly on the young man's shoulder, and asked him if he really wanted a field for heroic work, and if he was equal to bearing the persecution of the world to-day for the sake of helping on a noble cause. George was eager to prove himself capable of any effort toward a noble end. " Then," said the doctor, " make yourself the champion of woman's rights—woman's social and political emancipation. There are few young men in that field, and not one, sir, who does not stand, morally and intellectually, head and shoulders above the average young man of the period. You may think you cannot do much, but you know the ocean is made up of drops of water. Advocate the equal rights of human beings whenever you hear opposition. Go and hear speakers on the subject ; study it up well. My library is at your disposal, and I will direct your reading." George's assent was earnest and prompt. He showed, indeed, that he had given some little attention to the subject, which pleased the doctor greatly, and he talked to him then, more as an equal, and thus flattered the ambitious young fellow, who went away carrying two of the doctor's books under his arm, one of which was Mills' work on *Liberty.* " Read this first," said the doctor. " You can finish it this week. Bring it back next Sunday, and stay to dinner with us." When the doctor gave him his hand at parting, he told him he might perhaps as well call on Annie that evening. " No doubt she'll be ready to forgive you," said the wily doctor. "Women are more merciful than men, and too good for us by half." George thanked him with emotion when he told him where Annie was, and went away in a much happier mood than he had expected during one part of the doctor's sermon. As for the doctor, he was well satisfied with his Sunday morning's work. " It is with the young," he said to himself, " that reformers must work. New transit lines of thought in their brains are easily established ; while the brain in the old is like a dense forest of fossil California cedars." And so thinking, the doctor walked rapidly to the home of his " girls," as he called Clara and Susie. They listened to the account of the interview with George Storrs with great delight, and when they found he was coming that evening to see Annie, Clara clapped her hands with joy. " Susie, dear," she said, " we'll wrap her in my white cashmere dressing-gown, relic of former splendors," she added, laughing. " You shall do up her fine hair, and Master George shall see a creature very different from that poor, forlorn girl who cried to him in vain for help."

" Was there ever a woman in this world," said the doctor, laughing, " who was not a match-maker at heart ? "

" He don't deserve her," said Susie, warmly. " While I am arranging her hair, I'll give her a lesson in the art of receiving penitent lovers."

" Well, Min," said the doctor to the " long-haired angel," as he sometimes called her, " between these two match-makers, I shouldn't wonder if we had a wedding. What do you think ? " Min climbed up on the doctor's knees while giving unqualified assent to the proposition of a wedding ; her idea of it, as further conversation with her showed, being a " frosted cake with two birds on it." This information Min had some way gathered from her observations at the baker's.

Whether Susie gave the lesson she proposed on the art of receiving penitent lovers or not, it is certain that, after the meeting of Annie and George, the course of love "ran smooth," and the reappearance of George thereafter on Sunday nights, was characterized by a very exemplary regularity. Annie recovered safely from the shock to her system, and proved a " blessing in disguise," as Clara predicted. It was in the busiest part of the season of winter flowers, and as Annie was quick to learn, she proved a great help. As the poor girl's wardrobe, when she arrived, was of the paradisaic order, everything had to be supplied mostly from Clara's, as Susie was much shorter of stature than Annie ; and as Clara was rather of the heroic type of woman, there was some merriment over the fit of her old dresses on the thin form of Annie. Annie, however, was pleased with everything. To be among the refined, cultivated, gentle people, that heretofore she had met only in books, to be respected and loved by them, to be able to please those about her, and have no fault ever found with her efforts to do so, and then to be able to see George, to love him without shame or concealment—all this was so different from the life she had known, that at times she feared it could not be real ; that it was a heavenly dream, out of which some-time she might wake to the cold, hard world, in which she had struggled and suffered. No wonder the poor girl's heart went out to her new friends, in a kind of affection bordering upon worship. One fear alone re-mained, and this she mentioned to her friends : that her father might find out where she was and force her to return, as she was under age. To avoid this, the doc-tor had prevented her real name from getting into the local papers, in the items about the attempted suicide ; and as Annie was anxious to let her mother know that she was well, and above all things to return the two dollars she had purloined, she gave her letter to Clara, who enclosed the money, and had the letter posted in Boston.

Only one annoyance resulted from befriending Annie, and this was the disaffection of the Irish servant, Ellen, who had heard outside, of the " abandoned woman who had lived at old mother Torbit's," every item of truth going hand in hand with a dozen falsehoods and exag-gerations, as is usual in such cases. Ellen declared very insolently to Clara, that it was more than her char-*ac*-ter was worth to stay in the same house with such a girl. Clara graciously condescended to explain that these stories were false ; and though disgusted, endeavored to awaken some better feelings in Ellen, but without success. " Let her go, Mrs. Delano," Annie said, when she heard of it. " There is nothing she does that I cannot do. I have stood at the wash-tub, at home, from sunrise till after-

noon, and then helped do the ironing the same day. If
you can spare me from the flowers, I will take Ellen's
place. It is not hard. Why, I have not worked at all
here. I have been playing the idle lady."

"My dear child," said Susie, "you have worked much
harder than you will by and by, and much harder than I
ever wish to see you; but Clara, I think we will dis-
miss Ellen. We can send out the greater part of the
linen, and I can do the rest."

"I have never done any washing," said Clara, "but I
am a great bringer-in, sprinkler, and folder of clothes. I
used to do that for Dinah; so count on me for that part.
I do not like the system of servants. It jars upon my
nerves to have any one in the family who has no interest
in it. We have decided, Annie," she continued, glancing
at Susie, "to make you a partner in our flower business,
if, after a year, you are as well pleased with us and the
flowers as you are now. Meanwhile, I· see no better
adjustment of matters than to pay you a salary, as we
are now doing."

"Oh, you are too kind to me!" said Annie. "I do
not feel that I can ever deserve so much as you are doing
for me."

"Not too kind; that is absurd," said Susie. "We
both came into the business without any capital but our
willing hands. Why should not you, also? Our idea
is to build up a great industry for poor women who wish
to gain an independent position." At this point in the
conversation, the doctor came into the conservatory, where
the three women, and even Min, were busily engaged.
Susie was cutting tube-roses and other flowers, while Min
held a basket to receive them. The other two were

15

making bouquets. Clara told the doctor that the firm intended to make Annie a partner.

"Well, that's a good chance for you, Annie," he said, as he shook hands with her. "Have you quite forgiven me for that resurrection?"

"Indeed, sir, you know I am glad that I live, and every hour of my life is pleasant to me. If some good angel had only sent me here that night when I sat on the Common——"

"It was not written, Annie. By the way, have you paid that hotel bill?"

"Certainly she has," answered Clara. "She paid it the first time she went into the street."

"You do not say who gave me the money," replied Annie.

"Why, no one," answered Clara. "You borrowed it, and have already paid me. You need financial training, I see."

"It is hard for me to feel that my work is worth anything," said Annie. "I am used to working for nothing, or for my board and clothes."

"You must lose no time in learning," said the doctor, "that labor has made all the wealth of the world. Money is nothing but the representative of that labor."

"Have not gold and silver any value in themselves?" asked Annie.

"Intrinsic worth, you mean. Yes; and therefore they are not fit representatives of wealth. Political economists are beginning to see that there is no more necessity for money, the measure of wealth, to have intrinsic value than that the yard-stick should be made of gold, or set with precious stones. But I've no time to discourse on finance just now—not time; at least, to make myself clear."

"You forget, doctor," said Susie, with some pride, "that we have been reading up on this subject. We see clearly why children or savages should be unable to comprehend abstract questions; and until they do, they are swappers and barterers, not financiers. The savage wants bright beads and gorgeous feathers for the buffalo robe he offers you. He deals only with the concrete. Civilized people see the need of a medium which, without value in itself, may simply stand as a record of the values exchanged, the basis of the exchange being confidence in each other's honesty."

"The question of money," said Clara, "has always perplexed me. I have worked out several systems in my mind; but when I apply them hypothetically in practice, they don't work perfectly. It is like the clearing of algebraic equations by substituting $m + n$ and $m - n$ for the values of x and y. All goes on smoothly, and you solve lots of problems, until you come to one where your substituted values only involve x and y more and more, instead of eliminating them. Just now it seems to me that the government should issue all the money necessary for the transaction of business, this money being simply a guarantee of exchange based simply upon the national wealth and credit. But then, for the balancing of accounts in our exchange with foreign nations, paying interest on our bonds which they hold, we seem to need something else."

"Hence the Board of Brokers," said the doctor, "who grow rich on the ignorance and mutual distrust between nations. You see that specie does not solve your difficulty. A gold dollar has intrinsic value, and is worth, actually, just as much in England or France as it is here; and yet you attempt, when there, to pay your grocer or milliner with an American gold dollar, and they refuse to take it; so you have to take it to a broker, and suffer him to pocket a certain amount from you just for giving you another piece of gold or silver of the same value! This is simply the continuance of the old ignorance which made the Turks call all other nations barbarians, as the Chinese do to this day. But despite the pessimists, the world is improving. Railroads and steamships and telegraphs are bringing nations daily into closer relations and mutual interdependence. See! We have only just now effected a national currency in this country. Before that, we had a most vile system. Bank-bills, of banks located at Eastern commercial centres, were at a premium in the West; while those of Western banks were at a discount, and frequently refused, in the East.

"That was indeed a miserable system," said Clara. "How often I have had to wait in shops, while clerks pored over the bank detector, to find out if my bank-note was genuine or counterfeit, or if the bank that issued it was still in operation! and then the counterfeiters always managed to keep a little ahead of the bank detector, which, of course, could not be republished daily, and so keep ahead of the counterfeiters."

"I am not so impatient over the slowness of progress as I used to be," said Susie. "Nations are only a body of individuals, and governments can only improve gradually as the individuals improve. The important thing always, is to give the children the conditions for development, so that they may become good citizens, who are always a 'law unto themselves.'"

" Yet," said Annie, who up to this time had been silently listening, as she went on tying tube-roses on the end of little sticks, " I think the wickedest man I ever knew was an educated one—at least, far from what would be called ignorant."

" What Susie means by conditions for development," said the doctor, " comprehends moral training as well as intellectual. But you are opening into deep waters. I must go, and leave you ladies to flounder about alone."

" Masculine presumption ! " said Clara, smiling.

" Feminine assumption, rather," replied the doctor. " I did not mean worse floundering, because alone ; but only less in quantity because one flounderer the less. How quick women are with their suspicions. If the management of affairs should get into their hands, as it is now in ours, the compensation would be terrible."

" Wouldn't it ? " said Clara. " We'd be fearful tyrants, having so old a precedent before us, or rather behind us. We'd get all the wealth into our own hands, and when our sometime lords wanted money, we'd ask how much, and what for, and quibble about the amount, and recommend home-made cigars instead of Habanas. We'd give them donkeys and a side-saddle to ride on, lest immodesty and ambition should be fostered by riding astride of fine horses. We'd have them do hard work all the time, and yet we'd kiss only the hands that were soft and white. Then we'd set up our ideal for male chastity, which should be almost unattainable, through our own system of tempting them ; and then we'd laugh at the presumption of any who presumed to demand the same standard for us. If they wished to vote, we'd howl at and persecute them for getting out of their sphere, and show them they had no need of the ballot, because we, their heaven-appointed protectors, represented them at the polls."

The ladies laughed, but the doctor's face was quite grave. "That is about what you would do, and about what we should deserve; so we will take care that we rise together."

"I should think—" Susie began.

"No, I will not hear what you think. I will have one right that you tyrants are bound to respect, and that is the right to tear myself away from your eloquence. Goodbye, flounderers!" and the doctor passed rapidly out to the gate, Clara following for one more word, just to teaze him. There was Min, demurely seated on the narrow seat of the "sulky."

"Minnie's going to ride with her doctor, she is."

"Is she, indeed? Here's another tyrant of your sex," said the doctor, and hurried as he was, he drove the child around the Common, as usual, before going his professional round.

CHAPTER XXXII.

THE DISTINGUISHED VISITOR.

ANOTHER year has passed—a busy and prosperous year for the firm of " Dykes & Delano, Florists." Miss Galway, the modiste, still continued to dispose of the small bouquets, and for two years, finding the supply constant and the demand certain, she had devoted one of her windows exclusively to them, furnished it with a little fountain, and given it into the hands of the little girl, her sister, who sold a part of Susie's first installment on the Common. On the promise of Miss Galway to devote the whole proceeds of this window to the education of the little girl, our florists had agreed to continue the supply two years more, though they now had their own showroom and order department in the city, conducted by Annie, now Mrs. Storrs, assisted by another woman as book-keeper ; for the firm of Dykes & Delano were "sworn," as the doctor declared, to never employ a man when a woman could be found to do the work required. The conservatory had been extended and supplied with new heating apparatus. The wedding of Annie and George had taken place as the doctor predicted, and Min had a lion's share of the wedding-cake, having munched it at intervals for a month after the event. She was now nearly five and a half years old, for it was April, and somewhat more than a year since Annie found her new and better world through the good and great heart of Dr. Forest. George had kept his promise to the doctor, to enter the lists as the champion of women, and under the influence of his reading and the society of Annie's friends, he had greatly improved. His secret ambition was to become an author; and though he continued to gain his bread as a compositor, and was expert in the art, he spent all his spare time writing or studying. Annie proved in every way a treasure to him, and had implicit faith in his success. She wrote every week to "Madame Susie," as she called her, or to Clara, giving the most careful and minute account of the progress of her wing of the business. Orders came in constantly, after the first six months; and although the firm had opened business relations with a great English nursery establishment in another part of the State, which supplied them with young shade-trees, shrubs, and evergreens from rare foreign invoices, they could hardly supply the demand. Ten acres of Minnie's legacy from Mrs. Buzzell had been put in order as a nursery, and the propagation of shrubs and trees was progressing finely. Clara and Susie became more and more enterprising and ambitious. The taste in Oakdale and neighboring towns for lawn and park cultivation, was rapidly increasing, and the young firm looked forward to getting their supplies directly from England, instead of receiving them at second hand. One man was now constantly employed in the nursery, and other help indoors and out, when the busier part of the season demanded more hands.

One morning, as Clara was busy in the conservatory,

Susie brought her the card of a gentleman who was waiting in the sitting-room.

"Frauenstein?" said Clara, looking at the card, on which was written, in pencil underneath the name, "sends his compliments to Mrs. Delano and her partner, and would esteem it a favor to be admitted into her conservatories."

"Bring him in, Susie. I cannot present myself in the drawing-room in this rig. Don't you think I shall make an impression on his countship?" she asked, glancing at her looped-up dress and bibbed apron.

"Why not? You are beautiful in any dress."

"You wicked little flatterer! Well, send in his Exalted Highness, the Count Von Frauenstein."

Before Clara had scarcely glanced at the face of the count, she was strongly impressed with the distinguished air of the man. He wore a dark-blue circular, reaching nearly to the knee, and as he stepped through the folding-doors into the broad, central passage in the conservatory, he removed a very elegant shaped hat of soft felt, and seeing Clara, bowed silently, with a simple, courtly air, seldom attained except by men of the Continent. Clara returned the salute, but remembering the European custom, did not offer him her hand.

"Madam," he said, "I have had several glimpses of your flowers from the outside, and I greatly desire to have a better view, if you will pardon my presumption."

"I am very glad to see you, sir," Clara replied. "My father has often spoken of you, for he is one of your ardent admirers."

"He flatters me greatly. I am proud of his good opinion, for it is worth more than that of other men."

After passing, in a few minutes, those meaningless and unremembered preliminaries, inevitable between those meeting for the first time, and conscious of affecting each other and of being affected by a new and strange power, the count said : "To-night I hope to meet Dr. Forest at the Kendrick reception. You, madam, do not patronize the society here much, I think, or I should have had the pleasure of meeting you." Clara's perfect lips curled slightly, as she said, "No ; I am nearly always at home since I returned to Oakdale."

The count had called for no other purpose than to delight his senses with the sight of flowers, of which he was excessively fond ; but standing there among the magnificent array of colors, and breathing the delicious breath of jasmines and heliotropes, he saw nothing, was conscious of nothing, but the presence of a charming woman, whose every movement, every outline, was a study, from the poise of her regal head to the step of her beautiful feet. As the conversation continued, his wonder increased that there should be found in an out-of-the-way, unknown niche of the world like this Oakdale, a woman of such rare intelligence, such grace of bearing, and that clear and concise expression of thoughts, found very seldom among women, and not often among men, except a choice few. Then there was a modesty surrounding her like an atmosphere—not the modesty that is supposed to belong only to refined women, but the modesty of the philosopher, and which is as charming in men as in women, and equally rare in both. Yet she was self-poised, sure of herself, and when she raised her long, dark lashes, and flashed her splendid frank eyes upon him, he felt a diffidence in her presence, arising from his keen desire to please her and which was as new to him as it was charming.

While they were talking, Min came to the door and stopped, watching the count. As soon as he saw her, she made him a courtesy—a thing she seldom did impromptu, though she practiced it often before Clara and with her, Clara considering it an art, like musical execution, not to be attained except by commencing early. Min somewhat overdid it on this occasion, but the count returned the salutation very gravely and impressively. Min laughed. This just suited her, for she was, as the doctor said, a born courtier. "This is your brother's child," said the count, addressing Clara. "Why, she is wonderfully beautiful!"

Minnie opened a conversation with the count, which soon developed so many purely family matters, that Clara suggested her going away.

"Oh, do let me stay, auntie dear. I won't talk so much any more." After a little silence on her part, during which Min watched the count as a cat would a mouse, she asked, "Do you know what my name is?"

"I do. It is Minnie."

"What is your name? please."

"It is Paul."

"Oh, that is a nice name. Paul, are you going to stay to dinner?" she asked, insinuating her hand into his.

Both smiled at this outrageous freedom in the child; but Clara said, "Minnie, you must know——"

"Now, auntie dear, *please!*" and she pressed her dimpled fingers tightly over her lips, as much as to say, "Not one more word shall they utter."

"My child, auntie does not wish you to keep as silent as a statue, only you must not do all the talking; that is impolite." The count pressed the little hand still resting in his, and the little hand returned the pressure with interest, but fearing to be sent away, she maintained her silence, evidently by a most gigantic effort, and the conversation continued until Min, hearing the doctor's gig drive up, flew out of the conservatory like a streak. When she returned, it was in the doctor's arms. He set her down, and greeted the count with more deep heartiness than Clara had ever seen her father manifest to any man, and this cordiality was fully reciprocated by the count. "It does me good to see you again," said the doctor. "I was going to bring you to see my daughter. You must know it has been a long-cherished desire on my part that you two should meet. Knowing the opinions and tastes of both, I could predict that you would find much to like in each other."

"Permit me to say," said the count, "that you do me great honor. I have passed a more delightful hour than I ever expected to in Oakdale."

"That is good!" said the doctor, delighted to discover an unmistakable sincerity in the count's face, and he looked towards Clara.

"I see you expect me to be effusive, also," she said, blushing. "Well, then, I am too embarrassed to be original. I can only echo the sentiment of your friend, papa."

"My doctor," said Min, who could not keep silent any longer, "Paul won't stay to dinner; and we are going to have caper-sauce, and 'sparagus, and pudding."

"How can he resist such a *ménu?*" said the doctor,

smiling, but are you not rather presumptive in calling the gentleman Paul ? "

" No," said Min, decidedly. " He calls me Minnie."

" Indeed ! " replied the doctor, amused at Min's justification.

" We shall be very glad to have you dine with us," said Clara, " if you will do us that honor ; and papa can stay also, perhaps." But Von Frauenstein, knowing his invitation was more or less due to Min's unofficial cordiality, declined, saying he was expected to dine with the Kendricks, which was the case, though he would willingly have forgotten that fact, had he felt perfectly free to obey his inclination. He added : " But if you will permit me, I will call again to see your flowers. You must know I have thus far given them no attention whatever." The look that accompanied these last words could not fail to flatter Clara. The count had the most charming voice imaginable, perfectly modulated, and in its low tones as indescribable as music itself.

Clara knew well, and every woman understands how, though it can no more be expressed by words than can the sensation experienced at the sound of delicious music, that this was not the last time she was to see the Count Paul Von Frauenstein, and the certainty was a deep satisfaction to her. As for him, as he walked away, breathing the delicate perfume of a little bouquet in his button-hole that he had begged from Clara, he wondered simply that there was such a woman in the world ; but he, a man of the world, acquainted with men and women of the best rank in many countries—he knew well the secret of the charm that invested her : it was her freedom—a quality found very seldom in women, and for the best reasons. He met her as an equal on his own plane, and knew by instinct that no wealth, no social rank might win her hand, much less her heart. There were no outposts raised by feminine coquetry, to be taken by storm, or by strategy. If she could love a man, she would turn to him as naturally as the flowers turn to the sun. During the rest of the day, the count's thoughts continually kept wandering back to that pleasant hour among the flowers ; to the beautiful child, whose liking for him was so quick and frank in its expression ; and especially to Clara, a worthy daughter, he thought, of one of the most admirable men he had ever met. And he thought of her, and saw her mentally, in other lights than simply as the noble daughter of an honest and clear-thinking man ;—but of that hereafter.

That evening the parlors of the Kendrick mansion were brilliantly lighted. A pleasant wood fire burned in the open grates, and everywhere there was a rich odor of flowers pervading the air. Mrs. Kendrick, still young in appearance, wearing a black velvet dress with a train, and her thin, white hands sparkling with jewels, received the guests in a rather solemn manner that said, " Man delights me not, nor woman either; " but the guests were in no way troubled, for they did not expect any manifestation of exuberant cordiality on the part of any of the Kendricks. There were but very few invited, all being " solid " men and their wives, with the exception of the Forests. It was a special gathering, having a special object—that of bringing Frauenstein and the solid men together for a special purpose : namely, the springing of a trap to catch the count's money for a grand life and fire insurance company, of which he was to be president.

The count had often talked as if he would some day settle in Oakdale, though the suave, impressible cosmopolitan had talked the same thing from the Atlantic to the Pacific coast, whenever he had been pleased with the enterprise, industrial advantages, or location of places; but Kendrick did not know this; and as the count's only relatives in America were the Kendricks, except the Delanos in Boston—and Boston the count hated—and as it was certain that Prussia was no *vaterland* to him, the chances did look rather bright. But the idea of tempting Frauenstein with the presidency of a great joint-stock insurance company, showed that Kendrick knew as little of the man as Satan did of the One he took up "into an exceeding high mountain." Whoever is acquainted with the Mephistophelian penetration of Satan, must wonder at the shallow device. How could temporal power flatter One who said, "Blessed are the poor," and taught that we should take no heed of the morrow?

The count was apparently without any ordinary ambition. He had made his immense wealth by what proved to be shrewd investments during and before the war. He had bought and sold cotton, turned over gold in Wall Street, bought stock in many enterprises, and instead of commanding two millions, as Kendrick believed, he had actually at his control five times that amount and more. Society, especially fashionable society, was duller to him than a twice-told tale. He saw too well its miserable want of high purpose, its petty jealousies and rivalries, its instinctive worship of idols that to him were a vanity and vexation of spirit. One thing his wealth gave him, and that he enjoyed—the power to utter frankly his opinions on all subjects. No one criticised *his* radicalism; in him, it was only charming eccentricity, at the very worst. The only exception was Miss Charlotte, whom he had always highly esteemed. They had been fast friends for many years.

When Mrs. Forest entered the Kendrick drawing-rooms, the first thing she saw was Miss Charlotte Delano talking with Von Frauenstein. The latter she expected to see; but Miss Delano's presence was a surprise that gave her great uneasiness. This, however, was of short duration. Both came forward and greeted her; the count, with an easy courtesy, and Charlotte, much to Mrs. Forest's astonishment, rather more cordially than ever before. The three talked together for a few minutes, until Miss Louise Kendrick carried off the count to the piano. Then Mrs. Forest sought to relieve her over-burdened spirit. Seeing that Charlotte was not likely to broach the subject, she said:

"I have not seen you, Miss Delano, since the unfortunate separation of Dr. Delano and my daughter. I can assure you it was as terrible a shock to my family as it must have been to yours."

"It is to be regretted, certainly," answered Charlotte; "but I trust it will prove for the best. I don't think Clara is to be blamed in the least."

Now Mrs. Forest had counted on a right dismal, mutual howl over the disgrace to the two families, and the sympathy she expected, from the moment she saw that Miss Charlotte was not disposed to avoid her, was totally wanting. Mrs. Forest began to fear that the whole world was lapsing into loose and latitudinarian sentiments. Pretty soon the fact was revealed that Clara had visited Charlotte in Boston since the separation.

By great effort Mrs. Forest concealed her annoyance. Clearly there was a secret kept from her by the doctor, for, of course, whatever Clara did he would know. To vex Mrs. Forest still more, Charlotte said that she had never really been acquainted with Clara until the separation, and that it was owing to the trial Clara had gone through that they had been drawn together. Here then was an anomaly ; the very thing that had alienated her own mother from Clara had cemented the friendship between Clara and Dr. Delano's only sister ! Mrs. Forest was at loggerheads with herself and the world generally.

While the count played an accompaniment for a duet by the twins, the solid men were talking in the further parlor, hidden from the piano by one of the folding-doors. The principal one, after Kendrick, was Mr. Burnham, one of the bank directors—a bald, clean-shaven, oldish gentleman, whose whole air suggested stocks, bonds, investments, and high rates of interest. He sat in an uncomfortable straight-backed chair, for lounging or ease was something he had never cultivated. Like Kendrick, making money was the only interest he had in life ; not so much from any miserly feeling perhaps, as from long habit of thinking and scheming in that one narrow field. As many women grow by habit into household drudges, until they come to feel uneasy in pretty dresses and momentary release from the housekeeping treadmill, so these men felt uneasy, and almost out of place any where but in the counting-room. After a while the solid Burnham said : "I don't see, Kendrick, that we are to get a chance at the count to-night."

"Upon my word," said another, "he is as fond of woman's talk as a sophomore."

"A wise fool, eh ? " said Kendrick. " Yes, these foreigners are funny dogs ; but Frauenstein has a remarkably clear head, financially, though he's all wrong in
politics—believes in female suffrage, for example. All
the women like him, that's certain."

"H'm ! Not difficult to find a man agreeable who is
a count and a millionaire. Singular there should be so
much attraction in a title in this democratic country."

"Frauenstein maintains that we are not a democratic
country," said Kendrick ; " that there never has been a
democratic government in the world's history, because
never one where all citizens have the ballot."

"Haven't they in this country? I should like to
know," said Mr. Burnham.

"Why, women have not, and they constitute more
than half of the adult citizens. I tell you, Burnham,
you can't argue that question with the count. He's
armed at all points."

"I've no desire to ; but I don't feel like waiting much
longer for him to get through his opera squalling and
dawdling with the women."

Now it was a part of Kendrick's plan to broach the
insurance scheme, not in a set business way, but to
spring it suddenly upon the count in a general conversation when the ladies were present. He knew that
many men, ladies' men especially, would be more vulner-
able under such circumstances—less apt to manifest any
closeness where money was concerned. The opportunity
was soon found.

With the collation, or after it, coffee was brought in—
a thing never dreamed of at night, except when the
count was present ; then, indeed, it was available at

almost any hour, for he was, like most Europeans, very
fond of it. The solid men joined the group of three or
four around a table, where the count was sipping his
café noir.

"Wouldn't you like some cognac in your coffee,
Frauenstein?" asked Mr. Kendrick; and a glance at
the waiter caused an elegant decanter to appear. The
count measured out two tea-spoonfuls. Kendrick and
the other gentlemen drank a tiny glass clear, and while
Frauenstein was talking to Mrs. Burnham and Mrs. Kendrick about the beauties and merits generally of Oakdale,
the solid men added valuable information about the increase of population and the enterprise of the town. This
led up to the subject neatly, and Kendrick introduced
the insurance scheme, and hoped the count would
examine it. "We ought to start," he said, "with a
capital of half a million—say a hundred shares, at five
thousand dollars each. The truth is, everything is ripe
for a heavy insurance business and the capital can easily
be doubled in a short time. The heaviest buyer would
be the president, of course."

"That should be you, count," said Burnham, rolling
the tiny stem of his glass, and looking boldly at a point
between the count's eyes. The golden bait was not
snapped at. On the contrary, Frauenstein threw cold
water on the project. He said he did not believe in
private insurance companies. The government should
insure all its citizens. "Now this scheme," he said,
"will benefit a few at the expense of the many. Make
it a mutual affair between all the house-owners in your
town, and I will 'go in,' as you say."

"How?" asked Kendrick, not liking to discourage

any advance on the part of the count, whom he had just pronounced sound on questions of finance. "Give us your plan."

"Well, issue for a month, in your daily paper, a call to the citizens to prepare for taking steps to form a mutual banking and insurance company, and announce a meeting at the end of that time, when they will have discussed the matter very generally. Let the president and board of directors be chosen by the popular voice. Trust the majority for knowing who the honest men are. Let the shares be sold at one dollar, and limited to ten for each buyer, until a certain capital is raised. Above this amount, let any citizen deposit as much as he chooses, at the legal rate of interest, for the banking business. I will take all the stock of this part of the interest, if you like ; for I am pretty nearly ready to set on foot a grand enterprise here in your midst—or just over the river, on the fifty acres of land I've bought there."

By this time all were eager to know what the count's proposition was ; but he did not show his hand at once. He was, in fact, waiting for Dr. Forest, who, from the nature of his professional demands, was excused for coming at any hour. Mrs. Forest and her daughters had already retired.

Kendrick did not ask directly what the count's enterprise was. He only remarked upon the nature of the land, its soil and so forth, and while he was talking, Miss Delano, who was seated next the count, pulled back the little bouquet that was falling forward from his buttonhole, and said :

"How fragrant these are still ! Where did you get them, Paul ? "

"At your florists' here—the firm of Dykes & Delano. I was in their conservatory an hour or so, this morning, and had a very interesting conversation with Mrs. Delano. Why, she is a very cultivated, very charmiug woman. Why is it, Mrs. Kendrick," he asked, looking squarely at that lady, "that I have never met her at your receptions?"

Mercy! What a graveyard silence met this fatal question. Kendrick was fidgety; Burnham annoyed that the conversation had drifted away from business. Mrs. Kendrick, out of respect to Charlotte's presence, could not answer as she wished, so she looked into her coffee-cup, and the silence grew more and more oppressive. Charlotte did not consider herself called upon to speak. At length Mrs. Burnham said, smiling: "You ask, sir, for information, and I do not see why you should not be answered. Since Mrs. Delano came back to Oakdale, she has not been received in society."

"Indeed!" replied the count, sucking the coffee-drops from his long, silky moustache, and using his napkin. "Indeed! then all I can say is, so much the worse for your Oakdale society. Madame, that lady's presence would grace any society, however distinguished."

Mrs. Kendrick saw clearly, by the attitude and expression of her husband, that he was expecting her tact to guide the conversation into a smoother current; so she said quickly, and with some embarrassment, that it was not so much the fault of Oakdale society as of Mrs. Delano herself, who evidently wished for seclusion, and therefore her motives should be respected.

This did not satisfy the count. He saw clearly the same spirit that he hated and had fought all his life—

the sacrifice of honest fraternal feeling to conventional forms. He knew, without a word of explanation, that this Mrs. Delano had offended society, and had been unforgiven ; and further, that this offence could hardly be her separation from her husband alone, since such separations are of common occurrence. He knew Dr. Delano, and after meeting Clara, he was at no loss to understand the cause of the discord between them. He gave his opinions, therefore, very concisely and pointedly, upon the folly and short-sightedness of society, in refusing fellowship with any honest citizens whose education and refinement gave them a natural right to admiration and respect ; and then he gave his opinion upon the special claim these women florists had upon the community, because of their brave effort towards gaining an independence through means which added much to the refinement and education of the people.

"You are a true friend of our sex, Paul," said Miss Delano ; and addressing Louise Kendrick, she added, "You know Frauenstein means 'ladies' rock,' so he is rightly named."

"And on such rocks," said Kendrick, "I suppose they would build their church."

"There are not enough, unfortunately," replied Miss Delano, "for a grand cathedral, so we must build little altars here and there, wherever we can find a Frauenstein."

"You do me a very gracious honor," said the count, "but one I am far from deserving. I believe, though, I am always on the side of women as against men. I see very few really happy women ; and they never can be happy, until they are pecuniarily independent. All fields should be freely opened to them. They are quite as capable of enterprise as men are, and of filling offices of trust. They should have the same education that men have. Men should give their daughters money, as they do their sons, and send them abroad to continue their education. Every man knows how culture and experience adds to the attractiveness of a woman."

"For my part," said Mrs. Burnham, petulantly, "I don't see the use of bringing up our daughters to be modest and home-loving, if just the opposite qualities are to be most admired."

"My dear madam," replied the count, "do you suppose a woman is less a true woman and a devoted wife because of her culture and experience?"

This led Mrs. Burnham to say that every one was aware that Clara Forest was well educated, and "considered" very superior, intellectually, but that she had not certainly been a model wife.

"You are wrong," said Miss Delano. "I find it very distasteful to me to discuss such a subject, but it is my duty to say that my brother, and not his wife, is at fault. The plain truth is, he did not show that he could appreciate her devotion."

"Why can't they make it up, then?" asked Burnham. "It looks bad to see wives cutting out in that way."

"If women were independent, as I desire to see them," said Von Frauenstein, "there would be much more 'cutting out,' as you call it, than you have any idea of. But, by the same token, it would make men more careful to carry the illusions of love into matrimony."

Here Dr. Forest was announced, and the conversation took a different turn.

CHAPTER XXXIII.

THE doctor only stayed a short time, which was mostly employed in discussing the famous enterprise of the great French capitalist at Guise—the *Familistère*, or Social Palace. The count had been there on a visit, and he was eloquent in the praise of the work, which he called the most important and significant movement of the nineteenth century. "It points unmistakably," he said, "to the elevation and culture of the people, and to a just distribution of the products of labor." None present, except the doctor and Miss Delano, had ever heard of the great enterprise, and they listened eagerly, as if the count were telling an entrancing tale of some other, and more harmonious world.

"It won't work, though," said Burnham. "The equal distribution of wealth is a chimera."

"But, my dear sir, it *does* work," said the count. "It has been in splendid working operation several years, and pays six per cent. on the invested capital. Do not lose sight of facts; and then, I did not say an equal, but a *just*, distribution of the products of labor, or wealth, for all wealth is that and nothing else. Depend upon it, we are living in an age corresponding to that of puberty in an individual. There are no very marked changes from childhood up to this period, except that of increase in size; and then, everything being ripe for it, there is a marvelous sudden transformation in six months or a year, and the child assumes all the characteristics of the man or woman. Ask yourself why the man who makes your plow, or tills your ground, should be inferior to you who muddle your lives away in counting-rooms or offices? You can't answer it, except to say the chances ought to be in favor of the one who has the most varied exercise of his muscles and mental faculties. I tell you, with the increased facilities for education among the people, and for travel and intercommunication, they are beginning to feel their power."

"Building palaces and living in hovels begins to strike the workers as something more than a joke," said the doctor; "but up to this time they have done it very composedly. They have woven the finest fabrics, and clothed themselves and their children in rags, or mean and cheap materials. Bettering their condition was next to impossible when they had to work from sunrise to sunset to gain a bare living; but shortening the hours of labor will work wonders. It will give men time to read and improve their mental condition."

"Yes, if it would only have that effect; but will it?" asked Kendrick.

"Of course it will not," said Mrs. Kendrick. "There are the three hundred workmen of Ely & Gerrish. They struck, you know, and got their hours reduced to ten; and I hear that most of them spend their extra time in bar-rooms and billiard-rooms."

"Well, madam," replied the count, "do you expect men who have been drudges, to suddenly turn out philosophers, and give their spare time to algebra and political economy ? Why, many of them are no doubt so degraded by their lives of unceasing toil, that the bar-room is a culture to them, and getting drunk a luxury. But you must remember you have not collected the facts upon which to formulate a judgment. I do not believe the greater part of them, as you say, spend their time in bar-rooms and billiard-rooms."

"Oh, no doubt of it ; no doubt of it," said Burnham.

"My dear Kendrick, you must have doubts," said the count.

"Not the slightest, upon my honor."

"Well, then, let us decide it in the English way. We have had a bet, you and I, before this. I'll lay you three to one, on any sum you like, that not one-third of these workmen spend more time in drinking-saloons or billiard-saloons than they did before their reduction of hours."

"Done !" said Kendrick, very sure of his money. "Let it be two hundred dollars."

"Oh, shocking !" said Mrs. Kendrick. "You are like two dissolute young men. I do not approve of betting."

"I don't approve of it either, madam," said the count, "but this is to establish the honor of the ' hodden grey ;' and to make the transaction more respectable or excusable in your severe eyes, let us further decide, Kendrick, that whoever wins shall donate the money to your new hospital."

"Oh, that will be nice !" said Mrs. Kendrick, brightening. She was one of the board of managers, and had in vain tried to get her husband to subscribe anything further than the pitiful sum of fifty dollars at starting. The doctor also, highly approved of this disposition of the money. He had long agitated the subject of a hospital, and Mrs. Kendrick at last had come to be, he said, his "right-hand man." He was one of the committee to draw up the prospectus then under consideration. He wished especially to have the hospital so organized that not only the poor could avail themselves of it, but those in better circumstances—for the private family, he said, was no place for a sick person. He could not receive the necessary care without feeling himself a burden, which vexed and irritated him, and so retarded recovery.

After arguing upon the method of collecting the facts about the workingmen of Ely & Gerrish, and after calling out the count at some length on the particulars of the working of the *Familistère* at Guise, the doctor left, and Kendrick and Burnham returned to the charge of the insurance scheme. Burnham insisted that the growing enterprise of Oakdale, and its steady increase of population, made everything favorable for a "big thing" in the insurance line.

"I see," said the count, "that you are not disposed to take my suggestions about making your insurance a mutual thing among your citizens. Now, the longer I live, the more I am interested in the independence of the people. Your rates of insurance, in private joint-stock companies, are too high for the poor man, who needs insurance infinitely more than the rich do. Now, as for Oakdale enterprises, I see none so worthy of consideration as this well-managed flower business of Dykes & Delano. That is something worth taking stock in." Here Burnham turned away with ill-concealed impatience, not to say disgust; but Kendrick, anxious to keep on the right side of his rich guest and relative, said, smiling blandly.

" Well, count, one like you might invest in the Dykes-Delano paper, and still have a balance for our little insurance enterprise." The count did not at all like the covert sneer in this speech. " Kendrick," he said, "your heart is as dry and crisp as one of your bank-notes. It is not touched at all by the struggle of these women, while to me it is inspiring. You never even told me of it, and I have had to learn the facts outside. They commenced with absolutely nothing but a few plants in a friend's bay-window. One of them sold her watch and jewels, I hear, to help build the second addition to the hot-house. I tell you, they ought to be encouraged and helped in every way."

" Pity they couldn't have kept respectability on their side. That would have been the best help," said Mrs. Burnham. Old Burnham could have choked her; not that he had more charity than his wife, but more policy.

" Respectability !" said the count, thoroughly aroused. " I wonder that women do not hate the very word. No woman ever becomes worthy of herself until she finds out what a sham it is—a very bugbear to frighten slaves. No woman knows her strength until she has had to battle with the cry of 'strong-minded,' 'out-of-her-sphere,' 'unfeminine,' and all the other weapons of weak and hypocritical antagonists. I tell you, a woman who has fought that fight, and conquered an independent position by her own industry, has attractions in the eyes of a true man, as much above the show of little graces, polite accomplishments, meretricious toilet arts, and the gabble of inanities, as heaven is above the earth. She is a woman whom no man can hold by wealth or social position, but only by the love his devotion and manliness can inspire."

No dissenting word followed this burst, which was Greek to the solid men. The count was a little daft anyway, on the subject of women, according to them. Mrs. Kendrick, after a moment, offered some safe, negative remark, and Burnham, anxious to neutralize the mischief his wife had done, said he thought a woman might, at least some women might, "work up" a business and yet remain feminine. Men were not so hard on women, it was their own sex. This roused Mrs. Burnham, for she knew well he talked very differently in the bosom of his family. She took up the thread of conversation. "I am sure," she said—and here occurred a little jerky interruption to her speech, the cause of which no one knew but her lord, who had kicked her foot under the table, which meant, in his delicate, marital sign language, "Hold your tongue!" But like many of the slaves, as the doctor called married women, she made up in perversity what she lacked in independence; so glancing spitefully at her "lord," she continued, "I am sure I think women have a right to all the money they can honestly gain, and if Miss Dykes had conducted herself properly, I should have much sympathy with her success."

"Was it her fault, Mrs. Burnham," asked the count, "that the man who won her affection did not marry her? ——"

"My dear Louise," said Mrs. Kendrick, begging the count's pardon for interrupting, "I think you had better retire. It is getting rather late for you."

"No; let her stay, my dear madam. I am not going to say anything that the Virgin Mary herself might not hear. Let her stay. I see she listens intently, and if tonight she gains a broader conception of the true position of her sex, you will hereafter rejoice in the fact. She is a pretty, a charming girl, just coming into the glare of the footlights on life's stage, with bandaged eyes. This is what you mothers all do ; and then if they stumble for want of eyes to see the trap-doors of the stage, you blame them—not yourselves. Teach a girl to know herself—to consider all her functions as worthy of admiration and respect ; teach her to be independent, proud of her womanhood, and she will turn as instinctively from the seductive words of selfish men, as from the touch of unholy hands. Now, this little woman, Miss Dykes, had no such teaching, no knowledge of the world whatever, no standard by which to measure the honor of men's motives ; and, for believing and trusting, you, Mrs. Burnham, and other Christians, would stone her to death. But Nature is kinder than you are, madam, for it pardons her weakness, and compensates for her suffering by a most precious gift. Her child is one of the very brightest and loveliest I have ever met."

"It is certainly a very charming little thing," said Mrs. Kendrick, "and her mother's conduct is now, I believe, every way exemplary. I am truly sorry that her child is illegitimate."

"Illegitimate!" repeated Von Frauenstein, as if speaking in his sleep. "Why, all children must be legitimate. How *can* a child be otherwise ? I must be a barbarian. I can see nothing in the same light that others do. Well, by heaven ! I'll adopt that child, if her mother will consent. I'll take her abroad and educate her. I'll give her my name, and present her at a dozen royal courts. There'll be no question then, whether she is begotten by law or by the more primitive process of nature." The company were astounded.

"Good heavens, count!" exclaimed Mrs. Kendrick, breaking the silence that followed this speech. "Would you really do such a thing?"

"Yes, my dear friend. I'll do it—so help me God! and I'll bring her back to Oakdale, when her education is finished, a perfect queen of a woman. You call her illegitimate, madam, and yet the time may come when you'll be proud to kiss her hand!"

Mrs. Kendrick rose from the table, and the others followed. Miss Charlotte had retired some time before.

Kendrick, who could not imagine for a moment that the count was serious, was disposed to take the matter as a good joke. "If your knightly passion is the adoption of bastards, why have you never adopted any before? I think this is the first. Isn't it?"

"Yes; because I have never known a case where the mother, being poor and uneducated, rose out of her disgrace so nobly. The doctor tells me she is a great student—reads and studies regularly, while working like a martyr to get the flower business on a safe footing. I mean to go and see her to-morrow, and if she wants capital, I'm her man. It is just as safe an investment as your insurance business, though it won't pay so high a rate of interest." Kendrick could have strangled him. Burnham and his wife retired with sufficient discomfiture for any amount of conjugal infelicity. Burnham declared, as soon as the door closed behind the happy pair, that but for her "gabble about those women, Frauenstein would not have made such a fool of himself."

Mrs. Burnham assumed the silent air of the martyred wife. So they went home to their grand house, second only in cost to the Kendrick mansion, and laid their heads to rest on two contiguous pillows, with as much justification for the proximity as the law allows. Meanwhile a very similar conjugal harmony expressed itself in the grander home of the Kendricks; but Mrs. Kendrick did not play the rôle of the silent victim as Mrs. Burnham did. As her husband was removing his cravat, she said, "Now here's a fine mess you've got into with the count."

"*I!* Well, that's cool. What do you mean?" asked Mr. Kendrick, not for information, as his wife knew; so she answered somewhat impatiently:

"You ought to know Frauenstein well enough to see that he would never sympathize with any narrow social distinctions. He's seen Clara Forest, thinks her unjustly treated, and so he has gone over to the enemy."

"Seen Clara? I should say he had seen the other, by the way he talked. Shouldn't wonder if he fell in love with that brat, and the mother too."

"That's as much as you know. Men never see anything. I'm perfectly sure that he is smitten with Clara. That's the way it will end. You'll see," said Mrs. Kendrick, bitterly. She had long cherished the hope that Louise might win the count; but she spoke very despairingly about it now.

"Oh, I always told you that would never work. Men like that, know too well what a woman is. Louise has arms and legs like spermacity candles."

"Well, I must say, for a father to speak like that, is shameful," answered Mrs. Kendrick.

"It's all your own fault; you took her away from the high-school because she got hurt a little in the gymnasium, and sent her to that namby-pamby seminary of half idiots at Worcester. Didn't I always want her to work in the garden and in the hot-house, and develop her muscles? She'll always be sickly, just as she is now."

"I'm sure she has had a great deal of exercise, and her health is as good as mine was at her age, and she is not a bit thinner in flesh." Mr. Kendrick made no denial, and his wife continued: "Working in the garden spreads out a girl's hands, and makes them red; and what man, I should like to know, ever likes hands and arms like a washer-woman's? You were always praising the smallness and whiteness of mine. I mean before we were married, of course." Still Kendrick was silent, but his thoughts were very busy. Someway the world was out of joint, and he was wondering if, after all, these radicals, with their talk about making women free and teaching them to depend on themselves, were not pretty near the truth. Here was Frauenstein, for example, rich enough to put a wife in a palace, and surround her with attendants, and he was always admiring women who worked. This he expressed to Mrs. Kendrick, and said that it certainly was commendable in Clara, since she would be a fool and throw away her rights as Delano's wife, to take care of herself, instead of coming home and living on her father.

"Of course," said his wife; "and we ought never to have cut her. You heard what the count said."

"Who's to blame for the cutting? Not I. Men don't cut women, my dear."

"Well, Elias, I think you can take the palm for sneaking out of a responsibility. Men don't cut women, indeed! I know they don't; but they insult them worse than we do. I know you bow as graciously to Clara as if she were a duchess; but would you let Louise visit her? You know you wouldn't. That's the way men take the part of women whom their wives and daughters avoid." Mr. Kendrick thought silence the best reply to this just reflection of his wife. He thought he could trust her to bring harmony out of the discord; for while he wanted to keep the count's money from straying away from the family, she, on her part, was equally anxious to secure his name and rank for Louise; and he knew she would hang on to that hope to the last.

The next morning, after breakfast, which had been a serene affair, showing no trace of the perturbation of the previous evening, the count drove over to the doctor's. The doctor was out, but would return very soon. Frauenstein waited, and spent the time mostly at the piano. The twins were both delighted, though timid, especially in the presence of such a lion. Linnie, after they had sung, asked him to say frankly what he thought of their voices. "Do you allow your sister to speak for you, Miss Leila?" he asked, turning his fine eyes upon hers.

"Yes—no," blushing and laughing just like nothing in the world but a young girl. "I mean yes, in this case," she finally managed to say.

"Well, then, yours has most power, but it is wiry. Miss Linnie's is more flexible, more emotional. She feels more than you do, or, rather, more than you *seem* to, when she sings. If you were both equally to cultivate your voices, and also continue your practice for the next

five years, Linnie would win more applause for her singing, and you for your playing. That is my opinion; but
I ought to add, as the French do, *maintenant je n'en sais
rien.*" Then the count made them both speak French, he
carefully constructing his sentences as much as possible
after *Fasquelle's French Course,* which he knew was their
text-book, they having no idea of the reason why they
were able to get along so well with him. He understood
their worst sentences like a Parisian. Any foreigner
who has been in Paris will understand that. He will
recall how, in his abominable murdering of the language,
sentences which he could not for his life have understood himself, written or spoken, were instantly seized
and graciously and gravely replied to, as if they had been
models of elegance. When the count finished singing a
charming aria in his best style, Linnie said, with enthusiasm,

"Oh, I wish my sister Clara could hear you sing!"

"She shall hear me sing," he said, looking up to Linnie, who stood on his left, with an expression in his face
that she had never seen there. It affected her senses like
a caress.

Pretty soon the doctor entered; and after greeting the
count, he said, "What a fusillade of French! What a
state of excitement these girls are in! I believe you are
bewitching them both, Frauenstein."

"On the contrary, I am the victim of both, and I dare
not stay another moment. I have come to take you over
the river. I want you to see my fifty acres, on which I
am going to build a social palace, if the gods are pro-
pitious."

It was a clear, balmy day in the first week of April

that the count sought this interview with the doctor. So
far in his life, he had never found a man who was so
much "after his own heart." He believed in him fully
from the first hour he conversed with him, since when
they had corresponded, expressing their views fearlessly ;
and thus far had found them in perfect accord. To say
they loved each other like brothers would by no means
express the sentiment existing between these two men, so
unlike in many respects, yet so closely in sympathy that
thought answered to thought like the voice of one's own
soul. During the drive, for they went past the fifty acres
away into the country, neither asking for what reason,
the count gave in detail his plans. "If I build this palace," he said, "I shall do it with this clear granite sand
of the river. I know the secret of making stones of it—
bricks, we call them—which, moulded in any shape, and
tinted any hue, will last for centuries. I can have a man
here in three days to conduct the work. He will guarantee that they shall be finished this summer. If I do it,
it shall be a magnificent structure, beside which the
palace of Versailles will seem the work of a 'prentice
hand.' I can profit by the original palace at Guise, and
make it much handsomer, though that is truly splendid.
The apartments must be larger, and the whole should
accommodate about two thousand people. Now, I have
already one industry for its occupants. What is your
idea for a second ? "

"Making these very bricks," said the doctor, "if only
you have got at the secret of their perfect durability, as
you have, I know, or you would not speak so positively.
But this industry would not suit all. You want one
more."

"Of course. One that will employ women. What shall it be? I have thought of silk-weaving, for a certain reason of my own. It is proverbial, you know, that those who make the silks, laces, and velvets—pure luxuries, and the most costly—are the worst paid of any laborers in the world. Look at Spitalfields, England, and Lyons, the great velvet manufacturing centre of France. In India, those who make the fabulous-priced Cashmere shawls are the most pitiably paid of all. I am willing, if necessary, to lose a considerable fortune to prove that good wages can be paid to silk-makers, and yet have a fair profit on the product. I should go into that manufacture with some advantages. I have a first-class steamer already plying between San Francisco and China. I can get silk as cheap as anybody."

"Good!" said the doctor. "Let the third industry be silk-weaving." The count had not mentioned the first, but the doctor knew well he meant floriculture.

"There's only one thing lacking, doctor, and that is— the motive: the motive for the first step. That depends——" And suddenly checking himself and turning his horse in the road, he asked, abruptly, "Doctor, have you ever been in love?"

"With a woman—no; with a man, yes."

"I understand. You have met a man who responded to all the needs a man could respond to, but never a woman to respond to what you need there. That is my own case exactly, though I have loved, of course—few men more, I think."

"If men only knew," said the doctor, "how they cramp their own growth by making idols of women!"

"By idols, you mean slaves. Only free women are

worthy of free men; and the time is not come, though it is near, when they will be emancipated. Then we shall see the dawn of the Golden Age. Men think they are free; but they are bound by many shackles, only they have thrown off some which they still compel women to wear."

"And some they cannot throw off," said the doctor, "until women are recognized as their political equals. I have great patience with the women; they are coming up slowly, through much tribulation."

CHAPTER XXXIV.

THE SLAVE OF THE LAMP.

ON the way back to the village, the count left the
doctor at the house of a patient, and then he went
after Min, intending to take her to ride; but the time
was all consumed in conversation with Clara and Susie
about the organization of the social palace. He was
struck especially with the practical ideas of Susie, and
drew her out at length.

"Remember," he said, "that nothing is absolutely decided yet; but when I once decide, you will see a rattling
among the dry bones of Oakdale. You and Mrs. Delano
will be of great assistance to me, but you cannot grasp
the thing in a manner sufficiently broad. You ought
both of you to go with me to Guise, and study up the details for a certain time. Could either of you undertake
that mission? We would take Minnie along, of course;
that will be the commencement of her education; and
the very best thing would be to leave her there in the
schools until our own home is ready. And here I want
to say to you ladies, both of you—for this child belongs,
I see, hardly more to one than to the other—that whether
we build the palace or not, I want to adopt Minnie as
my daughter, and take charge of her education. Understand that I am serious; that I never make a positive

proposition until I have fully counted the cost, and made my conclusions definitely."

Susie listened to the count with breathless interest, and looked, almost stared, at him with a painful intensity; then she took Min in her arms, hid her face on the child's breast, and wept silently. Min looked wonderingly at the count, and then at Susie, and then at Clara, for explanation.

"How would you like, Minnie, to have this gentleman adopt you as his own little girl?" asked Clara.

"That would be *so* nice, auntie! but will he 'dop' mamma and you too, auntie dear?"

"Yes," said the count, smiling; "I will, as you say, 'dop' your mamma and auntie, if they wish. You will never lose any of your friends; but I should want you, by and by, to go abroad and attend school. You will be called Minnie von Frauenstein, and you can come home every year."

"Oh, sir," said Susie, "how *can* you be in earnest? How can such a blessed good fortune be in store for poor Susie's child? I never dreamed of her going from me yet for some years, and I did not know how much pain the very thought could give me; but I can forget myself entirely for her good. We are getting on well with our business, and I think we could provide very well for her; but under your protection her advantages would be greater than we could ever hope to give her." And after a pause, Susie rose and gave her hand to the count, saying, with great emotion, "It shall be as you desire. I cannot thank you for the honor you do me and my child—words fail me utterly." The count said, "You show the true feeling of the mother. Nothing shall be abrupt. You have ample time to think it all over, and to change your mind, if you wish. In a month we will consider the matter fully, and make our final decision."

To see so brilliant a future opened before the darling who had been unwelcome in this world, and regarded in the eyes of all, except her little circle of friends, as a child of shame and disgrace, no wonder that Susie was overcome with her emotions. "Think, Clara," she said, throwing her arms around her friend, "think what you have done, you and your noble father, for Susie! But for you, I might have been struggling to gain bread for myself and Minnie, in the kitchen of some of these women here who turn their eyes when I pass them in the street. I can think of no harder fate than that."

"Oh, you would have risen even without us, dear. Your heart of gold was sure to be recognized, sooner or later." Susie's tears could not be controlled, and apologizing for her weakness, she pressed the count's hand again and left the room. Minnie went with her, not exactly understanding why her mother cried so. Pretty soon she came back, and climbing up in the count's arms, said, "I thought dear mamma was unhappy, Paul; but she says she cried only 'cause she is so happy; and she kissed me and kissed me and kissed me. I'll give you just one of them;" and taking his head between her hands, as she knelt on his lap, she kissed it pretty much all over, ending with the lips.

"Mercy! Do you call that *one*, Min?" asked Clara. Min laughed, and asked Paul if he liked kisses.

"That is a leading question, mademoiselle;" but seeing she would have an answer, he said, "I know of but one thing sweeter than a little girl's kisses."

" What is sweeter ? "

" Why, a lady's kisses."

" Are they, Paul ? "

" That is my opinion."

" Well, that isn't *my* 'pinion."

" You think chocolate drops sweeter. That is your 'pinion." Min readily assented, and Paul told her that he was going away the next day to New York, and when he returned he would take her to ride, and be her "slave of the lamp." Of course the inquisitive child wanted to know all about the slave of the lamp, but the count excused himself, and promised to tell her the story of *Aladdin, or the Wonderful Lamp*, when they should take their ride. Min reluctantly consented to wait for the story, and then she asked "Paul" to stay to dinner. Clara answered, "Minnie, you are insufferable. I was just on the point of asking the count to dine with us. He will think all the hospitality of this house is confined to you."

" No, he won't, auntie. There's a lot o' *hostality*. Isn't there, Paul ? "

" Now go instantly, Minnie, or you will find there is hostility in the house," said Clara, laughing. " Will you stay ? " she asked the count. " I ask you only for your society, for I fear we have nothing to tempt you, gastronomically."

" Madam, I shall be most happy," he answered, " but I shall have to ask you to excuse me immediately after, for I have a great deal to do."

Min, who had got as far as the door, clapped her hands and shouted with great satisfaction. She went now to carry the news to her mother, and to " help," for she considered her assistance very important. In fact she could never see anything done without having a hand in it. Whenever the cloth was laid, she must pull it a little this way or that, by way of nice adjustment; so with the plates and everything she could reach.

Susie was a little anxious about the dinner on this occasion, and chose to make the flower decorations for the table herself. Min succeeded, however, in getting permission to make a little bouquet for " Paul," which she did not fail to inform him was her work as soon as he entered the dining-room, where both the wide folding-doors were thrown open, exposing a beautiful array of flowers and plants. The count's place was assigned him by Susie, on the opposite side of the table, in face of the conservatory. The count was charmed with everything, and Susie, who was at first a little embarrassed, soon gained perfect composure, as every one did in his presence when he chose. During the dinner the conversation was mostly about flowers, and the count said to Susie, "I have been urging Mrs. Delano to invest more money in your business. Nothing would give me more pleasure than to supply any amount you wish for extending your operations. I speak in a pure business way, you understand," he added, fearing the implication of charity as a motive. "I am perfectly satisfied that the investment or loan would be quite safe. Mrs. Delano seems to hesitate. How is it with you, madam?"

" I do not hesitate in the least, sir," she answered confidently. " I want to import our stock directly from England; but heretofore we have not had money enough to do so. We have orders now that we cannot fill, and they are increasing daily, especially for certain shade-trees and hedge-shrubs." Clara was a little surprised at the daring spirit of Susie, to whose lead in business, however, she always submitted. The little woman was developing a most wonderful executive ability. She was heart and soul interested in her business ; and so it came to pass that the count honored, what Mr. Kendrick called, the "Dykes & Delano paper."

"I confess," said Clara, smiling, "that I do tremble a little at the idea of giving Madam Susie ' a wider swing,' as papa calls it."

"Madam Susie," echoed Min, "that was what Annie always called mamma."

"And so does auntie also, when she speaks of her outside," said Clara. This relieved the count of an uncertainty, for he did not like to call her Mrs. Dykes, and politeness forbad him to call her Miss. Not noticing these last remarks, Susie said: "There has been a great demand here for pot-plants this spring, and I must confess we ask outrageous prices, but you see there is no competition, and as we've got so fine a start, I do not fear a rival, unless some one appears with unlimited capital."

The count laughed. "Commercial magnanimity," he said, "is a fiction, and commercial honesty is little better than playing confessedly with loaded dice ; but it does me good, Madam Susie, to see women getting hold of the dice-boxes that men have so long wielded."

"Almost all men believe," said Susie, "that women's industrial and commercial capacities are restricted by nature to very small, safe, light, feminine operations, like the conduct of a peanut stand. Now I've been haggling with Betterton, the importer, about hedge-shrubs for the last month. He has made us his last offer, and I *know* he thinks we are at his mercy. To-night I give him my answer. I shall write, thanking him for his slight concession in the matter of price, and decline, on the ground that the firm of Dykes & Delano have decided to open negotiations with foreign houses direct." Susie's eyes were bright with triumph.

"Good! Good!" exclaimed the count, as they rose from the table. "I haven't enjoyed such a satisfaction for years as that speech affords me. Go ahead boldly. Upon my honor, I'd rather lose out and out a million than to see you fail. But you must not fail. I pledge you to that amount that you *shall* not," and he gave Susie his hand. Clara was very silent, but Susie could not conceal her triumph. It beamed from every part of her, like the light from a flame.

After dinner they walked through the conservatory, and over the nursery plantation, where some men were engaged taking young pear-trees from their "heeling-in" rows, and packing them in bundles for the buyers. Susie looked at the little wooden labels tied on each tree.

"You wrote these?" she said. The man assented. "They are not written distinctly enough. Please come to me to-morrow morning and I will give you models." She spoke in a low, decided, but respectful tone. The count noticed everything. He talked with her a great deal, for he was greatly interested; but he noticed meanwhile every movement of Clara, and joined her in the walk back to the house, Susie remaining to look after something that needed attention.

"You are a little troubled, I see," he said, in a very gentle tone. "I know exactly the reason. You do not feel so sure of yourself as Madam Susie does, and you fear I may possibly lose money through your firm. I wish to reassure you. I am a very cautious man in business. Everything is favorable here. I admire your partner exceedingly. She is capable of conducting enterprises to any extent. Let me advise you to trust her head just as you tell me you do her heart," and stopping in the walk and turning his eyes full upon hers, he added, " Believe me sincere when I say again, I would rather lose money in this woman's enterprise than gain any amount in any other. Do not think I could ever regret a loss incurred here."

" I do not think you will lose," she said, " but the new responsibility weighs upon me a little at first ; " and her eyes, that had met his fully for a moment, fell before the magnetic power of his. That moment decided the location of the Social Palace. Not a word was spoken, not a glance that could show that these two were ever to be dearer to each other than friends ; but some subtle movement in the brain destroyed the poise of nicely-balanced motives, and Oakdale was destined to witness a mighty enterprise.

The next morning Susie had decided upon a business trip to Boston ; but feeling the importance of her presence at home, she asked Clara to go instead. Miss Charlotte Delano was to return by the first train, and so Clara readily assented. That being settled, they talked of the count, and rejoiced mutually over the prospect of extending their enterprise. " This day," said Susie, " atones for all I have suffered—for every tear I have ever shed. I have been happy many times, but I have never felt the stimulus of pride. To-day, oh, Clara, my friend, I am both proud and happy, and my cup is full. Contrast this hour with that when you came to my room at your father's. Do you remember? I can scarcely believe I am the same person. Still, whatever satisfaction I enjoy, whatever prospect of future happiness, I owe all to your blessed father and you."

"You will insist upon inflicting me with your gratitude. You make me ashamed of doing so little. What was it, after all, but a little human decency? Now, you shall not talk of it. Tell me of the count. He spoke so admiringly of you. Are you not already in love with him?"

"I don't know whether I could ever fall in love again. He seems to me something to be adored by me, not loved, in the common sense; but though my admiration for him is almost perfect, it will not be quite so, until he does one thing more."

"What is that, Susie?"

"Until he wooes and wins Clara," said Susie.

"Oh, you dear girl! I believe you are capable of anything. If you loved him, and could do so, you would sacrifice him to me."

"I would; but there is nothing of that kind to be. We are to be, he and I, good friends; but Heaven has designed him for you and you for him. I feel sure of it."

"Do you forget that you are talking to the legal wife of Dr. Delano?" asked Clara, with a very confident voice at the beginning, but with something very like a sigh at the end.

"Oh, well; Fate can tear down a shanty when it has a palace to build."

The count left in the same train with Miss Charlotte and Clara, and during the journey an incident occurred which should be mentioned, because it shows something more of Clara's nature. On changing cars at the railroad junction, the two ladies took a seat, the count occupying the one in front of them, and another gentleman. the one behind. This gentleman was just putting away a time-table, which Clara politely asked to see. The gentleman thereupon made some remark, which Clara answered, and they continued talking for some minutes. Miss Charlotte was a little shocked at such unconventionality. To her mind, it proved very conclusively that Clara had no intention of making a soft impression upon the count, else she would be more careful of her actions. The count kept on reading his paper, not seeming to notice anything—not even the fact that the stranger gave Clara his card just before he left the train, whereupon she promptly returned him hers. Miss Charlotte could not forbear remarking upon the strange proceeding.

"Why should we treat strangers with suspicion and reserve?" asked Clara. "It is my ambition to be treated by strangers exactly as one gentleman treats another; this is Susie's idea, also, and Miss Marston's. Gallantry is a wretched substitute for that respect that comes from the sense of equality."

"You are right, madam," said the count, with great earnestness, as he folded his paper. "Every such act as this on the part of women, teaches men a lesson—one they are slow to learn—that women are not necessarily and by nature simply pretty, dependent dolls, to be flattered and caressed ——"

"And despised," said Clara. "I have noticed always and without exception, that the men who bow the lowest before us, pick up our fans, when dropped, with the great est alacrity, and make the most adulatory speeches, are just those who respect us least. I can give you a good illustration, Miss Charlotte," continued Clara: " the last time I was in Boston, as I was passing up Court Street, a poor old apple-woman had her stand upset. There were many men passing, and I noticed that every one of the elegant low-bowers, or fan-servants, passed on without the slightest show of sympathy. One, only, a very young fellow, rather poorly dressed, I found helping me set up the poor old woman's stand and pick up the scattered fruit."

" Did you give him your card ? " asked Miss Charlotte, smiling.

" I did ; and allowed him to walk on beside me while I gave him my notions of a true gentleman ; and more, he has written to me twice. His name is Edward Page. I will show you his pretty, enthusiastic letters ; and still more, Miss Charlotte, when I found he was a poor boy, struggling against fate alone in Boston, I offered him, with Susie's consent, of course, constant employment with Dykes & Delano, and he is coming next week to take the place."

" Bravo ! " exclaimed the count. " I must beg your pardon, Mrs. Delano, for believing, heretofore, that Madam Susie had more business capacity than her partner. You will always choose your assistants wisely. You will make them devoted to you, and secure faithful work. This is the great secret of success as a leader of industry."

" I have been brought up so differently," said Miss Charlotte. " The talk of you radicals sounds to me as if it came from another planet ; and still I find I have to agree with you. I confess that when I have, on the

17

street, refused a courtesy from a stranger, as, for instance, the offer of an umbrella in a shower, I have always felt a little mean." The conversation followed this strain until the train reached Boston; and then the count left the ladies at the door of the carriage waiting for Miss Delano.

CHAPTER XXXV.

THE SLAVE OF THE LAMP OBEYS.

MISS DELANO had persuaded Clara to defer her business in Boston until the next day, and spend the intervening hours with her. "Albert seldom dines at home," she had said, "and he comes in, generally, late at night ; so you will not run much risk of meeting him." Clara replied that she believed she could meet him without the slightest discomfiture, and would even like to prove it. While they were speaking the street door opened, and a minute after Dr. Delano entered the presence of Clara and his sister. He showed unmistakable signs of confusion when Clara rose and greeted him with the simple friendliness of a common acquaintance. At dinner he spent most of the time looking at Clara. She was gay and chatty, handsomer than she had ever been. Was this the woman who had, as it were, clung weeping to his feet, imploring the return of his lost love ? Was this smiling, happy woman, who sat facing him, discussing the dinner with excellent appetite, and coolly talking of extending business operations, the same soft, dependent, adoring creature who had slept in his arms and lived only in the sunlight of his smiles and caresses ? He could scarcely believe it. Certainly he had never known her, then. This could not be his wife : it was a grander presence, an imperial, commanding woman, the glance of whose strong eyes, his own could hardly support. She inspired him with something like awe; and just in proportion as she seemed unapproachable, did the desire to approach her increase. Clara noticed the interest she excited in him, but she read his heart like an open book; she saw not love, not tenderness and regret, but the hope of conquest. Had she read tenderness there, her triumph would have been robbed of all its worth. This triumph was much to her. This man had used her most helpless fondness as a weapon against her, and had met her despairing tenderness with that mocking, superior calmness that only indifference can create. It was sweet to her to be able to meet his gaze proudly, to smile upon him, while her eyes said plainly, " You are nothing to me now."

During the evening Clara kept close beside Miss Charlotte. Dr. Delano was vexed that he could get no moment alone with her. Of course he could have asked for a private interview. Clara expected that he would; but he could not bring himself to do this, and the only other alternative was to go boldly to her room, after she retired. This he decided to do. It was characteristically marital and wholly cowardly, though very natural to such men as Albert Delano. Not two minutes, therefore, after Clara entered her room, she heard a well-known step approaching. The instinct of the slave for self-defence caused her quickly and noiselessly to slide the bolt of her door. The act was hardly accomplished when he knocked softly.

" Well ? " with the rising inflection, was the only answer.

" May I come in, Clara ? I wish to see you."

" No, Albert, you cannot see me here."

" Why ? "

Clara felt the blood mount to her cheeks at his want of pride.

"I feel a repugnance to the idea of seeing you here. Is not that enough?"

"Oh, do not be unreasonable," he replied, concealing his anger, but not his impatience; and with this he turned the knob. Up to this moment Clara had secretly reproached herself for bolting her door, not daring in her heart to really believe that he could be guilty of the baseness of forcing himself upon her. All fear of being unjust to him, now vanished like tissue in a furnace. She answered, with forced composure, "Go down into the library, and I will join you there. You cannot see me here, Dr. Delano." He could not possibly mistake her meaning, and he went without a word. "She shall pay for these airs," he said to himself as he retreated, determining to play the part of the impassioned lover, which he believed she would never be able to resist. He thought he knew her weakness; but his calculation was all wrong, since he failed to see that her weakness had been her strength of love; but now her strength was in the weakness of that love, and she was no longer the potter's clay in his hands that she had once been. The moment she confronted him in the library he was conscious of her power, and felt that no acting could deceive her. For a moment she stood silently looking at him, and then she said, in a slow, measured tone, "I have had some hard thoughts of you, Albert, but I never believed you could be guilty of such baseness, as trying to force yourself upon me when I had told you you were not desired."

"Permit me to say that I have never had any hard thoughts of you, and could not believe you would ever apply such a term to me. It does not strike me as a crime to wish to see my wife in her room."

"I am not your wife, and you know it; nor are you my husband."

"The law would hold a different opinion; and, allow me to add, a somewhat less sentimental one."

"Was it ever our mutual understanding that we were husband and wife, simply because of the ceremony of marriage?" asked Clara, growing more calm as her excitement increased.

"Our mutual understanding had not, nor has it now, any power to annul the fact."

"Then let it be annulled as soon as possible. I have heretofore been very indifferent whether you got a divorce or not; but, in Heaven's name, wait no longer, since you take so low a view of what constitutes marriage. I have deserted you, you know," she said, with a bitter smile, " and that is ground for a divorce."

"The complaint is already filed," he answered, " but I think I shall stay the proceedings."

" Suppose you do me the honor to consult me in the premises."

"I beg your pardon, Madam Delano. Will you favor me with your opinion on this subject?"

"You cannot irritate me by your mocking tone. I have learned that existence, and even happiness, is possible without your caresses."

" So it seems, madam; and if it will do your pride any good, I will add that I am very sorry for the fact."

"I should be glad to know for a certainty, that you *are* sorry for the fact. It is not pride, Albert," she continued, in a gentler voice, "but the sense of justice, which makes me wish you to confess that you cheated me, when you gave your love in return for mine. You never loved me grandly—never comprehended how you were loved by me. I never left you because of your infidelity; and for months I tried to reawaken in you something of the tenderness for which I was almost dying. I would have you admit this. Why should there be any misunderstanding? Why should we quarrel like the vulgar, because we are no longer lovers? I can never forget what you have been to me, and would remain your friend under all circumstances."

It seemed to dawn upon Dr. Delano's mind that the woman for whom he had thrown this pearl away, was very small beside her; but there was nothing of the hero in his nature. He felt a momentary self-contempt at the retrospect of his own conduct—at the cold, dictatorial letters he had returned for Clara's impassioned appeals; but he had gone too far for anything now but a temporary reconciliation. He had already committed himself to marriage with Ella, as soon as the divorce was granted. Of this fact Clara was ignorant.

"I can scarcely believe that it is you, Clara, standing there and discussing our future friendship so coolly," he said.

"No; you think my natural place is at your feet. Love makes us infinitely humble, infinitely dependent. Oh, Albert! you never saw anything but the surface of things. I could not make you understand how I have mourned my dead illusions. When I first knew that my heart had cast off its anchorage in yours, I could have died from grief, only grief does not kill the strong. Sleep but renewed my strength to suffer, as I suffer now

—not for the return of your love—I have outlived all
desire, all need for that—but from very pity for myself,
thinking of the long, long agonies I have endured;"
and Clara hid her face in the arm that rested on the
mantel-piece and sobbed. This was the supreme moment
Albert had desired. He did not believe her own explanation of her sorrow. He approached her triumphantly,
and put his arm around her and spoke gentle words.

"Thank you," she said, releasing herself and smiling
upon him. "You are very kind to try to comfort me. It
is over now;" and as he tried to hold her, she gave him
a chilling reproach—"Have you not understood what I
have been saying to you, Albert?"

"Oh, it is not true, darling; you have not ceased to
care for me."

"I care for you only as a friend. I told you I had
outlived all my illusions, just as positively as you had,
when after a few months of marriage you were wholly
drawn to Ella. Let us preserve our mutual regard by
the utmost candor. We cannot deceive each other, and
any attempt to do so is an outrage upon truth and
honesty. There is nothing left of our mutual passion
but a cold and bare skeleton, which we can never clothe
with the flesh and fire of life, do what we will. I would
not see you humiliate yourself;" and not wishing for a
reply, she turned quickly and left him. He stood gazing
after her as if dazed. At last he knew beyond question
that this woman was beyond his reach. He had once
called her love a "suffocating warmth," but even now,
he could not see how far she was above him, through
her fervid sentiment of the passion of love, and her
grander idealization of its object, which had made her

faithful, not from any sense of duty or consistency, but from necessity. To him, love was a luxury like rare wine, which might be substituted, when wanting, by an ordinary quality. To Clara, love was her religion—the one necessity of her higher life ; and when its object failed, her imagination constructed an ideal upon which her exuberant fondness lavished itself in thought, for she never dreamed of the folly of common souls, who satisfy the heart with stones when it asks for bread.

The next morning Dr. Delano breakfasted in his room, and Clara and Miss Charlotte had a long confidential talk over their coffee in the luxuriant morning-room of the latter. Clara told her friend of the scene between her and Albert.

"I have long given up hoping for a reconciliation," said Charlotte, " though it would be a great comfort to me. When he marries Ella, I shall quit the house, though where I shall go is uncertain. Maybe," she added, smiling, " I shall yet go to live in that Oakdale Social Palace. Nothing would irritate Albert so much, for he hates the count, though it would be difficult to say why. I have always been deeply attached to him. He is the most honorable man toward women I have ever met, and the charm in his friendship is, that he never misunderstands you. This is why his friendship is better than the love of ordinary men."

During the conversation Clara asked her if she thought Ella really loved Albert.

" No," said Miss Charlotte, decidedly. " She is too selfish to know what love means ; but in her way she is fond of him, and will keep her empire over him, by her coquetry with other men, principally. You lost your power over him simply by loving him with too much devotion. He fretted a good deal at first because you did not return to him. I told him you would never return, for you had ceased to love him. Upon that he showed me your letters. He could not bear any one to think him incapable of doing just what he pleased with you. Those were the first genuine love-letters I ever saw. I cried over them like a child ; and my deeper esteem for you dates from that time. They showed so unmistakably that you cared nothing for Albert's position or wealth. I had not counted on so high a virtue, and could not understand why he should be so worshipped for his gracious self alone; though, of course, he is a very elegant man, and most women find him irresistible."

Clara was rather silent. She was thinking of Albert's vanity in showing her passionate letters, simply to prove his power—to say virtually, " You see her heart is under my feet." There was something so indelicate, so coarse in this, that it almost made her hate the thought of him.

While the ladies lingered over their coffee, Albert was in the library walking up and down, fuming. He had worked himself into a very unenviable state. He had not slept well during the night. It was a new experience to be shut out from this superb woman, who was but a little while ago so caressingly fond of him, so sensitive to his slightest attentions. It was a humiliation that he could not endure with equanimity, and when a little later she entered the library, a scene occurred impossible to describe. Clara, with the fresh information of his engagement to Ella, was amazed at the state he was in. In his anger, he threw off every rag of decent reticence on the subject of his feelings, and said, without shame, that there was no reason why they should deny themselves the pleasure of being together, simply because they were not so ineffably sentimental as they had been. As he spoke, he was conscious of outraging all Clara's high sense of refinement, and he even enjoyed it as a kind of revenge.

"Stop there! Dr. Delano," she exclaimed, with furious indignation. "You compel me to despise you utterly. You talk to *me* of pleasure in what the soul can have no part. Oh, shame! shame! Until now I have never known you. Your peers are not honorable and chaste women, but those who may barter their favors, like merchandise, for wealth or social position."

"I am a physician," he said, "and don't pretend to understand so much about soul as you do. I have found that, as a general thing, men are men, and women are women. The natural functions exist, and demand their natural play quite independent of any bosh about soul."

Clara was never so amazed in her life. She was too excited to move from the spot, and she gave vent to her horror of his baseness in most unmeasured terms, ending a volley of eloquence with a fervent expression of gratitude that there had been no children to perpetuate such moral degradation.

"Children?" he sneered. "You need not count on their advent in your case, under any circumstances. Children are born of the body, not of the soul, or you might be the mother of an army of phantoms—the only kind you will ever have. That I can promise you as a physician."

"I despise your wisdom as a physician," retorted Clara, her face crimson. "You should have only brutes for patients. Children, in my opinion, are not well born, who are not the offspring of the soul as well as of the body. I have not the slightest fear that, if I should ever—." Clara stopped short, angry with herself that she should lower herself to answer at all.

"If you should ever marry a soul, you mean you would prove very prolific," he said ; but even he was conscious of going too far, and he added, "but I am sorry my temper has made me say rude things to you, Clara. I am really ashamed of myself, but I know you will not forgive me. But no matter now. One thing you forget. The divorce I get from you, not you from me, remember that. I shall be free to marry, 'as though the defendant were actually dead,' but the defendant will 'not be free to marry until the plaintiff be actually dead;' so the document will read, madam," and with these words, he left the library just as Miss Charlotte entered. She asked him if he would be in at dinner. "I shall try hard to do so," he said. "I would not deprive madam of the pleasure of her husband's presence. Ta! ta! *mon ange*," and he actually kissed his hand to Clara, who stood staring at him as at a monster. When the door closed behind him she told Charlotte all he had said.

"What then does a divorce mean ? " asked Charlotte. "How can you remain bound to him, when he marries another wife. It is not common sense."

"No," answered Clara. "It is not common sense ; it is law, it seems ; " and she poured forth a storm of indignant protest against laws made by men without the consent of women. Miss Charlotte replied :

"I wish I could see some of my friends, who say they have all the rights they want, standing exactly in your place. It is enough to make women insane with rage. Such injustice ! such barbarous tyranny. My doubts are all gone. The women's-rights agitators are right. Don't be surprised if you find me hereafter a 'shrieker,' as the press insultingly calls those women," and looking at herself in the glass over the mantel-piece, she added, laughing, "See ! an old maid, somewhat over thirty-five, tall, spare, with a thin, prominent nose. I should grace any suffrage platform in the land." Clara smiled, but she was too sad to enjoy the pleasantry of Miss Charlotte, and soon after took her leave, and dispatching with all speed the business of the flower firm, she was glad to get home to Susie, in whose never-failing sympathy she found a rest, which grew more and more to her with the experiences of life.

In a few days Von Frauenstein returned, and Min had her promised ride. It was quite a long one, and part of the course was through the fine grove of the Kendricks, which joined the doctor's fruit orchard ; and the Forest family, by the invitation of the Kendricks, always used it as freely as if it were their own. On this occasion Leila Forest was leisurely sauntering through the central avenue with a book in her hand. She looked up with a beaming face when the count stopped his horse and greeted her ; but seeing the child, whom she readily recognized, her countenance fell. He did not appear to notice this, and asked her if she would not join him in the ride. She declined with girlish stateliness. He divined her motive instantly, and said, "Miss Leila, I think you do not know this young lady by my side. Permit me to introduce you to Mademoiselle von Frauenstein, my adopted daughter."

"Ah!" was all that Leila's amazement could find for expression, and the count bowed gravely and drove on.

"She don't like Minnie, does she, Paul? But Linnie does. Linnie comes to see auntie, and she kisses me too."

"Does she? Paul will remember that."

When Leila reached home, she told her mother of the meeting in the grove. Mrs. Forest was not inclined to believe the adoption of Minnie anything but pleasantry on the count's part, but she said it was very unwise to refuse the count's invitation to ride with him.

"Why, mamma!" exclaimed Leila, "of course I wanted to go; but I thought you would never approve of it. I think he's horrid to make so much of that little crazy imp."

"She is nothing but a baby," said Mrs. Forest. "The count has certainly a right to choose his acquaintances. My dear, I fear you did a very unwise thing"—thrown away your chances, she would have said, if she had expressed her thought exactly. Leila was puzzled. This was a new phase of her mother's character, or new, at least, to her, and she replied, a little sourly, "Of course he has a right to choose his acquaintances; but supposing he had been riding with the child's mother? Why, I should have felt insulted if he had recognized me."

"Oh, now you are merely foolish. He would not do such a thing."

"Why not? The child is no better than the mother, is she?" Mrs. Forest assumed an icy silence.

Linnie, to whom her sister soon conveyed the intelligence of the meeting in the park, took a very different ground. "You did right, sis," she said; "for if you had accepted the invitation against your sense of propriety, he would have read your mind like a book, and despised you for it, as he will now, no doubt, for your airs."

"Well, that's a comforting dilemma, I must say."

"I don't care, Leila. The truth is, Susie was not treated well, nor Clara either. I like Susie. I've been there, lately, ever so many times, though you needn't tell mamma."

"Goodness me! I thought so. You're infected with the Forest radicalism too. I wonder what *you'll* come to?"

"A sensible person, I think. I mean to. I would not have refused to ride with the count. I should respect any one he chose to honor. Now you are smitten with him; you can't deny it. But I can tell you one thing: he's just as radical as papa is."

"Well, men don't like radical women for wives. They never choose them; and if they do, they don't like them long."

"You mean Clara. Now, Miss Wisdom, I'll give you a little file to gnaw: There are three Forest girls in the market, or will be when Dr. Delano gets his divorce; and if either of the three ever becomes the Countess Von Frauenstein, it will *not* be the least radical one."

"Well, I'm sure *I* don't want the honor."

"No, I understand exactly how afflicted you would be, if he should ask you. Poor child! I hope you *will* be spared that blow!" And Linnie laughed in the most exasperating way.

Min was in a fever of delight during the ride. During the first part of it the count had given her a very charming version of Aladdin ; and when he drove back to the town, he led her like a queen into the finest ice-cream saloon, and seating her in a chair, took his place opposite to her and said, as he removed his hat and gloves, " Now, my golden-haired mistress, what will you have ? Remember, I am your Slave of the Lamp."

" Well, my Slave of the Lamp," she answered, gayly, " I should like some chocolate lady-fingers, and some strawberry ice-cream, and some cocoa-nut pie, and some almonds, and—"

" Mercy ! " exclaimed the count, laughing. " If you eat all that, instead of taking you to the toy-shop for that doll, I shall have to stop at Simpson's, the undertaker, and have you measured."

" Well. Is that the way Slaves of the Lamp behave, I should like to know ? "

" Now, Min," said the count, " let us compromise. The Slave of the Lamp is terribly afraid of your auntie, and so he must not make you ill. You take the cream and the chocolate nougats, and the rest we will have put in the carriage, for home consumption when the Slave is gone."

" All right ! " said the little girl.

When they reached home it required the count, Clara, and Min combined to carry all her purchases into the house.

" Oh, auntie ! auntie ! See ! I've got such a lovely singing-bird ! " And she insisted, whatever became of her other treasures, on carrying the cage in herself.

" My child ! " exclaimed Clara, amazed at the quantity of parcels and boxes, " Surely you have not begged all these from the count ? "

"Why, don't you know, auntie, he's my Slave of the Lamp? Everything I want he has to get for me."

"Be gracious to me, Mrs. Delano," the count said, in his most winning voice. "You do not know how much pleasure I have taken in gratifying the caprices of this pet of yours. Do not chide us."

"Oh, I will not," answered Clara, smiling. "But what will become of Min, if another spoiler is added to the list?"

"Depend upon it," replied the count, "those children have the best chance of being lovely in their lives, who are most caressed and loved in their early days. 'Spoiled,' is generally only an excuse for not studying children's needs, just as parents deny them sugar on the ground that it is not good for them, when everybody knows they require it ten times as much as grown people."

Clara offered no opposition, for these were her own opinions. She asked the count in, and conversed some time with him. It was a conversation full of charm to both of them, but Clara was at times troubled with a vexing, ever-recurring thought. Von Frauenstein, master of human nature as he was, studied in vain to get at the secret. At length he said: "There is something that vexes you, and you are half tempted to tell me about it; that is because you know me so little. Pardon what may seem a vanity, but I am sure you will come to trust me with your confidence. Nothing should be hurried, nothing forced, among friends. We have a right only to what we can win; and there are some prizes too infinitely precious to be lost by careless play." He looked at her eyes a moment, and then asked her to play. "I feel certain, he said, as the music ceased, " that you do not wish to sing for me. I have never heard your voice."

" You are a magician," she replied. " You read my feelings so clearly that I sometimes almost tremble in your presence. I have not heard you sing yet, you know, and I much desire it."

" Do you? That is very sweet. Let me try." But when he had played the prelude to a song he stopped short. His hands dropped from the key-board. " I cannot," he said, turning to her with eyes full of unspoken words. " I am under a spell. Will you send for Madam Susie, and let me talk business?" Clara assented, and a minute after Susie entered.

" Oh, madam," he said, holding her hand, " I have the weight of Atlas on my shoulders;" and placing her in an arm-chair, he took a seat near her. Susie looked at him tenderly, like a divine little motherly soul as she was, and going to him, said, " You are tired. Now, make yourself perfectly at ease while you talk to me. I wish you would lie down on the sofa here, and light your cigar."

" I wish I could," he said; " but somehow I cannot lounge in a lady's presence—not even when she desires it. It comes from my European breeding; but I will take a cigar, if it is not disagreeable to you."

" Papa always smokes here," said Clara, " so you need have no hesitation. We both rather like the odor of a nice cigar. I am very used to it, you know ——"

Like a flash it entered the count's mind that Dr. Delano was the cause of her preoccupation; and strange as it may seem, this was almost the first moment that he realized her position with regard to that man. He had never thought of her before as bound to any one, though he knew, of course, the fact of her marriage. He gave himself, however, no time to think of it, but commenced at once to " talk business," as he had called it.

" You know," he said, " the Social Palace is passed the Rubicon, and with me there is no turning back. To-morrow there will be fifty men at work on a temporary building for the brick-making. The chief of that part of the work, a man of immense executive ability, I sent here the day after I left. He is at the hotel, and has done good work since he was engaged. In three months we can commence the walls ; but long before that, the subterranean air-galleries, cellars, sewers, and so forth, will be built. I have the general plan, which I brought from Guise, but as to details I am less fortunate; besides, you know I am to make this on a somewhat larger scale, though the original accommodates fifteen hundred. I put the limit at two thousand for this. I want you ladies and the doctor to go with me to-morrow and fix the exact location and position of the palace, the manufactories, the gardens and pleasure-grounds, and the nursery and conservatories."

Susie's eyes gleamed as he talked ; when he paused, she jumped up and walked the floor in excitement. "Oh, this is glorious, Clara ! See what a magnificent thing it is to have capital—no, not that, but to have the soul to use it nobly for the amelioration of honest, laboring people."

" You want to kiss me, Madam Susie. I see it in your eyes," the count said, laughing.

" That's just my desire," cried Susie; and coming beside him, she put her arms around his neck and kissed his forehead. In return, he kissed both her cheeks, saying, " You are my right-hand man, you know. I leave you this plan to-night, which you will study, and here is a magazine having a pretty full description of the original. In a short time I must go to Guise. I shall take Min, my daughter," he added, gravely, as if there was no possibility of questioning his right, " and you must look about for a nurse to take charge of her. I should think Linnie would like that place; and understand, I have a special reason for hitting upon her. You will go—that is, you *can*, can you not? You see, Min must go, for I wish her to stay, if you are willing—not otherwise, of course; and as this is a business expedition, you must be totally relieved from nursery duties."

Susie's head fairly swam. " Yes, you can go as well as not," said Clara. " It will do me good to work into your place. I will commence with new responsibilities at once, so I may be used to them. Young Page, the new assist-ant, is going to prove a great acquisition to us."

" Oh yes, I remember," said the count. " I must see him."

" Can you not come back with us from the prospecting expedition, to-morrow? " asked Susie. " You and the doctor, and take lunch with us. We have taken Page right into the family, you know. He is really a nice young fellow—so well bred and modest." The count accepted, and then bade the ladies good-morning.

CHAPTER XXXVI.

THE next day was rainy, and the prospecting expedition, as Susie called it, was deferred; the count meanwhile employed the time in completing the purchase of a farm of sixty-five acres, adjoining his original fifty, and now he held all the land he wanted. This farm was under cultivation, while twenty acres of the other land was a forest of large oak, chestnut, and maple trees. This was to form a pleasure-ground, for which it offered singular advantages, since it had, near its centre, a beautiful lake, fed by never-failing springs, in a hill on its further and northern boundary. The following day was magnificent, and though the distance was very short, the party set out about nine o'clock in an open carriage, for the count never walked, except on pleasure excursions; then he was equal to the strongest. He and the doctor occupied the front seat, and the ladies the other. Pausing on the high ground that sloped down to the bridge, they surveyed the scene before them. Along the river, on the opposite bank, which was quite steep and skirted with large trees, except immediately on either side of the bridge, there lay a broad, level field, straight beyond which was the twenty acres of forest, level at first, and rising gradually toward the north-western hills. The count turned on his seat, and asked "Madam Susie" where the palace should rise—"Speak, and I obey you; I and the other 'slaves of the lamp,'" he added, smiling.

"I would have it set back two-thirds the distance toward the wood," answered Susie, promptly. "The front, on right and left of the avenue, extending from the bridge, should be a park and garden, in which should stand first, after the bridge, the theatre."

"Easy of access to our 'transtevere' neighbors. I see your idea; go on," said the count.

"I have no very definite ideas further," said Susie, "except that I would have the silk manufactory to the right or east, reserving the west as much as possible for our view."

"The brick-making establishment," said the doctor, "could be placed still beyond, further to the right."

"Yes, I agree to all that," said the count. "Now that lake in the woods, I find is just high enough to carry the water to the third story of the palace. You see there is land enough, so there is no object in having it higher. I tested the water yesterday. It is perfect, and will amply supply all our needs. Now, behind the palace are your nurseries and gardens, and in these, and near the palace, we must build our grand swimming-baths. I propose two apartments, one for women and children, and the other for men. In the women's there must be a movable platform, like that at Guise, which will rise at one end to within six inches of the surface of the water— made to rise by simply turning a bar."

"That is for the little children," said Clara. "How fine a thought that was of Mr. Godin! In the centre of each bath we might have an island, about twelve feet in diameter, for flowers."

"A good idea; we will not omit that," said the count. "The palace will be four immense buildings, standing like a Greek cross, with a vast glass-covered court in the centre, about two hundred feet square. Each quadrangle also, will have a glass-roofed court, but not so large. The great central court must be a grand hall for great celebrations. Now what shall we do with the others? The corners of the four buildings lap some ten feet, you understand, and communicate on every story by passages or corridors."

"One of these courts," said Susie, "I would have for a winter conservatory."

"That is my thought exactly," said the count, "and all things are working together admirably. I have spoken for a palm-tree, fifty feet high, and many years old, which is an elephant drawn in a lottery to its owner, and which I can have for the tenth part of what it will be worth for the centre of this court. It once belonged to Gouverneur Morris, of Pennsylvania, I am told."

"Why, I know the history of that tree," said the doctor. "Is that so? Can that be obtained? Well, how all things do conspire to success when you operate on a grand scale! Now, in your great subterranean-ventilating galleries, you are to place hot-air furnaces for warming the palace. One of these galleries can run directly under the court, and hot-water pipes, from a furnace located directly underneath, can warm your conservatory, Susie."

"The swimming-baths are the most difficult to warm, I think. The silk works we will place nearer than we intended, and use the exhausted steam of the engines for the purpose. Baths there must be in the palace as well;

but these swimming-baths I want to make a great feature. Nothing is so refreshing after labor as a swim. It makes the body supple and elastic. I don't think water, as a moral agent, can be over-estimated. Make a community thoroughly clean outside, and the inside will soon set itself in harmony. People will never be moral so long as baths are a luxury."

"Oh !" exclaimed Susie. "I can't believe I shall live to see all this ; or if I ever do see it really accomplished, I shall die of pure joy. Think of it ! Hundreds of poor families having all these luxuries, these splendid conditions for culture and refinement, and all for no more money than they now pay for their miserable tenements ! *Can* it be done ? "

"It certainly can," replied the count ; "and hereafter it will be by labor organizations themselves."

As they drove down over the old wooden bridge, the doctor remarked the necessity of having a new one.

"Yes, I have already thought of that, doctor. I was closeted with your town council yesterday afternoon. I offered to build them a new iron bridge—have it all completed in forty days. You see I have peculiar advantages, for I am a large owner in the Phœnix Iron Bridge Works, in the Schuylkill Valley, Pennsylvania. I proposed to your town council to issue to me small notes, to the amount of fifty thousand dollars, receivable for all taxes and town dues of all kinds. I will endorse them myself, if necessary. With these I can pay the workmen."

"That is a capital idea, Frauenstein," said the doctor ; "but you won't need to endorse them. Those notes will circulate perfectly. Everybody wants the bridge. It has been discussed seriously for over three years."

"When these notes come into the town treasury, it can burn them. They can easily be all redeemed and burnt in the course of a year, and your citizens will have their bridge without feeling the cost in the least."

"Kendrick & Burnham, the bankers," said Clara, "are members of the council. They will of themselves turn the balance, for they know you will have a good deal of banking business, which they expect of course to do."

"Exactly," said the count; "you see how all things work for our interest. I am promised an answer at their next meeting, which is to-morrow night."

Thus discussing the plans, the party drove to the edge of the forest; and as there was no road through it, they walked to the lake on the hill, following the course of a pretty brook that wound down through the woods, across the land, and emptied into the river. It was noon when they returned and drove to the spot where the temporary building for the brick-making was going up. As the carriage approached, the "boss" of the operations came forward and saluted the count with great deference. The count gave him his hand cordially and presented him to the rest of the party. "This is Mr. Stevens, Dr. Forest, with whom you will soon be better acquainted. He is a scientific man, as well as an accomplished artisan, and to him we look for the transformation of this sand into stone bricks." Then the count presented him to the ladies separately, saying, "These are the heads of the firm of Dykes & Delano, Florists, of whom you have heard." He had not, in fact, but did not confess that, as he took the offered hands of the ladies. "They will conduct the florist and nursery industry of our future social palace." While the count was talking and listening to

18

the conversation of the rest, his eyes were busy with the scene before him. There, on piles of lumber, on the ground, on carts, everywhere, the men, some alone, some in small groups, were seated, each one with a long, narrow tin pail or kettle, out of which they were eating their principal meal of the day. Frauenstein looked at Clara. There was an appeal in his eyes that she understood.

"Mr. Stevens," she said, "where you have so many workmen who will be engaged here regularly for months, would it not be practicable to have a table set for them in the building you are putting up? It would seem so much more fraternal and——"

"Human, you would say, madam. Ah! madam, that is the way I ate my dinner for years."

"By ——, it's a shame!" exclaimed the doctor.

The count asked permission of Mr. Stevens to speak to his men ; and driving near a group of three seated on a pile of boards, he said,

"My friends, I wish to ask you a question—not out of curiosity, believe me, but from a motive which you will approve."

"Go ahead, sir," said one of the men, tearing off a piece of tough meat with his teeth.

"I want you to make me an estimate of the cost, the average cost, as near as you can come at it, of a working-man's lunch, such as you are eating to-day."

"I think mine, boss, costs about as much as that you give your dog every day," said a low-browed rough man seated near the group addressed.

"Sure would ye spake to a gintleman like that, Mikey? It's onmannerly in ye, onyhow."

"I'm not offended with Mike. I like his protest. He

is not satisfied, and that is the first thing we want when we propose a reform." Here the intelligence was in some silent, mysterious way communicated from man to man that this black-gloved gentleman was the great capitalist, of whom there were circulating fabulous stories about his untold wealth, and his project of a Social Palace for workingmen. Many of them were incredulous, and suspicious of the intentions of all capitalists; but as the knowledge of the count's presence spread, many of the men rose and doffed their hats to him and his friends, as they gathered round the carriage. After trying again, the count found the lowest average estimate he could get was ten cents. They agreed that if they could have the same for that amount, they should not bring their kettles. The count and Mr. Stevens talked together in a low tone for some minutes; and then the count, rising in his seat, removed his hat and gloves and commenced to address the workmen. Suddenly every voice was hushed and every eye intently studying the elegant face and form before them:

"My friends," he said, "you know my name is Frauenstein, and you have heard that I am a capitalist, which some of you take to be about equivalent to 'enemy.' [Cries of "No, no!"] Now some of you, doubtless, belong to the International Workingmen's Association, and other labor organizations, and you know, as well as I do, that no man can own a million of dollars which he has earned by any industry of his hands. [Cries of "Hear, hear!" and "That's true!"] Some of mine I inherited; but most of it I have acquired by investing it in great industrial enterprises in various parts of this country, of which I am a citizen; and some of it I have acquired in Wall Street, by what is called gold speculation. You know that every dollar of this wealth is the representative of a dollar's worth of productive labor, performed by laboring men like yourselves. I also have done some labor, actual productive labor, and I think I should not exaggerate if I say that in this way I have an honest title to about five hundred dollars ! [Laughter and cries of " Good for you, if you are a count !"] Yes, I am a count, as you say, but I came honestly by that, if I did not by my property, and I confess to a certain pride in my name, for it is an honorable one ; but a thousand titles cannot make a man a true nobleman. In my opinion, he is noblest who most loves his fellow-men. [Great applause.] Now, my friends, it is the desire of my life to do a great work for industry ; and understand well, I do not come to insult you with charity. Every true man despises charity, and wants only a just and fair compensation for honest labor performed. A man wants to have a home of his own ; leisure for studying social and political questions ; he wants baths whereby to keep himself clean : good clothes for himself and family ; he wants his wife freed from the wash-tub and the cooking-stove ; he wants a guarantee of support in sickness and old age ; and especially does he want to see his children educated, and brought up to be noble men and women, who may be an honor to their country. [Immense applause.]

" Now, we propose within the next three years to offer all these advantages, and many more which I have not time to name, to two thousand people, or say five hundred families. When your bricks are done, you will see rising on this spot of 115 acres, a grander palace than your richest citizens have ever dreamed of. It will cost, with all the improvements of the parks and grounds, and the silk manufactory, which will be an industry to support the establishment, about $4,000,000, and I mean that those who build it and those who come to live in it, shall buy it and own it through the rents they pay. Say there will be one thousand working adults earning, on an average, $300 a year. That will be $300,000 a year, which will pay for the home in less than fifteen years.. There will be ample work in the silk manufactory and in the cultivation of flowers for the women, and also for the children during hours that may be spared from their schools. I think, therefore, fifteen years is a fair estimate of the time it will take to purchase your magnificent home. And here I want to say that no credit is due to me for this idea. It is not mine, but that of one whose name you should teach your children to pronounce with reverence, as soon as their lips have learned to utter their first words. It is the name of a Frenchman, who has done already for his workmen what I propose to do here. I allude to Monsieur Godin, the great labor reformer and capitalist, in the town of Guise, in France. [Immense applause, and cheers for Godin rent the air.]

"In a few days I shall put into your hands a pamphlet which I have translated from a part of Monsieur Godin's book, called *Social Solutions*. That will give you a clear idea of the organization and working of the first Social Palace ever founded. The second is the one on which you are now engaged, and I am sure you will work with new spirit now that you see what is expected of you. You are not working to build a stately palace for the rich, while you keep yourselves and your children in hovels, or mean tenement houses. The palace you are to build is to be your own home and that of your children after you. A capitalist builds this, but hereafter labor organizations will build them for themselves, all over the world, until, as I hope, it shall become one fair garden from the Atlantic to the Pacific, and from China to Gibraltar.

"Finally, I come to say the few words which I rose to say, for I did not intend to branch out in this way, and cheat myself out of a few moments of your valuable time! [Laughter and applause.] Your chief here, Mr. Stevens, who is a labor reformer, and whom I trust you will come to love as a brother [cheers for Stevens], thinks it practicable to construct in this temporary building an oven and range, where every day a quarter of an ox or so may be cooked, with loaves of bread and a plenty of good coffee, and that this can be furnished you every day for ten cents each."

Here the count was interrupted by applause and the volunteering of the men to build the range for nothing after working hours.

"That's the right spirit, boys. I know you work hard, and I would not ask it, nor would Mr. Stevens, but I will not dampen your ardor. It shall be as you wish, and I will send you the bricks and lime to-morrow morning. [Cheers.] Some of you are carpenters, and can put together with these rough boards a couple or more long tables. The necessary crockery and table-linen I beg you to allow me to present you, as an offset to your giving your labor to making the oven and the tables. One thing more, and I have done. I met yesterday in your streets, crouched on the pavement, crying, a poor Chinaman, who can scarcely speak a word of English, and who was suffering from hunger. I told him I would give him work, and the way he received my slight kindness, touched my heart. Some boys had been insulting the poor fellow in his poverty and wretchedness, and I took the occasion to read them a lecture. I found out that the Chinaman could cook and wash. Now, what do you say to his coming here to do this cooking, setting the table, and keeping the table-linen clean ? [Applause and assent.] Meanwhile, you see, he can learn our language, and I have no doubt he will prove very useful—perhaps he will take charge of our great steam-laundry, which is to be a part of your Social Palace, and which will free your wives from the wash-tub. [Great applause.] I hope you will treat him well. Never by any carelessness teaze him about his cue, which you know is an honor in the Chinaman's eyes. Respect, you know, always begets respect and confidence, and no man is worthy of the name, who thinks he is better than another, because he dresses differently or happens to be born in a different country.

"I said I would not offer you charity, and I will not; but when this great Social Palace is finished, I will show you that, capitalist though I am, I have one right that you are bound to respect. That right I mean to exercise in organizing a festival and ball on a grand scale, to celebrate the completion of our work ; and if, after I have accomplished all this, you will forgive me for being a capitalist, and consider me a brother, I shall have all the recognition I desire. In conclusion, I propose three cheers for the Social Palace, in the name of liberty, equality, and fraternity."

The three cheers were given with the most deafening enthusiasm. Then followed cheers for the count, and the heartiest wishes for his health and prosperity. Clara, and Susie, and the doctor, were as enthusiastic as any of the men. They cheered and clapped their hands with the men all through the speech, and the carriage turned away and drove off, amid cheers for Dr. Forest, whom all workingmen recognized as a friend, and then cheers for Dykes & Delano. To this Clara and Susie answered by waving their handkerchiefs.

"I had no idea you could be so eloquent," said the doctor to the count, " though I was prepared for a telling speech the moment you opened your mouth." Susie was profuse in her demonstrations of admiration, but Clara was silent.

During the drive home, the doctor took from his pocket a copy of the Oakdale daily and read: " Dr. Forest presents his regards to his patients of Oakdale and vicinity, and hereby announces that he will suspend his medical practice from the first of May, 18—, until the completion of the Social Palace, when he will take charge of the medical service of that institution."

"I fully expected that," said Clara. " I knew papa would have a large hand in that workmen's palace; but what place are you to take, papa? Just before the Chinaman appeared in the programme, I was counting on your volunteering to take the office of *cordon bleu*."

" Which I would do, willingly," said the doctor, " if I could be most useful there."

" By the way, let us stop at the hotel as we are passing, and see what *Too Soon* is doing. That's the name of our celestial brother," said the count.

In a small room in the upper part of the hotel, they found Too Soon seated on the floor, busily sewing. As they entered, he rose and pressed the count's hand to his forehead, and then showed what he knew of western etiquette, by bowing very low to the rest. It was very difficult to talk to him, but by dint of pantomime and a few English words, they found that Too Soon had sewed all night, and had nearly finished his wardrobe, consisting of baggy, thick, linen trowsers and two nondescript jackets. The count tried to convey to him an idea of the function he was to fill over the river, but without success. However, after lunching with Clara and Susie, he returned for Too Soon, took him in his carriage, and drove to a hardware and crockery store, and then to a dry-goods establishment, where he made all the purchases for the new *cuisine*. The moment Too Soon saw the table-cloths, he showed by pantomime that he wished to hem them. He understood, evidently, that the count was going to establish a restaurant somewhere over the river; but he was as devoted as a slave, and ready to do whatever was required of him.

The work went on bravely. Stevens set every man at work who could drive a nail, and in less than a week the building was in use. The cooking arrangement was admirable. The tables built, Too Soon's well-stocked china closet filled and locked, and all the washing and other paraphernalia ready for use. " To-morrow," said Mr. Stevens to his men, "lunch for fifty and over will be spread here. I expect the count will be here. Understand you are all free to act as you usually do—take your own lunches to the table, or bring nothing. A good plate of meat, with gravy and potatoes, will be furnished for six cents; a large cup of coffee for two cents; (Too Soon has already roasted it in the new oven, which works to a charm,) and bread, as much as you want, for two cents more. That makes ten cents. Too Soon will hereafter sleep here, and keep all safe. There will be water and towels provided, so that every man can make himself so presentable that any one, seeing him at table, will be surprised if he don't eat with his fork just like a gentleman. Now I ain't afraid of offending you. I am a workman like you, and used to eat with my knife, which was all right when we had to use a two-pronged fork, and I confess, boys, that I shall have no little pride tomorrow at this lunch."

"Boss, I guess some of us would know a silver fork if we had a good square view of it," said one of the men.

"All right," said Stevens, laughing. "You know very well there are some people who think a workingman must be a boor, anyway. Von Frauenstein is not one of them, I promise you. On the contrary, he expects rather too much of us." The men said nothing; but evidently they determined, each and every one, to perish rather than forget and put their knives in their mouths. This piece of policy was rather nicely managed on the part of Stevens, for there is nothing on which people, who have been deprived of refined breeding, are so sensitive as this very subject of manners.

The next evening Burnham and his wife were at the Kendricks. Mrs. Burnham enquired for the count.

"Oh, he's running and driving everywhere," said Mrs. Kendrick. "We scarcely ever see him. He apologizes, and says he don't like to make our house a convenience; but I won't hear of his going to a hotel, of course."

"Why, the whole town is talking of nothing but Von Frauenstein and his great workmen's palace," said Mrs. Burnham; "and, do you know, there are over fifty men

at work already, and to-day they had a banquet. My
boys were over there, and all the afternoon they've been
dinning *Too Soon* into my ears. He wanted to know the
names of everything, and it wasn't enough for them to
tell him, but they actually helped him wipe his dishes.
I've forbidden them to ever go there again."

"Oh, let them go," said Burnham. "I haven't seen
Charlie so well for months. The excitement is innocent, and much better than he will get in the streets."
While they were talking, Kendrick was very uncere-
moniously walking up and down the drawing-room with
his hands behind him. Pretty soon he stopped short
before the company.

"Burnham," said he, "we are old fogies. We've let
the world get way ahead of us. I saw a sight to-day
such as I never expected to see, to say the least."

"Oh, you were over there too, were you? Do tell us
about it," said his wife.

"Why there were tables set for over fifty—snowy
linen, napkins, silver forks, beautiful white china, and
I'll swear if most of the men didn't eat as decorously as
those at my own table."

"I shouldn't have thought they would like spectators,"
said Burnham.

"Spectators! Bless your soul! I was invited to
lunch with them."

"Goodness! Did you ever hear of such assurance!
What did you do?" asked Mrs. Burnham.

"Why, I accepted." The ladies both uttered exclamations of amazement. "What could I do? There
was Frauenstein just about to sit down. I couldn't
pretend I had lunched. Everybody knew better, and

wherever Frauenstein could hob-nob, I ought to be able to."

"But you couldn't eat anything, of course," said Mrs. Burnham.

"On the contrary, I had a very satisfactory lunch. In the first place, the coffee was as good as I ever tasted anywhere. The beef was roasted to a turn, the gravy perfect, and the baked potatoes also; and as for the bread, Mrs. Kendrick, I would much like to see as good in my own house."

"Why, how on earth could it be done? A Chinaman beggar couldn't do all that!"

"Yes, he's a cook; besides there's a French baker in the gang of workmen, and he showed the Chinaman how to make the bread and the coffee."

"For my part, I think Frauenstein will get himself into a scrape. What will Ely & Gerrish's men say? There's nobody to give them such a dinner every day. Why, don't you see it will raise wages?"

"Oh, no, Burnham; no gift about it. The men built the kitchen and tables at odd hours, and they pay for the food just what it costs, with enough over to make up the Chinaman's salary."

"Why, it is that horrid dirty Chinaman, I hear, that we used to see about the street trying to sell matches," said Mrs. Burnham.

"No dirt about him now. He had clean new clothes, his cue neatly braided, and his skin, and even his nails, were as clean as yours or mine."

"And the conversation was very edifying, I suppose," said Mrs. Burnham.

"Just about as good as the average. I'll be blest if I

haven't heard worse at my own table.   To be sure, some of them spoke bad English.   One of them, at the further end of the table, where Frauenstein and I sat, got up, and asked to speak, if his fellow-workmen and the distinguished guests were willing."

"That was putting it rather neat," said Burnham. "He made a telling speech in very good English."

"Do repeat it," said Mrs. Kendrick, as curious as if her husband had just returned from a visit to the South Sea Island savages.

"Well, he said, among other things, that Count Frauenstein's address to them a week ago had touched them deeply, even independently of the magnificent promise of the Social Palace, which was something they could not yet realize as possible—touched them deeply because he had recognized the dignity of labor, and the rights of laborers to a just share of the products of their industry."

"Oh, he's filling their heads with that stuff, is he?" said Burnham.

"Not all stuff.   No man could talk to men and win such unbounded admiration without talking soundly.   I tell you, I'm more than ever convinced that we are old fogies.   This laborer said workingmen knew perfectly well they were far below the educated gentleman in refinement, in manners, in culture—in everything, perhaps, but heart.   He thought no men had more heart than workingmen, and workingmen knew their true friends just as quickly as they knew the true gentleman from the sham. 'I felt,' he said, 'as the count talked, that I could not do enough to express my gratitude that God had sent us so true and noble a friend—a man disclaiming the idea of charity, and avowing that the best help a workman could have, was that which gave him a field wherein he could help himself. I felt, as he talked of our building ourselves a palace, that I would work my own fingers off to build him and his a palace, for he deserves it, God bless him !' and the man sat down, quite overcome."

"Oh, I wish I had been there," said Mrs. Kendrick. "He must be a sensible man."

"Did Frauenstein say anything ?" asked Burnham.

"Oh ! He was on his feet like a flash. He said the man's sentiments did him honor—his emotion did him honor. With men having such comprehension of their rights, and such faith in the honesty of their fellow-men, he could trust the building of the palace. And then he drew a picture of life in the Social Palace—the labor, which would not be drudgery, but a pleasant exercise, that would preserve the health of both body and mind ; the nursery and schools for the children ; the grand festivals in the vast, glass-covered court, festooned with banners and garlands of the flowers their women and children would cultivate ; the music, the societies, the theatre, where the children would learn elegance of bearing and address—O Lord ! Burnham, I never heard anything like it. You see, he has studied this subject profoundly. If he succeeds, you will see one grand thing—the happiness of the aged, for they will have a sphere just as the children will. Now, life is organized for the strongest— that is, for adults. No doubt about it. Children are not happy, nor healthy, as a general thing. They are in the way ; so are old people. Well, he only made a little speech, ending with a depreciation of war, and some touching remarks on the cultivation of the sentiment of the brotherhood of man. War, he called a stupendous imbecility, as a civilized way of settling disputes, and he offered a gracious tribute to Christ and Dr. Forest."

"Oh, shame!" exclaimed Mrs. Kendrick.

"I don't mean, you know, that he mixed them together. He spoke of Christ when talking of the brotherhood of man, and he said, but for Dr. Forest, one of the best and noblest, as well as most learned men he had ever met, the first Social Palace would have been built in some other place. I never saw men so earnest. Why, they already adore the man. They would do anything for him. He'll get good work out of them, you may be sure."

"Well, I should think he might, if in working for him, they are building up a grand home for themselves," said Mrs. Burnham.

"Cost $4,000,000, you say, Kendrick. I tell you, it will never pay," said Burnham. "So much ornament, you see. Now what on earth do poor people want of an astronomical observatory, and a theatre, and library, and billiard-saloon? It's all nonsense. Such people want nothing but a decent home and decent things generally."

"Well, that has been my view; but Frauenstein says you won't know the second generation of the Social Palace as what we understand as laborers' children."

"But don't you see, bringing them up in such luxury, baths, and amusements, and accomplishments, and all that," said Burnham, "they'll feel themselves too good to work?"

"That's just exactly what I told Frauenstein; but he says they will certainly have an attraction to luxuries, just like the rich, but they will have another attraction

the rich lack, and that is a love of labor, not drudgery—
you know the distinction he makes—a love of productive
labor, that will be second nature to them ; so they will
despise idleness, and honor no one who leads a frivolous
life."

"Why, you are quite a labor reformer," said Mrs.
Burnham. "That Count Von Frauenstein bewitches
everybody."

"Well, I see one thing. He is a happy man. It's a
luxury to see a happy man. Now, I'm not a happy man.
You are not a happy man, Burnham. We are just business machines—animated ledgers, you might call us.
Frauenstein has the fervor, and enthusiasm, and freshness
of a boy ; so has Dr. Forest and that man Stevens ; and
I swear, that Chinaman is happier than I am !"

"Dear me, Elias !" said Mrs. Kendrick, not knowing
what to think of her husband's mood. "I'm afraid you
are not well."

"Yes, I am. I've only been awfully stirred up, that's
all. If things *could* be so that a man could make a lot
of people happy while putting money in his own pocket,
business would have more life in it."

"Well, Kendrick, we'll see how this thing works.
Time enough to talk then."

"How about the bridge ?" asked Mrs. Burnham.

"Oh, that's settled ; the notes are to be issued at once
—are ready now, I believe."

"That is a good idea," said Burnham. "I'm pleased
with that ; we shall get the bridge and not feel it at all.
That's a sound idea of Frauenstein. Well, maybe he'll
make his big scheme work, and get his money back in
fifteen years, but I don't see it yet."

CHAPTER XXXVII.

POETIC RETRIBUTION.—GROG-SELLERS INTERVIEWED BY
WOMEN.

ON a perfect morning in early May, the very day of
the departure of the count and Madam Susie for
France, a man prematurely old by dissipation, and destitute through wasting his substance by gambling, approached the town of Oakdale, which once had been his
home. His last cent had been spent to bring him to a
railroad station some miles distant, and from sunrise
until ten o'clock he had walked, weary and almost fainting at every step.

He arrived by the least frequented road, and when a
few rods from the house once owned by Mrs. Buzzell, he
sat down under a tree by the roadside. The birds were
singing and chirping in the branches, the sun was warm,
and the air balmy and delicious. As he sat there, a little
child approached and stood silently regarding him with
evident curiosity. It was a lovely child, whose soft,
golden hair descended to her waist from under a quaint
little mushroom-shaped hat of white straw. She was
dressed very coquettishly, her stockings nicely gartered
above the knee, short white dress with embroidered
flounces, and pretty bronzed gaiter-boots. Her dress was
protected by a jaunty white apron, with bib and pockets
trimmed with crimson braid. Her blue eyes showed

traces of tears, and the man looking at the charming little picture before him, soon discovered the cause—a dead canary-bird whose tiny claws and yellow tail peeped out of one of her apron pockets.

"Well, I never before saw a little girl with a canary-bird in her apron pocket," he said, trying to smile.

"You never had a birdie die. *You* never did; did you?" she asked, almost ready to sob.

"No, I never had a birdie. I am sorry yours died."

The child took the dead bird from her pocket, and sitting down on a stone beside the man, caressed it and moaned pitifully, "Oh, birdie! birdie! I am so sorry Minnie gave you chocolate drops! Oh, birdie! birdie! How can I leave you in the cold ground! I shall never, never see you again!"

The child's distress touched the rough gambler's heart, and he tried to console her. "What a beautiful thing this child is! Some rich man's spoiled darling," were his thoughts, and he sighed heavily.

"Poor old man!" said the little one, forgetting her own trouble for a moment. "What is the matter?"

"Do you think me so old? How old are you?"

"I am six years old."

"Six years old!" repeated the man, and then he asked her name.

"My name is Minnie von Frauenstein. I am Paul's little girl, you know, and he gave me my birdie. Oh, it sung *so* sweetly! and I gave it chocolate drops. Poor birdie! Minnie was so silly;" and the child sobbed again.

Dan, for of course the reader has guessed that it was he, though he was broken in spirit and weak and exhausted by fever and chills, from which he had long suf-

fered in the West. had yet in his degradation something
more of human softness than he had ever had in his
strength. When this beautiful little girl told him she
was six years old, the thought flashed upon him that his
and Susie's child would be, if living, about this age; and
something in her face appealed to him like a half-forgotten picture. Mrs. Forest had never once alluded to Susie
in her letters, and in the short notes he returned, at long
intervals, in answer to his mother's tiresome, pious com-
munications, he asked no questions, though he had often
determined to do so, or write to his sister, or even to
Susie; but he had never done so. Susie might be gone
away or dead, for all he knew, and the child too. This
one was no such child as would spring from him and
Susie, he thought. This was some proud, petted beauty,
whose birth had been heralded as a blessing, and when
she told him her name, his speculation ceased, but every
word and motion charmed him. She seemed like a creature of some purer, higher sphere than that to which he
belonged, and when he spoke to her he softened his voice
and manner as by instinct.

"I must bury my birdie and go back," she said, "for
I am going away with mamma and Linnie and Paul.
The ship is waiting for us, papa says, in Boston, and it
sails on the great ocean to-morrow morning. We are
going to France, you know, to the Social Palace."

"Who's Linnie? Not Linnie Forest?"

"Yes; Linnie Forest, my doctor's girl. Don't you
know Linnie? She is my nurse now."

Dan saw at once that this Frauenstein must be some
great nabob, or his mother would never let Linnie go in
such a capacity—a relative, he thought, of that million-

aire count, of whom he had heard in his youth. As the child ran on, talking of many things, she mentioned her mother as "Madam Susie."

"Susie!" echoed Dan. "Is that your mother's name? What is her other name? I mean, what was it before she was married?" But he could get no satisfactory reply. "Is this Mr. Frauenstein, then, your father?" he asked.

"Yes," said Minnie. "He wasn't once, you know, but he made me his little girl. He isn't Mr. He's Count."

"Who is your real father?"

"Oh, we don't ever speak of him. He was a naughty, bad man. He didn't love me nor mamma. He went off and forgot his little girl; but Paul loved me, and is so good to me. He is my Slave of the Lamp, you know." Dan covered his face with his hands, and hot tears of shame and remorse poured down his face. Minnie patted his head with her soft little hands, and told him not to cry. "Come home to my house," she said, "and we will give you something to eat."

"Thank you; I am not a beggar."

"Well, you are poor, ain't you?"

"Yes, poor enough, God knows."

"Well, then, you can work for Auntie Clara while we are gone; and she is such a darling auntie, and she is very kind to all poor people. So is mamma too, and Paul, and Minnie is too." While she was talking the count approached, being anxious to know why she stayed so long. Dan rose totteringly from his seat when the elegant gentleman appeared. "My child," the count said to Minnie, who ran towards him, "your mamma is anxious about you. Go quickly and get ready. The train leaves in a few minutes." And taking her up in his arms, he kissed her tenderly. She had not buried her bird. Her heart had failed at the last moment. She would leave him with auntie, she said. As she ran back toward the house, the count turned to the man and said,

"You look ill, my friend. You had better go to Dr. Forest, just across the Common."

"I know where he lives," said Dan. "That is where I am going." And the count took the poor, broken-down man's arm, though Dan tried to refuse, and walked with him back to the Common, telling him on the way that Dr. Forest would be able to set him all right, and then would give him work, if he desired it. "Tell him Frauenstein sent you to him, and you will be well taken care of. Or, better, come to the house with me. The doctor may be there by this time."

Dan declined as politely as he could. His emotions were varied, to use a mild term, at being recommended to the charity of his own father by a great nabob, who had adopted his child, and was just at that moment starting on a European tour with that child's mother. Dan supposed, as a matter of course, that Susie had married this man. His head was in a dazed condition, as, from behind a great tree on the edge of the Common, he saw the party emerge from the house. Susie, and the child, and Linnie received the parting embraces from Clara and the doctor, who then handed them into an open carriage. The count lingered a moment at the porch, holding Clara's hand. Susie looked more mature, and much more beautiful to Dan than ever before, and through her tears shone a radiant happiness. The count came forward, embraced the doctor, jumped into the carriage, which immediately drove off, Min throwing kisses to the doctor and Clara till it was out of sight.

Shame, regret, self-reproach, and jealousy, gnawed at Dan's very vitals, as he stood there, a poor, forlorn wretch, witnessing a bliss that might have been his, but for his own folly. He felt strangely attracted to the beautiful child. He could feel still her little hand patting his head, and pitying his sorrow. Surely if ever there was an exemplification of poetic retribution, Dan Forest experienced it that day.

He stood supporting himself against the old tree for some time after his father and sister entered the house, and then he went to his mother. She wept over him, and accepted without question his representation of the causes of his sad condition. According to this representation, he was the innocent victim of an untoward fate. He said not a word about gambling or drinking; and as he was certainly cadaverous in appearance from his intermittent fever, as well as from hard drinking, she attributed the effect wholly to the causes he assigned. She gave him a biscuit and a glass of wine, and then made him take a warm bath, and don the clean linen she prepared for him. While they were at lunch, the doctor came in. He looked searchingly into Dan's face as he held his trembling hand, and the quick eye of the physician read the secret of the terrible life his son had led; but he uttered no word of reproach. He sat down to the table and listened, with Mrs. Forest and Leila, to all that Dan had to say of the beauties of California, and the scenes through which he had passed, carefully omitting those in which he had played a disgraceful part, or presenting *his* rôle as that of a third party. Mrs. Forest thought the state of society must be dreadful in California, and wondered that her son could live in such a moral atmosphere !

On a subsequent and private examination, the doctor found Dan's system even more shattered than he had expected, and told him he must leave off drinking, or there was no hope for him. Dan promised faithfully to follow the regimen the doctor prescribed, seemed very reasonable and grateful for his father's kindness, and that very day, late at night, a policeman brought him home in a beastly state of intoxication.

Poor Mrs. Forest had been touched to the heart that her only son should have returned on foot, like a beggar, to the home of his youth, and she had supplied him generously with money, a fact she now regretted. Dan, in his weakness, illustrated well the truth of the old saying, *in vino veritas.* He was maudlin to the last degree. He raved about his "dear child," his "beautiful Minnie"—how she looked with the dead canary in her apron pocket, and how cruelly she had been torn from his protection by that "swell, Frauenstein," whose head he seemed very anxious to "punch," as he declared. Mrs. Forest was disgusted beyond measure by the low words Dan used; but the doctor studied him, as the naturalist would some strange species of animal. After Dan had wept copiously over the wrong he had suffered in being robbed by the count of Susie's love, he ordered champagne and then "cocktails" of his mother, whom he took for the mistress of an unmentionable resort; and then the doctor managed to get him up-stairs and on the bed, when he removed his boots and left him.

"How awful! How awful! What shall we do with him?" exclaimed the mother, as the doctor re-entered and threw himself on the lounge.

"I don't know, Fannie. He's only one step from *delirium tremens.* He ought to go at once to an inebriate asylum." Mrs. Forest was shocked at the idea. "It couldn't be so bad as that. She would have a long talk with him. Doubtless he had met old friends and they had induced him to drink."

"My dear, he is already over the bay. His nerves are shattered. He has no power to save himself. Talk to him! I should as soon expect to stop the thunder by beating a tam-tam."

"I know. Those are your fatalist views. You don't believe in free-will, so of course you will say he can't save himself."

"What is free-will? One of our greatest scientists characterizes it as the 'lawlessness of volition.' The will is not a faculty. It is simply the state of mind immediately preceding action, and that state is determined by motives; by circumstances and attractions which we do not create."

"Yes, we do. We create them in others. We constantly affect their motives and their actions; and so we may act on ourselves, and change our motives. We can make weak ones strong."

"What do you mean by *we* acting on *ourselves?* But I will not quibble, Fannie. What is the result, when you put two pounds in one scale of a balance and one pound in the other? Dan's desire for the excitement produced by alcohol is the two-pound weight; his resisting force is the other."

"I am sure there can be no pleasure in the excitement he is now under, for example."

"Oh, yes; a subverted pleasure. He felt himself a hero as he talked about his wrongs, and he had strong hopes of conquering Frauenstein, whom he thinks his enemy. You see it is insanity; but many insane people are happy. This is often the case when insane enough to be ignorant of their condition. Some madmen enjoy years of a triumphant career as Julius Cæsar, Napoleon, and so on."

"Well, then, you think Dan happy, and that we had better do nothing to save him," said Mrs. Forest, with a sad irony. "For my part, I shall do all I can to avoid the repetition of this."

"Do all you can, dear. You should know, without my telling you, how I feel about our son; but I see no possible way to save him, except the one I suggested. How do you propose to keep him from getting in the same condition to-morrow?"

Mrs. Forest was silent a moment, and then she went quickly out of the room. Pretty soon she returned. "Just look!" she said, holding some crumpled money in her hands and counting it. "Two dollars and eighty-four cents, out of twenty dollars that I gave him to-day. Well, he can't get any liquor to-morrow; that's one satisfaction. Such a shame! Such a disgrace to us!"

"Rather worse than Clara's leaving Delano, eh?"

"Oh, don't mock me, doctor. It is a hundred thousand times worse." This concession was quite new on Mrs. Forest's part, and the doctor did his best to comfort and reassure his wife. Dan, however, did come home the next night in much the same state, after seeming so peni-

18

tent, and promising his mother that she would never see him intoxicated again. In sore distress Mrs. Forest then went to Clara. It was the first time she had crossed the threshold in seven years. Clara received her in the sweetest, most filial way; took her all over the conservatories and nurseries, and presented young Page to her. Mrs. Forest was greatly pleased with this happy, modest young fellow. She looked at his fair complexion, his light, boyish moustache just appearing, and thought of her own boy, before the wicked world had degraded and ruined him. He wore a straw hat, shading his girlish complexion, and a brown linen blouse, buttoned to the throat. Mrs. Forest stayed and took lunch with her daughter, when there appeared at the table three of Clara's flower-girls and this young Page, now divested of his blouse, which left exposed a fine linen shirt, printed all over with dogs of every species. It was a new experience for Mrs. Forest to sit down with working-people; but then she was getting old, and had had strange havoc made lately with all her "settled" notions of things. She watched these young people narrowly; noticed how clean they were, even to their finger-nails, and that their manners at table were unexceptionable. Clara called them her children; and it was pleasant to Mrs. Forest to see the affection and harmony existing between Clara and them.

During the lunch the conversation turned on the woman's-rights convention, which was to sit at Oakdale the following week. Mrs. Kendrick had actually signed the call, and Mrs. Forest had been almost tempted to do so, but that was before the count's name had been added, or she would not have resisted. These adolescents seemed to have very decided views on the subject of equal political rights, especially young Page. Mrs. Forest asked him where he obtained his first convictions on this mooted question. " From my mother, ma'am," he answered, promptly. She had had at one time a very successful millinery industry in a large village near Boston, and her husband ruined it through drinking. Mrs. Forest did not see how the ballot in his mother's hands could have prevented her husband from drinking.

" I think, madam," he replied, " that the ballot in the hands of women would shut up the rum-shops. Would you not yourself vote to have them all cleaned out of Oakdale ? "

This was touching Mrs. Forest in a tender place, but the young man knew nothing of her special interest in the question.

The doctor came in afterward, bringing Dan with him, and they held a family council on the subject of his weakness. He defended himself for awhile, declaring that he did not drink more than other fellows, but finally he broke down like a child—confessed he could not resist drinking, and said he meant to put a bullet through his head. Clara was very gentle to him. She soon hit upon the strongest motive that could be brought to bear upon him—his regard for Susie, and the hope that she had not wholly ceased to care for him. He told his mother if she hadn't treated Susie like a dog, making her eat with Dinah instead of with the family, he should not have been ashamed of his love for her, and would have married her before ever Clara came home from school ; by which all understood he meant before the appearance of Miss Marston. Dan seemed greatly relieved when he learned that Susie had gone abroad solely on business, and that there was no idea of marriage between her and the count, though he had adopted Minnie. Dan said if Susie would forgive him and care for him, he could stop drinking; and Mrs. Forest, seizing this hope, inspired Dan with it, though Clara said she did not believe he could ever win her—certainly not as a dissipated man. Dan was pretty sure of himself, and made a strong vow to abstain from drinking and follow the doctor's directions until he looked "a little less like a corpse," as he said. He seemed to be well pleased that Susie had not seen him in his present condition. Of course the poor fellow was sincere in his resolution; but in three days he came home reeling. Again Mrs. Forest sought Clara for advice.

"I have thought of a plan," said Clara, "that might do some good. If you will go with me, we will visit every drinking-saloon in town; see the keepers and appeal to them. Perhaps we can get them to promise to stop selling Dan liquor." But Mrs. Forest was not equal to the task. She said she should sink with shame to enter such places. Clara urged her most earnestly. "I am sure it will do some good at least. Mrs. Burnham, perhaps, will go with us. You see how intemperance is ruining not only Dan, but many young men. Burnham's only son, not yet twenty, is a drunkard. Now, Mr. Burnham goes for shutting up the drinking-places. They are discussing this in the town-council, and the dealers are having their fears aroused, and could easily be persuaded to make some compromise. Do go, mamma! You would not see me go alone?"

"No, I would not; but ——"

"How can you say 'but'? I should think you would gladly make any effort to save Dan."

"Well, go and see Mrs. Burnham. Let us see what she says."

"Why, mother dear, it is for you to go. You and Mrs. Burnham both have sons ruined by drink. You can appeal to her as I cannot; and besides, I am so driven by my business."

Of course, any one who waits for others to move, can never be counted on for any heroic work. Clara had to go to Mrs. Burnham herself. Mrs. Burnham believed in the move, and said she would consult her husband. She did so, and he told her to not "make a fool of herself," which was the best thing he could have done, for it roused a spirit of defiance, and no sooner was he out of the house than she ordered her carriage, drove over to Clara's, and announced herself ready. On the way they called for Mrs. Kendrick, who joined them, and Mrs. Forest also at the last.

In some of the places they visited, they saw sickening scenes; but Clara's noble presence, her commanding eyes, her frank, womanly speech, gave the rest courage. She asked in every instance for a private interview with the heads of such establishments, and this interview was often had, for want of a better place, in back rooms piled with casks of liquor, demijohns, and bottles. Clara leading, the three elegant ladies followed, looking neither to the right nor to the left, but rather to the floor covered with sawdust, to absorb the tobacco-juice, ends of cigars, and dirt. The air was sickening in the extreme. Clara laid the case before the proprietors, appealed to their humanity, even when she had little faith in the existence of the sentiment, and pictured to them the suffering of mothers and wives and sisters, at the sight of their loved ones ruined for all good in this world. Some of the men affected contempt for any one who didn't know "when he had got enough." Mrs. Burnham occasionally put in a word of indignant protest that the town should allow poisonous liquors to be sold to young men, and boys in their teens. At one place a burly-necked, brutal man told Clara she had better go somewhere else to preach temperance, and suggested, with a leer, that a good place for her talents was among the "shriekers" at the approaching convention. When they left this place, their cheeks burning, Clara said, "Which of you ladies will tell me you have all the rights you want? These men, my friends, are your masters. These make the laws that control your property and your happiness. These men would teach *us* our sphere, and make us forever dependent upon them, and the laws they make without our consent."

"Oh, don't!" exclaimed Mrs. Burnham. "I am so angry already that I could burn up every rum-cask in town, and, I had almost said, these brutes with it."

"But don't forget this, Mrs. Burnham: we are on a mission of strategy. We are not the political equals of these men, and every sign of anger you show, betrays your impotence to help yourself, and weakens our chance of success. Here we are at the next saloon. Now do be calm, Mrs. Burnham."

It was a long and arduous task, but at last, without flagging, they finished the rounds. A great number of the liquor-dealers promised to cease selling intoxicating drinks to those known as drunkards, or to make an exception in the case of Dan and young Burnham. Clara often asked them to promise "upon their honor," which always flattered a certain class of these men.

It was a good lesson in woman's rights to these women who went with Clara, and it greatly increased their admiration for her personally. The effort did much more good than they expected; for though Dan, young Burnham, and others, occasionally went home intoxicated, the occurrence was rare, and gave Dan a chance to follow up his father's treatment and recover his health. The doctor, in the count's absence, had the full control of the works over the river, and after a month or so, Dan went daily with his father, and becoming interested, did good service in the preparation of the parks and gardens.

Mrs. Forest was very grateful that Clara had persuaded her to go on that "terrible excursion," as she called it. "You are a noble girl, Clara," she said, with expansion, "and I feel that I have not always been just to you. If I had my life to live over again, I should do many things differently."

"Oh, mother dear," Clara replied, embracing her, "you have done the best you could. Clara has no fault to find with her mamma;" and seizing her mother in a weak moment, asked her, as a great favor, to attend the coming convention !

"Well," said Mrs. Forest, resignedly, "I will go. There can be no harm in it. Many of our most respectable people have signed the call. But," she added, with a sudden sign of terror, "you don't suppose I should be called on to sit on the platform, or offer a resolution or anything, do you ?" Clara laughed. "Oh no, mamma. There will be no backwardness on the part of women, to do all that is required. I myself am going to read an address."

"You, Clara! Well. I begin to believe it is 'written,' as the count says, that you are to do everything you set out to do. I might as well yield at discretion. The prospect of some time seeing you on a woman's-rights platform used to be my nightmare. That also is 'written,' you see."

CHAPTER XXXVIII.

PROGRESS OF THE WORK.

DURING the spring and summer the work over the river went on so grandly and surely, that the most skeptical doubted no longer that the great enterprise would be accomplished. Bricks, of many shapes and colors and forms, were ready by hundreds of thousands. The forest was laid out in broad winding avenues, according to the plan ; the water-main from the lake was laid, the sewers and drains leading to the river in their places, the great subterranean galleries for ventilation constructed, the cellars completed, and the broad stone foundations of the immense palace and buildings were all completed. Every mail from France brought letters from the count giving the most minute directions, and so harmoniously did everything work, that scarcely a day's labor was lost by any change of details in the plan. The bridge had been completed long ago, and Oakdale was well pleased. with the light, elegant structure placed there as if by enchantment. For when the piers were laid, the railroad disgorged at the station, one evening, a quantity of strange-looking iron-ware, every part made exactly for its place and fitted to its neighbor part. Some strangers, men from the Phœnix Works, accompanied the charge, and in an incredibly short space of time, lo ! the bridge was laid and carriages bearing curious visitors and heavy carts were passing over it. The jocose Social Palace laborers declared that they passed over the river to their work in paddle-boats one morning, and at night returned by the bridge !

The scrip issued by the town authorities to aid the building of the bridge, passed everywhere without question, from the banking-house of Kendrick & Burnham to the farmer's stall in the Oakdale market. In fact, the people rather preferred it to "greenbacks," though at first they had eyed it suspiciously, and asked questions. Then it came to be called "Bridge Scrip," and the "count's money," and was everywhere the text of crude, or deep, financial theories. Said Kendrick, one of the town-council, "This paper is out to the amount of fifty thousand dollars. The taxes have just been collected, but the people took no pains to pay their taxes with it. They did so only in a few cases. I don't see why it might not be kept forever in circulation."

"Only," said another, "we stand committed to burn it as fast as it comes in."

"Of course. I know that, and don't intend to prevent it; but I only say, why would anything but good come by keeping it in circulation ? The men who built the bridge are paid. Von Frauenstein was paid by this paper. He has got it all paid out to his workmen. The scrip has done its work, and it still keeps on working. I only ask, why not let it work for us—that is, the town? It is not only as good as it was at first, but a good deal better, for the town is rich, as everybody knows. What do you think about it, Dr. Forest ?"

"I ? I think specie basis all rot. It is simply a relic of barbarism—when there was no commerce, only barter.

Then, when civilization advanced a little, and men wanted to sell their ivory, and the buyer had not rhinoceros hides, or whatever was wanted in exchange, there arose the necessity for something, to give in exchange for the ivory, that would buy what the seller wanted. Naturally the first money was bright beads, bright metal coins — things of intrinsic value. As civilization progresses, barter ceases, and commerce commences. We have arrived then at the conception of value, and use a mere symbol of it. We don't want money now that has intrinsic value, any more than we want a figure nine with nine positive strokes in it, or a yardstick made of gold."

"But you must have a basis of wealth," said one of the listeners. "I know we don't want coin for business purposes. It is unhandy and cumbrous. The commerce of to-day could not march a step without bank-notes and checks. Now the United States issues our paper-money; but it must keep specie in its treasury vaults to the amount of the paper issued, according to some."

"Which it does not do," said the doctor, "and everybody knows it. You are mistaken in supposing that. It is required simply to keep a certain specie reserve; that is all."

"Why don't we bust up then?" asked an awkward new-comer, who felt the heavy responsibility of citizenship.

"We can't 'bust up,' my friend," said the doctor, with a very broad smile, "because we have a much better foundation for this paper-money than rhinoceros hides, wampum, or gold coin. That foundation is the wealth of the nation, and the credit of the people."

"I don't understand," said Kendrick, "how you would fix your basis."

"My idea," said the doctor, "is that of many who have studied the subject profoundly : that the basis should be the cereals and certain other commodities necessary to the support of life and comfort. Average their prices during twenty years, in order to get at your unit of value, or dollar."

"Ah ! but that of necessity would fluctuate ; one year is fruitful, another unfruitful."

"But the averaging process would preserve the equilibrium," replied the doctor ; "and gold ! you forget how that fluctuates. Why, the discovery of a cheap method of extracting the gold from quartz and gold-bearing sands, liable to happen any day, through our constantly-increasing knowledge of chemistry, and your gold would become ten times as plentiful as it is now. You see that is not the scientific basis. The scientific basis should be the products of industry : the wealth of the nation."

"My dear friend," said Kendrick, "this question of a proper circulating medium has bothered philosophers from the foundation of the world, and we shall not be likely to settle it in ten minutes on a street corner." Kendrick had good reasons for being puzzled. As a banker he was getting into deep water ; but no alarm had been sounded yet. As he took the doctor's arm and walked toward the new bridge, the doctor said :

"Nothing tends more directly to the demoralization of the people than a fluctuating currency. It upsets all our ideas of probity. A man buys, for example, a quantity of cotton to-day for a thousand dollars, payable in three months. In three months gold has 'gone up,' as they say, and instead of paying one thousand, he has to pay eleven or twelve hundred. You see the result is dis-gust, distrust, and loss of nice moral balance. A state of things making an inflated currency possible, creates our stock and gold gamblers—makes men see little harm in influencing Congress to favor great monopolies that oppress and rob the people. From this, only one step to corrupting Congressmen with shares in enterprises which they have then a direct interest in favoring. Now what must be the effect of this on the laboring people, who are beginning to see where they stand? I tell you they are everywhere being roused to desperation. Go into any of the labor organizations here, and listen to what is openly said. If you don't come away with a vivid impression that this deep muttering foretells a coming storm, all I can say is, you can't read the signs of the times."

" I've thought of all this, doctor, but what can we do ? Leave off banking and all other business, and go to build-ing social palaces ? I think I'll wait and see how this one works after a few years. How do you know these workingmen will be better satisfied ? They want luxury and idleness. That's what they want."

"Well, Kendrick, you might sympathize with them a little in that. But that's all rot. The workman will be well pleased when he has a good home, which he can pur-chase with his rent ; when he has real luxuries for him-self and family ; when he sees his children being nobly educated ; and above all, when he knows he will have a pleasant home for his old age, or if he dies before that, that his wife and children will be well provided for. To not believe that, is to believe in the natural depravity of the human heart."

"Well, I swear, the longer I live the more doubts I have on that point," said Kendrick, rather ambiguously.

But while men talked and speculated, they watched with eager interest the development of Frauenstein's great project. Stevens, the doctor, and all the chiefs of the operations, declared that their men worked with a devotion unparalleled. The social lunch became the rule, and the men ceased carrying their tin-kettles almost without exception. Too Soon had as much as he could manage among the brickmakers, and so the doctor put up another temporary building, about halfway between the site of the palace and the woods, and a similar lunch provision to that for Stevens' men, was established for the others. Too Soon, however, could not be outdone, or even rivaled, by any one the doctor could find. The Chinaman became a favorite with the men and with the idle boys, that were at first a pest around the building, attracted by the unusual state of things, or by the chance of getting something to eat, in exchange for taking a turn at chopping Too Soon's cold meat and vegetables, for he was an economist by the transmitted instinct of generations. He saved his gravy and dripping, and produced a hash every other day, which became famous for its excellence.

Too Soon was wonderfully neat and methodical. He would not do the slightest thing for the boys until his work was all done; but when they had helped him clear the tables, wash the dishes, lock them away in the pantry, and sweep out the place, he would entertain them by the most wonderful jugglery or slight-of-hand feats. He spun tops up inclined planes, and strings, made paper butterflies, that, under the influence of his fan, acted for all the world like live ones endowed with reason; and Young America soon learned that it was in its very swaddling-clothes in the art of kite-flying. Too Soon was now a hero, and the boys fully atoned for their former meanness to him, when he was a forlorn wretch in their streets. They would do anything so that he could get his work done. Sometimes they actually crowded him away from his washtub, and rubbed out the napkins and table-cloths themselves. The way he dampened his clothes, preparatory to ironing them, was great fun. To this end he used to fill his mouth with water, and, by some trick they never could imitate, send it out over the linen in a fine mist. One or two of them partly learned the secret, and astonished Biddy at home by what they knew about clothes-dampening.

Times were good in Oakdale. The only trouble was with certain great manufacturers, whose men would desert and go over the river to work even for less wages, because it was "jolly" there, as they said. Men came from neighboring towns and besieged the doctor for work, or, failing, took the place of deserters in the window-sash and blind factory of Ely & Gerrish; and so hundreds of families moved into the town. Ely & Gerrish, however, did not lose many of their workmen, for they had provided some years ago a "workmen's home," a very superior tenement-house, which had been constantly full of tenants; but some other firms had to stop business.

The bet between the count and Kendrick was decided after considerable difficulty in getting at the facts, in which they were finally aided by a commission appointed by the town-council, who were persuaded that statistics of this nature would be valuable. Kendrick lost, and the hospital profited accordingly.

"I'm very sorry, Elias, that you did not win," said Mrs. Kendrick.

"Are you? I should not have supposed it possible. All you women are so devoted to Frauenstein."

"If you had lost, you know the hospital would have received twice as much," said Mrs. Kendrick.

"I thought it mighty strange," said Kendrick, "that you could be on my side against the count. That explains."

During this conversation Mrs. Kendrick asked her husband if he did not believe that the count had put money in the flower firm of Dykes & Delano.

"Of course I do. Clara has been rushing things since he left. There has arrived invoice after invoice of foreign trees, which she has set out as thick as reeds in a swamp ; and she has a dozen men there at work all the time, beside the women she employs."

"The trees and shrubs, and all the new hot-house plants, are for the grounds and hot-houses over the river, I am told," said Mrs. Kendrick. "I wonder you don't go and see them. I never saw anything so fine in my life."

"Oh, I don't care to. It would only make me more disgusted with this affair of ours, that costs so much, and gives so little satisfaction to anybody."

"Well, you don't manage it right. You should have somebody who understands it. I wish I could do it myself, or make Louise interested ; and she would be, if they were where they could be seen, or if you had a place for them clean enough to wear a decent dress into, or wide enough to pass through without knocking down the pots. I'm sure I can't bear to go into it. I'd rather have a little twelve-foot conservatory opening from my drawing-room than all your hot-houses, even if they did produce five bunches of grapes with only seventy-five tons of coal! That little room opening out of Clara's dining-room is perfectly lovely—one mass of color and perfume; and then the oiled floor is so clean, and the place so roomy! Why, you can sit there with the largest arm-chair!"

Kendrick said that nothing ever pleased his wife, and he meant to give up the hot-houses. They were a great expense for nothing. Mrs. Kendrick was sure she hoped he was not keeping them up for her sake; and after a good many cutting speeches on both sides, they ended in secretly pitying each other, seeing that they obtained so little pleasure out of this world. Then they gravitated into an indifferent conversation about the convention, and Mr. Kendrick inquired about Clara's address.

"I must confess it was very interesting," said Mrs. Kendrick. "She was applauded a great deal. I enjoyed the whole convention very much." Kendrick told her she was becoming radical. "I think men are greatly to be blamed," said Mrs. Kendrick, "for the little interest we take in great questions. You, for instance, never talk to me of them. Why, I actually did not know that women voted in Wyoming Territory. I was never more astonished at anything than at a letter which Clara read from one of the judges there, about the women jurors. It seems they give the greatest satisfaction, except to the rumsellers and dance-house keepers. Did you know this fact?"

"On the contrary, I read in the paper lately that most of their decisions have been set aside."

"Well, this letter was written only three weeks ago, and the judge says everything favorable ; that the morality of the place is greatly improved ; that before the women sat on juries it was almost impossible to convict men for murder or manslaughter, and the laws against drunkenness and gambling were disobeyed with impunity. Now this is all changed, and he says particularly that not a single verdict, civil or criminal, has been set aside where a part of the jury has been composed of women. What do you think of that, Elias ? "

"Why, my paper must have lied. I have long thought a man might almost as well do without a metropolitan paper. They don't seem to be conducted in the interest of any decent principle. But I don't understand about those Wyoming juries. Would you really sit on a jury ? I assure you, men consider it a great bore."

"I can't say I should like to ; but don't we owe it as a duty ? Whatever is a duty should be done, whether agreeable or not." Kendrick's secret thought was, that such a sentiment of devotion to duty, would certainly tend to promote justice ; but on that subject he said nothing. He asked his wife how she would vote intelligently for political measures ? How she could decide, for example, whether free-trade or protection was the right principle.

"How does the plantation hand decide that, Elias, and the ignorant foreigner ? I should not dare to vote as carelessly as they do. For my part, I think it a great responsibility."

"Well, how would you decide ? "

"I should certainly study up the subject, and if I had

not time for that, I would go to the wisest and most up-right man I knew, and ask him to instruct me on the principles of free-trade and protection. That is what *I* should do."

Kendrick pondered over this naive speech of his wife for a long time. Any person who could take that trouble to do the best thing for the interests of the country, might, he thought, have as good a right to political free-dom as the newly-enfranchised slaves! But then, even he was becoming tinctured with radical ideas.

Not long before Susie's return, she wrote to Clara a long letter, describing life in the Social Palace at Guise. "I am," she said, "so impatient of this slow process of communicating my thoughts and feelings, and I long to sit down by your side and talk a few volumes. Truly I am a fortunate being, in having the rare advantage of coming here. It is something to think of with pride and delight, as long as I live.

"The people who live here are most of them nothing but poor, uneducated working people, and you can tell at a glance those who have but just arrived from the older residents. A single year, surrounded by such order and beauty, such social advantages of every kind, works won-ders. The women at first, some of them, set up their cook-stoves, and wash and cook in their apartments; but the first time they take their linen to the laundries, they see the advantage of washing there, and the custom is soon established. So of cooking; they find that the great public kitchen, cooks better than they can, and they are glad to send there for their soups and meats, which are so cheap, that it does not pay to broil themselves over their own stoves. This, alone, is a most important thing in the emancipation of women. Mr. Godin has thought of everything. But the nursery and the schools! Oh, Clara, I wish you could see them. I said everything was free; there is one exception. No one can keep his children out of school. Every child is bound to have a good practical and industrial education.

"One thing struck me as strange: all drink wine at dinner, even to the small children; but for these it is diluted with water. Yet I have not seen a case of intoxication since I have been here—not even in the café and billiard-room, where there is much discussion and lively conversation. The best comment on the temperance and order of the place, is the fact that there has not been a single police case in the Familistère since it was founded, and yet there are over a thousand people living here.

"I sit in the council of twelve (women), whenever they meet, so that I may learn how they conduct business. There are often very spirited discussions, but never disorder or any discourtesy. This council directs the internal interests, nurseries, schools, oversees the food and other supplies, but it is not limited to these; it can discuss all matters. By natural attraction, it is found the women's council gravitate to this business. Sometimes the council of twelve men meets with and deliberates with the council of women.

"One thing strikes every visitor: the exquisite cleanliness of the apartments, the windows, the corridors, the courts, the schools, and the gardens and parks. Then, too, there is very little illness among the children. Why should there be? They have the conditions for growth and happiness. In the nursery of some seventy *poupons* (three or four years old), and nearly as many nurselings,

there is no racket, though plenty of play and laughter.
All these pretty babies go to bed without rocking, and
without crying, and wake in the morning the same way,
waiting each his turn to be bathed, and dressed, and fed.
These are their first lessons. If a new-comer sets up a
'howling,' as Min says, all the rest look at him with
wide open eyes, and he can't long stand against the public opinion of his peers! Their pretty little iron cribs,
canopied with snowy muslin, have each a sacking bottom
filled with bran; over this the sheet goes. Let me tell
you how these beds are kept sweet and fresh. Any
moisture in this bran immediately forms a lump, which
is taken out, and after a few days, more or less, the whole
is replaced by fresh bran. The *nourrisons*, or nursing-
babies, are very fond of watching the *poupons*, in the
same immense room, and only separated from them by
a little railing. They see them march to music, and try
to imitate their little gymnastic exercises. Their ambition is to become *poupons*, which they do at about
two years, or a very little over. One indispensable quali-
fication for this promotion is, that they shall have
learned to keep themselves clean—to use their neat little
earth closets adroitly, like their big comrades, the *poupons!* The *poupons* are marvelously accomplished in the
eyes of the *nourrisons*. In their turn, the *poupons* look
up to the *bambins*. Oh, it is such a delight to see all
these blessed, happy children! All the way up from
the nurse's arms to the highest classes, they are disci-
plined and educated for a high and useful career. It
is instilled into them from the first, that they must
respect the rights of others: the infant should not cry,
because he will disturb his little comrades who wish to

rest! In eating, he must not be greedy, for that offends
the good taste of his companions, or robs them of their
share. In meeting any one in the grounds or courts,
he must bow gracefully, for all have a right to courteous
treatment; and so on all the way through, the rights of
others are respected. There are no punishments, except
withholding the disorderly or refractory child from the
organized plays and sports in the parks and ground.
This is found all potent. But I could go on all night.
Let me sum it all up in this: Monsieur Godin has discovered and applied the laws of social harmony, and
therefore he deserves immortality.

"I see very little of the count. He is very busy. One
day he is in Paris, the next in London, and so on; though
he is kind enough to write me very often. Min is in the
bambinat all day. She is perfectly happy, and the whole
bambinat does her reverence as a distinguished visitor!
She is learning French as only children can."

Clara constantly received letters from Susie; long, delightful letters, full of enthusiasm, and tenderness, and
hope for the future; but the count was silent. He did
not even mention her in his letters to the doctor, and
although this pained her, there was a possible meaning
in it, sweeter than all the conventional remembrances in
the world. Once only he wrote: "I have not written to
you, dear friend, from a motive you may regard as very
boyish; but I should never attempt to express anything
but the exact truth to one like you: the reason of my
silence is simply, not knowing what to say. Would you
believe me so much a child? I can only answer: you
are responsible. You have thus affected me. When

I am in your presence, I can talk of indifferent subjects. I cannot write of them.

"There is a mystery in my life, or rather in my character—a riddle I am waiting for you to read. I am tempted to disclose it, and yet dare not; therefore I sit with the ink drying on my pen.

"I believe in you in all ways. I trust your delicate insight to understand even this awkward attempt to approach you, as I trust your generosity to deal patiently with my weakness. You also have been silent, my friend, and sometimes I am vain enough to ascribe that silence to a like cause with mine; but I dare not be too bold. There are some hopes that must not be rashly cultivated; their disappointment would destroy my power to do the work which no other can do for me. In two weeks, if the gods are kind to me, I shall stand in your presence.

"Believe me, with sincere devotion,
"PAUL VON FRAUENSTEIN."

This, to some, might seem a very singular missive from a man of the world like Frauenstein—a man sure of himself, confident of his power, and accustomed to the caresses of women. But there are others who will understand from it, that Paul was deeply in love; and that just in proportion to the strength of this passion in certain high natures, while there is any doubt of its meeting a perfect response, there is always great weakness, and a humility that creates self-distrust. The fear that his love might fail to awaken a perfect response, at times overwhelmed him and made him as weak as a little child. He had wooed other women boldly; but this one, he could not approach. To trouble her serene soul with his passion seemed like an impertinence. He saw himself, like Adam in Paradise, standing naked and trembling before a divinely superior being, who held his fate in her hands. He could do nothing but wait some sign from her—some unmistakable, slight sign, that so gracious a lady must know well how to convey. Could she hesitate because of a dead legal tie? That should not hamper free expression of sentiment in a grand, self-poised woman, the daughter of such a man as Dr. Forest, though it might hinder the fruition of hopes. Busy as Paul was with his pressing responsibilities, it was impossible to banish the thought of Clara from one of his waking moments. Between him and every object, her fair face appeared, and the memory of her tender eyes, her entrancing smile, the play of her mobile features, and her soft voice, were dearer far to him than all the realities of life. "Some time she *must* love me!" he said. "A grand passion cannot exist when one object is passive. It is not her beauty that draws me; it must be love answering unto love."

About the time Clara received her first letter from the count, there arrived a formidable legal document from Boston—a copy of Dr. Delano's divorce. What he had said to her during their last interview, proved no idle prediction. Clara ran her eye down the page of "legal-cap" until she came to the last paragraph, which read: "*And it is further ordered and adjudged that it shall be lawful for the said complainant to marry again, in the same manner as though the said defendant were actually dead; but it shall not be lawful for the said defendant to marry again until the said complainant be actually dead.*"

"This, then, is law," thought Clara. "No wonder Charlotte said it is not common sense." She showed the instrument to her father, but he hardly glanced at it. He was very glad. "That's one good piece of business finished," he said. He was full of care and anxiety about the work under his direction, and talked only of that, so Clara forbore to call his attention to her own vexation. In her ignorance of legal forms, she regarded this as a perpetual barrier to her ever marrying. A little while ago, she would have given herself but slight trouble about such a thing, being quite persuaded that she would never love again. It was different now. The letter she had just received from Von Frauenstein opened a new world to her—a world never to be entered. It was like shipwreck in full view of the Happy Isles.

Whenever Clara recalled this divorce, she felt humiliated, wronged, the victim of a hideous farce. How could she be bound to one who was free to marry again, "in the same manner as though" she were actually dead? The question recurred continually, and day by day it seemed more difficult to speak to her father about it; and then he had no power to change the decree, and why trouble him for nothing? Meanwhile Albert made prompt use of his freedom. He married Ella and established her in the family home. Miss Charlotte then quitted it, as she had determined, and went to live with the Kendricks in Oakdale, until she should decide on a permanent residence. Ella pouted terribly at the conduct of Miss Charlotte, in leaving the very day after the wedding, for her presence was necessary to give tone to the union. There had been ugly stories abroad about her and Dr. Delano, connected with his separation from his wife; and the departure of

20

Charlotte, especially her going to Oakdale, where Clara lived, seemed to confirm them. Many of the older acquaintances of the Delanos "put on airs," to use Ella's expression, and were at best only coldly polite ; and so it happened that her triumph in marrying Albert was robbed of all its sweetness.

CHAPTER XXXIX.

AN HONEST WOMAN.

A YEAR had passed since the count's return from
Guise, and still he and Clara had not spoken of
that which filled them, and made the music and the
poetry of their lives. To Clara's heart there never came
a doubt that she was loved. To doubt Paul would be to
lose faith in the operation of natural laws. True, they
had not confessed their love in words, and though it was
sure to come, Clara almost dreaded it, as though it might
break the spell that surrounded her like an atmosphere.
He was in all things her ideal : high in sentiment, devoted to humanity, and, like her father, appreciative of
all things, impatient of nothing, because he exemplified a
grand faith in the " mills of God "—in the ultimate triumph of the best. When you gained his friendship you
forgot his rank and wealth, and thought only of the man.
No one ever felt the grasp of his hand without a sense
of pride—that honest pride experienced in awakening an
interest in one superior to his kind. When he spoke to
you, it was impossible to avoid feeling flattered. He
gave you his whole attention for the time, and his fine
eyes rested on your features as if they would let no
slightest movement or expression escape, and at the moment, you were compelled by a power over which you had
no control, to express the highest and best that was in

you ; and then his beauty was something exceptional, for it delighted men almost more than women.

After his return, he had been more with Clara, though not much alone. The something that he had remarked as troubling or oppressing her, he still noticed with great pain ; but he could not ask her for her confidence. Some time, he knew, she would give it unsolicited, and meanwhile he refrained instinctively from pressing himself too much upon her notice, leaving her time after time with a mere pressure of the hand, more delightful in its magnetic effect than all the caresses of the many women he had known. In his creed, it was woman's prerogative to call ; the lover's to answer. By no sign yet had Clara shown him that she desired or needed more than she received ; and nothing could have been more impossible to a nature like his, than to sue for any grace for his own sake ; so he waited, and he prevented himself from too great anxiety by forcing all his energy into his great work. He had brought with him from Guise several of the most accomplished workmen, who had aided in the building of the *Familistère*, and the enterprise went on rapidly and surely. The walls of the palace and buildings were all completed, and the palace was to be ready for its occupants in the early fall, and the great inaugural festival was set down for the following June; both the count and the doctor agreeing that the time for a public jubilee was not when the palace was done, but when the schools, the theatre, the library, and all the details of the new social life were in full working order.

With the count's retinue came, also, or rather returned to this country, the only remaining member of Von Frauenstein's family, the son of his father's sister, named

Felix Müller. He was an accomplished gentleman, about forty-five years old, who had lived many years in New Orleans, and had lost his fortune during our civil war. He was a scientific chemist and geologist, and Paul wished him to direct education in the Social Palace; so he came with that view, if the prospect should please him. He always considered himself more an American than anything else, being, moreover, a naturalized citizen; and he had made himself very obnoxious to the government minions in Berlin, on account of his doings and sayings as a leading member of the *Internationale*. He was threatened with arrest and imprisonment, when his cousin Paul came to the rescue, and smuggled him out of Berlin and into Guise, where he studied the organization of the *Familistère* with great enthusiasm.

The count's responsibilities in directing the Social Palace enterprise often took him away for several days at a time. Now, whenever he was absent, he wrote to Clara. He knew she read whatever he wrote with interest, and it was much to connect himself with her thoughts in any way. In one of these letters he said: "There can be no real satisfaction except in the divine joy of love's perfect answer to love's needs. When one is longing for the touch of magnetic hands, and for words that are like caresses, the gratitude of thousands whom he has made happy, the adoration of the world even, falls upon his heart like the tongue of a bell in an exhausted receiver. What if a man gain the whole world, and lose his own soul—if he gain all things except the one blessing which alone could answer the cry of his heart! I am without soul, without inspiration, almost without hope to-day, or I could not write in such a strain to you. Do not heed it. Do not let your pure heart be troubled by my raving. You know I trust you, and whatever you think, or feel, or do, will be wisest and best."

To this Clara wrote, by the next mail: "If I could reproach you for anything, it would be for daring to say you are 'without inspiration, almost without hope.' I know it is only a mood, that has passed long before this. I know well that you are happy, for you can have no real doubt that Clara loves you with all her heart. See how presumptuous she is!

"If words can make you happier, dear Paul, frame any declaration, even the most extravagant, and I will make it my creed.

"You should know that I have passed a terrible ordeal, that left my heart torn and bleeding; and one like me does not recover rapidly from such a shock. The first moment my eyes rested upon you, I read, as in an open book, what my father in other words predicted long ago—that you were my destiny: that you could waken every possibility of tenderness, of devotion, of high purpose, of which I am capable; and I knew well from the first, how strongly you were drawn toward me. Yet had you wooed me then, as lovers woo, I should have hidden myself from you, if for nothing else, for the pleasure of torturing myself, so strangely subversive does the power of love become by the wrongs it may have suffered! But you did not do this. In no way have you ever offended me, even in the slightest word, or tone, or motion. In all things you are adorable in my eyes. Surely *you* can understand—if not, there is no one else but me who can—that love may sometimes be too intense, too deep for any of love's ordinary expressions. I am only waiting for a saner moment, a more simple and common impulse ; and therefore, when I can, and as soon as I can, I shall hold out my arms to you."

When Clara next met Paul, three days after he received this letter, she was riding over the river with her father and Susie, and met him returning. Clara's quick eyes divined, in his, an expression of triumphant happiness which was entirely new to them. She allowed her hand to rest longer than usual in his, though in the presence of others. Both those hands were gloved, but the warmth and magnetism with which they were charged would have passed through a substance much thicker or more obdurate than kid. That evening he called on Clara, and found Miss Delano with her. Miss Delano had just returned from Boston, and, in speaking of her brother, she said he was almost morose over his disappointment in not having an heir. "He is the last male member of a long line," she said, "and I don't believe he will ever have children. To be sure, he has been married to Miss Wills only about a year and a half."

"Nature seems to have a spite in such cases," remarked the count, "when the family name is represented by only one man. If I were you, Charlotte, I would marry. You are still young, and a son of yours might continue the name." The count offered it as the most natural suggestion in the world ; but as Miss Charlotte was inclined to treat it as a joke, he appealed to Clara. "I quite approve of it," said Clara. "Miss Delano should marry."

"You think," replied Charlotte, "that it would teach my brother a lesson. He has a great contempt for old maids, and," she added, laughing, "I believe he would have a poor opinion of any one's taste who should choose me for a wife."

" And then, if the rest should happen ! " said Clara, " I confess I am wicked enough to take a certain delight in the thought. It would be what papa calls poetic justice."

"I know my cousin Felix might become strongly attached to you," said the count, addressing Charlotte. " He is very fond of talking of you to me—says he should never imagine you to be over thirty."

" So you have been talking of my age. What impertinence ! "

" He asked me your age," replied Paul.

" Did you tell him I was sixty ? "

" I told him your exact age, thirty-six. That is really just the flower of life, and it may be written that the family name shall be continued through you, though perhaps Müller would have objections to adopting any other than his own. There is no justice in a woman's losing her name by marrying."

" Well, I don't think I would ask him to change his, on the slight and frail expectation of future heirs ; that is, supposing there was any question of marriage, which is absurd," said Miss Charlotte, blushing like a girl in her teens. That blush was a revelation to Paul ; but he quickly changed the subject by asking for music. While Clara was singing, and while he was listening too, his mind was busy with a matrimonial scheme for the benefit of his cousin and Miss Delano.

One evening a few days later, after Paul had left, Susie scolded Clara for being so cold to him.

"Cold ! Susie. Why, it seems to me that every word,

every tone and look of mine in Paul's presence, shows clearly that my heart is under his feet, as the Irish song has it."

"Well, dear, they don't show any such thing. He loves you with adoration; but he is too proud to accept any love that can be won by begging."

"It is just that spirit in Paul that makes me worship him. Oh, Susie! you do not know what he is to me. You cannot know, even after all I have told you. He knows I love him. Why, child, I have fairly, frankly confessed it in a letter not yet two weeks old. He understands me."

"I'm sure I would not make *such* a man unhappy. He is the only one I ever met whom I would marry instantly, whether I loved him or not. If he wanted me, I should say : take me. You deserve all things, and the greater includes the less."

Clara looked at little Susie, as she spoke in her earnest, soulful way. "Are you very sure that you do *not* love him, Susie? You have been with him more than I have. Happy woman! to be taken to Europe by him. Why, he has actually kissed you! I don't know what would happen, if he should kiss me."

"Would you 'dissolve into an Israelite?' as Linnie says. By the way, have you not noticed the flirtation going on between young Edward Page and her?"

"Yes; I spoke to the witch only to-day, and she told me that her heart was breaking for the count, and she was only flirting as a 'mockery to her woe.' I think mamma is well pleased. She has no longer high ambition for her girls; satisfied if they can only marry honest, temperate men. Poor mamma! She is so changed. Think of her going to our convention and listening to my address ! She is by no means converted, but she can look at reforms now without any contempt. She said it troubled her, in spite of herself, to see me there making myself so public, and in the committee-room being addressed by men, entire strangers. She would have felt different if I were married. A husband always gives countenance and support to a woman."

Susie laughed, and asked Clara what she answered. "I told her I was going to be married, and, making her promise to keep it a profound secret, I told her, to the Count Paul. 'Has he asked you, my dear?' she said, greatly excited. 'No, mamma,' I said, 'I told you I was going to marry *him.*' I do love to astonish mamma. Then I told her it would burst upon her some time; that there would be no pomp of circumstance, only just the steps necessary to make it legal. I am sure, conventional as she is, she would be so overjoyed at being the mother-in-law of Paul, that she would say nothing if the marriage ceremony should consist in jumping over a broomstick ! "

"Well, now, to change the subject, Clara, what am I to do with Dan ? "

"I cannot advise you, dear. He acts like a very goose."

"I pity him so. He loves me as much as he can love ; but it is only a feverish desire, not a sentiment having only my happiness at heart. He should respect me because I have grown beyond him, but he does not. It has no effect to tell him that I have not the slightest inclination to marry him. He doesn't believe it. He thinks I can love him just as of old, if I only will ; but I cannot *will*, and I have told him so. It makes him crazy to hear Minnie call Paul her papa. He is not glad, as I am, at the advantages the child has in being adopted by such a man."

"It is too bad, Susie ; but do not be induced to marry him out of pity. A woman wrongs herself when she does that."

"There is no danger. The very thought is horrible to me ; but what a position I am placed in ! Here is your mother, coming here nearly every day, and treating poor Susie like a daughter, because she thinks, of course, I shall marry Dan. Oh, it is simply dreadful !" said the good little Susie. "She has taken so to Minnie too."

In fact, everybody did that, and especially was Min popular among the children. She went everywhere to their parties, and picnic excursions, and everywhere introduced a new play, which she called the "Social Palace game." One day when she had collected about a dozen children and twice as many dolls, on the front porch, and was marshalling them in true autocratic style, Dan came through the gate and sat on the steps. Min told him she could not have anybody in the Social Palace who was idle.

"Well, then, if that's the case, you may give me some office." Min looked at him a moment, her chubby hands in her apron pockets, like a stage soubrette, evidently studying what place he was fit to fill in the play.

"You are so big," she said, "I don't know what to do with you." But a lucky thought struck her, and she told him he might be *Monsieur Godin.*

"Well, what does *Mongshure Godang* do ? " he asked, trying to imitate her French pronunciation.

"Why, don't you know ? He does everything. He is the chief."

"Oh, yes, I know. But that is a pretty difficult part for me."

"Oh, no ; you just sit there on the steps, and whenever you see a chicken come in under the gate, you go and drive him out. The chickens, you know, are the bad people who want to ruin the Social Palace."

Dan promised, immensely attracted to the child and all her ways, and thinking how he was wronged, because she was not taught to call him father, or to know that he was so. Min then went on with what she called "ognizing." The little dolls formed the nursery, the big ones the *pouponnat*. This girl must be head-nurse, this first-assistant-nurse, a larger girl leader of the exercises in the *pouponnat*, and so on. She made them all call her, as she had been called abroad, Mademoiselle von Frauenstein. There were three little boys present, and one of these she made head-gardener, and set him at work, with the next in size as assistant, in the flower-garden, with her little hoe and rake. The other, a very little boy, complained that she gave him no place.

"You wait till I *ognize*, and I'll put you somewhere," said Min ; but pretty soon he got tired of the tediousness of the "*ognizing*" process, and called loudly for office.

"Well," said Min, "you may go into the *pouponnat* as the biggest *poupon*, marching at the head. That will be quite nice."

But the little boy thought the honor of head *poupon* a very questionable one, especially as the *poupons* were all big dolls, whose marching powers he held in contempt, and he told her so in very plain words. Then the autocrat informed him that he "shouldn't be nothing;" whereupon he raised a revolt, and Min announced that there would be no more Social Palace that day. She was highly disgusted at the rebellion of her subjects, and even scolded Monsieur Godin for the lax manner in which he had repelled the encroachment of the enemies, who constantly were allowed to come under the gate.

"I know I haven't done very well," he said, humbly, "but I am a novice; never played Social Palace before, 'pon my word."

After the children were gone, he called her to him, and tried to interest her and make her like him; but she submitted to his kisses with a bad grace.

"Don't you know that you are my little girl?" he said.

"Yours! Is your name Paul von Frauenstein?" she asked, with withering scorn. Dan confessed it was not.

"Then I am *not* your little girl, for I am Paul's; and you are a saucy man, and I don't like you;" and with this she shot into the house, leaving Dan a prey to very bitter reflections. The result was his going to Susie, and reproaching her for teaching "his child" to hate him. Susie was offended at being obliged to justify herself against such a charge.

"I have never said the slightest word that should even make her indifferent to you. You can have her confidence if you can win it. I see no other way." Dan could not control himself. He burst forth in a torrent of complaints at Susie's coldness, and at her being unwilling that his child should love him. Then he became serious, and played the rôle of mentor—told Susie what was best for her to do, which was, of course, to marry him forthwith.

"Don't you see, Susie, that is the only thing to do. That will make you at once an honest woman in the eyes of the world, and we can bring up Minnie like a lady, and no one will dare to treat her with disrespect." This was too much for even Susie's sweet temper.

"I wonder at your assurance," she said. "You, who trampled my love for you under your feet, who deserted me in my agony of disgrace, when I had not one friend in this world—you, who had not the manly decency to conceal your love for another woman when I was in such a condition, by the basest, most sacrilegious act of treachery a man ever perpetrated ; then after all that, leaving me for six years to fight the battle alone, never during that time sending me one word of sympathy, or even taking the trouble to enquire whether I, or your child, or both, were dead ; after all that, and after by toil such as you never dreamed of, and by a long and unremitting struggle, I have conquered independence, won friends among the noblest and best, and compelled even my worst slanderers to respect me and my child, *you—you* come to me and offer to make me an honest woman, by the offer of your debauched self. If that is honor, give me dishonor for the rest of my life."

Dan raved and threatened, still talking in a very authoritative style about his child.

"Thank Heaven ! she is not your child, she is mine. There's one bit of justice which the law offers to a dishonored mother. *My child is mine!* You cannot take her from me, as you could if I should marry you. What do you suppose I care for a lost honor that can be restored by any jugglery of law ? Now drop that subject forever, if you wish me to retain the least friendliness toward you.

I should not dream of marrying you—no: not if you were to become emperor of the world."

Three days afterward Dan was brought home by two policemen from one of the lowest dens of the town, where he had been robbed of purse, cravat, handkerchief, and hat. In a day or two, by the united efforts of the family and friends, he was forced to consent to be taken to the Binghamton Inebriate Asylum. The doctor went with him, treated him very kindly, and labored to show him that by staying two years, leading, as he would, a temperate life, he might entirely overcome the passion for intoxication. "It is most important, you see, my son, for you are still a young man, and you may yet be useful to the world." Dan was much affected when his father left him, and promised to follow his advice, and turn his attention to some scientific study. He expressed sorrow for having given him so much trouble, and added, "I ain't worth saving, I fear. If you had drowned me like a blind kitten, when I was little, you would have done the best thing for me."

"Oh no, Dan. Don't feel that way. Your life has not been in vain, and I have by no means given you up. When I'm an old codger, with one foot in the grave, I believe you will be my comfort, and atone for all the heart-aches you have caused me."

"God knows, I hope so," said Dan fervently; "for no scapegrace of a boy ever had a better father than I have." This was the first and only manly speech Dr. Forest had ever heard from Dan, and it touched him deeply. When he was gone, Dan spent an hour or so walking rapidly back and forth through the fine grounds of the Asylum; and then he went into the billiard-room, and began to make the acquaintance of the patients. He was quite astonished, and immensely gratified, to see that they were not low fellows, but, on the contrary, real gentlemen in appearance and manners, almost to a man. Dan, conscious of looking very "shaky," from his late three-days terrible debauch, made some apology to a fine-looking fellow who handed him a cue and challenged him to a game of billiards. "Oh, don't trouble yourself to make any apologies," said the gentleman, laying his hand kindly on Dan's broad shoulder. "We are all drunkards here, every one of us!" After this Dan felt at home, and began to enjoy himself far more than he had ever done before. For the first time in his life, he spent several hours a day reading, and at last conquered a real love for it; also, he became, from the loosest, most uncertain and unsatisfactory of correspondents, a very tolerably exemplary one. He wrote every week to his father, and quite often to the other members of the family, giving long accounts of life in his asylum, and talking hopefully of the future. "Don't forget to tell mother," he wrote, after he had been there about six months, "that there is a little decanter of brandy kept here on the mantel-piece, with a wine-glass beside it, and that I have never once tasted it. I want you to tell her this, because it will please her. You, sir, will understand very well that it don't prove any remarkable virtue, for you understand the philosophy of drunkenness. Your real victim don't drink for the taste of liquor, but, as an old soaker in California used to say, '*for the glorious refects hereafter.*' So, when you haven't enough for these 'glorious refects,' you find it mighty easy to resist a single glass."

CHAPTER XL.

ONE beautiful day in August, about a month after the events just narrated, Miss Charlotte came over to see Clara. She was looking quite radiant with some new happiness, and Clara noticed that the plain Quaker-ish knot in which she was wont to confine her really pretty dark hair had undergone considerable change in its structure. It was less rigidly twisted, and from the mass depended several natural curls. She wore a pretty silver-gray barège, flounced to the waist, and with the upper skirt open, short, and looped up at the sides with ribbon.

Seating herself in an arm-chair, she said, " Now stand right there, Clara—no, just behind a little, and fan me while I tell you something." Clara obeyed.

"Dear me ! How shall I ever commence ? I begin to repent."

"Take your own time, Miss Delano. I will wait as long as you wish."

"No ; I won't wait. If I do, I shall never tell you— *The old maid is going to make a fool of herself. There!*"

"Oh, that is splendid ! You are going to marry Paul's cousin Felix. This is most agreeable news. From all I hear of him, he is an admirable gentleman."

" Yes ; but I wish he'd cut off that terrific Blue-Beard moustache. Do you like moustaches? I can't endure them. They are too signal a confirmation of Darwin's Origin of Species, according to which I believe we lose our hair as we advance to higher types. Is that so ? "

" Papa says," replied Clara, laughing, " that the coming man's head is going to be as smooth as an ostrich egg ; but I think, myself, the moustache will change. I think it is ugly just in proportion as it hides the contour of the lips."

" I see you are thinking of Paul's blonde, silky affair. Well, that is very different. It stays where he puts it. At table a little twist of his fingers, and his mouth is free ; but Felix—well, I'm sure I must be in love with him, or I should never have consented to marry him after seeing him eat soup every day for a year."

Miss Charlotte then told Clara they were to be married in a month, and move into an elegant suite of apartments in the left wing of the Social Palace. She was going to Boston in a day or two, to choose the most charming furniture she could find. Felix was to organize the schools, and she was to have a share of that work. The idea of having something useful to do, seemed to inspire her. " In my old life," she said, " I used to spend days and days helping to get up articles for fairs for charitable purposes ; but there was never the right kind of satisfaction about it."

" How could there be ? " asked Clara. " Charity is an insult to human nature. What we want is to give the poor the conditions for a comfortable, independent life. Now my mother and Mrs. Kendrick have won a reputation for benevolence on about the poorest stock of virtue

imaginable ; though of course they have acted from good
motives.   They ride around in their carriages among the
poor, and carry food and clothing—cast-off garments of
their own children and themselves.   My father has been
trying for years to get the ladies here to establish a *crèche,*
as they do in foreign cities—a place for poor women to
leave their little children when they wish to go out to
do work.   This would enable them to keep their elder
children in school, instead of at home to nurse the little
ones.   Then he would have them establish some industry
by which the poor women could earn money ; but he
could never get them to do it."

" No," said Charlotte ; "women's lives are so narrow,
their ambition so dwarfed, that most of them actually
enjoy going in their carriages and rich clothing into the
homes of the poor and patronizing them.   I confess I
always felt like a fish out of water, and generally contrived to give money, and let somebody else do the rest.
You may palliate wretchedness by charity, but you can
never raise the condition of the poor by it."

" Dependence and degradation are synonymous," said
Clara ; " and now you see why this workingmen's palace
is a mighty work.   There, for their labor, all the industrious can have comforts and luxuries beyond even the
power of the rich to enjoy, while their rents go to pay for
their homes."

" Oh, it is a noble work ! " exclaimed Miss Delano.
" I am catching, imperceptibly, the great enthusiasm of
Paul and Felix.   I see what must be the educational
influence of these daily baths, these walks in beautiful
gardens and groves, with music, and rare greenhouses
filled with exotics, the splendid schools, the reading-

room, the library, the societies. Why, it is enough to inspire the coldest and most selfish heart."

"And you see clearly, if all this was given to the people as a charity——"

"Why, it would not have a thousandth part of the good effect. The hope of owning all this, will so elevate the honest pride of these people, give them such strength and courage to work. Why, they will not care how much rent they pay."

"No; the count says the great trouble will be, that these laborers will deny themselves leisure and proper clothing, and put everything into their rents; but he is sure that it would not be well to have them own it too soon. They will be so much better able to appreciate and enjoy the ownership after ten or fifteen years, when the new and better educated generation will come on the stage to help preserve the order and prosperity of the institution. It does my heart good that you are going to live there and help on the education."

"Oh, you needn't say anything to inspire or encourage me. I tell you I am a radical, a social reformer of the deepest dye," replied Miss Charlotte gayly, as she took her leave.

Later in the day Paul came. He walked with Clara and Susie through the greenhouses and nurseries, now largely occupied by the stock for the Social Palace. Already thousands of trees had been set out in the new grounds, and were doing well, while the great conservatory in the court of the right wing was being rapidly filled, under Susie's direction. The great palm, of historical fame, was in its place, having borne its journey in May without the slightest injury. The great pink blos-

soms of Susie's banana-trees had long since fallen, and
the bunches of young fruit were ripening, while the rich
perfume of exotics in great variety filled the air. Passing
back to the house, through the old conservatory, the
little one first built, and which Susie kept now only for
flowers in blossom, the count expressed great admiration
for the two quite large orange-trees, laden with blossoms,
and he asked her how she managed to make these flower
so long after the usual time. "Why, it is very simple,"
said Susie; "by keeping them back; that is the techni-
cal term for denying them water and plenty of sunlight.
Then when you are ready, you bring them right under
the glass, in a warm room, and sprinkle them lavishly
every day at sunset. They can't resist; they are powerless, and must send out their blossoms, whether they like
it or not."

When they re-entered the house, Susie left them. The
count stayed only a short time, during which Clara tried
to overcome her repugnance to speak of the divorce—that
hideous divorce, that was ever in her thoughts; but she
could not. If anything outside of themselves could have
broken down the invisible barrier that separated these
two, Min on this occasion certainly would have accomplished it. As Paul rose to go, she climbed up on the
head of the sofa beside where he stood, and taking the
ends of his long moustache in her dimpled hands, she
pressed her little lips to his very demonstratively. Then
jumping down with a bound, she ran to Clara, and
standing on tip-toe beside her chair, she kissed "auntie,"
laughing, as she exclaimed, "Oh, auntie, am I not
good?"

"Why, my child, are you specially good just now?"

"Because I've given you the *sweetest* kiss ! Oh, you don't see," persisted Min. "Why, I've given you Paul's own kiss, and you didn't know it !"

"You insufferable magpie !" exclaimed Clara, blushing in spite of herself. "Go away now and don't come back—hear ? " Min, much discomfited, shot a Parthian arrow as she edged toward the door, where she turned while hunting for a chocolate-drop in the bottom of a little white paper-bag, and having crammed it into her mouth, said, "I don't care, I don't; auntie don't like Paul's kisses, but Min does ; so !"

The count laughed quietly, and commenced at once to talk of some new plans for the stage of the theatre. "May I bring them for you to see this evening," he asked.

"I should like to see them ; but do not make any excuse to come. Come freely whenever you wish. That will please me best."

"I thank you. That is very gracious, but the margin is wide—whenever *I* wish. You do not know," he said, passing her hand to his lips, "how boundless and insatiable are *my* wishes. I even wish to create wishes sometimes ; but that is when I am not wise. You know the one supreme desire of my heart, embracing and holding in abeyance all others, is that I may be worthy of Clara. The dear words that you wrote me, the written page just as I saw it, is burned into my memory. I can imagine no sweeter praise than that 'in no way have I ever offended you in the slightest word, or tone, or motion.' You see how I remember." He would have said more, but Clara was troubled. He could almost hear her heart beating as she answered, without looking directly in his face, as she spoke,

"And yet it was only a negative praise. It seems to me there were other words more worthy of remembering."

"You are right; but not even a lover's vanity could justify him in repeating those."

"You have no vanity, Paul. You have *no* imperfections; or if you have, it will be my fault if you ever manifest them—no, I don't mean that: I mean if you ever manifest any faults, they must be new possibilities created by my folly. No—don't answer. Go now and return by-and-by." Paul kissed her hand again, and with the pressure of his lips came the words, just above a whisper, "*Tu es adorable.*"

"Oh, he's getting very bold," said Clara to Susie, who entered the moment the count left, and she involuntarily looked at the fingers of her right hand.

"Because he kissed your hand? Oh, that is nothing for a gallant foreigner. It is, indeed, only a mark of respect and obedience, such as that due to queens."

"But he said 'Thou art adorable.' Surely that is more than a gentleman would say to a mere queen," replied Clara, delighting, like all those in love, to linger over the trifles that make up their bliss, when they are so fortunate as to have a friend wholly worthy of confidence.

"Did he say '*tu es*,' really? Then you are lost," replied Susie, laughing. "He must feel very sure of his position, or he would never dare *tutoyer*."

"Oh, Susie!" said Clara, embracing her friend, "I am going to be wonderfully sweet to Paul to-night—that is, if I can. He is coming back."

"Are you? I doubt it. You are so cold to him. I would not be so cruel as you are. I should appreciate such respect, such delicacy. Most men, when you show them the slightest favor, behave like bears."

"Do I not know that well ? If men only knew where their power lay ! You know papa says, in the Golden Age women will always take the initiative in love. You believe that, Susie ? "

"If the coming man is to have a head like an ostrich-egg, I think he'll be incapacitated for gentle, seductive arts," said Susie, laughing.

"When you speak of women taking the initiative in love, vulgar people think you mean proposals of matrimony, or caresses at least. The initiative is that which the word implies—the first movement; it is but the slightest thing. When Paul has pressed my hand, I have always drawn it away after a few seconds. He is waiting for me to leave it in his just one second longer. I have never given him a really tender glance. If I were to do so, the 'bear,' as you say, would instantly be developed ; though I should not apply that word to him. He is the perfect gentleman in everything. He *could* not offend. I mean to speak to him about that hateful divorce, which forbids me to marry 'until the said defendant be actually dead.' I say I mean to ; but I have not the slightest certainty that I shall have the courage. I don't believe you can imagine how I feel about it."

"Yes I can, dear. Don't trouble your precious soul about it. Only be sweet and good to Paul, and everything will be well. You are not going to wear that dress ? Do put on that lovely white organdie. Will you ? I will loop up the skirt with ivy."

The vision that met the count's eyes as he entered Clara's parlor must have charmed the most fastidious taste. The white, gauze-like organdie was looped with ivy by Susie's cunning hand. It was that rare, silver-edged ivy, with a light crimson flush in some of the leaves. Over the low corsage she wore a Louis-Quinze basque of white dutchess lace, the graceful folds of which fell over her exquisite hands that were without ornament of any kind. In the coronal roll of her hair, which fell in many curls from the mass behind, she wore a tiny bouquet of mignon-nette and white Neapolitan violets, relieved by a border of green. The basque was closed at top of the corsage with a beautiful cameo of her father's head in profile. Paul knew she had dressed for him, and the thought was deli-cious. He expressed warmly his admiration for her toilet —a thing foreign gentlemen are as careful to remember as Americans are to forget; not that they are not sensi-tive to the beauties of woman's dress, but it is a habit with very many to ignore the fact that dress can enhance beauty; and then, perhaps from a feeling of delicacy, for American gentlemen are among the most refined in their sentiments toward women. With the older civilizations, dress is a pure art, and artistic effects are always a fit subject for study.

Edward Page and Susie were present when the count entered, but after a half hour or so Susie left, and the young man soon followed. The conversation then turned upon the engagement of Miss Delano and Felix Muller. "It will be a very happy union," said Paul. "If the theory of opposites hold true, they are well suited to each other, and they are certainly much in love. They are constantly together. They sit up evenings after all are abed, and then take long strolls in the park before break-fast. It is a most happy courtship. They are both

21

among friends who give them full sympathy, and there is never a straw in the way of their bliss."

"The old adage, then, about the course of true love, is likely to prove false in this instance," said Clara ; and then changing the subject abruptly, as women are wont to do—when they see fit—she asked the count if he had brought the theatre plans.

"Ah ! I forgot them. From the time I left you until I returned, I don't think I was once conscious of the existence of business. Are you disappointed ? "

"In what ? In which ? " asked Clara, a little mis chievously, perceiving that his question was susceptible of ambiguity ; but she repented in a moment, seeing how gravely the count regarded her, and added, " I know you mean the plans. I don't care to see them to-night. I wish you would sing to me."

Paul sat down to the piano almost hurriedly, and as his deft fingers ran over the key-board, he said—the music making his low words even more distinct—" Hear what Paul says to his love." He looked at her as she stood on his left, but her eyes were studiously fixed upon his hands.

The consciousness of a well-trained voice, able to express with divine eloquence words that may not be fitly spoken without music, is perhaps the proudest gift a lover can possess. Paul played the prelude once, and then repeated it, as if waiting for the certainty of self-control. The music he was playing Clara had never heard ; but she knew that it was his own ; for there was a certain latitude of interpretation in Paul's style, when playing his own compositions, which he would not pre-

sume to attempt, in following the masters. Paul sang
the words of some poet unknown to Clara.

> "O meadow-flowers, primrose and violet!
> Ye touch her dainty ankles as she moves,
> But I that worship may not kiss her feet.

> "O mountain airs! where unconfined float
> Her locks ambrosial, would that I were you,
> To wanton with the tangles of her hair.

> "O leaping waves! that press and lip and lave
> Her thousand beauties, when shall it be mine
> To touch, and kiss, and clasp her even as you?

> "But she more loves the blossom and the breeze
> Than lip or hand of mine, and thy cold clasp,
> O barren sea! than these impassioned arms."

The last line of each stanza was repeated. Clara realized that Paul had never sung to her before. "I don't
like your song," she said, but doubtless with that glance
which, according to her confession an hour ago to Susie,
she had never given him; for he rose with a cry of tenderest passion, clasped her in his arms, and pressed his
lips long and silently upon her hair, holding her head the
while softly against his breast. Clara heard his heart
beating loud and fast. There they stood. Neither could
desire to speak or move. It was heaven enough to know
that the supreme moment that revealed them fully to
each other, had come at last. From this close embrace to
the folding-down of Love's kiss upon the lips, in "perfect
purple state," as Mrs. Browning says, "the transition
was easy," which Mrs. Browning does not say. The
kisses of these two were different from nearly all others.
It was soul meeting and mingling with soul, and the

sensitive lips were only the medium. That may seem obscure to philosophers who are always seeking in vain for the seat of the soul. Lovers of the nobler and finer type, emotional beings, who will not have their altars profaned by the contact of unholy offerings, never have any doubts about soul. To them it is not an entity which may be found here or tnere ; it is life—the one thing infinitely precious, and they are not to be disturbed by nicely-studied definitions. Are not lovers of this rare type the truest philosophers ?

It is like an impertinence to try to describe the unutterably perfect state of Paul and Clara as they stood there by the piano. A cynical observer would probably have said that they uttered more nonsense in the short space of ten minutes than he would have believed possible; but he would only thereby show his ignorance of the mysterious power they possessed of

" Kissing *full* sense into empty words."

After a time, Susie's light step was heard passing the partially-open door, and Clara called her and said, as she entered, " Come and see how cold and cruel I am to your friend."

" Oh, this is too good ! " exclaimed Susie, embracing both with effusion. " My cup of joy runneth over. If you and Paul had not turned to each other, as naturally as flowers to the light, I should have lost faith in providence ; but I never had any doubt. But come, my precious lovers, you will grow faint on your diet of the ineffable. I knew by intuition that you two would find your souls to-night, and so I have prepared a little feast in honor of the occasion. Edward and I, I mean, but it is not quite ready yet. In about fifteen minutes I shall call you. Into that fifteen minutes you have full liberty to crowd all the bliss you can. I know your capacity in that direction must be miraculous," she added.

"What could be so gracious as this dear girl's sympathy?" exclaimed the count, bending down and kissing her forehead.

"Why, when we love our friends dearly, we must naturally enjoy most that which makes them most happy. C'est bien simple," said Susie, and with that she left.

When Paul and Clara entered the dining-room they were amazed at what Susie had accomplished. The folding-doors of the conservatory were flung wide open, revealing that fairy-like effect which all have noticed who have seen foliage and flowers lighted from beneath. The light of the central hanging-lamp was dimmed by the light of numerous sections of wax-candles, set in the earth under the plants and small trees. In the dining-room the table, decked with flowers, was laden with a choice collation.

"Am I in the land of fairies?" asked the count.

"How have you done all this in so short a time, you darling Susie?" Clara asked. "Why, it is like enchantment!"

"Why, we have had time enough," answered Susie, glancing at young Page, who stood by the folding-doors enjoying the effect of the surprise. "We commenced," he said, "when we heard the count's beautiful song."
"Yes," said Susie, "we knew then it was time to prepare for the bridal feast."

"You see, Paul," said Clara, "you are Orpheus, working magic through the music of your voice."

"May I not meet the fate of Orpheus," said Paul; "but I think I should be more patient than he was when his Eurydice was coming out of Hades." Clara looked at Paul thinking her own sweet thoughts.

"Now you must be just as happy, just as free, as children; yes, a hundred times more happy. We are all lovers. I am in love with several people, and Edward, he is also, but with one especially. Is it not so?" Susie added, turning to the young man, who blushed as prettily as a girl as he answered, "I should be very sorry to contradict Madam Susie."

"That is not a frank admission."

"Then I admit frankly."

"That is as it should be," said Paul. "I sympathize with Claude Melnotte, who would 'have no friends that were not lovers.'"

"Oh, we must have some of that delicious *Sauterne* that *we* brought from France," said Susie, addressing the count. "Red wine alone will never answer." Edward disappeared in search of the wine.

"Why, Susie is as happy as we are, one would say," said Clara.

"You think nothing but the prospect of marrying Paul ought to make any woman happy."

"How sweet she looks, Paul!" said Clara, her whole face breaking into dimpling smiles. "I should think you would want to marry Susie too."

"I do, of course," answered the count gallantly; "but you know the wicked world has such prejudices! Susie had trouble enough abroad to convince people in hotels and *auberges* that we required separate apartments;"

and he laughed, remembering certain scenes that had caused her vexation.

"Well, you know that was all Min's fault; she was forever in your arms. Here comes our *Chateau Yquem.* What! who on earth can be ringing the door-bell at this hour?"

"I know that is my father," said Clara, going to the front door. Edward, for some reason, disappeared at the same time.

"Now tell me what I am here for," said the doctor, after laying down his hat and saluting the friends. "I sat in my studio for an hour, and resisted the impulse to come over. It is ten o'clock, and you know I never came here, or anywhere, at such an hour, unless I was called."

"Well, you were called," answered Susie, who loved to nurse little superstitions.

"Count, what do you think of it?" asked the doctor.

"I will not say it is impossible for us to act upon each other at a distance. I have known several instances that would seem to prove it."

"We were so happy, papa," said Clara, putting her arms around her father tenderly. "I think my own joy must have filled the world like an atmosphere, and so it embraced you, and you being a '*sensitive*,' responded."

"Papa's own girl is radiant to-night," he said, kissing her. "I never saw you look so well," and glancing at the conservatory and the table, and then at Paul, he read the mystery. "Why this is very irregular," he added, gayly. "Are my paternal rights to be disregarded? Are you going to marry my girl without my consent?"

"I trust not, sir," said Paul, confidently.

"Oh, do you not know, papa, I cannot marry any one?"

"Why not, pray?" But as Clara did not answer her father's question, Susie explained the clause in the divorce.

"Why, this is what has troubled you, darling," said Paul, in his tenderest voice. "Be reassured. It is only a form. By marrying you might be liable to a charge of contempt of court, the penalty of which is only a fine. No one ever notices this injunction; at least, I never heard of a case."

"Is that all?" asked Clara, amazed and almost ashamed that she had been so long disturbed by a mere bugbear. "But women are so ignorant of legal matters."

"The Social Palace will make a wiser generation of women," Susie said. "The children will learn politics in their cradles."

"And *bambins* will commence to exercise the franchise by balloting for their little industrial leaders," said Susie. "But come, our *Chateau Yquem* is waiting. There is only one thing wanting. If these two dear ones could only be married to-night, and have the bother all over!"

"Papa," said Clara, "I must have inherited from you my repugnance to ceremonies. I would never get married in the world, if it wasn't for my love for Paul," she added, looking at him.

"We will have no ceremony, dear one," he said. "The marriage contract, duly attested, is all that is necessary; besides, any one can perform the marriage ceremony. It is not necessary that it should be a priest, for marriage is a civil contract."

"Why, let us draw up the contract now," said Susie, forgetting the waiting *Sauterne*. Here is my desk and all proper materials."

Paul did not need any urging. The contract was duly signed in less than ten minutes. As Clara signed her name, she exclaimed, "Why, I am a victim to a conspiracy! My consent to this precipitate act has not been even asked."

"But there is your name," said Paul. "It is too late for retraction. I shall at once assert my prerogatives."

"Come, my children!" said the doctor, "let us have a gloriously radical marriage ceremony, after our wicked latitudinarian hearts."

"Oh yes, do, Clara; just to make Susie happy. Here is Edward come for another witness."

"You know my sentiments on this matter," said the count, addressing the doctor. "As any one may perform the ceremony, I should choose you from all the world."

Clara would have postponed further action after the signing of the marriage contract, but there was no resisting the enthusiasm of Susie, the doctor, and Paul. Susie would have them married in the little conservatory, among the flowers. And so it happened. There was no need of orange-blossoms, for the happy lovers stood beneath the two blossom-laden orange-trees, that dropped their fragrant petals on the united hands of Paul and Clara, as the doctor said, in his deep, solemn voice, "Paul von Frauenstein, do you take this woman to be your lawful and wedded wife?" Clara was a thousand times more deeply affected than she had been at her former marriage, when her heart was in rebellion all the time against the "show," as the doctor called it. She

sobbed in the doctor's arms for some time, and his own
eyes were hardly dry. At last he said, handing Clara
over to Paul, "I will not comfort your sorrowing wife
any more. *That* is one of your prerogatives, unquestionably."

"Sorrowing, papa ; what a word," replied Clara, looking divinely beautiful through her tears at her father,
and then at Paul. "If this is sorrow, may I never be
comforted ; " and then, while the rest left the conservatory, she listened to words from Paul, which were far
too sweet for repetition.

Susie was wild with delight. She poured out the
choice *Sauterne*, proposed toasts, made everybody reply,
and was so gay in her *abandon*, that her friends scarcely
knew her.

In the midst of the hilarity there was heard in the hall
the patter of little feet, and the next moment Min,
aroused by the unusual noise, opened the door, in her
long white gown, looked at the lighted conservatory,
and then at the *convives*, exclaiming with a very grave
air :

"What is all this row about ? I should like to know."

"You little ghost ! " said the doctor. "Where do you
come from ? " Min curled herself up in the doctor's
arms, and then directed her attention to the attractions
of the table.

"Min, somebody is married to-night—can you guess
who ? " asked Susie, colloquially if not grammatically.

Min looked at Edward. "It isn't you," she said,
" 'cause Linnie isn't here."

"Ah ! a cat out of the bag ! " said the doctor, noticing
the vivid reddening of the young man's fair face.

" And it isn't you, auntie, 'cause you don't like Paul's
l. ses."

" Oh, but I do, Minnie. I have found out how sweet
th y are," replied Clara, archly.

" Well, you were a long time finding out," said the
spoiled pet, changing her place to Paul's lap.

It was difficult to get Min back to bed, but the promise of a ride with Paul the next day finally proved a
sufficient inducement. Edward left soon after Min, but
it was some time after midnight when the doctor took
his hat to go. Clara handed Paul his.

" What ! " exclaimed the doctor. " You to be sent
away, Paul ? That is wrong." Susie wickedly con-
firmed the sentiment, but Paul, noticing a kind of distress in Clara's face, said, as he held her a moment in his
arms, " We do not recognize rights, dearest. All the
events of this evening, so crowded upon each other, have
quite unstrung your nerves. See, doctor, how cold her
hands are ! "

" Well," said the doctor, taking his daughter's hand,
"you are right—right, I mean, in leaving all things to
her ; but you know how instinctively women cling to
precedents. You may find this a dangerous one."

" I have no fears," replied Paul, embracing Clara tenderly. " Does she not love me ? and is not love sure to
respond to love's needs ? Her desire is mine always."

CHAPTER XLI.

"What I do and what I dream include thee
As the wine must taste of its own grapes."

THE doctor, on his way home, saw a light in the printing-office, which was at the corner where he separated from his newly-made son-in-law; and at the latter's suggestion a notice of the marriage was left there for the morning paper. So the next morning, as Mrs. Kendrick, Louise, Miss Delano, Felix, and the count, sat down to the table, they were electrified by the exclamation, "Good God!" proceeding from Mr. Kendrick, who came forward to take his place at the table.

"What is it? Do read it?" said Mrs. Kendrick to her husband, whose eyes were riveted on the morning paper.

"Married—Sept. 10th, at the residence of the bride, the Count Paul von Frauenstein to Clara Forest Delano——" Kendrick stopped short and looked at Paul, who was very composedly taking his cup of coffee from Mrs. Kendrick's trembling hand.

"What silly joke is this?" he asked, addressing Paul.

"My dear sir, I beg you to not consider it a joke. It is a genuine announcement of a genuine fact," replied the count, with a serious gravity that could not be mistaken.

"But you slept here last night. I heard you come in."

" So did I," said Miss Delano, " but it was shockingly late—late enough to have accomplished any folly, I should say ; marriage among the rest." But Charlotte felt secretly hurt that when she had given her confidence freely to Clara the day previous, Clara had withheld hers. Louise turned very pale, but sipped her coffee without any serious manifestation of the rage she felt.

" My dear cousin, I give you joy ! " said Felix, grasping the count's hand warmly, and adding, in French, " I must suppose you have good reasons for keeping your confidence from me."

" The very best reasons, my dear Felix—reasons certain to prove satisfactory," said the count, in English.

" Good God ! " said Kendrick again. " I never heard of such a thing. Married, and then go home coolly to your bachelor quarters ! " This was spoken in a very incredulous style.

" Even so," replied the count, throwing back his head and laughing at the inordinate excitement caused by a simple event. " We have not yet completed our domestic arrangements ; but to save my honor in your eyes, Kendrick, I should add that my leaving was at the desire of the bride, whose wishes, according to my code, should be the law of a gallant man."

" I like that, Paul," said Charlotte, not daring to look at Felix, but meaning her approbation to be a lesson for him. Paul's answer to Felix's question had convinced her that the marriage was an impromptu one ; therefore her heart lost all its hardness towards Clara, and she added, " I will call on the Countess von Frauenstein this morning." Paul thanked her with his lips, but still more cordially with his eyes.

"*I* shall do no such thing," said Mrs. Kendrick, whose face had been flushed ever since the reading of the marriage announcement. "I think, when people marry, they should show decent respect to——"

"To their friends, madam," said the count, rising from the table. "Are you so unquestionably a friend of my wife that she has wronged you by not asking your presence at the ceremony? Did you give her your womanly sympathy when your ridiculous Oakdale aristocracy frowned upon her, in her days of sorrow?"

All this was said in a very low, quiet tone, but it cut Mrs. Kendrick like a two-edged sword. She saw she had been too hasty, and a glance at Kendrick, who seemed ready to faint, terrified her, recalling, as it did, the fact that he had told her the bank could not tide over its present crisis without the aid of the count.

"Pardon me, count," she said, rising. "This was so unexpected, so alarming, I may say, in the way it burst upon me—of course I know you will do things differently from other people. I shall, of course, be happy to call on your wife. I will go with Miss Charlotte and your cousin. Do you forgive me?" she asked, offering him her hand. The count had noted well Kendrick's anxious look at his wife, and though he despised the policy of Mrs. Kendrick, which forbade her the pleasure of enjoying her spleen, he answered, urbanely,

"Certainly, madam. Excuse me, also, for alluding to an unfortunate omission on your part, which I am sure you regret; but I beg you to not call on my wife as a concession. If you do that, our friendship ends there."

Before Miss Charlotte and the Kendrick party set out for their call on Clara, Miss Charlotte took care to post a copy of the paper to her brother, with the marriage notice duly and conspicuously marked. It reached him the next morning. His surprise was great, and his feelings of a very mixed character. He naturally thought that, in justification to himself, Clara should have married some very common kind of man; and then her winning the love of one so high in the social scale was balm to his vanity, and a just punishment to Ella, who hated Clara, as little minds do hate those they have wronged. He had come to despise Ella for her mean spite against Clara, shown unqualifiedly whenever he had spoken a word in praise of her; and his home was anything but a happy one. He found out, as many a man has done before, that Ella having become his wife, considered him her inalienable property, and only a subject for consideration when there was no other man about upon whom to lavish her smiles and pretty coquetries. Why should she dress for him, or practice her winning graces on one who was hers already, and that forever? In short, he learned by bitter experience the difference between a true, loving, devoted woman, whose sweetest smiles and gentlest words were ever for him, and a mere thing of fashion and convention called a wife, but no more a real wife than the first eye-winking doll in a shop-window. If any power on earth could have annulled the past, and given back Clara to his arms, after six months of Ella Wills, he would have been a happy man; but he made the best he could of his life, and was not unreasonable over Ella's faults, except when she spoke ill of Clara, as she did on the occasion of his reading the notice of her marriage. Not knowing of Ella's former flirtation with the count at Newport, and her extreme vexation at that time over her signal failure, he set down everything she said to her spite against Clara.

"He hasn't much pride, if he is a count," she remarked, "or he wouldn't take up with anybody's cast-off wife."

Dr. Delano was disgusted. He replied savagely, and a stormy scene ensued, in which both descended to the bitterest recriminations. They mutually confessed that their love was a farce, and then they separated coolly, the doctor going to his office and Ella to discuss a love of a ball-dress with her *modiste*.

The marriage of the count was a nine-days' wonder in Oakdale, and there was terrible commotion in the breasts of scheming mammas, some of whom found a large grain of comfort in the fact that "Louise Kendrick must be terribly cut up." And she was indeed, poor girl! and her chagrin was all the more bitter from the consciousness that her hopes had been built on a foundation of the most flimsy nature. There is very little true sympathy in the world for hopeless love; many people, indeed, who pass as educated or cultivated are capable of reproaching the unhappy lover, or even laughing at him, thus showing themselves, in refinement of sentiment, on a plane with the barbarian. Sympathy of a common and lower type is everywhere freely given to heroic suffering; but if any one would know which of his friends not only loves him most sincerely, but has the highest and finest nature, let him make an unqualified fool of himself.

Despite the portentous rumors touching the unsoundness of the great banking-house of Oakdale, it weathered through the storm, and the Kendricks and Burnhams held their heads as high as ever. As long as Oakdalers might have seen any future possibility of a marriage be-

tween the count and Kendrick's daughter, the recovery
of the bank's credit might be comprehended; but as
things happened, it remained a mystery, rather augmented
than lessened by the fact that there had been a "run"
on the bank very soon after the marriage. And the won-
derment of Oakdale had an extraordinary vitality. Why,
among all the wealth and beauty of the town, had the
count chosen the radical daughter of the arch-radical Dr.
Forest; and a woman, too, with a history, a thing so
deplorable in a lady? In a less advanced age it would
have been set down to witchcraft, or Satanic interposi-
tion; but the thing was done, and there was no way of
escaping the inevitable. Those who had exchanged
courtesies with Clara after her separation from Dr. Delano,
took consolation in the fact that they ought to be on the
cards of the count thereafter; those who had not, said
spitefully, that no doubt the count would take up his
residence "among those working-people over the river,"
where the cream of the town would scarcely care to visit.

It did not become known who the "officiating clergyman" was, in the marriage that excited such commotion,
for the notice in the paper had barely announced the fact
and the place of occurrence, and no one would have
dared to ask such a question of any of the interested parties. Indeed, minor circumstances sank into insignificance beside the one marvelous fact that Clara Delano,
whom society had dared to snub, had suddenly risen to
such an enviable position in the social scale. Poor Susie
Dykes, as the bosom friend of Clara, rose mightily in
importance also; but the Priest and the Levite were
deterred from approaching her now, from consciousness of
their past attitude toward her, or rather, from the fear

of inconsistency—that bugbear of little minds. The most conservative, however, were pretty ready to admit that the kick-her-down policy was not the wisest after all, and that love and sympathy might be due even to a "fallen" sister.

But even the excitement caused by the marriage of the count and Clara, and the influence it promised upon the fate of Susie, could not long hold the attention of Oakdale from the mighty enterprise "over the river." Architects and builders came hundreds of miles to see the great work, whose renown was daily widening and extending. Oakdale palatial residences sank into insignificance beside the vast pile. Capitalists looked on with wonder, and great manufacturers grumbled at the growing discontent of their workmen over the high rents they had to pay for their poor accommodations. The Social Palace workmen talked with outside laborers, and the natural result was dissatisfaction. Ely & Gerrish took the wisest course— they, who less than the other manufacturers felt the need of conciliating their employés, having years before built improved homes for them. This firm called their workmen together, and urged them to wait patiently, and see how the Social Palace worked. No one could say yet that it would not be a failure. To be sure, that in France had worked well, but French people were very different from free Americans! If this enterprise worked, of course it would become universal in this country; and from what they, Ely & Gerrish, had already done, their workmen might expect them to try to keep up with the demands of the time.

Other manufacturers were not so fortunate. They were insolent to their workmen when the latter grew dis-

contented, and the result, in some cases, was disastrous
to their industries, and provocative of hatred to the millionaire, whose wealth enabled him to ride over smaller
capitalists rough-shod.

"You see," said the doctor, to one of these, "our financial and industrial system is a regular cut-throat affair.
Anybody who can see an inch before his nose must admit
that in order to carry on that system successfully, you
must have but two classes—masters and slaves. The
moment you give the people schools and newspapers, you
teach them revolution against a state of things which
keeps them poor while their labor makes others rich."
In fact, it was very little consolation to talk to the doctor,
though in the end he never failed to show that if he had
sympathy for the laborer, he had also for the small capitalist, and could see exactly his difficulties and vexations.
Burnham seemed wonderfully interested in the great subterranean galleries for ventilating the Social Palace, and
these were his theme whenever he talked of the great
enterprise. "This question of ventilation is an important
one," he said. "It's safe to say that, up to this time, no
architect has ever successfully ventilated even a school-
room; but I believe this Frauenstein, or Godin before
him, has hit it."

"Is it true," asked a listener, "that he is going to put
hot-air furnaces in these galleries under the palace, and
so heat up the whole thing at the same time he carries in
the fresh air?"

"Yes, that's so. He went yesterday to New York to
make arrangements for the furnaces."

When the silk industry was in operation, Mrs. Forest
and the twins went over to see it. Linnie had for some

days declared that she was going to learn silk-weaving, and when she saw the actual operation she was fully decided. The factory was a beautiful building, only a little less ornate than the palace itself, and Mrs. Forest was so charmed with the polished oiled floors, the immense, deep-set windows, and the exquisite cleanliness of everything, that she pronounced it "so unlike a factory! Why, I almost want to weave silk here myself," she said. Leila declared if Linnie came to weave, she also would. "It will be setting a good example, you know, for the independence of young ladies," she added, half in irony. Mrs. Forest did not fail to remark that a great many of the weavers were quite respectable young girls, and finally she gave her consent that Leila and Linnie should learn —there could be no harm in it. They were already both engaged to teach in the Social Palace schools, but these would not be organized yet for two months. The doctor's apartments were already selected, and Mrs. Forest went to see them on this day. She had not expected to find them so grand.

"What do you think now, mamma?" asked Linnie.

"Why, I suppose we shall only reside here temporarily. We are not to give up our house," said Mrs. Forest, very gently but positively.

"Oh, the house will be given up," said Leila. "I expect you, mamma, will become one of the council of twelve. I shall see you presiding, no doubt, and gravely giving the 'casting vote.' What a woman's righter you'll become," she added, laughing. "There's no use trying to resist such an outside pressure. We'll all have to become radical reformers like papa and 'Papa's Own Girl.'"

"Papa's Own Girl" was in a state of beatitude these days, that shone out from her beautiful face, and lent a divine softness and tenderness to her every word, and act, and motion. Susie, who loved to give wings to her imagination, declared to Clara that there was often a halo about her head, like those crowning the saints in the pictures of the old masters. Paul, when absent now, did not sit with ink drying on his pen. He wrote freely, from an overflowing, all-absorbing happiness, great enough to fill even his great heart; and if he hesitated now when writing his beloved Clara, it was not for lack of words, but rather from the impotence of all possible combinations of words, to express the half that he felt. The first letter that he wrote her after their happy union, or parts of it, may be given here, for the benefit of lovers; others may find it extravagant and out of character as an expression of the passion of love in a practical, philosophical gentleman like Count Frauenstein, and so they can pass it over unread:

"DEAR HEART:—Ah! dear indeed, since it has answered mine. Jean Paul sighed that he had lived so long and had never seen the sea. Like his longing was mine, to find my love—and I have found her! For me there is no more sighing—never any more; for I have seen the sea, the broad, the deep, the infinite. It broke upon my vision with a sweet surprise, and my mind and heart went out to measure it; but I knew that on and on, beyond the purple limits, it still extended in its earth-embracing mystery. Erewhile I had heard but its far-off echoes answering to the whisperings of my heart, as one who listens to the sea-shell. But now my eyes have seen its changing beauty. I have heard its murmurings and its laughter. I have swayed with its flux and reflux; and its waves—ah ! dear, they have overflowed my soul ! Everlasting sunlight is spread upon its bosom, on which I have floated into rest. The sunshine is abiding. I have taken it away in my heart—my satisfied, contented heart—and the music of its waves I shall hear forevermore ! ❋ * ❋ All things should bless you for loving me, since with the remembrance of that sweet loving with which my heart is full, I touch more tenderly even the dear earth that has been made young again for me. It seems as if every one should notice that something has happened to me ; as if the little children should gather about me, believing that I could bless them ; as if the flowers should turn to me for sunlight. Oh, what have you done to me, my darling, that I am so happy and so strong, that I have such tenderness in my heart, and that such heavenly peace sits upon my forehead. ❋ ❋ ❋

"I try in vain to still my beating heart into some more temperate mood. They might as well have attempted to presume upon sanity who were visited with the Pentecost." ❋ ❋ ❋ ❋ * ❋

The next day Paul wrote :

"To-day, love, the furnaces for our Social Palace are on the way to Oakdale. For three days I have been attending to the most prosaic details of business, feeling myself all the while a thing distinct and apart from the mortals with whom I discussed smoke-flues, heating capacities, and combination-boilers ! I believe I have accomplished everything with an exemplary sanity ; though as I talked I found myself surprised, from time to time, that none of these business men discovered the great mystery of my other and deeper life, which I know my whole manner and expression might have betrayed.

"Yesterday being Sunday, I stayed nearly all day in my room, that I might luxuriate in my happiness. For a long time I lay on my lounge in a half dream, my heart, and lips, and my whole body thrilling with the very memory of your kisses and caresses. With what difficulty I rose to write you. It was so sweet to simply remember!

"Do you know, sweet one, that I am yours by the most absolute surrender of myself to you—not a surrender once for all, but a surrender repeated with every pulsation of my heart. It seems to me that I never lived until I knew you; all before that seems to me a vague, half-forgotten dream; yet I realize that for years I had been trying to work out some plan that might leave the world better for my single effort, but I needed an inspiration that would not come to me. I stood within the great temple of humanity, and studied the mummeries of the priests, and the silent, unsatisfied seeking of the devotees. When I felt your divine presence there, the atmosphere was no longer cold to me; and when your lips had touched mine, the fretted arches of the temple burned—a fire was lit upon the altar, every symbol became life-giving, and the miracle was wrought for me which I had waited for so long in vain.

"To me now everything is endowed with new life, and every human face, however coarse or degraded, wears a new significance.

"This evening I visited an industrial reformatory home, instituted by some good Unitarian women, for the reclamation of 'abandoned girls.' I gave money to the fund, and the matrons called the girls together, that I might speak to them. It was a task to make up my mind to stand before them, until I thought of my precious one, and the brave step she took, when a young lady 'just out of school.' That gave me my text. I told the story of dear Susie's struggle and her final victory. I was played upon like a musical instrument by the magnetic force of those two hundred unhappy young girls. Nothing else can or could explain why I stood there and talked as I did—of what? Can you imagine? I talked of love, the subject that lay nearest their hearts, for they were women—of its beautiful mission in this world. I said women fell never from love, but from the want of it, and that by love alone could either women or men become a blessing to their time. As my audience became affected, many of them to tears, my own eyes became so dim that I could hardly see the faces before me, and then I knew I was eloquent. I described the love of a true, great-hearted woman, and the miracle her love could work in man's heart. I told them that the love of such a woman made the glory of my life, and to it they were indebted for the inspiration that made me come among them to speak words of encouragement. I said that, with such a love in my heart, every woman was sacred in my eyes, even though covered with rags and shame. I dwelt long upon the fatal error of any woman considering herself lost, whatever had been her history, or however great her degradation. 'Never,' I said, 'allow priest or layman, friend or foe, to convince you that you are not capable of a good and happy life, while there is yearning in your hearts, as

I know there is in every one of them, for a love such as I have described. It is a vile insult to human intelligence to presume that any one loves evil rather than good, or prefers the pity to the respect of mankind.' I then appealed strongly to their womanly pride and ambition, urging them to study earnestly in the classes established in the institution, promising to return in a year, and, if the directors would permit me, (here I obtained ready permission from the ladies on the platform) distribute certain prizes to those who had made the most progress in their studies and in their general deportment, and certain other prizes to all who had made any meritorious effort. The value and kind of the prizes being determined after some discussion with the ladies, I went on, and showed them the high importance of study as a discipline to the mind, and the value of education generally. I pointed out, in plain, simple language, the prospect opening before women through the recognition of her equal rights as a citizen, for I am always anxious, when talking to women, to show them the moral and political power they may wield by the ballot, this being the primal means to put them in the proper position to exercise a vast influence necessarily dormant without it.

"I was pleased to see the intense interest in the faces of these young women. I am sure I awakened them to a sense of innate womanly dignity, which cannot be crushed out by sudden misfortune, and to a firm resolve to work their way up to a better and more honorable life. There was great enthusiasm when I finished, and one sweet, silver-haired old lady came up and kissed me, with the natural simplicity of a little child. I was very proud of that. She then spoke of me to the girls, in a way that made me feel guilty, because I was not a perfect saint; and then calling one of the girls to the piano, I listened to some very pleasant singing by the whole company, and retired, feeling that I had deserved the approbation of her who is the joy and blessing of my life." ✿ ✿ ✿ ✿ ✿ ✿

CHAPTER XLII.

A VISIT TO THE SOCIAL PALACE.

NEARLY a year has passed, and it is summer again. Changes unheard of have been wrought over the river. The great palace dedicated to industry, rears its proud head toward the heavens, and joy and peace and plenty reign within its walls. Every apartment and every shop has been occupied over six months, and the tenants are voluntarily doubling and trebling their rents, for in this way they are paying for their magnificent home. The organization of the industries and of the domestic life, modeled after that of the great *Familistère* at Guise, must be scientifically adapted to the true laws of social harmony, for all the machinery works quietly, regularly, and satisfactorily. There is plenty of suggestion and lively discussion, but there is no discord. Even the narrowest and most selfish have learned that the happiness and continued prosperity of the individual lies in, and is indissolubly interwoven with, the happiness and prosperity of the whole.

As we cross over the neat iron bridge, we stop to admire the scene before us. On either side of the broad avenue leading to the palace, are green lawns, decorated with parterres of blossoming flowers, young trees and flowering shrubs, and winding roads and walks. To the left, beyond and stretching out of sight, are fruit orchards, fields of grain, and gardens in perfect order and luxuriant growth. On the left of the central avenue, and not far from the bridge, stands the pretty theatre, in colored bricks and very ornate in its style. Children from six to sixteen are passing in, for this is the last rehearsal, but one, of a great spectacular entertainment, to be given to-morrow afternoon, and repeated in the evening. To-morrow is the children's festival, which will end the grand inaugural celebration, beginning to-day—promised long ago to the workmen of the Social Palace. The count had intended to give this festival outright, as a testimonial to the devotion and enthusiasm with which the men had conducted their work; but they got together and discussed it, and ordered it in a better way, as he himself was forced to admit. At the last meeting of the two councils of directors (twelve of the ablest men and twelve of the ablest women chosen by ballot by all the members), they had united their session, and decided to advertise the festival widely, and to count on paying all the expenses with the proceeds of the refreshments, the entrance fee to the evening inaugural ceremonies in the grand central court, and the tickets to the grand ball that was to follow. The count was to make up the deficit, if there was any, and none but members of the Social Palace were to receive everything free on that day. Stevens, who had sent for his family and taken up his residence in the palace, was an influential member, and his prediction that even the great court, capable of seating five thousand, would not hold all who would come, proved correct. The day dawned magnificently, and extra trains on the several railroads were filled during the whole two days, and thousands came and went who did not stay to the evening celebration, but were shown over the palace and grounds, and lavishly patronized the luxuries furnished by the restaurant and the wine-cellar.

But we have just crossed the bridge, and are passing the theatre. Going in with the young actors are their big brothers—young men dressed in a very elegant and jaunty uniform. These are the corps of Social Palace firemen, whose ostensible office is a sinecure, but they are the conductors of all the muscular work at festivals. They are stage-dressers, ushers, box-keepers; and on this occasion, with Too Soon dressed in gorgeous Oriental costume, they wait upon the little tables, scattered everywhere in the vicinity of the palace, in arbors, and wherever there is a shady spot.

The grand façade of the palace, with its great arched doorway, presents an imposing appearance. The main color of the large bricks that compose the walls, is light granite gray, but the facings and arches of the doors and windows are of a dark slate tint; while in the walls, high up, are set in, like mosaics, smaller, brilliant-colored bricks, forming three words that resemble a mediæval illuminated missal. One of these words, reaching more than half way across the face of the left wing or quadrangle, is LIBERTY; on the middle building, the word EQUALITY; and on the right wing, FRATERNITY.

The café, restaurant, and billiard-room, as well as the great public kitchen, are in one building, behind the rear quadrangle of the palace, and connected with it by broad covered corridors on two different stories. On the left of this rear quadrangle, and connected with it in the same way, is the fine building containing the nursery and *pou-*

ponnat below, and above, the *bambinat ~* cnools ; still beyond,or to the left of the school bu..aing, and joined to it, are the fine swimming-baths, fed by the brook, and heated in winter by the exhaust steam of the silk factory, which, on after consideration, was placed at the left of the palace, instead of at the right, as first intended. Still beyond these buildings are stables, carriage-houses, and the steam laundry ; and still further, are the gasometer and the *abattoir*. From these buildings on to the forest, and extending right and left over a broad area, are nurseries filled with plants, shrubs, and young trees ; and here also are located the hot-houses and green-houses of the Social Palace. Finally, beyond, are the rising, wooded hills, now transformed into a beautiful grove with shady walks and carriage-roads extending to and around the lake on the summit. This is the grand resort of the children for picnics, boat-rides, fishing, and for skating in the winter. The most serious punishment of the children for idleness or any misconduct is the deprivation of this pleasure, which is allowed the first sunny afternoon of every week.

Flags and streamers are flying on the palace roof to-day, and music from bands in the open air adds its charm to a scene too inspiring for description. To-day the shuttles of the silk-looms are silent. The brick-making establishment is represented by a single guard, relieved every two hours ; for there must be some one there, as in the silk factory, to answer the questions of visitors. All the workmen are in their holiday dresses, and joy and happiness are on every face. Large numbers of the Social Palace occupants—all who are willing to assume the responsibility of making the visitors comfortable, or to assist in their entertainment in any way—wear a little

badge bearing the words "Liberty, Equality, Fraternity."
When they wish to escape being constantly appealed to
for information, they hide their badges for a time; but it
is rarely done, for they are as proud as princes of their
magnificent home and its surroundings.

Inside the palace, in private apartments, young girls
are busy laying out their dresses and finery for the
evening ball which is to commence at ten o'clock. No
single Cinderella is to stay at home for want of the proper
accoutrements. The fairy godmother, in the form of
Susie and the count's munificence, has already been working magic in the way of simple but beautiful ball-
dresses, and flowers have already been provided with
lavish hands. Not only is the inauguration to be cele-
brated, but another great event, which as yet is a secret to
the greater number; and those who know, will only give
hints of the birth of a child, the first that has seen the
light in the Social Palace.

By three o'clock in the afternoon not only strangers,
but all Oakdale, seems to be on the ground, or enjoying
the marvels in the interior of the palace; and carriages
and pedestrians are still swarming up the great avenues.

Mrs. Kendrick and Louise, with Mrs. Burnham, have
been all the afternoon with Mrs. Forest and her daughters, or with Charlotte and Felix. The doctor has spent
all the time he could spare from his various responsibilities in the direction of the festival, with his well-beloved
Clara, who is somewhat indisposed, but in an ever-present
and still ever-promising state of happiness such as rarely
falls to the lot of women. Not a cloud has ever darkened
the sky of her married bliss. She is grown even dearer
to Paul than ever, and to her he is still the hero of her

dreams. There is little danger that the illusions of love
will not endure in this case ; not because, after a year,
they are more ineffably tender to each other ; not because
there may be new ties to bind them, but because Nature
has attuned them to each other

"Like perfect music unto noble words."

The apartments of the count are in the right wing of
the palace, directly under the word FRATERNITY, emblazoned on the outer wall. The doctor's are adjoining, on
one side, and those of Felix and Charlotte on the other.
Charlotte's marriage had proved a very happy one, despite
the croaking of her brother and certain of her old friends.
On this afternoon, as Felix was absent, the doctor brought
Charlotte in to dine with his family and their visitors.
There were no signs of dinner as she entered, but in an
incredibly short space of time Dinah, in a gayly-trimmed
head-dress, and a ruffled white apron spanning her ample
proportions, produced a very elegant repast, without the
slightest sign of flurry or over-heating manifested in her
shining face.

Mrs. Forest saw that her visitors marveled at this suddenly and easily prepared table, and she explained :

" We scarcely ever do any cooking. When the table
is set, Dinah brings, or has brought, from the great *cuisine*
whatever we want. It is under the control of our French
citizens—we are all fellow-citizens, you know," said Mrs.
Forest, by way of parenthesis, and with a comical smile,
"and nobody can cook as they do."

" And so you are actually free from all the trouble of
marketing and overseeing the cooking," said Mrs. Ken
drick ; " but is it not very expensive ? "

"On the contrary," answered Mrs. Forest, "if we were to furnish all these materials, buying them at retail, and Dinah were to cook them, which she could hardly do in a whole day, even if she knew how, it would cost almost twice as much, calculating, of course, for the waste which cannot be avoided in a private family. Many a woman here used her cook-stove at first, but as the palace is all heated by the furnaces in winter, and the kitchen-stove fire not needed, they soon gave it up. Now, even the very poorest go or send their children to the *cuisine* for whatever they want. After dinner I will show you our wine-cellars. They are well stocked, and the very poorest may drink them. The count has contracted with certain great vineyards in France to supply us. They are of several prices ; some very good ones at ten cents a bottle, and fair light kinds for six--half bottles at five and three cents. You know it is his belief, and also the doctor's, that children should be accustomed to drink wine, diluted with water, of course, as the best and surest means of preventing drunkenness."

"Do you really believe that, doctor ? " asked Mrs. Burnham, who was naturally greatly interested in the subject, on account of her son's intemperance.

"I do believe it," he replied. "Who are the people whom we call 'shoddy,' and who make themselves ridiculous by overdressing ? Naturally, they are those who have been deprived of the luxury of dress in their youth. Who are the gormandizers ? Certainly not those who have been accustomed to plenty of excellent food from their childhood. Then again, the miser, who lives deprived of all the luxuries of life, that he may gratify an abnormal passion for hoarding away money ; he is in all cases, I believe, one who has been deprived of money in his youth, or may be he has inherited the passion from some unhappy parent. The same law should apply to drinking, though there is another cause at work here, too frequently overlooked : the passion for stimulation or exaltation. That, in my opinion, will vanish when we have a social life that answers our demands for natural excitement—society, music, games, dancing, dramatic acting, scientific pursuits, and flirting I will add, Miss Louise, for your sake, for I know you think I was going to leave out something important."

Louise blushed very prettily, and disclaimed all such shocking thoughts.

"Yet," said Mrs. Burnham, "you certainly have some members who are addicted to drinking."

"True, but there are no liquors sold in the café or billiard-rooms, and account for it as you can, men are not apt to get drunk on wine. To be sure the men wanted liquors sold in these rooms, and they voted for it pretty largely."

"Why, what hindered it being brought in then?" asked Mrs. Burnham.

"Why, don't you know the women vote here as well as the men?" asked Linnie, glancing at her mother. "I certainly voted against it, and so did mamma, and Leila, and just about all the women."

"Mamma is a female suffrager now," said Leila, mischievously. "She is one of the council of twelve elected by universal suffrage." Mrs. Forest reproved her daughter's garrulity, looking herself a little foolish, remembering her own stricture in times past, upon the claims of the women's rights agitators.

"What are the functions of these councils?" asked Mrs. Kendrick.

"The twelve men," said Mrs. Forest, "manage the industrial and financial matters, the buying of supplies, and so on. We attend to the working of the domestic machinery, the nursery and the schools, report on the quality of the supplies, call general meetings of the women, and discuss all matters. Nothing is done as a duty, and for nothing but the honor, except our work as councils of direction. So far, we have not seen fit to ask for pay, but our duties are not onerous. We sit an hour every week."

"Well, I must confess this Social Palace is the most wonderful thing," said Mrs. Kendrick. "If the people were all educated—of our own class, you know—I would try to have Mr. Kendrick sell out and come here to live."

"Bless you!" said the doctor. "Wait till you see our rising generation, who are being educated here; I was going to say you wouldn't know them from gentlemen and ladies; but you would, by three signs: superior refinement, superior education, and superior recognition of the rights of others. You'd better come as soon as there is a vacancy, but there are, at least, now on the books, a hundred applicants, and as the first applying have the first chance, yours are rather small." Mrs. Kendrick thought there was a slight malice in the doctor's tone.

"One word more about intemperance," said Mrs. Burnham. "Any of your members can go to Oakdale and get liquor. Now that your son is gone, and that Clara has moved away, the liquor dealers have broken their

promises. I believe my poor boy will be quite ruined.
I have been thinking of consulting you, doctor, about
taking him to Binghamton."

"The worst thing about that inebriate asylum there,"
said the doctor, "is that there is no industry for the
inmates. They actually spend days carving sticks and
bits of wood; but still, as it is the best thing that offers.
I should say send him there at once."

"So should I," said Mrs. Forest. "I believe our son
is quite cured of his habit. There is a decanter of brandy
standing in the sitting-room all the time, and he has not
once touched it. You know he is coming home on trial.
We expect him next week." And the mother's face
lighted up with joy at the thought of the restoration of
her first-born.

"You were going to ask, Mrs. Burnham," said Charlotte, "what we do when our members come home intoxicated. We say nothing, unless they disturb the quiet of
others, or unless their families complain to the council.
When this occurs, or any act of disorder militating
against public order and morality, the council publish a
bulletin of censure, and place it on the bulletin-board,
where all the acts of the board, and all general notices,
are placed. At first the name is not mentioned, but
accompanying the censure is an expression of deep regret
and the offer of sympathy to help the culprit reform."

"We have, so far, had but four cases," said Mrs. Forest.
"Our council attends to these questions. This bulletin-
board is a terror to the disorderly."

"And very naturally too," said Charlotte, "for it contains the decisions of the council they have chosen by
their own votes."

"We hear all sorts of stories outside," said Mrs. Kendrick. "One is, that the *bambins* study politics, and learn the uses of the ballot; but of course that is a mere joke."

"Not wholly," replied Mrs. Müller, or Charlotte, the name by which we have known her. "The children all have daily exercises in the open air, and even the little tots six, seven, and eight years old do quite an amount of useful work. They go out in bands of ten or twenty each, under a little industrial chief, girl or boy, chosen by themselves, by ballot. They have regular ballot-boxes."

"Then they do learn the use of the ballot-box even at that absurd age."

"Oh yes. Why not?" answered Charlotte. "The head gardener, or his assistant, Edward Page, provides them with little hoes and rakes, or other small implements, and points out the work to be done. Then the chief sets them to work after his or her example, and sees that the gardener's instructions are carried out to the letter. For this work, chiefs and laborers receive five cents an hour, which is their own money, and they can squander it just as they please; but as all the candies are of a simple and healthy kind, they can't hurt themselves. Some of them save their money. The height of their ambition is to amass a fortune of one dollar. That takes twenty days, for they are not encouraged to work more than an hour at a time. They show real judgment in choosing their leaders, and these little leaders are very careful to please their constituents. So, in this way, almost from the cradle they begin to learn the principles of popular government. Why, they use the terms ballot,

nominee, majority, candidate, constituent, just as intelligently as other children do doll and hop-scotch ! "

"Well, it is plain to be seen that girls brought up so
will never discuss the right to a voice in government. It
will seem as natural a right," said Mrs. Kendrick, "as
that of breathing."

"True," said Mrs. Forest, "and I wish we had all been
brought up so. If we had, it is my opinion that there
would not be a house of ill-fame or a drinking den in the
town. But let us go into the nursery."

The doctor excused himself, and the ladies, all except
the twins, went by themselves. Mrs. Forest led them
through the long, well-lighted corridor, to the angle of
the left wing, and seating them and herself in an elegant
elevator, descended to the noor below, and then passing
through the central court and the covered way leading to
the school building, on the lower floor, they were shown
into the nursery and *pouponnat*. Susie, who was one of
the council of directors, was there, giving some directions
or suggestions. She was dressed in a gossamer-like
organdie, and wore fragrant flowers in her blonde hair and
on her breast. The ladies noticed that Mrs. Forest and
Charlotte gave their hands to Susie cordially, and therefore they followed the example.

The nursery and *pouponnat* were in an immense, high-
studded, well-lighted and well-ventilated room. The
floors were waxed or oiled, and here and there were bouquets of flowers in pretty vases, on wall-brackets. There
were also busts and pictures. Everything was exquisitely
fresh and clean. The *pouponnat* was separated from the
nursery by a little balustrade, and the *poupons* were
marching to the music of their own songs, keeping time

meanwhile with their little hands to an accompaniment on a piano played by a young girl who was one of five who conducted the *pouponnat* exercises two hours every day. There were about eighty *poupons,* and some fifty babies, who were watching the *poupons* with great interest. There were toys of every kind, and little swings and various furniture for light gymnastic exercises. While the visitors were looking on, one of the *poupons,* marching somewhat awkwardly, fell and hurt his head. He uttered a loud sob and ran to the young girl, who took him in her arms and "kissed the spot," in a motherly fashion, and sent him back to his place in the ranks after a very short term of consolation.

Mrs. Kendrick remarked the child's restraining himself from crying.

"They very rarely cry when they are hurt," said Susie. "If any child 'yells,' as Min calls it, the others stare at him, and he cannot brave the public disapprobation of his peers. This is a thing that we have all wondered at. Children are not very sensitive to the criticism of grown people. They can only understand the motives and feelings of their peers. You see there is plenty of sound, of prattle, but no racket. It is the same thing in the nursery at Guise. There is no punishment there nor here for crying, and yet they do not cry unless they are suffering. Their wants, all of them, we try to supply ; and if they moan and cry, we know they must be ill."

"Yet certainly that is not natural," said Mrs. Burnham. "Children do cry when nothing is the matter with them."

"Their wants cannot be supplied in the isolated home," said Susie, very earnestly. "They suffer from lack of amusement, and especially for the society of those whom they can understand—their peers. It is difficult for those to understand this who have not seen the working of a well-organized nursery. When the mothers try to keep their little ones at home longer than a few hours, they worry and fret until they have to bring them back. The nurslings stay here all night for the most part; the *poupons* sleep at home. All the food for both these departments is supplied free. It is kept warm all day, and for the babies all night. There are several wet-nurses, and mothers who have not weaned their babies come at intervals and nurse them, and take them home generally at night. All is free. The mother can have her little ones here a part or all the time, or keep them at home all the time. But there is not a *poupon* in the place who does not pass some of the hours of the day here."

"When do they reach the distinguished honor of becoming *poupons?*" asked Louise, smiling.

"You may well say honor," replied Susie. "It is the ambition of the babies to enter the *pouponnat*. This they do when they can walk well, and have learned to keep themselves clean. The *poupons*, in their turn, aspire to become *bambins*, where they have higher exercises, and commence the Froëbel exercises, slate exercises, and reading. The nurslings are promoted when about thirty months old, and the *poupons*, at from four to five years old."

"Well, I must say I never saw children so happy—did you, Mrs. Burnham?"

"Never. Modern progress will eliminate the mother altogether by-and-bye, I suspect."

Some of the babies were crowing in their nurses' arms, some sleeping in their elegant little cribs, canopied with snowy muslin, many playing and rolling over each other on the floor, or practising their first steps in the "walker," an elliptical platform on castors, surrounded by a double railing just high enough for the little toddlers to cling to and lean on as they walked around between these railings. The first lesson in politeness, Susie said, was to wait in their cribs in the morning until their turn came to be bathed, and dressed, and fed, and the next to pass each other in the "walker" without jostling or crowding.

"I see you have no rocking-cradles. How do you get all these children to sleep?" asked Mrs. Kendrick.

"It is one of the prettiest sights you ever saw," said Mrs. Forest, "to see these children all put into their little beds at night without rocking, and there singing themselves to sleep without any crying."

"You don't really mean to say they do that?" asked Mrs. Burnham, incredulously.

"They certainly do, all of them, after they have been here a short time. The gas burns low all night, and the little ones who do not sleep all night are fed, of course."

"Well, wonders will never cease," remarked Mrs. Burnham, who then inquired how this forest of little cribs were kept so perfectly sweet and fresh. One of the nurses showed these beds. Each one had a sacking bottom, holding about a bushel of wheaten-bran, over which was laid a little blanket. Any moisture penetrating this bran formed at once a solid lump, which was removed, leaving the rest all dry and clean. Fresh bran was added from time to time. Each bed had a soft little pillow, and plenty of covering.

Other visitors came and went, while these stayed, determined to see if everything was really as marvelously satisfactory as people said.

Here the nurses prepared to take their charges, or numbers of them, into the swimming-baths, where the company followed them, wondering more and more.

CHAPTER XLIII.

'HAVE you noticed," asked Mrs. Kendrick of her friend, "how deliciously cool it is in here? and yet this is one of the warmest days of this warm summer."

"It is always cool here compared with other places," replied Mrs. Müller. "Great buildings, you know, keep their own temperature very evenly all the year round; and then these walls being of great thickness, and having an air-chamber between the outer and the inner, neither heat nor cold affects us greatly. Everybody was astonished at the small amount of coal used last winter in heating the building. The mercury in the great court hardly ever went down to fifty degrees."

The little ones were greatly delighted with their baths, which were in a large one-story brick-building, covered with a handsome glass roof. The floor of the bath in the children's room was brought up to within about three inches of the surface of the water at one end, and sloping down to two feet below at the other end. At the shallow part the babies rolled about and splashed and crowed, while they continually tried to dare deeper and deeper water, imitating the *poupons* and the *bambins*, some of whom, Min among the rest, swam like little South Sea Islanders.

Passing from this room into the next, through a thick partition some seven feet high, the visitors were in the presence of some two or three hundred bathers, men and women, dressed so exactly alike that it was often impossible to tell one sex from the other. At the upper end, where the visitors entered, the water was deep, for swimming ; while further down, beyond the island, the water was shallow enough for the most timid. Mrs. Forest explained that there were an unusual number of bathers to-day, because of the hot weather and because of the coming ball, this being the first part of the toilet of the dancers. Some took flying leaps and dives from different stages of a platform at the deep end of the bath, according to their temerity ; and some of the boldest were women. Sometimes young men and maidens—Linnie and young Page were among these—leaped or dived together, holding each other's hands, disappearing under the water, then reappearing and swimming a race to the little island. This was some ten or twelve feet in diameter, and covered with plants in luxuriantly-flourishing condition. Great African lilies opened their creamy spathes to the sun, and extended their enormous leaves over the edge of the island. In the centre of the island was a tall fern, and smaller ones at its base. This island was entirely left to the mercy of the bathers ; but as there were always some, and even many, every day, it was kept in perfect condition.

"Oh," said Louise to her mother, "how grand this is ! I would rather live here than in any place in the world !"

After a hasty survey of the laundry, cuisine, café, and other adjuncts, our visitors went back to the palace through the nursery, for Mrs. Burnham would have "one more peep at those happy babies." But many of them were now in their garden, playing on the lawn, watching the beautiful birds in a large aviary, or talking to the parrots. There was a balcony, protected by a balustrade, extending across the garden end of the nursery, and the little ones who could walk were continually passing through the glass doors on to this, where they could see the birds and flowers, and the sports of the children.

On returning to the doctor's apartments, Mrs. Kendrick found a messenger with a note from her husband, saying that Dr. Delano and his wife had arrived from Boston, intent on visiting the evening ceremonies at the Social Palace, and that they would probably expect something to eat. Mrs. Kendrick asked for her carriage.

"You will return with them?" said Mrs. Forest. "You may as well bring them and your husband here at once. They can just as well dine here, if they have not dined."

"Of course," said Charlotte. I will order dinner for them in our rooms while you are gone. Louise wants to go home and dress, I know, for she means to dance at the workman's ball."

"My child, is that so?" asked Mrs. Kendrick, gravely. "Why, you have no escort!"

"Oh, Felix will take care of her. He dances, and I do not," replied Mrs. Müller.

The three suites of apartments of the doctor, Paul, and Felix, extended through the wing from front to back, where they opened on the court of the quadrangle. In this court was the magnificent winter conservatory of the Social Palace. All these three suites of apartments were very elegantly furnished, especially those of the count, who could find nothing too rich or magnificent for the home of his precious Clara. On this second floor, around the three sides of this court, were the apartments renting the highest, being more spacious in their character. Every tenant had the right to finish or decorate his interior as he chose. He could fresco, or paper, or wainscot it at his pleasure. The count and Felix had had theirs frescoed by a skillful foreign artist; but most of the occupants were quite satisfied with the elegant "hard-finished," tinted walls of their homes.

In about an hour the visitors returned, bringing Dr. Delano and his wife and the two "solid" bankers. Louise was in a state of great excitement. There were to be many Oakdalers at the ball, but none, so far as she knew, of her own particular set, except the count, and he would probably only dance once, and then retire to his "idol." But Louise was seized with a democratic mania. She was anxious to see how young men who actually worked all day would deport themselves in white kid gloves, and she told Ella she expected rare amusement. Ella decided that it would be exceedingly "nice," and only regretted that she was in her traveling dress.

As the party drove over the bridge, Ella was amazed at the sight of the magnificent structure before her, and asked what it was.

"Why that is it," replied Louise.

"It?" fairly screamed Ella. "Do you mean to tell me that is your workingman's home? You can't make me believe it."

"You should have been with us to-day," said Mrs. Kendrick. "The outside is nothing to the spacious elegance and comfort inside; and it is so deliciously cool there!"

"I should think it would be stifling like a big hot-house, under those glass roofs of the courts," said Dr. Delano, addressing Mrs. Kendrick.

"Oh no; in the first place, those roofs are very high, and have openings, and then great volumes of air are constantly coming in from the underground venti-lating galleries; besides, I am told that all immense buildings, like St. Peter's at Rome, keep their own tem-perature very evenly all the year round."

"That a workingman's home!" repeated Ella, as if dreaming. "Why, the finest mansions in Boston would be lost inside of it!" And she sank back in the carriage as if exhausted. Such a palace for mere laboring people seemed to shock her sense of the fitness of things, like the sight of hippopotami on a grand banqueting-table.

Felix was waiting to receive them at the grand en-trance; and giving the carriage into the hands of one of the uniformed young men, he conducted his guests up the grand stairway, decorated with huge vases of flowers, along the corridor into his own apartments. Louise begged Charlotte to take them at once into the back parlor opening on the great conservatory. The long fold-ing windows were open, and through these they passed on to the balcony surrounding the conservatory on three sides; for it extended quite through the end of the quad-rangle toward the south-east, where it ended by a double wall of glass. Dr. Delano seemed struck dumb by the magnificent spectacle before them. The air was laden with rich perfumes, and the colors of the foliage and flower, were dazzling in their beauty.

"This," said Charlotte proudly, "is our tropical conservatory. There are several others in the nursery
grounds. The whole is under the head direction of
Madam Susie, but there are many skillful florists under
her."

The great palm stood in the centre, and reared its
huge trunk and wide-spreading fronds toward the glass
dome, which the rays of the setting sun still emblazoned.
The wide passage around this centre was laid in handsome colored tiles, like all the floors of the balconies, so
that water could not injure them. The visitors looked
down from the balcony on to this walk, where people
were continually passing. "See!" said Dr. Delano,
calling the attention of Ella. "Do you see those two
young ladies in white under the palm-tree?"

"No—where? There are so many."

"Why, there on your right, in ball-dress, with their
cavaliers. Those are the Forest girls—twins, you know.
How very pretty they look!"

"I must say this is magnificent!" exclaimed Kendrick, who was studying the conservatory, being much
interested in the subject, from his own experience. Plants
seemed there to forget what latitudes they were born to.
Huge century plants from Mexico crowned vases set on
high pedestals, and spread out their long polished leaves,
as if enamored of their foster climate. Around these
pedestals climbed the many-tinted velvet foliage of the
lovely *Cissus discolor.* There were poinsettias from
Australia opening out their giant crimson bracts, the
papyrus from Egypt, clerodendrons, and a wonderful
variety of calladiums, whose broad leaves reflected the
most brilliant colors. There were climbing plants in

great number; large orange-trees, filled with flowers and fruit that had been growing under Susie's care at her old conservatories; banana-trees, on which hung heavy clusters of ripening fruit; pineapples, in the sunniest spots; and every plant, every leaf, in that vast court seemed to have found its own conditions for perfect growth.

"My dear Charlotte," said Felix, with the tenderness in his gray eyes that is seldom wanting in young husbands, "is not the dinner waiting?"

"Yes; but I cannot drag these people from the balcony by main force. See! they are clear out of sight, on the further balcony."

At this juncture some officials entered the conservatory, and at a given signal Felix gathered in his guests, and every window opening on the balconies was closed, while the promenaders below were warned to leave immediately, or take a drenching. From behind the French windows Charlotte's guests watched the artificial rain-shower which burst up from the hose, capped with rose-sprinklers, even to the very roof, and descended gently for some minutes on balconies, windows, walls, and on all the masses of foliage below. In a few minutes several women, armed with mops of white cotton waste and a bucket, passed round on the balconies and removed the water. Mr. and Mrs. Müller then succeeded in getting their guests to the table, which was spread with a profusion of delicacies and luxuries, and adorned with flowers. They were delighted with everything, and the same, or fuller, explanations had to be given as those at the doctor's table some hours before. By special request, Too Soon had been sent from the restaurant to attend Felix's table. The only assistance Charlotte had in her simple

23

household duties, as she explained, was a young girl whom she had taken from an orphan asylum in Boston, and who was attending the Social Palace school. To-day, of course, she had a holiday.

The sight of the gorgeous Oriental, and his quaint polite ways, amused Ella and Louise greatly. Albert went into ecstacies over a *sole au grattin.* "When I want a sauce like that," he said, " I have to go to the Parker House, though I have a cook at sixty dollars a month, and furnish him three assistants. I may add, that not even at the Parker House have I ever tasted mushrooms so delicious as these."

" You ought to live here, Albert," said his sister ; "because you are such a *gourmet.* Mushrooms are a perfect drug here, and we sell them by the ton. You see they grow under the flower benches in the dark. This is one of our great industries. Children pick them and pack them, and they are also very skilful in the handling of our cut flowers. They earn a great deal of money, though they all attend the schools. This is the one-thing obligatory. Every child must be kept at school."

" What do you think, Müller," asked Burnham, "about the occupants paying for this establishment ? "

" Why, we shall do it without a doubt, in less than ten years. The profits from the stores and the *cuisine* alone more than pay for running the establishment. On many of the articles of food there is absolutely no profit. This is to encourage the poor and the unskilled laborers, who do not earn so much, of course, as the skilled laborers ; but then their wives, being relieved from nursing and cooking, can help them put money in their rents. There are about two hundred women employed from two to eight hours a day in the nurseries and schools, in the stores, café, laundry, and in taking care of the flower business, and keeping the palace in order. Then there are many more in the silk factory and in the dairy."

Burnham asked what the articles of food were that were furnished at cost. Felix and Charlotte enumerated : crushed wheat, certain fruits, hominy, milk, beef soup, Graham bread, mashed potatoes, plain roasts, and some others.

"Why," said Kendrick, "that is a sufficient diet for any one. The economical can easily live on that, and make the support of the institution out of those who indulge in luxuries."

"That is true," replied Charlotte, "and we think it quite just. There is such a spirit of good-fellowship and honest enthusiasm here, that all goes on admirably. Our wheat and beef, we raise on the farm, and if any choose to live on simple fare, which is always excellent of its kind, they can do so on much less than one-half what it used to cost them."

While they were talking, the great conservatory was suddenly lighted up, and Louise and Ella precipitately sought the balcony. The walk below was quite dry, and filled with promenaders, while the crystal water-drops, that still hung on the great palm fronds, glistened like diamonds in the brilliant light.

While the gentlemen lingered over their wine, a grand swell of music echoed through the palace, announcing that the time for the inaugural ceremonies in the great central court had arrived. Felix and Charlotte then led their guests down one flight of stairs and into this court, and seated them on the platform reserved for the musicians and speakers, and for a few specially-honored guests.

The scene presented from the platform of this vast glass-roofed court was one of dazzling splendor. It was lighted by scores of gas-jets, projecting all around from the base of the three tiers of balconies or galleries, on which the apartments opened, now crowded with spectators. The centre was also filled with seats, not one of which was empty. Over the centre of the platform were gracefully draped flags of many countries, conspicuous among which were the tri-color of France and the " star-spangled banner." These flags were draped around an immense shield of delicate green mosses, in which were set a mosaic of half-opened rosebuds, tube-roses, white-violets, and scarlet-verbenas, forming the motto, " *Attractions are proportional to destinies.*" Opposite the platform, on the further side of the court, filling the space between the two upper balconies, was another flag-draped shield of the same kind, bearing the motto, " *The Series distribute the Harmonies.*" Long chains of rare flowers, looped with gay ribbons, completely festooned every balcony, the slender iron supports of which were covered with winding garlands of natural flowers. The whole air was deliciously perfumed. Great vases of flowering plants decorated each end of the platform ; and scattered among the audience were women in ball-dress, their shoulders draped with brilliant opera-cloaks. On either side of the court, half-way between the display of flags, were the words, in a mosaic of flowers, " *Liberty, Equality, Fraternity,* the first word being on the lowest gallery, and *Fraternity* on the highest. Murmurs of admiration were heard everywhere among the immense audience. Suddenly the court rang with shouts of applause, and the band struck up " *See! the Conquering Hero Comes.*" The count had entered the court. Ascending the platform, he advanced to the front and waited until the applause had somewhat subsided. He looked quite pale when he commenced :

"Friends, fellow-workers, and citizens :"—after a pause, which became even painful, he laid his hand on his breast, saying—" Can you bear with my weakness when I confess that my heart is too full for utterance ? To say that this is the proudest hour of my life, seems to me but a lame and impotent phrase. No words that I am able to combine, are adequate to express the emotion that fills me to-night. But as I am expected to speak, I will not disappoint you, and will do the best I can ; and as there are many strangers present, I must endeavor specially to make myself intelligible to them. To you, my fellow-workers, I need only say that the first Social Palace of America is finished, and I think it does honor to the hands that have built it." [Here the count was interrupted by cheers and protests against his modesty in giving all the credit to the workmen.]

" You do me personally too much honor. It is not much to advance capital for the building of an institution like this, following the example of one of the noblest lovers of humanity, who did *his* work without precedent, and against opposition and discouragement of every kind. [Cheers for Godin.] This palace is built on the model of the first one ever founded—that at Guise, in France.

That has been in successful operation now for several years,
and I wish every capitalist within the sound of my voice
to note well the fact, that it is a perfect financial success,
paying six per cent. annually on the capital invested,
which is as much as any commercially-honest capitalist
in France expects to make." Here the count gave a
detailed description of the organization and working of
the Social Palace system, and then he continued :

"You have gone over the palace and the grounds
to-day ; you have seen the flourishing industries, you
understand the provisions made for the children, the sick,
the aged and infirm, and you can judge whether this
institution furnishes the proper conditions for moral and
intellectual growth [prolonged cheers] ; but you may
not yet be able to comprehend what the children of these
industrious men and women will become, when they have
grown up under the influence of the means for education
and artistic culture which this grand institution supplies.
They will despise drudgery by instinct, for it leaves the
form bent and awkward, and the mind cramped and
divested of beauty ; and just as certainly will they honor
labor as the great natural function of the human race,
distinguishing it from the brutes. The reason why labor
has not been honored heretofore, is because it has always
been confounded with slavery or drudgery. With the
abolition of slavery, we are just beginning to learn that
man is not to be adapted to labor, but that labor, through
machinery and scientific organization, is to be adapted to
man.

"The primal object of society should be to make perfect men and women—perfect citizens. This cannot be
accomplished without scientific training for the mind,

and the free and harmonious development of the muscles
through labor, with gymnastic exercises and games for
the development of those muscles not brought into play
by the ordinary industrial occupations. When a man
continues many hours a day using only one set of muscles, as the blacksmith his arm, he must do it at the
expense of grace, and strength, and beauty, which we
should be taught to seek as a duty to ourselves and to
our fellow-beings, since we have no moral right to trans-
mit disease and ugliness to posterity. [Cheers.] No one
should dream of finishing his education until he dies.
Besides the exercise of the muscles by industry, every
human being should have time during the twenty-four
hours, for amusing games, for bathing, for dressing
elegantly and becomingly, for social converse, for music
or the drama, for regular study and drill in classes, and
finally for sleep. All this may not be accomplished for
the wronged and cheated adult generation of the present;
all this and more will be the proud heritage of the children growing up under the blessings of a nobly organized
social and industrial life. [Great applause.] Children
growing up under such conditions, will be strong and
beautiful, tender and wise. They will be strong through
constant exercise, a varied and plentiful diet, and the
natural stimulation of happiness. They will be beautiful,
because to develop their bodies harmoniously will be the
object of scientific study ; and their faces will be beautiful because they will be moulded, not by anger, and
cunning, and selfishness, but by generosity, candor, and
love. They will be tender, because they will be taught
to be proud of exemplifying the devotion of love, the
grandest of all our passions, for it is the only one that

exalts us the dignity of the creative mood. Finally, they will ⌐ wise, for they will have acquired the sentiment of the brotherhood of man.

> ' Wisdom is humanity;
> And they who want it, wise as they may seem,
> And confident in their own sight and strength,
> Reach not the scope they aim at.' "

Such enthusiastic and long-continued applause followed the count's address, that he came forward again, and said :

"This time, my friends, I will forgive you for taking more notice of me than I deserve, since it reminds me of a duty I owe to you. I wish to say to the thousands here present, and especially to the capitalists who may hereafter engage in the building of Social Palaces, that their task will be an easier one than they suppose; because men and women will work for their establishment with the same single-hearted devotion with which they have worked for this. I have been often pained to see the sacrifices that these noble workers have made. I doubt if one-half of them have taken the allotted hour at noon for their lunch; and I have seen carpenters, cabinet-makers, and decorators, seize a spade and dig in the trenches, rather than be a moment idle, when their own special work was interrupted by any accident; and be it said to the honor of labor, that the men who have done the most skilled labor on this palace, have never failed in equal respect toward those who have done the most mechanical and unskilled portions. A spirit of fraternal good-fellowship and unity of purpose has, so far as I know, characterized these men throughout every hour of

the work from its commencement. This spirit is based
on the sentiment of equality, the recognition of human
rights everywhere, and is most significant, for it is full of
promise for the future success of our great effort. And
here I will mention one thing, not out of malice, but
simply as a lesson. I am accused of advocating the
'leveling' principle. 'Frauenstein, you are a leveler,'
said a friend to me to-day. Well, there is some truth in
that : I would bring all the races and individuals on the
globe up to the highest level ; but I should be very sorry
to do anything toward bringing my artisan friends down
to the physical, intellectual, or moral level of certain
aristocrats whom I know. [Laughter and applause.] It
is undeniably the fact, that to-day the soundest views
on education, on politics, on finance, on social organization, are supported, not by those who hold themselves
above their kind—the drones of the community, who feed
on the mechanic's labor—but by those who have an
honest right to everything they own, and much more.
The more I associate with laborers, even those who have
had little advantage from schools, the more I am struck
with the saving virtue that is in them. I confess I am
almost disgusted with the very word aristocracy, for it
has been vilely degraded, until it is applied only to those
who would be ashamed to do an honest day's work of any
kind. And what is this aristocracy ? What are these
parvenues of two hundred years, who would cry down
the nobler aristocracy of labor, which is as old as civilization itself ? "

CHAPTER XLIV.

THE BIRTH OF THE HEIR.

AFTER the count's speech, there was a quartette performed by pupils of the school, and a solo by Leila, Linnie playing the accompaniment. Her cold, correct soprano voice was heard very distinctly throughout the great auditorium. She pretended to be very indifferent to the applause that followed, but secretly was much flattered. Mr. Stevens followed with a very neat practical speech on the subject of what he called penny-wise and pound-foolish investments of capital, and several times "brought down the house" by his quaint way of turning sentences. The audience were in a joyous humor when he ended, and called loudly for their great pet at public meetings, Dr. Forest. He said :

"My friends, I thank you for calling me, though I was intending to come without any invitation [laughter], for I have two announcements to make to you. During the latter part of the eloquent address of my son-in-law— That is pure vanity on my part. If he were not so distinguished a man, I should probably say, During the latter part of the address of Mr. Frauenstein.—[Great laughter and applause, during which the doctor tried to continue.] I was going to say, and would say, if you would only stop your noise and listen [more uproarious laughter], that three rich and honorable gentlemen in the audience sent me a note for the Count Frauenstein, asking for an appointment to-morrow morning. It is a profound secret, and so I will make no scruple in telling you that they propose a joint-stock company for the building of another Social Palace, in a neighboring town. [Applause.] I tell of this to please you, and then to make them feel somewhat committed to the enterprise, so that they can't back out so easily. [Laughter.] That, you see, is killing two birds with one stone, as the physician said who had two patients in the same street. [Laughter and applause.]

"Now, some of you being strangers may not understand, seeing the familiarity with which my fellow-citizens treat me, that I am a very grave and dignified person——"

The roars of laughter that greeted this quite prevented the doctor from continuing, and Mr. Kendrick, liking well to see the audience amused, rose and begged permission to corroborate the doctor's statement by an anecdote. "Some years ago," he said, "being seized by a sudden and severe illness, I sent for my friend Dr. Forest. He came, examined my pulse and my tongue, asked the ordinary impertinent questions, and seemed to study the case very seriously. Then he said, 'Kendrick, I don't see what the devil is the matter with you, *but I'll give you an emetic on a venture.*'"

As soon as the noise subsided a little, the doctor adjusted his spectacles and said:

"Allow me to say, my friends, in defence of my professional skill, that I was not wholly without a certain spiritual insight into my friend's case at that time. Knowing that his phrenological bump of Alimentiveness was seven plus, and considering that lobsters had just appeared——"

The doctor could not go on for the uproarious merriment, which was increased by the fact that Kendrick was a thin little man, with no appetite to speak of, and so the sentence was never finished. When he resumed his address, he went on in a far more serious strain :

"I have been asked many times to-day, if we do not suffer here from want of privacy. One lady told me she would like to live here but for the terrible 'mixing up.' Now that lady lives in one of the most crowded streets of one of our great cities. She cannot step into the street without entering a promiscuous throng. Here, she would meet only honest people, and her purse would be quite safe. The truth is, there is here the utmost enjoyment of privacy. There is but one law, and that is liberty. All the cooking, washing, and ironing, may be done in individual homes or in the cuisine and laundry, just as the people prefer. There is, however, a remarkable unanimity in preferring the latter. The world has generally believed that women are by nature devoted to the cooking-stove, the wash-tub, and the cradle. We have found out positively that this is a mistake. [Applause.] It may be different in a state of nature—among the Otaheitans, for example—but certainly I never found a civilized woman who did not wish to get away, even from the cradle, a few hours during the day. Why, one civilized baby is capable of turning an isolated household into a pandemonium [laughter] ; and how many of the very tenderest mothers are worn out with the care of a single infant. The child, however small, pines for the society of other children, and this is really the secret of many a

'cross baby.' The baby, by crying, is only expressing
the fact that its wants are not supplied. Explain it as
you can : cross babies cease to bear that reputation when
they are accustomed to our nursery ; and when brought
home, if kept after a certain time, they fret and worry
until carried back among their baby companions. Now,
if the children did not prefer the nursery, but cried to go
home, we should not decide that they were naturally
depraved, but that there was a screw loose in the organization of the nursery. We do not accept the doctrine of
total depravity. We know that if we give an acorn its
proper conditions, it will become a beautiful tree. If we
wish a chicken to grow into a strong and perfect fowl, we
study what its wants are, and then supply them ; and
but for the interference of theology, I think mankind
would have discovered, a little before this time, that
human nature is no more naturally bad than an acorn or
a chicken. We are depraved only through the want of
conditions for the normal and harmonious growth of all
our parts. But theology itself is finding out that it
cannot preserve its rigidity in the face of the progress of
the age. I find there are many priests who are very
excellent men [laughter and applause]; but then, these
have rotated out of theology into common sense. You
will find some to-day who would rather see a Social
Palace founded than a mill for grinding out parsons, or,
to speak more respectfully, a theological seminary. A
clergyman told me to-day that he was greatly pleased
with our Social Palace, but he regretted to see that we
had provided a theatre. You can judge what a labor I
had with that individual. [Laughter.] I would rather
build stone-wall all day, than have another two hours'

struggle with that man's powerful but theological intel-
lect. [Great laughter.] Of course I had to go back for
my premises among the monsters of antediluvian times,
where theologians and scientists differ radically as to the
conditions of our ancestors. [Laughter.] You see that
is such uncertain ground, that one can bully just as much
as the other. In short, I attempted to show that theological mind, that human nature was decent enough to
prefer beauty to ugliness, virtue to vice, and that what
he called depravity, was only false development, through
the want of the right conditions for true and healthful
development.

"Do you suppose we are willing, or that we can afford,
to have our children pining in the Social Palace for
amusement, and being driven to seek it in the questionable resorts of the city ? It is to avoid this, that we have
billiards and other games, and musical and dramatic societies. It is to avoid this, that we have a library and reading-
room. Our theatre is a special pride. You all know how
irresistibly the young are attracted to dramatic performances ; and out of our respect to human attractions,
we have built the theatre, and furnished it with an
extensive wardrobe of historical costumes and all stage
appointments. Those pupils take the first rank for polite
address and grace of bearing, are rewarded by becoming
members of the dramatic company; and there is no honor
more coveted and ardently sought for, than this. Many
strangers in these grounds to-day have remarked the
polite and easy address of some of the boys and girls, who
have sacrificed voluntarily their play to answer the questions of visitors, to bring them delicacies from the restaurant, or to show them over the grounds. [Applause and

cries of 'That is true!'] It gives me pleasure to hear you acknowledge this so readily. These boys and girls are competitors for dramatic distinction, and if any of them manifest very marked and promising histrionic talent, they will be furnished with the means to continue their studies here and abroad. To-morrow, at the one o'clock matinée, and at the evening performances, you will have an opportunity to judge, from what the dramatic company has accomplished in six months, whether or not it promises well for the future.

"The theatre and the opera are two of the greatest moral educators of the world, and they should in every community be under the control of the highest and most cultivated of the citizens. When controlled by the impulse of avarice alone, they are sure to become degraded and fail in their high mission, which is to stimulate the imagination to a love of heroism and virtue, and to cultivate and develop artistic taste. Mark well that the drama and the opera are democratic in their principle; rank is gained by study and high merit, and woman is recognized as man's equal, and receives equal or even higher compensation for her labor. Equality, you know, is one of our watchwords; and our institution is not a sham, but a real republic, where the voices of all citizens over sixteen years of age are heard in the making of our laws and regulations. This, in the opinion of some people, is too early an age for the exercise of the ballot; but it must be remembered, that long before that age, the children are thoroughly acquainted with its use, and with the general principles of democratic government. Woman's political duties are not onerous, and so far as I know, though every woman votes, not one has yet 'unsexed' herself. [Great laughter and applause.] You know certain weak, unscientific men, are dreadfully afraid of that calamity. [Laughter.] One reason may be that our voting is not conducted in dirty halls nor rum-shops.

" The education of the children from infancy up, is all free, and supported by our shops and industries. Every orphan will be adopted, educated, and tenderly cared for, as will the sick, the aged, and the infirm ; not as a charity, mark well, but as a natural right. We have educational classes for adults, and they are well attended, while the education of the children embraces a wide range of scientific and industrial training. You have seen to-day in the lowest class of the school proper, nearly a hundred children engaged in what are called the Froëbel exercises —seated at their long tables constructing houses, fences, furniture—innumerable tiny objects, with their blocks, and sticks, and plastic clay. Some of them already show great skill. Visitors called their occupation play. So it is, but a most important play ; so organized that skill and artistic taste are gradually developed, through friendly emulation and the natural love of beautiful forms.

" The right education of children is the most sacred duty of the world. Remember, you who have these dear little ones under your care to-day, how you fill their tender, impressible minds with effete creeds and unverifiable hypotheses. You may think you are doing them good, forgetting that we have seen the dawn of the scientific method of investigation, and that hereafter these children will rise up and reproach you for wasting their precious time. Teach them to see God, not as a greater man, subject to anger, repentance, and the various passions of men, but as the invisible, and to us, incomprehensible, power behind what we call phenomena. The religious aspiration is the aspiration toward universal harmony, and is literally, as well as in principle, the highest part of man. It is most normally excited by the study of nature—the mysterious laws that we see governing the springing grass, the unfolding flower, the growth and development of the child, and the great kosmic forces that control the movements of the planets, and suns, and systems of the universe.

" We are standing on the threshold of a brighter era for mankind, as I believe I can see, and I am not alone in this faith. Since the great success of the labors of M. Godin in France, we may confidently assert that the laws of social harmony have been put into practice; but it is to the coming generation that we must look for more significant results, for higher harmonies than we can effect—cramped and robbed of our birthright, as we have been, by false and imperfect conditions for the free development of our physical and mental powers. We look to the educational system of the Social Palace for the working out of the grand problem that we have stated; and hence the advent of every child here will be a signal for rejoicing, for he is born into conditions that should make him

'Grow in beauty like the rose,'

and become a blessing to the world.

" And now, my friends, thanking you for your courteous attention to what I have said to you, and out of respect to the thousand youthful feet that are impatient

to open the ball, I will end my remarks by the announcement of a joyful event. The birth of the first child in
the Social Palace, occurred this morning at sunrise: a
happy omen for our inaugural festival."

At this announcement the air was filled with long-continued shouts of applause and cries of " Whose baby is
it ? " " Tell us whose child it is," " Is it a boy or girl ? "
" Of course it is a girl," said a man in the audience.
" No boy would dare to take precedence here."

Ella looked at Dr. Delano, and whispered, " I'll bet
anything it is the count's ! "

" Nonsense ! There hasn't been time enough."

" Yes, there has," said his wife, with the confidence of
those most interested in being certain concerning such
matters.

The people would not be satisfied. They called loudly
for the doctor, who at last came forward and said :

" It is *our* baby. It is the child of the Social Palace.
Every man is its father, every woman its mother, and
every child its brother and sister. I will add that it is a
strong, beautiful child, perfect in all its parts ; but as
you will not be satisfied with this, I will say further that
it is the son of my dearly-beloved daughter and the
Count von Frauenstein."

" There, I told you so ! " said Ella. Dr. Delano sat
like a stone, and paid not the slightest heed to his wife ;
not even when she added maliciously, " You see some
people are not so wise as they think they are ! "

The demonstrations of delight at the announcement
of the birth, were nothing to those that followed the
knowledge that the idolized Frauenstein was the happy

father. The immense audience rose to their feet—even strangers, who neither knew nor cared anything about it, caught the infection—and waved handkerchiefs, and the shouts, "God bless the child!" "Long live Frauenstein!" "Long live the heir!" rolled through the corridors of the immense building, even to the ears of Clara, who lay in her luxuriant curtained bed holding her precious treasure in her arms, listening to words from Paul that were but the voice of her own heart.

Min sat in an arm-chair nodding, worn out with the excitements of the day, among which had been two rehearsals at the theatre, for she was to play a little part at the coming matinee, and this baby, over which her delight knew no bounds. She was fast asleep when Susie entered with the doctor.

"Clara," she said, bending over her friend, "he was there on the platform! He heard it all! and I know perfectly well, by the way his wife spoke to him, that she said, 'I told you so.'"

Clara's sweet face lighted up with a momentary triumph, and then she said softly, "I am very sorry for him."

"You wish everybody in this world had a baby, don't you, Clara?" said the doctor. "You see you bear ' anger as the flint doth fire,' as Brutus says."

"Well," answered Clara, taking the doctor's hand, and looking up into his face tenderly:

"*Am I not Papa's Own Girl?*"

FINIS.